New York Times and *USA TODAY* bestselling author **Jane Porter** has written forty romances and eleven women's fiction novels since her first sale to Mills & Boon in 2000. A five-time RITA® Award finalist, Jane is known for her passionate, emotional and sensual novels, and loves nothing more than alpha heroes, exotic locations and happy-ever-afters. Today Jane lives in sunny San Clemente, California, with her surfer husband and three sons. Visit janeporter.com.

Jackie Ashenden writes dark, emotional stories, with alpha heroes who've just got the world to their liking only to have it blown wide apart by their kick-ass heroines. She lives in Auckland, New Zealand, with her husband, the inimitable Dr Jax, two kids and two rats. When she's not torturing alpha males and their gutsy heroines she can be found drinking chocolate martinis, reading anything she can lay her hands on, wasting time on social media or being forced to go mountain biking with her husband. To keep up to date with Jackie's new releases and other news sign up to her newsletter at jackieashenden.com.

THE PRICE OF A DANGEROUS PASSION

JANE PORTER

PROMOTED TO HIS PRINCESS

JACKIE ASHENDEN

MILLS & BOON

First Published in Great Britain 2020
by Mills & Boon, an imprint of HarperCollins*Publishers*
1 London Bridge Street, London, SE1 9GF

The Price of a Dangerous Passion © 2020 Jane Porter

Promoted to His Princess © 2020 Jackie Ashenden

ISBN: 978-0-263-27828-6

THE PRICE OF
A DANGEROUS
PASSION

JANE PORTER

For my editor Megan Haslam.
So good to have you back!
You're a dream to work with.

PROLOGUE

New Year's Eve

SHE HAD RULES. Rules she never broke. There were no exceptions. Charlotte never mixed business and pleasure, never. She wasn't ever tempted, either…regardless of the value of her clients. All her clients were VIPs to her, clients who came to her for her sterling reputation. They trusted her to make the best possible decisions for them. They came to her because they needed her expertise in sorting out image issues, public relation snafus and social media nightmares. How could they trust her judgment, if her judgment was faulty?

If her judgment lost sight of the objective?

If she forgot why she was there in the first place?

Charlotte Parks knew all these things, and yet Brando Ricci was making it almost impossible to remember why these—*her*—rules were so important. She'd wrapped up business weeks ago, well before Christmas. All conversations and concerns with the Ricci-Baldi family had been handled, settled, put to bed. She was here at the Ricci family's grand New Year's Eve party because they loved to throw lavish parties and loved to include everyone who had helped them. And

Charlotte had helped them, having spent the entire autumn in Florence, working to smooth tensions following intense, negative media attention arising from the family's struggles with power, and issues from succession.

Not all issues were completely settled, but much of the tension was gone, and the family had come together to present a unified face to the public once again. Tonight's party was part of that unified face.

She shouldn't have come tonight. Her part was done. She'd been paid—well paid, too. There was no justifiable reason to have returned to Florence for a party.

The music changed, slowed, and Brando pulled her closer, his hand settling low on her back, her breasts crushed to his tuxedo-covered chest. "You're overthinking," he murmured, his breath warm against her ear.

"I am," she agreed. "Or perhaps I should say, I'm thinking. And I should be thinking. You are dangerous."

"I would never hurt you. That is a promise."

And she knew that. She knew he'd be amazing—in bed, out of bed. The chemistry between them was electric and had been there from the moment they'd met last September. But the chemistry is what also troubled her, because she'd never felt a pull like this... She'd never even considered throwing caution to the wind. And yet here she was, a half hour from midnight, wrestling with her conscience, wrestling with desire.

"I shouldn't be here," she whispered, fingers curling around his, her heart thumping too hard, her body warm, sensitive, exquisitely aware...aroused. She hadn't made love in over a year...perhaps two years... She hadn't felt this attracted to anyone...ever. Part of her was so tempted to give in to the heat, while the logical, disciplined part warned that it was a mistake, a mistake that could jeopardize her career, her reputation…

Her heart.

She looked up into his handsome face again. He was gorgeous…truly handsome, but it wasn't just beautiful bone structure. He was smart, fascinating, compelling. During the months of working with the Ricci family, Brando was the one who drew her, time and again. Even though he was the youngest in his family, he had the most wisdom and insight, and she'd come to trust and respect his point of view, even going to him when Enzo, Marcello and Livia couldn't agree on anything, hoping Brando could find a diplomatic way to bring his fractious siblings together. And he had. And he did.

She'd returned tonight to Florence for him.

For this…

Whatever this was.

"What are you afraid of?" he asked now, his narrowed gaze sweeping her face.

His scrutiny made her face tingle, setting countless nerve endings alight. "Losing my head. Losing control."

The corner of his mouth lifted ever so slightly. His hand slid lower on her back, nearly cupping the curve of her butt. "We're two consenting adults."

She could feel his sinewy strength pressed against the length of her. His hard chest, his waist, the powerful thighs. "Yes, but business and pleasure should always be kept separate—"

"We're no longer working together," he reminded, his head dropping, his lips brushing the side of her neck.

She shuddered, and closed her eyes, trying to ignore how her breasts tightened, nipples pebbling, desire coiling within her. It was becoming increasingly difficult to keep a clear head. All she wanted was his mouth on hers, his hands teasing, exploring the length of her. It had been so long since she'd been with anyone and yet she wanted him…wanted his weight on her, wanted his body filling hers, wanted the pleasure she knew he'd give. The pleasure she craved…not from just anyone, but him. Brando Ricci. Vintner. Entrepreneur. Billionaire.

Lover.

No, not her lover, not yet.

"We shouldn't do this," she whispered, air catching in her throat as his thumb stroked the side of her neck, lighting little tongues of fires just beneath the surface of her skin.

"We've done nothing wrong," he murmured. "We're simply dancing."

Done nothing wrong yet, she silently corrected, with *yet* being the operative word.

Charlotte tipped her head back to look up into Brando's mesmerizing silver eyes that were anything but cool, or cold. The heat in them scorched her now and she felt a shiver race through her. She'd fought this attraction for months, fought the sizzling awareness, suppressed the hunger, but tonight she was losing the battle. Just being in his arms was making her breathless and dizzy. Her body hummed, aching with awareness. Hunger.

"It's nearly midnight," she said, glancing over his shoulder at the enormous clock that had been mounted on the wall of the palace ballroom for tonight's New Year's countdown.

He glanced at the clock, too. "Ten minutes."

Her gaze took in the orchestra on the stage playing everyone's favorites, and the throng of beautiful people filling the dance floor. The seventeenth-century ballroom was packed with some of Europe's most glamorous, wealthy people. They were having a wonderful time, laughing, dancing, drinking, celebrating. When the clock struck midnight, the celebration would become deafening.

She'd always hated crowds, and normally avoided parties, but when the invitation came to attend the Riccis' party, she didn't say no. She couldn't say no.

"What are you thinking, *cara*?" Brando's deep voice was a caress.

Cara, darling. She felt another helpless shiver race through her.

She'd come tonight for him.

She wanted only him.

And yet, her rules. Her stupid rules.

She dampened her lips with the tip of her tongue. "I don't mix—"

"Business and pleasure," he completed for her. "I know. But tonight is not business. We're done with business, done with the family, done doing what others want us to do."

His lips brushed hers, a fleeting kiss that felt as if he'd set a thousand butterflies free inside her heart and mind. Wings of hope. Flutters of possibilities.

She always lived so alone, so controlled, so contained, but tonight… Tonight she felt as if maybe, just maybe, she belonged somewhere, to someone. Even if it were for one night only.

"Just tonight," she said hoarsely. "You must agree

this is just one night, and nothing more than that. Promise me, Brando."

His lips brushed hers again. "Fine. Tonight is ours. Tonight belongs to us."

"And tomorrow—"

"We won't worry about. It's not here."

CHAPTER ONE

CHARLOTTE PARKS TUCKED her long pale hair behind an ear, straightened the lapel on her fashionable coat and rang the doorbell on the tall, handsome seventeenth-century building in the heart of Florence, just steps from Ponte Vecchio. Originally constructed as a palace, the building had been turned into several private homes, including the town house for Italian tycoon Brando Ricci.

She'd been here twice before, once for business last October, and once for—well, *not* business—New Year's Eve. It was a large, lavish town house with three separate floors and the sheer size of it meant that it'd take a moment for someone to come to the door, and so she waited calmly, expression serene.

Charlotte was skilled at serene. She'd mastered stress and pressure, having learned how to adjust to instability and conflict early in life, as the next to youngest in a big, rather famous British family, her affluent, aristocratic parents marrying and divorcing with rather joyous abandon, giving her a dozen siblings, half siblings and stepsiblings. She'd been born in England, then hauled to Los Angeles for ten years with her mother when she married the roguish film director Heath Hughes, and then bounced back to Europe at fifteen for finishing school in Switzerland.

Charlotte's siblings and stepsiblings were quite famous in their own right—models, actresses, race car drivers, as well as beautiful, envied English socialites. The Parks-Hughes-horpe family even had their own reality TV show for a bit, before certain members of the family decried it as too common, too crass, too American. It didn't help that nearly half of the family was now American, and full of plans and ambition. Charlotte, having spent twelve years in America, the ten with her mom, and now the past two on her own with a lovely house in the Hollywood Hills, had come to appreciate American bluntness and the efficiency with which Americans tackled problems. Well, maybe that was overstating things. Affluent Americans, inevitably image conscious, were very good at hiring help for damage control, and Charlotte was very good at damage control, so good, she had her own little company that had become a very successful PR company with global clientele.

Her ability to solve problems is what brought her to Florence. She'd met Brando Ricci nine months ago when she was hired to sort out a public relations nightmare involving the legendary Ricci family, one of Italy's most famous families, known for their wine, their leather goods, as well as their modern fashion house.

The Ricci family business dated back to the turn of the century, when making a great Chianti was their claim to fame. Following World War II, the family expanded, adding fashion and luxury leather goods to their business. The three Ricci brothers, grandsons to the founder, grew and nurtured the business until they ran into a rather common problem—how would succession work in a family where the three brothers had been almost equals, and yet each brother had two or three children each? It was one thing to share leadership among three, but a corporation couldn't have eight leaders. She'd stepped in late last August to smooth over some of the negative publicity stemming from the internal family struggles, generating new media coverage that focused on the family's cohesiveness, but behind the scenes, the family was still rather fractious as succession hadn't yet been truly addressed. But she'd done her part. The Ricci family was out of the tabloids, and she'd been given a very generous payment for services, and that should have been that.

Except it wasn't.

Charlotte, who rarely made mistakes, made a critical tactical error on New Year's Eve. She shouldn't have spent a night with Brando Ricci. Yes, it had been an extraordinary night, but letting down one's guard, and breaking one's rules, had staggering consequences.

Now she was here, but she dreaded the moment she'd be face-to-face with him. Brando was brilliant, powerful, perceptive, exciting. He'd made her feel all kinds of things she'd never felt before, and that was while still on the dance floor.

Returning here, being carried up to his bedroom, had been earth-shattering. She wasn't a virgin but she'd never felt anything as exquisite as what she felt in his arms, in his bed. It was without a doubt the most amazing night of her life. The sex had been so good, so unbelievably good, that she'd flown home dazed and dazzled and completely swept away.

Thank goodness there was a huge distance between

them—6,188 miles to be precise—a trip that required at least one or two stops, depending on the airline and route, so it wasn't easy, or convenient to jet over to say hello. She returned home determined to focus on the future, not the past, or the bliss of being with a man who knew how to make a woman feel like the most glorious thing in the world.

There would be no reunions, no weekend escapes. They'd had their fling, and yes, it'd been the most exciting, sensual thing she'd ever experienced, but she wasn't going to lose her head over incredible sex with the sexiest, most sensual, most overwhelming man she'd ever met. That would be plain foolish, and she might be slightly, *slightly*, secretly besotted with Brando, but she was no fool. He was completely out of her league, and she'd told him so when he'd phoned to say he'd be in Los Angeles and hoped they could get together.

Just hearing his voice on the phone slammed her back to the night she'd spent in his bed in Florence. She felt his heat and strength again, and could picture his head between her thighs, his mouth on her where she was oh, so sensitive, his tongue finding every delicate nerve so that when she came, she came hard, and completely fell apart, dissolving into tears because he made her feel, so very much, and it was actually too much. She might live in California now but underneath she was still quite British and didn't enjoy being flooded with quite so much emotion. Emotion was wonderful in tidy bites and measured doses, but the emotion Brando made her feel, well… Really, there was no place for it, and no room in her life for dazed, dazzled and befuddled.

Which brought her to this exact moment, where she

waited on Brando's doorstep, her elegant swing coat hiding her secret, a secret she had to share, because there was no hiding it any longer. It was one thing to keep a secret when there was no physical evidence, but her bump was impossible to hide now, so here she was, steeling herself for a conversation she did not think she'd ever have. Because she'd been on the pill, and he'd used a condom, and yet…

And yet…

Charlotte's heart staggered and she exhaled hard, before drawing in a slower calming breath and ringing the doorbell again, pressing on the bell a little longer, and more insistently, than before.

The last time she was here Brando had almost made her believe in miracles. But there were no miracles, just bruised principles, and broken rules, and heart-wrenching consequences.

The front door suddenly swung open, revealing a tall slender young woman with long, dark tousled hair, red lips, her naked body barely covered by a white silk robe, the fabric so sheer, her dusky nipples shone through.

Charlotte recognized the model immediately. She was an Argentinean beauty taking the fashion world by storm.

"Si?" Louisa drawled as her robe slid off her shoulder and down her slender arm, fabric no longer covering one jutting breast.

Charlotte ignored the nipple. *"Brando è disponibile?"* she asked, utilizing the Italian she'd learned at her Swiss finishing school.

Louisa looked her up and down, a sly smile curving her full lips. *"È un po legato."*

He's a little tied up, Louisa had said, and from the

model's smug smile, Charlotte had a feeling the words were literal.

"Would you be so kind as to untie him?" she said politely in Italian. "Let him know Charlotte Parks is here. I'll be waiting for him in the grand salon," she added, stepping into the house and heading for the formal room halfway down the white marble hall.

Charlotte heard the door close hard, and then footsteps on the curving staircase that led to the second floor. Brando's bedroom was up there. Charlotte knew, because she'd been there, during that second visit to this house when he'd stripped her naked and turned her into a mass of quivering need. She'd been far too intrigued by him, and she'd been far too confident in her ability to manage him, just the way she managed everything else in the world. But one didn't easily manage Brando Ricci. He was a force to be reckoned with.

That force, all six foot two inches of him, entered the salon, dressed, thankfully, and looking casually handsome in faded denims that wrapped his muscular thighs, and a silver-gray cashmere V-neck sweater that hugged the hard planes of his chest. The cashmere sweater perfectly matched the color of his silver-gray eyes and paired a little too well with the espresso black of his hair.

He was tall, lean, honed and even more beautiful than she remembered. Her heart jumped, a quick staccato that did nothing for her sense of calm. Just that little glimpse of skin at his throat made her remember what it had felt like to be naked against him. His body didn't just look magnificent, he knew how to move it, and when he'd been inside her, she'd felt satisfied, more satisfied, more...everything...than she'd ever felt in her life.

Being intimate with him hadn't been just physical pleasure. She'd experienced a feeling of peace and wholeness, which made no sense since Brando had a history of breaking hearts. He didn't do long relationships. He didn't want commitments.

Which was why he should be fine with her proposal, relieved to hear that she would handle everything.

"Charlotte," he said, approaching her, and leaning down to kiss each of her cheeks. "What brings you to Florence?"

"You do." She smiled up at him. "I hope I haven't interrupted anything."

He gave her an amused smile, indicating he was aware that she was aware she'd obviously interrupted something.

"Shall we sit?" he suggested, gesturing to the chic armchairs in the white room with red and coral accents.

"Yes, thank you." She took the chair opposite his, the chairs a little closer together than she preferred, but it felt good to be off her feet as her heart had begun to race and all her cool, calm confidence deserted her now that he was here. Brando was larger than life, humming with an energy that she found potent and strangely addictive. Her family was filled with beautiful people, but Brando exuded a physicality and a virility that was all his own.

He'd more than impressed her with his virility six months ago in this very house.

New Year's Eve. What a life-changing night...

Heat rushed through her at the memory, and her stomach did a wobbly flip. The last thing she wanted to do was relive those intense memories now, here, with

Brando within arm's length and his lover upstairs waiting for him in bed. "I imagine Louisa must be growing
impatient," she said.

He smiled, a lazy, almost indulgent smile. "Louisa
is good at entertaining herself." He was still smiling,
but his silver gaze narrowed, expression sharpening.
"When did you arrive in Italy?"

"Today actually. I've left my bags at the hotel, but
haven't yet checked in."

"That eager to see me?"

"I wasn't sure if you'd be here, or at the country
house. If you were in the countryside already, I was
going to rent a car and drive out to meet you."

"I'm heading to the villa tomorrow." His gaze
skimmed over her, studying her intently. "You look
well."

"Thank you. I feel well." She hesitated, struggling
for words, her carefully rehearsed speech forgotten.
She'd convinced herself that he wouldn't care about
her news. She'd convinced herself that he'd be relieved
she was going to handle everything and do everything.
Suddenly she wasn't so sure and her heart had begun to
race, anxiety pulsing just below the surface. "Do you
mind if I take off my coat? It's very warm."

"Yes, your cheeks are quite flushed."

The moment her coat came off, he'd see. He'd know.
She hesitated, hands no longer steady, her confidence
shaken.

What if it didn't play out the way she anticipated?
What if he—

She stopped herself there, unable to imagine any
other scenario than the one she'd planned on. He was

a bachelor. A playboy. He wasn't father material. He wouldn't be interested in the domestic details.

"Charlotte, are you all right?" he asked.

Tell him. Just tell him now.

Instead, mouth dry, heart racing, she slowly, carefully eased her arms from the sleeves and then allowed the coat to slide off her shoulders and fall back onto the chair.

Her emerald dress was slim fitting, the soft knit clinging to her small frame, highlighting her bump. The baby gave a hard kick just then and she touched her bump, not sure if she was soothing the baby, or herself.

"I'm six months," she said quietly, steadily. "It's been an easy pregnancy, and there have been no complications. I didn't want to say anything until I'd made it out of the first trimester—" She broke off, took a quick breath and plunged on. "I wasn't showing until recently and then I just popped. I couldn't hide it any longer, and I didn't think I should."

"Should I be offering my congratulations?"

"If you'd like to include yourself in the congratulations."

There was a beat of silence. "Is this your way of saying it's mine?"

"Yes."

"And you're sure it's mine?"

"Yes."

His gaze held hers, the silver gray piercing. There was no judgment in his eyes, no censure, no shock, not even disappointment. "We took precautions, both of us."

"It seems we have a child that very much wants to be part of the world," she answered, sitting tall, shoulders straight.

"A child with determination," he replied.

She smiled, her most charming smile, aware that they were now both playing the same game. "It's an admirable trait."

"Agreed." He hesitated. "You never considered an abortion?"

"No." She eyed him cautiously. "Would you have preferred me to end the pregnancy?"

"I'm Italian. Catholic. So, no."

"I'm neither, but it was never an option."

His gaze held hers. "And now you're here."

"Yes." Her chin lifted, and yet she kept her voice even. As long as she maintained control, she'd be fine, and he'd be fine. Really, it was just a matter of needing time to work through the shock that he must be feeling. "It seemed best to tell you in person. I knew you would want to know, and you deserve to know. It didn't seem fair to just make all the decisions without consulting you."

Brando arched a brow. "And yet you haven't consulted me."

"I am now. That's why I've come."

Silence stretched and the silence made her pulse do an odd, uncomfortable thudding in her veins, a thudding she felt all the way through her. This was not the Brando she'd last seen. In fact, this was not a Brando she recognized. They were like strangers, and yet the last time she'd been with him they'd been incredibly intimate. She'd given herself all of him and had never regretted it...not until she discovered there were consequences for that night of passion.

"The pregnancy stunned me," she said after a moment. "It wasn't part of my plan, and it took me a few weeks to sort through all my feelings, but I'm actually now very much looking forward to motherhood."

"This consultation… What is your goal? You want money? Financial support?"

"No."

"What, then?"

Her plan was to offer him exactly what he didn't want—a chance to be a father. She'd give him the opportunity to co-parent, an opportunity she knew he wouldn't want, and when he balked, she'd gently offer to do it all herself, and he'd be relieved, and accept. Brando was handsome and brilliant but not ready to settle down. His sister had said so more than once. Brando was the least committed to family. Brando was the rebel and valued his independence. She understood that, though. Charlotte valued hers.

"I want you to be this child's father," she said quietly, "*if* you want to be his or her father, and if not, I am sure one day I will fall in love and marry a man who will raise this child as his. In the meantime, I recognize your rights, and I respect your rights, and would like to include you in the decision-making, should you want to be included."

"You were pregnant when I was in Los Angeles earlier in the year."

"Yes."

"Why didn't you tell me then?"

"It was early in my pregnancy, and I wasn't sure that the pregnancy was viable. My sisters have miscarried in the first trimester, and they warned me that it could happen to me."

"Your family knows, then?"

"No. I've managed to hide the pregnancy so far, but it's impossible now. I'm obviously expecting."

"Why haven't you told your family?"

"It's none of their business." She put a hand to her bump again, feeling another fluttery shift inside. "And if I was going to share the news with anyone, it should be you."

Charlotte Parks was every bit as beautiful as the last time Brando had seen her, naked in his bed, her long golden hair splayed across the pillow, her mouth swollen from his kisses. This morning she looked impossibly self-contained, as well as impossibly glowing. Pregnancy suited her. Her skin appeared more luminous, her eyes bluer, brighter, her long, golden blond hair shimmering in the sunlight that poured through the tall windows.

When Louisa had come upstairs to tell him there was a woman at the door, demanding to see him, he'd arched a brow, but hadn't been concerned. When he discovered it was Charlotte in the salon, he'd been intrigued. Charlotte, fascinating Charlotte, never made demands, and yet she'd been pure pleasure in his bed. But now he wasn't as sanguine. Apparently, she was pregnant. With his child.

He'd heard this before, years ago. Thankfully he'd asked for a paternity test, and the test had turned out negative. He couldn't have been more grateful.

Now… Now he didn't know what to think and Brando's gaze swept over Charlotte, skimming her fair hair, high elegant cheekbones, before dropping to her full breasts and her taut, round bump. She looked radiant, but not quite as serene as he'd first thought her to be. "Hasn't this been a difficult secret to keep?" he asked.

"No."

"Really?"

She shrugged. "I'm not one that needs to discuss things to make decisions, and I've never turned to others for advice. What I needed was time, and I had that time, which is why I'm here, ready to discuss the future."

"And yet this is all news to me."

Color swept her lovely high cheekbones, and her head dipped. "True." Her chin lifted and her gaze met his. "I expect you'll want a paternity test. I've already checked into clinics that do the testing here in Florence. It's a simple procedure, just a blood draw for both of us and then we wait for results." She hesitated a moment. "If possible, I'd like to get it done today. That way we'll have the results sooner than later."

"And if I am the father?"

"Well, you are the father, but please let me reassure you that I have things well in control. I'm not asking for anything from you. In fact, nothing in your world needs to change. I just wanted to be courteous—"

He laughed, a low husky sound that stopped her mid-sentence.

She glanced at him, winged eyebrows arching higher, her color even more heightened. "I wasn't trying to be funny," she said rather stiffly.

"Maybe not, but I found it comical when you said nothing in my world needs to change. *Bella*, everything in my world will change. It's already changed, if I'm to become a father."

"I'm obviously going to become a mother. But you...

You don't have to do this…or be part of this. I'm quite comfortable parenting on my own."

"Which would be fine, if it wasn't my child, but if it is my child, then I'm going to be involved."

Her lips parted and then pressed together. She glanced to the tall windows framed by large red-and-white-check silk curtains, the checked fabric a contrast to the marble terra-cotta parquet floor. She suddenly looked anxious and appeared to be struggling to find the right words.

"I'm surprised you're taking this so well," she said at last, looking over at him, her blue gaze clear. "We had one night together, little more than a fling, and yet you seem ready to embrace parenthood."

"I've always taken precautions to prevent an unplanned pregnancy, and yet now that we're here at this crossroads, it's not a tragedy, not something that needs to be overcome. We're mature and independent, able to provide a safe, happy home for our child."

Again, her lips parted, and again they pinched closed. Color washed through her cheeks, her eyes shone overly bright.

It struck him then that he'd caught her off guard. What had she imagined he'd say? No thank you, and goodbye?

That he'd wash his hands of his child?

"But maybe it's not mine," he said, thinking back to that other time where a woman had tried to trick him.

"No, it's yours. Without a doubt. But I didn't expect you to believe me. Why should you? We spent only one night together. Which is why I want the blood test done today. I'm only here for the weekend, and then Monday I head to England for a week, but we should get the results in seven business days, or three, if we pay to rush the results." She drew a breath. "I'd prefer to pay the rush fee, so I could return here and draw up custodial paperwork before my flight back to California."

"Custodial paperwork?" he echoed, thinking she'd certainly mapped it all out.

"The baby will live with me."

Her calm, crisp answer stirred his temper. "It seems we do have things to discuss."

"I just want to reassure you, Brando, that I have no intention of sharing the baby's paternity with anyone. This isn't anyone's business but ours, and the secret will be safe with me."

He lifted a brow. "Our child isn't to know I'm his or her father?"

"Do you want to be a father?" she asked bluntly.

"I don't understand the question, *cara*. If I'm the father, I am the father."

Fresh color swept through her face. "I suppose that is the part we need to discuss."

Was she seriously wanting to cut him out? Was she envisioning him as a sperm donor, but nothing more? He felt a surge of temper, but swiftly checked it. "It seems you and I do have a great deal to discuss," he said, "but I'd prefer more privacy. Now isn't the ideal time, not with Louisa here."

Charlotte glanced up to the ceiling, as if she expected Louisa to be there, on the hand-blown glass chandelier. "True." She slipped her coat back on, opened her handbag and drew out a slip of paper. "This is the nearest clinic that can do the blood draw. They can get you in this afternoon. I'll be going straight there when I leave here. If you could just call and make an appointment for today? Would that be possible?"

"I see no reason for us to delay the test."

"Good, thank you." She rose and tucked her purse beneath her arm. "And I apologize for barging in on you like this. I should have realized you might have a guest."

"It's fine. This was important." He couldn't imagine anything being more important, nor could he imagine any woman more beautiful than Charlotte Parks. He'd wanted her from the very first meeting. She'd been the elusive one, but he hadn't given up...not until she'd returned to Los Angeles and ghosted him.

He walked her to the front door now. "Where are you staying?"

She gave him the name of her hotel, a five-star property overlooking the river. It's where she had stayed before. There were smaller hotels, more affordable hotels, but this one took such excellent care of her the last time she was in Florence, it's where she wanted to be this time.

"Let me call a taxi for you," he said.

"I think I'll walk." She forced a faint smile. "The fresh air will do me good and maybe then I can get some work done."

"You're still working?"

"But of course." She flashed a smile. "It's what I do best."

"It's not too much at this stage of your pregnancy? It won't hurt the baby?"

"No. Everything is good."

The baby, Charlotte silently repeated as she walked back to her hotel. He'd referenced the baby in such a way that emotion fluttered in her, little wings of pain and heartache.

It was strange talking about her pregnancy. She'd kept the news to herself all this time, carrying the secret within her, just as she carried the baby, close to her heart, protective of the world's reaction. And yet in a matter of minutes she'd shared her news, and Brando had knocked away the walls of secrecy and made the news...matter-of-fact.

She paused at the curb, checked for traffic and dashed across, grateful for the brisk walk, needing the quick pace to help her process everything she was thinking and feeling.

All this time she'd thought she was most concerned about the pregnancy, about becoming a single mother, but seeing Brando had stripped away the pretense.

Seeing him made her feel naked and nervous and incredibly vulnerable.

She didn't have feelings for him, and yet...

Charlotte exhaled hard, and blinked even harder, and wondered why she felt so terribly discombobulated. Seeing Brando made her feel...strange.

Raw.

Hurt.

Which didn't make sense as he'd been nothing but polite, and respectful considering how shocking her announcement had to have been. She was grateful there had been no drama and he'd been quite cordial about taking the paternity test. The lack of drama made her suspect, though, striking her as too good to be true.

Maybe Brando was in shock. Maybe he wasn't as sanguine as he appeared, and underneath his veneer of calm, he was secretly rattled.

Or maybe he didn't believe her and was just waiting for the test results before challenging her...

Or maybe he wasn't even thinking about her news anymore and maybe he was back in bed with Louisa.

She blanched, and her stomach rose.

Oh, why, oh, why did Louisa have to be there today? And why, oh, why did Charlotte have to know about her?

Brando left the clinic across the street from Maria Beatrice Hospital and called Charlotte. It took her a few rings to answer the phone.

"It's Brando," he said when she answered. "Am I interrupting anything?"

"No. Just trying to write a press release but can't focus. I didn't sleep well last night."

"You should try to nap."

"Maybe," she said.

"What are you doing later?" he asked. "Do you have plans for dinner tonight?"

"No. Just more work."

"Have dinner with me."

"Did you have the test done?"

"I did, and we should have results in the morning. There is a lab here in Florence that will expedite testing for us."

"How? I heard three days was the fastest—"

"Unless you pay enormous sums of money to get something done."

"Ah."

He heard the wary note enter in her voice. "So, dinner?"

"What about Louisa?"

"She's not invited."

"Brando."

"Can we just focus on you for the time being? You're here, six months pregnant. Isn't it time we finally started communicating?"

CHAPTER TWO

BRANDO WATCHED CHARLOTTE emerge from the hotel's elevators and cross the marble lobby. Unlike this morning's form-fitting dress that had outlined her shape, she had chosen narrow black trousers and a stylish white tunic that skimmed her stomach, the tunic's natural fullness making the bump harder to detect.

Suddenly he flashed back to a different pregnancy with a different woman. It was years ago and when confronted by the news of her pregnancy, he'd been horrified. They'd had a brief relationship, and it had ended when he discovered she was not at all what she seemed, her vivacious, sparkling beauty a cover for an insecure, unkind, manipulative personality. It filled him with dread to think of her raising any child of his, and yet he'd promised her he'd support her and the baby... if the baby truly was his.

Thank God, the blood test came back negative. The child wasn't his. Adele had cried and protested, claiming the DNA blood test flawed.

It was only much later that he'd learned she'd manipulated some other wealthy man to marry her.

The pregnancy scare had been a wake-up call, and for a while Brando didn't date, choosing to be celibate over risking paternity claims. But after an eight-month celibacy period, he began dating again, and now here he was, waiting for the results of another DNA test.

He didn't like comparing Adele to Charlotte, though. They were nothing alike, and to be honest, Brando didn't need a paternity test to prove he was the father of Charlotte's baby. She wouldn't have come here, to him, if she hadn't been certain. Charlotte had money of her own, as well as a successful career. She'd even said earlier that she wanted nothing from him, and was planning on raising the baby in California, apart from him.

Which would be fine if it was someone else's child, but if the baby was his, since the baby was his, Brando was not going to be forced to the sidelines.

He'd taken the paternity test this afternoon to fight for his rights. He was going to be part of his child's life, and not as a distant figure on the periphery, but as a hands-on parent who was present from birth.

He moved toward Charlotte now, meeting her near the reception desk. "You look lovely," he said, greeting her with a kiss on the cheek.

She stiffened at the kiss, shooting him a suspicious look. "No need for compliments. This isn't a date."

"Would you prefer I had said something along the lines that you're very punctual?" he replied mockingly.

"Yes."

"Charlotte, good to see you. You're very punctual tonight."

She shot him another disapproving glance. "It's discourteous making people wait."

"You must have hated it when Marcello showed up an hour late for our first meeting."

"I wasn't impressed, no." And then her expression softened a fraction. "But you were on time. You're always on time."

"Speaking of time, we have a reservation in ten minutes. We can drive there, or walk, if you're feeling up to it. The restaurant isn't far." He glanced down at her feet. She was wearing pumps with a stylish kitten heel. "Would you prefer to drive, or walk?"

"I'd love to walk."

"Good. I was hoping you'd say that." Brando placed his hand lightly on her lower back and steered her out the front door, where he handed the keys of his car to the hotel valet.

Charlotte was exquisitely aware of Brando's hand on the small of her back as they left the hotel. He'd smelled heavenly when he'd kissed her in the lobby. It had been just a brief kiss on the cheek, and yet the warm brush of his lips and the light spicy scent he wore made her stomach curl and breath catch. He was sin on two legs, and her undoing.

"Where are we going for dinner?" she asked, trying to distract herself.

He named a restaurant she wasn't familiar with and for a few minutes they made small talk about Florence's cuisine. It was an inane conversation, she thought, as superficial as it could be, but also better than talking about what was really at stake.

The baby, and the future.

"You really think they will have results from the blood test tomorrow?" she asked, glancing from the golden sky to Brando.

"They said they might be able to rush something to-night, but we'd know for sure in the morning."

Charlotte wasn't worried he wasn't the father. He was the only one she'd been with in years, but she didn't expect him to take her word for it. After all, she'd slept with him on the first date. Why should he not think she did that all the time?

"Are you nervous?" he asked.

Her brow furrowed. "About the results? No. I think I'm more overwhelmed just seeing you again. It's… surreal."

"You had no plans to see me again, did you?"

She glanced up at him again, her gaze skimming his handsome profile. "No," she answered honestly. "I didn't. I don't mix business and pleasure, and once I'd slept with you, I wasn't going to be able to see you, or work with you, again."

"Why did you sleep with me, then?"

She mustered a small, tight smile. "I think you know the answer to that."

"If I did, I wouldn't have asked."

"I found you quite irresistible," she said, her voice lightly mocking. "And I thought, why not, just once, live a little? I should have remembered there are always consequences—" She broke off, stumbling, her toe catching in one of the cobbled stones lining the street. She didn't fall, though. Brando's arm tightened around her, keeping her upright.

"I've got you," he said.

He certainly did. His arm felt like a hot brand around her waist, his fingers sending forks of lightning through her middle. He was so very close and she felt completely overwhelmed by his nearness, creating an aching awareness she didn't want or need. Brando was already her kryptonite. If she wasn't very careful, she'd implode.

"Maybe," she said carefully, as she stopped walking, "I would be steadier without you."

"I don't want you to trip."

"I'm klutzy because you are close. I'd feel surer of myself if you didn't touch me." She tried to keep her tone light. "It must be a pregnancy thing where my center of balance is changing."

He looked skeptical, his silver gaze penetrating. "I was barely touching you."

Heat rushed through her, his words reminding her of the night where he did touch her, all over, giving her endless pleasure. She'd never felt anything like that, and doubted she'd ever feel anything like that again. He'd taken sex and elevated it to an art form. Making love with him had been transcendental…transformative.

"Nonetheless, I find it unsettling." The words sounded harsh, and so she added, "Take that as a compliment if you can. I might be six months pregnant, but you're still you, and apparently, I can't help responding to you."

Brando faced her on the street. "What we had was good, wasn't it?"

"Too good. I didn't trust it." She realized they were blocking the sidewalk and people were having to walk around them, some glancing at Brando and nodding, recognizing him. "We should keep walking."

Five minutes later they arrived at a building tucked off a hidden street not far from one of the famous squares. They took stairs down into the cellar. The walls were frescoed, the floor covered in thick tiles, the beams of the ceiling stenciled in shades of blue, red and gold. There were perhaps a dozen tables, almost all booths framed by rich burgundy velvet curtains. Italian glass chandeliers hung over each table, creating a mosaic of glittering light within each cozy booth.

They were seated at a table in the far corner away from the other guests. No one had paid them any attention when they arrived and Charlotte was happy to be off her feet, tucked into their booth, the cushion covered in rich, midnight-blue brocade with hints of gold thread, and yet her pulse raced and butterflies filled her. She couldn't remember when she'd last felt so worried. She hadn't been nervous when she'd arrived in Florence this morning, but ever since leaving Brando's house, she'd struggled. "I didn't think this would be easy," she said bluntly, "but at the same time, I didn't think it would be quite so difficult."

"Have I been difficult?"

"No. You haven't. But at the same time, I'm rattled."

"What is troubling you?"

She didn't know how to put her worries into words. She didn't know how to explain her feelings. They weren't making sense to her. How could they make sense to him?

She hadn't come to Italy expecting a declaration of love from Brando. She hadn't come imagining that he would even want to be part of her future. They'd had a one-night stand, and that was really all it was, and she'd had realistic expectations about what he'd say and do. And yet for some reason, seeing Louisa at the front door in that sheer negligee had maddened a small part of her brain, torturing her with a jealousy she couldn't, *shouldn't*, feel. There was no relationship between her and Brando, and certainly no commitment, or feelings of any kind, so why should remembering Louisa make her feel heartsick, and anxious, and angry?

And why should remembering Brando appearing in the salon, handsome and sophisticated and oh, so very calm, make Charlotte feel almost impotent with need, and pain?

That was the part that baffled her.

Why had she been so upset today?

Why did she feel cheated?

How could she possibly feel resentful, and played, when Brando wasn't even hers?

"I can't read your mind, *cara*. You'll have to try to use words," he said.

"It's ridiculous. You'll think I'm ridiculous—"

"I won't."

"No," she corrected, "you will, because I find myself ridiculous right now." She fiddled with the trio of stemware on the table, adjusting the glasses, forming them into a line. "I'm usually incredibly confident, and yet I've been rattled by your girlfriend Louisa." Charlotte glanced at Brando and shrugged. "I'm sorry. It sounds petty—"

"No, it doesn't. You're pregnant and feeling quite alone—"

"I wouldn't go that far. I'm excited about the baby. But seeing Louisa at your door made me realize how weird this really is. I should have called you first. I shouldn't have just shown up."

"It's fine."

"Louisa must be upset."

"She doesn't know. I haven't said anything to her."

"That makes sense, especially as you need to wait for results from the DNA test."

"I'm certain the results will show I'm the father."

She nodded. "They will." She hesitated. "And then you'll tell her?"

"No one needs to know anything, not right now."

She sighed with relief and felt some of her tension knotting her shoulders ease. "Thank you. I'm not ready for the world to know."

"I agree."

Charlotte then had another troubling thought. "But Brando, if you keep the information from her, it's going to cause trouble, it has to."

"Louisa and I are having fun. It's not a serious relationship."

"Do you ever have serious relationships?"

He cocked an eyebrow. "Do you really want to discuss my relationship history tonight?"

Charlotte grimaced. "No. I'm quite sure that's more than I could handle."

Brando laughed softly, the sound low and husky. "Before we put the subject of Louisa behind us, let me just reiterate that Louisa is lovely and fun, but we're not serious, or exclusive.

"You and me being here, having dinner together, isn't problematic, nor is it deceptive. We're not going behind Louisa's back. She knows I'm out with you tonight, just as I know she's with others tonight. So, you don't need to worry about her, or fear that you're stepping on toes."

"And yet she opened your front door almost naked."

"She's a bit of an exhibitionist. She enjoys the attention. Don't let her overly upset you. You've come a long way to meet with me and address the issue of co-parenting—"

"Co-parenting? Is that what you're thinking?"

"I'm the father."

Charlotte's chest squeezed. Her pulse began to race. Panic set in. "What if you're not?"

He gave her a look that made her stomach somersault.

"You are," she said lowly, "but I didn't think...didn't assume..." She couldn't finish the thought. She felt sick. Her limbs felt cold. She struggled to find her center and breathe. *Keep calm, keep calm, keep calm.* "You're a bachelor, living the bachelor lifestyle."

"You're single, as well."

"But I'm not dating others, and not sleeping around—" She stared at him horrified, and yet unable to take the words back. "What I mean is, we live really far apart. It's not as if we can fly a baby back and forth across the Atlantic."

He said nothing, but she felt the weight of her words between them as well as the accusation.

He was still sleeping with others. She was upset that he was sleeping with others. She hadn't even phrased it as nicely as that. She'd made him sound like a tomcat.

She waited for him to speak. And still he kept silent. She went hot and cold, hating to now be on the defensive. "You are a bachelor. You can do whatever you please. I apologize if I sounded critical of your lifestyle."

"Is that why you've waited so long to tell me about the baby?"

"No." She forced herself to meet his silver gaze. "No, I promise. I waited because... I didn't want to share the news."

"Share the news, or share our child?"

It felt as if he'd struck her in the chest. She inhaled hard, pain splintering her heart.

"I live in California."

"And I live here."

She picked through his words, processing the meaning. "Do you truly desire to be part of our child's life?"

"Absolutely. Any child of mine will be raised by me."

Another blow that made her throat thicken and her eyes sting. "By you?"

"My father was a hands-on parent, and I intend to be the same."

"How can you be so sure you want to do this?"

"I would never walk away from my responsibilities." He hesitated. "Would it make you feel better if I offered to be the custodial parent? I'd raise our child—"

"*No.* Not an option."

"Then why is it an option for you to be the sole custodial parent?"

"Because I'm making this baby. I'm carrying it right now."

"And you wouldn't be making a baby if it weren't for my sperm that found a way to reach your egg."

"I don't need the biology lesson, Brando."

"And I will not permit you to cut me out. I might not be carrying our child, but I am as committed to his or her future as you are."

Things had escalated quickly, she thought, dazed. She sat back, stunned, and uncertain as to what to say in response.

The waiter appeared with a bottle of sparkling water and after a few words from Brando, cleared away the wineglasses.

Silence stretched and Charlotte's eyes stung, hot and

gritty. Six months ago, she'd had sex with Brando, sex that resulted in three unforgettable orgasms, and one very unplanned pregnancy. "I didn't want any of this to happen," she said quietly. "I've never mixed business with pleasure, never, ever, until you, and now everything is a mess."

"Not that much of a mess," he answered. "We're two capable adults. We will sort things out and come up with a plan that puts the baby's needs first, because in the end, that is the important thing."

It wasn't a question, but a statement. It crossed her mind that she was seriously in over her head, because she'd had a plan, a good plan, but he'd just tossed it out and now they were starting over, and she had a feeling she wasn't going to like the new plan at all.

"There's no reason to rush, though," she said after a length pause. "We should take time to consider all the different options. The baby won't be here for three months, and that gives us time to discuss the pros and cons of each option. The last thing we want to do is let our hearts overrule our heads."

He studied her from across the table, the glittering light captured in his narrowed silver gaze and casting shadows beneath his high, hard cheekbones. Brando was no longer smiling. His jaw was hard, lips pressed firm. "Time will not change what is right. My duty is to my child, and the needs of my child come first now."

"I just thought you might want more time… You've only just learned about the pregnancy today. I worry you're being impulsive—"

"You didn't expect me to assume responsibility?"

"I—" She broke off, glanced away, the tip of her tongue moistening her dry lower lip. "I thought you'd be more ambivalent. I thought there might be more resistance."

"Why, if it's my son or daughter?"

"It took me weeks to get to the place you've reached in hours."

"Sex is how babies are made. I've always been cognizant that sex, as pleasant as it is, leads to procreation."

The waiter returned and there was no menu to read. The waiter rattled off the house specialties and Brando recommended the *bistecca alla Fiorentina*, claiming it was the best Florentine steak in the city.

"I won't be able to eat very much," she answered, "and I'm craving pasta. I thought I heard *crespelle* mentioned. Is that the dish that's similar and stuffed with ricotta cheese and spinach?"

"Yes. It's good here, too."

"I'll just have the *crespelle* and salad."

Brando spoke quickly to the waiter, placing their order. The waiter topped off their water glasses and left them alone.

"You didn't order wine," she said.

"You're not drinking so I won't drink," he said.

"I don't mind if you drink. You're a vintner."

"I'm not giving up wine forever. I just don't need any tonight." He studied her, expression hard. "Did you really think I'd agree to let my child be raised on the other side of the world?"

"I thought you'd react differently, yes."

"What did you expect?"

"That you'd be noncommittal, ask for a pregnancy test and then make me wait while you came to terms with the fact that I'm truly carrying your baby."

"Did you ever think it might possibly be someone else's?"

It was a fair question. It shouldn't put her on edge. She felt defensive, though. "No. You have been the only man I've slept with in the past year."

There was a subtle shift in his expression, his black lashes dropping ever so slightly over his piercing gaze. "Why?"

"I only sleep with someone I'm profoundly attracted to." She lifted her chin, smiled wryly. "I was profoundly attracted to you."

"Surely there are other men who catch your eye."

"Apparently not often enough." She pushed back a long pale strand of hair, tucking it behind her ear. "On the plus side, it made the question of parentage easy. You've been the only one I've slept with this year, so, you're it."

"Yet we used birth control."

"My pill, plus your two condoms." She felt hot bands form across her cheekbones. "Obviously, my pill wasn't effective."

"Nor were the condoms."

"I blame myself," she said. "Not you. It's why I'm on the pill. So there are no oops, no mistakes."

"And yet we still have an oops baby."

Her eyes met his and held. "I'd like to raise the baby at my home in Los Angeles. I have a lovely garden and I'm close to the ocean—"

"I don't live in California, *cara*."

She ignored the endearment as she held her breath, silently counting to ten. She needed to remain calm. "Perhaps you could buy a place near me. Perhaps you could make Southern California a second home."

"But it's not, nor will it ever be."

"I'll be there, and the baby—"

"Or, I kidnap you, keep you locked up at one of my estates."

She waited for him to smile or laugh. He did neither. "You wouldn't do that."

"You don't think so?"

Her insides did a nervous flip. He was being outrageous and she wasn't worried he'd kidnap her, but she understood the point he was making. He wasn't just going to walk away from them. He was asserting his rights. Brando would be a permanent part of their lives, and that was what made her heart race, and her anxiety spike. Brando wasn't one to be managed. Brando Ricci tended to do the managing. "No, you wouldn't do something illegal," she said lightly, feigning calm. "It would be bad for business, and we both know you're very serious about your family business and protecting your family's reputation."

"But even more protective of my child. If I'd go to great lengths to ensure the safety of the business, imagine what I'd do for my son or daughter."

Her pulse jumped yet again and she felt downright nauseous now. This was not going well. She'd thought she'd been prepared for these conversations, but clearly she'd forgotten Brando's strength and focus. "The point being that you'd never do anything to risk your reputation, and that includes your child's."

"Which is why I should whisk you away to keep you out of the public eye until we've figured out what we're going to do."

"I wish I could say that being whisked away sounded appealing—and yes, it does have a certain *Roman Holi-*

day sound to it—but I'm only here through the weekend. I fly into London Monday early afternoon."

"So soon?"

"I was actually worried that three days was far too long." She glanced up at the hard planes of his striking face, her gaze briefly meeting his, the silver-gray irises piercing, before looking away. Just that brief look into his eyes made her feel hot and tingly. If she could go back in time and change the past, she would. She would have never given herself to Brando, never allowed herself to imagine that she'd be able to handle all the complications of a night spent with him. "Why did I need to be here for three days? We'd have a conversation, you'd get a blood test and then we'd talk after the results were in. But it's not going like that. We're talking now as if we know the results—"

"Because we do. It's my child."

"But that doesn't mean we have to decide everything tonight. We have months—"

"No. We're not putting this off, and we're not going to try to negotiate with you in California. We're going to come to an agreement now, while you're here, and we get it in writing, and notarized, so that it's legal and binding."

"I'm not a runaway bride, Brando. I'm not going to disappear on you."

"How do I know that?"

"Because I'm giving you my word."

"That's a start."

"You don't believe me?"

"You waited six months to tell me I'm going to be a father."

"As I said this morning, I wanted to be sure the pregnancy was viable."

He said nothing for the longest time, and then, "Are we going to need lawyers? Should we just take it to court—?"

"Why would you say that? We don't need lawyers, and we don't need anyone else telling us how to do this. We're smart and reasonable. Surely we can come up with a plan between us."

"So, you'd be willing to live here?"

"I don't think that's necessary."

"You'd rather a newborn baby spend its first year in the air, flying back and forth between Los Angeles and here? That must be eleven hours or more in the air, without connections."

"No, of course not. That's why I think the first year the baby should be with me."

"And then you hand the baby over to me for a year?" he asked, expression blank.

She shuddered. "*No.* I'm not ever handing my baby over, not to you, not to anyone."

"So, we do need lawyers."

"Don't go straight there. Can't we at least try to talk this out?"

"I think you should live here the first few years. Your work is flexible. Your work isn't tied to a place. Whereas I'm a vintner. I can't abandon the grapes."

"Not all your work is in Chianti. You have other business endeavors—"

"So, let me get this straight. You want me to know about my child, but not be involved. You don't want support, either. You just want me to pretend this child doesn't exist, and let you do whatever it is you want?"

Her stomach cramped. She balled her hand into a fist. "That's not what I'm saying."

"Then how are you including me? Where is the space for me, *cara*?"

She didn't answer the question, but then, how could she? Her answer wouldn't have been positive, or flattering, but at least Brando understood Charlotte's intentions. She was doing the correct thing—informing him of the pregnancy—but then she was shutting him out. She didn't truly want him raising the baby with her. She wanted to be mother and father on her own.

That wasn't an option, but he chose to change the subject to keep her from jumping up and leaving.

He asked about a publicity campaign she'd been part of last winter, and as the subject changed, so did the tension. After a few minutes, he could see her relax. They discussed friends they had in common, as well as what was happening with the Ricci business right now.

Dinner arrived and conversation died as they ate, but at least it wasn't an uncomfortable silence. If anything, Charlotte looked thoughtful. He caught her looking at him several times, her brow furrowed, lips pursed.

"I hope you know that I would have never not told you about the baby," she said quietly after Brando ordered a coffee. "I wouldn't have ever kept his or her existence a secret from you. I'm not duplicitous. I genuinely needed time to wrap my head around the pregnancy, and the ramifications. Being a single parent will take work, but we can make it work."

"Why didn't you ask me to come to you in California?" he returned.

"And what would I have said to lure you there?"

"That you're pregnant. That you need me."

She ducked her head, but he could see the wash of hot pink in her cheeks. "I don't generally need people," she said after a moment. "They need me."

Suddenly he understood her in a way he never had before.

Charlotte wasn't playing games. She wasn't trying to cut him out—not in the way he'd first imagined—but she truly believed she was better off trusting no one, relying on no one, and just taking care of everything herself. It wasn't out of cockiness, or arrogance, but survival. This was how she functioned. This was what had allowed her to be successful.

"People make messes and I clean them up," she added with a faint smile, but the smile didn't reach her eyes. "I'm good at problem-solving. Rather exceptional, if I do say so myself."

"It's why we hired you last summer," he answered. "You were exceptional."

"I still am."

This was why he'd been so drawn to her. She was smart, articulate, gorgeous and passionate. The one night only hadn't been his rule, but hers. He hadn't liked making rules, or liked letting her make the rules, but he'd agreed because he'd wanted her that much.

He still wanted her, but everything was different now. This, between them, was no longer about sex, but family, and commitment. He couldn't think of her as an object of desire, but as the mother of his child.

"You might not like admitting it, but you do need me, *cara*," he said quietly, "and our child needs me, too. Let me in. Try to trust me a little bit."

"I will try, but it's not easy."

"You said you fly out Monday."

"Yes."

"It's Friday. That gives us the weekend to talk and make plans. Let's go to my house in the country. It will be quiet there, and we can discuss the future undisturbed."

She hesitated. "I don't know if that's a good idea. Being alone together created this situation we're now in."

"I'm not going to seduce you, if that's what you're worried about."

"I don't expect you to, not when there are other women in your life now, but I think we have to be clear in our intentions. Yes, I'm carrying your child, but I'm not yours, and you're not mine, and we don't have a relationship. We've never had a relationship. We had sex."

"Your point being?"

"One night of intimacy doesn't equate a relationship, so it's going to be very difficult for me to imagine a future where we do anything together, but I will try provided you realize that I'm not going to give up who I am, and what I want to do, just to please you."

Charlotte tried not to fidget as they waited for the bill to be brought. Her pasta had been excellent, but her nerves had kept her from eating too much. Their waiter, who had been attentive during the meal, now seemed to have disappeared, perhaps going on a dinner break of his own. Worse, she and Brando weren't speaking.

They sat at the table looking in opposite directions when he suddenly reached for his phone, tapped the screen and read something.

"The results are in," he said, his tone without emotion. "I am the father."

"There never was doubt at my end," she answered.

"Nor mine." He put away the phone. "But at least we have definitive confirmation, because people will ask."

"You mean, your family will ask."

"Of course they'll be interested."

"Even though it's none of their business?"

"That's where you're wrong, *cara*. It is their business. My child will become part of the business. You of all people, having worked with my family, should know that."

After returning Charlotte to her hotel, Brando drove home, and parked his car in his garage, but couldn't make himself go inside, his thoughts too tangled, his emotions intense, to the point of being overwhelming.

He was going to be a father.

A *father*.

It wasn't a hoax this time, or a game. The paternity test was positive. Charlotte was carrying his baby.

His.

Brando pocketed his car key and walked away from his house, heading toward the Arno, which flowed through historic Florence on its way to the sea. He walked along the riverbank to the medieval Ponte Vecchio with its multitude of shops.

Brando knew Florence intimately. He'd grown up here, not far from this very spot, just as his father had, and his grandfather before him.

Now he'd be a father, and he could raise his child here, too, or maybe in the countryside, maybe at his *castello* in the Chianti Valley.

Either way, his child would know and love Tuscany, just as he loved Tuscany, and the soil and grapes of Tuscany.

It was what it meant to be a Ricci. Passion. Perseverance. Commitment.

CHAPTER THREE

CHARLOTTE SLEPT BADLY, her sleep restless with dreams of Brando. Kissing him, making love with him…fighting with him, hiding from him, dreaming one dream after the other.

And now he was back at her hotel, driving the same classic sports car he'd driven to her hotel last night. It was a sleek glossy black car, a collector's car no doubt, a car that matched his sophisticated style and impossibly handsome face.

"I left the roof up," he said, "but if you prefer, I can put it down."

It was a beautiful early June day, the warm weather hinting at the summer heat to come. There would be no rain, nothing but gorgeous blue sky all day. "Is it too much trouble to put it down?" she asked.

"Not at all. You won't mind all the air?"

"I'd like it. It might help blow the cobwebs out of my brain."

"You didn't sleep well?"

"I'm having a hard time adjusting to the time change. I don't usually. Not sure what's changed," she said lightly.

"I do," he answered, "and I think you do, too. Maybe

it's time to stop pretending everything is 'normal.' Nothing is normal. Nothing will ever be quite the same again, either."

She stiffened, even as dread swept through her. What did he mean by that? It sounded so ominous, and yet Brando wasn't negative, or pessimistic. Perhaps she was just overreacting. Perhaps her exhaustion was making her overly prickly. "There will certainly be some changes," she answered, "but nothing problematic. Nothing I can't handle," she added.

"That's a good attitude," he said.

Charlotte fought the urge to scream. She was losing control, wasn't she? It wasn't her imagination. Brando was slowly seizing the upper hand, bit by bit, smile by smile, encouraging word by encouraging word.

She'd come to Florence expecting tension, and drama, especially after the results of the paternity test came in, but Brando was anything but tense, or angry. He wasn't cold or detached. He was kind…calm. Solicitous. He was managing her, versus the other way around, and that would end badly. She knew it'd end badly. She'd seen how he worked, and how he turned situations to his advantage.

She should have had a better plan.

She should have remembered how smart he was. How strategic.

"I was worried about you flying at this stage of your pregnancy," he added, his hand light on her back as he walked to his car, and yet the possession was clear. He was acting as if she was his, and the baby was his. He was acting as if they belonged to him. But they didn't.

She stepped away from him and gave him a pointed

look. "No touching," she said under her breath. "Remember?"

"*Cara*, I do this for every little old lady, including my grandmother."

Annoyed, she bit her tongue and gave her head a short, sharp shake.

"I might as well be a cane," he added soothingly.

She wasn't soothed. Her nerve endings tingled. She felt hot all over, hot and incredibly aware of him, as well as aware of the night spent together. It wasn't all that long ago. Just months ago. And it had been the most sensual, memorable night of her life, a night so full of passion and sensation that she didn't think she'd ever be the same.

She certainly didn't think she'd have to be here, now, dealing with him.

She'd allowed herself to do everything because she hadn't thought she'd ever see him again…

"What's wrong?" he asked. "Why are you aggravated?"

"I'm not aggravated. And I'm not a senior citizen, Brando, nor am I in need of assistance. I'm strong, and capable, and really happy not being helped," she answered tersely, hating herself for wishing his hand would return to her lower back, wanting the press of his fingers against the curve of her spine. Her body felt even more sensitive now that she was pregnant, and for some reason her libido was even stronger than before. She dreamed erotic dreams at night. During the day, she found herself wanting more, fantasizing about making love, and since that wasn't an option, she'd pleasured herself once, and the orgasm was so intense she'd worried that she might have hurt the baby, and so she hadn't done that again…even though she still craved touch and sensation. Satisfaction.

Brando opened the car's passenger door, and she settled into the sports car's low seat, feeling decidedly awkward. Her center of balance was changing, and her narrow skirt hindered her movement. Brando waited patiently, though, before closing the door behind her even as the hotel bell captain finished putting her bags in the trunk of the car.

Brando then went to work putting the convertible top down, which required just a couple of adjustments on his part, and then he was done.

"Was the international flight taxing?" he asked, returning to the driver's side and sliding behind the steering wheel.

He was dressed in a pale gray linen shirt and gray linen trousers, the shirt open at his throat, sleeves rolled back on his forearms. His throat and chest were tanned, the same burnished color of his arms. It took effort for her to focus on his words and not his lean, powerful body.

"I flew business here so I had my legs up," she answered, "and that definitely helped. But this is probably my last international trip until the baby arrives."

"Do you know if we're having a boy or girl?" he asked, shifting into Drive and pulling away from the hotel to merge into traffic.

She tensed all over at his use of *we* and she glanced at him, studying his profile as he focused on the congestion ahead caused by a truck delivering sleek modern leather couches to an interior design store. The truck was blocking a lane and drivers were honking. "Does it matter to you if I'm carrying a boy or girl?" she asked.

"No."

She wasn't sure she believed him. "Would you really love a daughter as much as the son?"

"I might love a daughter more," he said with a faint shrug.

She didn't know why but his words made her heart ache. Her father hadn't been unloving, but he hadn't been particularly affectionate, or attentive. She'd always thought if she was a horse he would have loved her more. He adored his horses.

She'd once wanted to be adored. She'd wanted him to miss her the way he'd missed them when away for too long.

He never did, though, and her mother had never really missed her, either, not even when she'd gone to Switzerland for boarding school.

Charlotte had learned to fill her time, and she'd learned the art of distraction. Don't think too much, don't feel hardly anything. Work, focus, achieve.

Those three things had become her mantra, and her mantra had made her successful.

She could still be successful as a mother. She'd certainly be a more devoted parent than either of her parents. She'd make sure her child knew he or she was loved and wanted.

Finally, Charlotte would have a family of her own. Finally, she'd have someone she could shower with love...

"There are no disadvantages to being a girl." Brando's deep voice drew her attention.

Charlotte glanced at him, heart suddenly too tender. "But there might be with a boy," she said.

He lifted a brow. "How so?"

She adjusted her seat belt around her middle and tried to make herself more comfortable. The interior of the sports car was small and Brando was close, his hand resting on the stick shift just inches from her knees. She could smell whatever he was wearing—aftershave, cologne, body spray. It was light, and sexy and very masculine. Between his heady scent, and the warmth radiating off him, she felt painfully aware of him. "I don't want to quarrel. I'm too tired today to quarrel—"

"Why would we quarrel?"

"Because if I'm carrying a boy, you might feel differently about being…involved. It might influence you somehow."

"How so?"

She swallowed hard. "This isn't the best time. I don't want to do this now—"

"Do what? Discuss the future?"

"Yes."

"But that's why you've come to Florence."

"But you're taking over, dictating everything—"

"You've had six months to be in charge. It's time I had a say, don't you think?"

She gritted her teeth, battling her anger, battling fear. She wasn't just losing control, she'd lost it. She'd been a fool to come to Florence without a proper plan, a fool to think it'd go any other way. For a split second she wished she'd never come to Italy, wished she'd never told him about the pregnancy, but just as quickly as the thought came, she smashed it. It wasn't right, or fair, not to Brando, and not to their child. Their child had a right to a father as much as a mother. "I hate this," she whispered. "I hate all of it."

He said nothing for a long moment, his jaw hard, his

eyes narrowed as he concentrated on the road. And then after an interminable silence, he said, "You hate me."

Her eyes burned. It hurt to swallow. "I don't hate you." Charlotte blinked back the sting of tears. "I hate that we're going to be playing tug-of-war with our baby. I hate that he or she will never have what I always dreamed of—a stable, unified, loving family. A family that stays together, sticks together, through thick and thin."

Silence followed her words. Charlotte knotted her hands in her lap, feeling raw and exhausted. Was it only yesterday she'd arrived in Florence? Was it only yesterday she'd knocked on Brando's door, feeling confident of her plans?

"It doesn't have to be acrimonious between us," Brando said, breaking the silence. "There's no reason we can't be unified, and supportive of each other, and when the baby is with me, he or she will have a supportive and stable family. A loving family. The Riccis might argue over succession within the business—"

"Might argue? Brando, you all hired me because your fights were making headline news."

He shrugged dismissively. "We're Italian. We're passionate."

"It's more than being passionate. Your family is in the middle of a battle over leadership, and the Riccis don't separate business from family. You might call yourself the Ricci family, but it's truly about the Ricci business."

"Your point being?"

"I don't want my child to be dragged into that. I'd hate for our child to become part of that scramble for power and position."

"Any child of mine will automatically become of the Ricci family, and thus the Ricci legacy. Boy or girl, he or she will play a role in the family—"

"Business," she added.

His broad shoulders shifted again. "You're right, in my family, it is one and the same. Family. Business. We're one family working together to succeed."

"Except you all weren't working together. You were at odds with each other—"

"We were, until you came along and helped shift the focus on what we weren't doing right, onto what we were doing right. You helped us focus our vision, our mission and our internal communication." He glanced at her, lips twisting. "We're stronger than we were before, thanks to you."

His words gave small comfort. She put a hand to her taut belly, uneasy, and worried. "Will an American child be welcomed into your very Tuscan, old-world family?"

"You're not American. You're British."

"I like living in America, though. I plan on remaining there, raising the baby there, so yes, the baby will be—"

"No."

She stiffened at his brusqueness, and for a moment there was just silence before she said quietly, "You like America. You have many American friends, particularly in Napa Valley."

"Yes, I do, but I'll never agree to my child being raised apart from me. That's not even an option."

Her pulse kicked up a notch. "Since we're being honest, tell me. What would you do with a small baby?"

"The same thing you'd do." He glanced at her, features hard. "I'm an uncle to a half-dozen nieces and nephews and we get together a lot. I've been part of their lives since they were born."

"Being an uncle isn't the same thing as being a father. Parenting is full-time work—"

"Which is why we should do it together, not forcing the baby to bounce between us."

"Well, the baby won't be bouncing anywhere for quite some time. He or she will need to be with me since I'll be nursing."

"I have no desire to separate the baby from you, but no Italian court will decide to give you custody based on breastfeeding."

She gripped her hands tightly together to hold back the whisper of panic. She hadn't flown all this way to lose her child. She hadn't begun this trip to be told she'd have only partial custody, either.

In her heart, she believed that babies belonged with the mother. It was her mother who did all the heavy lifting when Charlotte was small. Well, her mother and the fleet of nannies and housekeepers who were employed to keep the family running.

She blinked hard, fighting emotion she didn't understand.

He shot her a swift glance. "You should have come to me right away, you know. You should have told me the moment you knew you were pregnant. Instead you've had all this time to imagine life the way you wanted it to be, versus what it must be."

"You don't have to want the baby," she said under her breath.

"But I do."

She turned away, glancing out at the river, and the light bouncing on the bridges and elegant historic buildings. "During the ultrasound, I was asked if I wanted to know the baby's gender, and I said I didn't, because it doesn't matter if I'm expecting a boy or girl. I'm simply excited about being a mom, and the goal is a healthy baby."

"Agreed," he said. "But that baby is going to need a family. A healthy family. Neither one of us can do that on our own."

Brando drove, concentrating on the road, and Charlotte watched the city suburbs give way to rolling hills of gold and green.

For the next forty minutes, Brando drove the narrow, winding road that connected Florence to Siena, a road famous for its scenic beauty through hills and valleys dotted with villages and vineyards, while Charlotte admired the beautiful landscape. This was the renowned Chianti Valley, an area famous for its wines, olive trees and medieval villages.

She knew about his estate, but had never been there, and she was curious about the undulating hills, and the picturesque villages, each with its own bell tower rising above tiled roofs.

They were between villages when a tire blew in a loud pop and the sports car pulled sharply right. Brando slowed, and parked on the shoulder of the road, before climbing out to inspect the damage.

"It's just the tire," he said, opening her car door to speak to her. "Stay put. I can change it while you're in there."

She watched him roll his sleeves higher on his arms. His arms were sculpted of corded muscle. His skin the loveliest shade of bronze. "I heard it was dangerous to do that," she said, remembering how his shoulders had been equally powerful, and his torso endless lean muscle.

"You'll be safer in the car than standing on this narrow road."

"But what about you?" she asked, shading her eyes to look up into his face.

"Nothing's going to happen to me. You're the one I'm worried about." He closed the door firmly and she turned in her seat to watch him go to the boot and pull out the spare tire, the jack and tools.

He made changing it look effortless—well, except for the part where he lay on the ground, partway under the car to check the jack's position, and then he was out again and the car up, the lug bolts off, tire swapped, lug bolts replaced and car back down. Brando stowed the flat tire, dusted himself off and returned to the driver's seat, flashing her a wry smile. "Hope I didn't keep you waiting too long," he said.

His olive cheeks had a dusky flush and his eyes were bright from exertion, but he looked sexier than ever, and she thought a man who knew how to do things with his hands was incredibly appealing.

"That was impressive," she said, smiling at him as he buckled his seat belt.

"You must be easily impressed, then."

"Actually, I'm not. I have very high standards."

He shot her an amused glance. "Then how did I get you into my bed last New Year's Eve?"

It was her turn to blush, and she felt herself go hot all over. "Can we blame the champagne?"

"You weren't drinking that night. Everyone tried to hand you a glass of something. You refused."

"I rarely drink." She wrinkled her nose. "It's not that I don't like alcohol, but I'm a control freak."

"I see. You lost control, hated yourself for it and then promptly ghosted me."

"I didn't *ghost* you."

"What would you call it, then? No calls, no emails, no communication?"

"We didn't have sex to start a relationship. We had sex because we were attracted to each other and we were curious to see if it would be good."

One of his black brows lifted mockingly. "I hadn't realized I'd left you disappointed."

"You didn't. You know that night was incredible. But it wasn't something that we could do again. I was hired to work for your family, not bed the rebel son."

"I'm no longer the rebel son. I've become the good son."

"Then why do Enzo, Marcello and Livia all work together at the Ricci headquarters in Florence and you have your own office? And why are they no longer involved in the wineries, and you alone manage that arm of the Ricci business?"

He shrugged. "Because I have an affinity for the land, and they don't."

"Marcello told me you're the smartest of them all, but they worry about you doing your own thing."

"Because I don't do things by consensus, I do what I think is best. They don't like it—"

"Because you're the youngest?"

"And because you've met them. You know how it is. Too much discussion. Too much tension. It's a waste of time and energy. If something needs to be done, I'm going to do it. End of story."

"You don't feel isolated?"

"No. I love it. It's far better now that they are out of the fields and winery, and they can focus on fashion, and merchandising."

"And yet I saw the report Enzo had prepared for our meetings last August. Your wineries are outperforming, and outearning, what the three of them do...combined."

"Now it does. It wasn't always that way."

"But you have to be pleased."

"I'm not competitive, at least, not with them. I like to be successful, but not at their expense." He glanced at her, black lashes framing those startling silver eyes. "They're my older brothers and my sister. I look up to them. I respect them. I just want to do my part now—" He broke off, drew a breath, "It's time to do my part, to ensure my family's success."

It wasn't a villa, but a proper castle, she realized as they turned off the main road and began driving up a hill to the castle with a square tower in front of them, while tidy rows of grapes covered the hillsides.

"That's your home," she said, because it was the only building nearby, and what an impressive structure it was. The tower was made of stone, while the plastered walls were a soft creamy yellow, surrounded by tall stone exterior walls.

"It is," he agreed.

The *castello* was positioned on a hill with sweeping views of Val di Greve, and with access to both Florence and Siena, it had most likely been a strategic stronghold for centuries.

"From the square tower, it must date back to the eleven hundreds."

"There are some disagreements regarding the age of the *castello* itself, but historians all agree that the central tower is from the twelfth century. Some sources claim the castle as it is today dates from the early fourteen hundreds. We know from ancient records that the *castello* has been inhabited since 1456, and it was during that time period it earned its name, Castello Mare Scotti, for a descendent of the Medicis."

"When did you buy the property?"

"It's been almost ten years. The castle and grounds were a mess, in need of serious restoration, and while the vineyards were still producing grapes, they also needed to be replanted. Overhauling the orchards made sense—and those have become quite profitable. The restoration of the *castello* is more of a labor of love, an ode to Tuscany. I've lived many places now, but nowhere else is like this place. Chianti Valley is without a doubt home."

"More so than Florence?"

"I enjoy Florence. It's elegant and filled with art and history, but I've discovered I prefer the country over the city. My family had a big estate outside Florence when I was growing up, and my brothers have divided it between them, but that estate has never resonated with me, not the way Castello Marescotti resonates. From the first time I walked the property, I knew it was meant for me." Brando flashed a wry smile. "The family said I was crazy. Livia emailed me a half-dozen listings of available properties featuring palaces and villas in excellent condition, many with land attached, but none of them were right. Marescotti was mine. I often spend weeks at a time here. One day soon I hope to live here full-time."

JANE PORTER   67

"What about your house in Florence?"

"I'll still go for a special night, or a weekend, but once I have children—" He broke off and shot her a meaningful glance as he slowed to pass through the ten-foot stone walls with the huge iron gate. "I'd like to raise them where there is space to run and play."

Staff appeared as Brando parked. Someone claimed the luggage. Someone else took the car keys and then the car. A housekeeper ushered them through the front door, offering to show Charlotte to her room, but Brando said he'd take her himself.

Sunlight poured through the windows flanking the front door, and the staircase rose in the middle of the great hall, the staircase three levels of dark gleaming wood against pale yellow walls. Framed oil canvases hung on the walls while an enormous Venetian glass chandelier cast sparkling light everywhere.

She followed Brando up a flight of stairs to the second floor. They walked down the hall to the second door on the left. Her bedroom was luxurious as well as spacious, with plastered walls and thick dark beams set into the ceiling. The rose silk curtains framed tall windows, and the bed was covered with a matching silk coverlet. Fresh roses filled a vase next to the bed, and more roses nestled in a low bowl on the antique dressing table.

"Would you like a brief tour of the house and gardens?" Brando asked. "Or are you too tired?"

"Not too tired. I'd love to see your place. I heard so much about it last fall."

They exited her bedroom, stepping back into the hallway, which was sunny and bright thanks to a trio of tall windows lining the wall. The windows overlooked fertile vineyards and tidy orchards.

"How much of this land is yours?" she asked, pausing at one of the hall windows.

"Almost everything you can see from this spot." He pointed to a distant hill topped with another castle. "See that *castello*? That is my nearest neighbor, and his property starts at the bottom of his hill and continues for one hundred and ten acres that way. Everything from here, to that hill, is mine."

"How many acres do you have?"

"A little over two thousand, but it's in chunks and clusters as I've purchased available property in the valley."

Her eyebrows arched. "That is significant land for this area, isn't it?"

"I've been buying land when I can. Most of it is devoted to grapes, but not all. I also have a large olive orchard, and we have bees, and produce honey, too."

He led her back downstairs through the reception rooms and grand salons and smaller sitting rooms, as well as through the dining room, and the kitchen staffed with a head chef and an assistant. They walked through kitchen gardens, their shoes crunching the gravel paths, before entering a small orchard with fruit trees. At the back of the fruit orchard were the beehives, and they found one of Brando's gardeners, who also was the chief beekeeper, just finishing repairing the rain cover on one of the hives. Brando greeted him warmly and introduced Charlotte before they continued, returning to the path with the worn tiles. The smooth red-tiled path led them away from the house to a small chapel with its own square bell tower. They peeked into the chapel with its stained glass and dark wooden pews, before he led her back down the path, cutting through rose gardens and a topiary garden to end up at an enormous infinity pool with a jaw-dropping view of the valley. Elegant wrought iron loungers lined one side of the pool while a fountain happily splashed away in a far corner, creating tinkling sounds.

The valley was that of dark green rolling hills and picturesque villages and grapes. The terrain was more rugged than Napa, with high mountains in the distance. "You have a bit of paradise here," she said.

"I'm quite partial to it. I focus well here. In fact, I enjoy my work so much that it doesn't feel like work."

"That's the best sort of work, when it feels more like a passion."

"Do you feel that way about your work?"

"Sometimes. It depends on the clients. And the crisis." She flashed a smile. "Sometimes the crisis element overwhelms everything else and all I feel is adrenaline."

"Did you feel that way working with my family?"

"No. The Riccis are pragmatic. None of you liked the bad press, and you were able to come together to downplay the succession issue." She made a face. "Not that the issue has gone away. It's just smoothed over for the time being."

"I think we've at least begun to whittle away at the issue. We aren't burying our heads in the sand anywhere. Something has to be done."

"But you personally don't think Enzo's son is the one to lead the Ricci company in the future."

"I think he should be involved in management, but Antonio isn't a visionary, and he's overly cautious, which leads to a fear of making decisions. You can't have your CEO afraid to make a decision."

"And what of Marcello's and Livia's kids? Anyone there look promising?"

"Livia's daughter, Adriana, is brilliant. She's strategic and has this rather dazzling ability to 'see' the future while very much coping with issues of today. My vote would be for Adriana, but that won't be popular with my brothers. They both have sons and they're both grooming their sons to head the company." He paused and looked down at her. "And who knows what our child's strengths will be, but I'm hopeful he or she will also embrace the family, as loud and fierce and complicated as we are."

"Yet you all love each other," she said after a moment. "I think that is the thing that struck me most. You quarrel rather passionately, but that's because you all care so much." Her family was the opposite. The quarreling wasn't warm and loving. The quarreling was incredibly divisive, so divisive that Charlotte was more comfortable with her stepbrothers and sisters than her own siblings.

He shrugged. "We're family. Family sticks together." Or not.

He looked at her, silver gaze assessing. "You don't agree?"

"My family isn't as neat and tidy as yours, so I'm not sure how I feel about 'family.' It's not a simple question, nor a simple answer."

His expression eased, and he smiled. "Then how about I pose a simple question. Are you hungry? Lunch should be served soon."

"I am hungry," she admitted. "Lately I feel like I'm always hungry."

"Then let's walk back to the house, and you can freshen up before we meet on the terrace for lunch."

Brando escorted her back to the sprawling *castello*, where he left her at the foot of the stairs—on her insistence, as she didn't need to be walked all the way to her bedroom door—but as she climbed the stairs to the second floor, she couldn't help thinking of what Brando had said when they'd first arrived, that Castello Marescotti is where he'd want to raise his children, because there would be room for them to run and play. He was right, there was plenty of room here, both indoors and out. The stone house was huge, almost too big for a game of hide-and-seek, but she'd been raised in such a place herself and had thought nothing of the grandness, or the sheer amount of space. It's what she knew. It was home.

In her room, she took a brush to her hair, combing through the long blond strands until they were smooth, and then touched up her makeup. As she reapplied her lipstick, Charlotte tried to imagine this house as her baby's home and felt an odd prickle of pain and her hand shook. She had to draw a breath and steady her hand before putting the cap on the lipstick. It wasn't that this grand medieval house wasn't comfortable, because the interior was stylish and yet welcoming, a place both grown-ups and children would be at ease, but rather it was the idea of the baby being here without her...that her baby would have a whole life without her...

Sudden tears stung her eyes and she blinked hard, clearing her vision. She wasn't usually emotional, and yet all she felt right now were emotions, strong, intense, overwhelming.

She loved her unborn child rather desperately, and every fiber of her being wanted to protect the baby. But how could she do that if she wasn't with him or her?

How could she bring a child into the world and then not be part of his or her life…even part-time?

She put away her lipstick and slid the makeup bag and hairbrush into the top dresser of the pretty vanity, and then squared her shoulders. She could do this with Brando. She could be civil, and calm, and make him understand that she wasn't going to let a baby grow up without her. She didn't know the answer to "sharing" the baby, she just knew she was going to be with her child full-time, end of story.

CHAPTER FOUR

BRANDO WAITED FOR Charlotte on the terrace, the sun warm overhead as he stood at the balcony overlooking the valley. It was perfect weather for lunch al fresco, the temperature warm, the air fragrant, smelling of roses, citrus blossoms and jasmine. The table was set for two, and a lush bouquet of pale pink and creamy white antique roses created a charming centerpiece, especially when paired with the fine china and delicate Venetian stemware.

It was a table setting that hinted at romance, but there was nothing romantic about his intentions. Brando had never been a man of romance—he was far too carnal, far too practical. He loved women and loved sex, but so far, he'd been careful to avoid commitments, much less serious entanglements.

And yet despite his best efforts to avoid entanglements, he was facing one now, an entanglement with lifelong implications.

He'd known that one day he'd have children—Italians were family oriented, and he had a wicked soft spot for his nieces and nephews, who made it clear they adored him—but marriage and children was down the road, far, far down the road, because marriage was forever. Marriage required complete commitment, as well as a suitable partner who one could grow old with, and hopefully, still like decades later.

His parents had had such a marriage. His parents married in their twenties, and had just celebrated their sixtieth wedding anniversary when his father passed away. Heartbroken, his mother had almost immediately moved to her widowed sister's house in Cinque Terre, where she and her sister found happiness being under the same roof. They missed their husbands but found endless opportunities to see their children and grand-children.

Livia and Enzo had grumbled about their mother moving to the coast, to a place that wasn't easy to reach, but Marcello agreed with Brando that it was good for their mother to have an identity of her own, that she needed to have adventures and fun, adventures that had nothing to do with the rest of them.

Brando smiled thinking of his mother. She was a spitfire, full of endless energy, and she was always happy to see her family, but he respected her for not wanting to sit around her house, just mourning the death of her husband, and waiting for death to come. Life was meant to be lived. Life was meant to have passion, and gusto, and if anyone in the family had gusto, it was his mother.

But he also knew what his mother would say if he knew he'd gotten a woman pregnant. Her first ques-tion would be, "How will you make this right?" Not because a pregnancy was shameful, but a pregnancy represented life, and love, and family. He didn't think of himself as a traditionalist, but the idea of someone, *anyone*, having his child and raising that child far from him made his skin crawl. Maybe Charlotte was comfortable picturing a world where her baby—*their* baby, he corrected himself—shuttled back and forth between two homes, but he wasn't.

He knew her family had numerous marriages, divorces and out-of-wedlock babies in it. They took the idea of commitment far more loosely than his family did. There hadn't been a divorce in his family for generations. Nor had there been a baby born out of wedlock.

One of his older brothers had married when his girlfriend was pregnant, and it had been a rather hastily arranged wedding, but they were still together, and had added three other children besides that first unplanned pregnancy.

Brando hadn't been thinking of marriage, nor had he thought he was ready to settle down, but if Charlotte was pregnant, this was serious. This was a game changer. This impacted everything. Either she would agree to give him custody of the baby—which he didn't see her ever doing—or she would agree to marry him. Those were the only two options he saw. He wasn't about to have his firstborn raised in a bohemian household in California, or at one of the sprawling estates owned by her family in England. Her family seemed to spend as much time in England as they did in France and that was not acceptable, not for a Ricci. His family was Italian, and proud of their heritage. He wanted his child—son or daughter—to be raised immersed in his culture, his language, his family.

Bottom line, he wanted his child to be part of his family.

And put like that, it did make him sound conservative, and old-world. But the Riccis were family oriented, and family came first, and last, and they understood what it meant to stick together, through thick and thin. It wasn't that her family or culture didn't count, but her culture was a mishmash of English, American, French, and then there were those years from the Swiss boarding school, years where he suspected young women were taught how to snare the world's most eligible bachelors, rather than how to live a successful, independent life.

Charlotte, though, was probably the exception. She'd started her own business and had created a name for herself. She was financially independent, and success- ful. She'd be a good wife. Once he convinced her it was the right thing to do.

He thought of her, stubborn, proud, confident—and then just like that, she was there, stepping through the glass doors out into the Tuscany sunshine, blond hair spilling down her back, a hint of rose in her cheek, fire in her eyes—and he knew it would take some convinc- ing, to get her on the same page.

She wasn't going to want to marry him, but having weighed his options, it was the only real option before them.

Lunch was leisurely, with small courses being re- placed by other courses, and the portions were perfectly sized so that Charlotte enjoyed everything as much as she could, considering Brando kept watching her with an intensity that she found dizzying. Every movement reflected his physical strength and grace. He was not a man of leisure. One didn't get a body like his with- out hard activity. She had a sudden flash of memory, of his hips arching against hers, his body filling her so completely that she wanted nothing more than to be his, again and again.

The vividness of the memory, the picture of his beautiful naked body above her, filled her with heat and a breathlessness that made it impossible to take another bite of her custard dessert.

She pushed the small plate away, hot, flustered, confused, and put a hand to her hot cheek, as if to cool herself.

"Is it too warm in the sun?" Brando asked, immediately noting her gesture. "Would you prefer to sit in the shade? We can move to the umbrella—"

"I'm fine. The sun is gorgeous."

He didn't appear convinced. "I don't want to fatigue you."

"I'm pregnant, not eighty, Brando."

"Yes, you're pregnant," he said darkly. "Which is why I won't have you overly tired. Perhaps we should go inside—"

"I'm *fine*. Trust me."

"You're flushed."

Yes, because I'm thinking about making love to you. Thinking about your body. Thinking about the amazing things you did with your body...

She didn't say it, though, but she blushed, exquisitely aware of him.

"If you truly are comfortable where we are, I think it's time we talked about why you've come to Italy, and what we're going to do." Brando's deep voice was firm, his gaze direct as it met hers.

"I suggest we marry. Soon. A simple ceremony, followed by an intimate dinner with our immediate family—"

"Excuse me?" she interrupted, brow creasing.

"The sooner the better," he concluded.

"Your wife?" She stared at him aghast. "Please tell me I'm misunderstanding you."

"No. You are understanding me perfectly."

"I am not going to marry you."

"Why not?" he retorted calmly.

"There's no reason for us to marry. We're not living in the Dark Ages, or the Victorian times. There is no reason we can't have a child without being married—"

"There is in my family."

"Maybe your family needs to adapt, then. Maybe it's time the Riccis evolved."

"It's not just about my family's values, or morality," he answered. "It's about the business. Our child won't have any hopes of heading the family business if we're not married."

"Well, I sincerely doubt our child would want to head your family business, not if it's that archaic." She gave him a long look. "And I know your family is archaic. It's why I was called in to mediate in the first place. The Riccis still live in the nineteenth century, but it's time they caught up with the rest of the world. Children do just fine in single-parent homes. Children thrive—"

"When raised in a stable home, with two loving stable parents."

She eyed him for a long moment. "You and I are stable, and we will be loving parents. But it's not necessary to be in the same house together. In fact, that's asking for disaster. I can guarantee that will create more instability than anything."

"Why?"

"We're not meant to be together, Brando, and regarding a single home, you don't live in just one house. You bounce between your properties, never in one place long."

"But you've already heard me say that this place is home, and this is where I intend to raise my children."

"You're not settled here yet, and babies are adaptable. Obviously it's different once children are in school, but that's years from now. Five or six years."

"I hadn't planned on settling down quite yet, but your pregnancy changes everything. It changes both of us. I'm prepared to make the necessary changes." He hesitated a beat. "Are you?"

She felt her shoulders rise, and a quick hot retort rush to her tongue, but she held the words back and forced herself to count to five, and then ten. "I already have. I'm preparing a nursery in my home. I've begun taking birthing classes."

"All without me?"

She choked on an uneasy laugh. "I'm not planning my future around you, no."

"You should be. I'm planning my future around you, or more correctly, I'm planning my future with you."

If her heart wasn't racing she'd get up and move. Flee. But as it was, she didn't feel steady enough to even get up and walk. "I don't think we're on the same page," she said hoarsely.

"*Cara*, my love, children need security, traditions and a familiar routine."

She suppressed a shiver at the husky rasp in his voice, as well as the endearments. She wasn't his darling, or his love, and she hated that he sounded so reasonable, so patient, when everything in her screamed in protest. "That's where we don't see eye to eye, Brando, as I had very two very different families and very different traditions with each family, and it didn't hurt me.

If anything, it was good for me. I learned to be flexible, and adaptable."

"You say that now, but I'm sure you felt pain when your parents divorced, and then your mother remarried and moved you to California."

"It was a change, and yes, it was hard being ten with chaos all around me, but I'm stronger because I've had to deal with challenging circumstances."

"But if you had your way, is that what you'd wish on your child? Challenging circumstances? Or would you want to protect him, or her—"

"Now you're just being unfair. I would always want to protect my baby. I want to do what's best for the baby, which is why I'm here, trying to include you, but there's a big difference between including you and becoming your doormat!"

"How is marriage making you a doormat?"

"Because it's giving up everything I want, and need, to do what you think is best. But I don't believe it's necessary for us to marry, and I most definitely don't believe it's the best thing for us. We can provide stable homes independently of the other. You provide a home here in Italy, and I'll provide one in LA—"

"You can't possibly be serious about raising our child in Los Angeles."

"What's wrong with Los Angeles?"

"What is right about Los Angeles?"

She pressed her lips together, frustrated and unwilling to say more. She counted to ten, and then she couldn't remain silent any longer, and blurted, "There is much to like about Italy, and much to love about Tuscany, but you're a little too smug about being Italian—"

"I'm proud of my heritage."

"But it's not the only heritage in play here. I have my own."

"You've run away from yours. You left it behind. You're just like everyone else that has run to Los Angeles, looking to reinvent themselves."

His scorn stung and she bit into her lower lip, trying not to focus on his criticism. He was fighting for a place in their child's life. He was fighting to be included. She understood that. She respected that. But he was giving her no middle ground and middle ground is what she needed. "There is beauty in reinvention," she said quietly. "And beauty in change. I appreciate you wanting to do the right thing by offering to marry me, but I must decline, must most adamantly decline. I will not marry because it's the morally right thing. If I marry it's because I'm in love and want to spend the rest of my life with someone, rather than being trapped with someone out of duty or misplaced obligation."

"Now that is old-fashioned."

"To marry for love?"

"Love marriages end in divorce when the dopamine fades. You and I both know that. Children can help parents bond, and marriages can last because of oxytocin. We make a choice, and then choose to be committed, and we have a marriage that endures."

"For a moment, I thought you were speaking of grafting grapevines. That is another asexual propagation technique."

"Yes, but I believe our procreation technique was sexual. I believe you're pregnant because we couldn't get enough of each other."

True, true, true.

Charlotte closed her eyes, held her breath and prayed

for something witty to say, because right now she just felt trapped.

"We still have two days," Brando said quietly, "two days before you fly to London. Let's say no more now, and let you have some time to yourself. We can discuss this again at dinner."

Her eyes opened and she looked at him a long moment before she gave her head a short, regretful shake. He was beautiful, and fascinating, but not the man she'd marry. Not a man she could plan a life with, either. He loved women, loved sex, loved his freedom. He'd be a terrible husband, and he'd break her heart because she wouldn't be able to share him, nor would she be able to forgive him for being in other women's beds. "My feelings won't change."

"Neither will the facts. We're having a baby. We have to put aside our differences—"

"I don't think we can."

"Let's leave it for now. We have tonight."

In her bedroom, Charlotte curled up in a chair near the window, pressed her fist to her mouth and stared out the window at the valley trying to calm herself and yet unable to relax, annoyed by Brando's high-hand-edness, and frustrated by his inability to listen to what she wanted and needed.

This was why she didn't date powerful men, or pow-erful, wealthy men, and this was why she didn't want to become part of a powerful man's family...or any fam-ily that made edicts and rules and told her how she was supposed to live and behave. She wanted to be herself. She wanted to be her own person.

How did she become so good at handling family

strife? Because she'd grown up in it. Immersed in it. And would have drowned in it if she hadn't figured out how to rise above.

The point was, she understood family dynamics, and family politics. But just because she understood it didn't mean she wanted to spend her future answering to others. It was bad enough that she still had her own family to contend with, but to marry Brando, and to suddenly have to deal with the Ricci family, as well?

No.

It wasn't going to happen.

His family were not bad people, and she'd enjoyed them as an outside consultant, but Riccis were very strong and opinionated, and passionate, and forceful with their thoughts and feelings. Her family, on the other hand, were quieter, and judgmental, and distantly disapproving. One still had to measure up, but the interactions were different, and the expectations were communicated differently. She didn't know what was worse: the fierce, expressive discussions that took place in passionate families, or the cool, disapproving silence of her family. Either way, she preferred the calm of living alone, on her own terms, able to make the decisions that were right for her.

During dinner Charlotte felt as if she was on pins and needles, waiting for Brando to launch into another persuasive speech about why marriage was the right choice for them, but he didn't. Instead he asked her how much she knew about the wines of Tuscany, and when she said she knew very little other than Chianti was considered the most popular red wine from Tuscany, he gave her an interesting history of winemaking in Tuscany, explaining that Sangiovese, the most commonly plated red grape, and the basis for Chianti Classico wines, was such an ancient grape in Italy that many considered it indigenous to the area. "It's a grape that has a very long growing season, budding early, and then needs time to ripen. In the industry, we say it's slow to ripen."

"Not all grapes are slow to ripen, then?" she asked.

"We have mutual friends in Napa Valley, and their Chardonnay and Pinot Noir are both early ripening grapes. Cab, Merlot, Sangiovese are late varieties."

"Is that what brought you to California last year?"

"No." His gaze met hers and held. "You did."

"Me?"

"Mmm-hmm. I'd hoped to see you again."

She felt herself flush. "We agreed there would be just that one night."

"Most women don't mean it."

She grew hotter, her skin hot and prickly across her cheekbones, her lips tingling, too. And just the tingle in her lips made her remember how good his mouth had felt on hers, and how his kisses had drawn her in, pulling her under, seducing her like nothing she'd ever known before. "I'm not sure how to respond to that."

"You're remarkably good at compartmentalizing."

But ah, she wasn't, and she hadn't found it easy to put him behind her. She'd felt almost desperate with desire, and she'd craved him for weeks after her return to Southern California. The desire and her emotions had been so intense they'd scared her, making her feel alien even to herself. In the end, being with him that night hadn't been a release, but a bond, and now the ties to that bond were tightening. Her stomach did an uncomfortable little flip and she forced herself to respond, feigning a cavalier attitude she didn't feel. "You mean, good at compartmentalizing for a woman?"

"I'm not sexist."

"Oh, you most definitely are. You're the one expecting me to move here. You're the one that won't even consider other arrangements."

"Nothing is in stone. I'm open to discussion, open to suggestions. How should we make this work, *cara*?"

Again, she bristled inwardly at the endearment. He said them so easily, dropping them like overripe cherries, even as he neatly turned the tables on her. "There is no simple solution. It's one of the reasons I've waited to come to you. I needed to accept what's happening, and then problem-solve. And I'm here now, because I believe that at least for the baby's first year, the baby should be with me—"

"Then how will our baby bond with me?" he interrupted, his expression still pleasant but there was a new, steely edge to his voice.

"Fathers bond with their children later… They're never fond of the baby stage and tend to feel useless until babies are weaned and able to have more independence and mobility."

Brando looked at her for a moment before laughing, and not just a little laugh, but a big, deep laugh as if he'd never heard anything half so amusing. "I don't know where you get your information from, but it's wrong."

"It's common knowledge."

"Is it?"

Again, he made her hackles rise. "My father had no use for babies. My brothers are useless until the toddler stage, but even then, they hate it when the children cry for Mummy."

"Maybe it's cultural, then, because my father was very hands-on, from day one. My brothers all helped with the night feedings by changing diapers, bringing the newborn to their wives and then burping the newborn before returning to bed. Marcello and his wife have a young baby now, and they're in the middle of the sleepless-night phase. Marcello is exhausted but he said he wouldn't trade this stage for anything. It's when he feels closest to the bambino, and the most needed."

His words filled her with a strange yearning feeling, which was so strange since just a moment ago she felt fierce and angry. She hated the rioting within her making herself feel as if she were a living kaleidoscope. "You paint an idyllic picture."

"Well, I've left out the colic, and the baby that won't sleep at night, but insists on napping all day, or the exhaustion from trying to cope with an inconsolable infant who won't stop screaming."

She just looked at him, unable to think of a thing to say because it struck her for the first time that he might know more about newborns than she did.

"It's easier to parent as a team. I think we should work as a team," he added. "I think we'd be most successful as parents that way."

She suddenly needed air. She needed to move and breathe and she couldn't do it in the dining room, as elegant as it was. "Would you mind terribly if we stepped outside? I'm feeling overly warm."

"Let's step outside and walk a bit. It might be a little cool, though."

"I'm sure it'd feel good."

It was cooler outside, but not cold, and there was a light breeze that carried the fragrance of flowers, freshly cut grass and warm soil. It was rich and ripe and pungent and Charlotte breathed deeply, drawing the layered scent in, reminded of her family's country house in Sussex.

"How are you feeling now?" Brando asked her as they walked along the pea gravel path that led from the house and into a long, rectangular walled garden, the pale gray stone walls lined with neatly pruned boxwoods, the center dominated by an ornate fountain that looked as if it had been there for hundreds of years, and two ornate flower beds. The light was just now fading, painting the garden shades of lavender and plum.

"A little better," she said.

"That doesn't sound very convincing," he replied.

She didn't answer, and he said nothing. They walked the length of the walled garden in thoughtful silence, and then did another lap, completing a full circle of the garden.

"I'm just scared," Charlotte blurted, stopping next to the fountain. "I feel like everything is moving faster and faster, and I feel like I'm losing control."

"You're entering the final trimester. It won't be long until the baby arrives, and that is a loss of control. Everything will be different, for both of us."

The baby gave a kick just then and she inhaled and put a hand to the side of her bump.

"Moving?" he asked.

She nodded. Impulsively she reached for his hand, and placed it where hers had been, pressing his palm to the spot she'd felt the kick. For a moment nothing happened, and then it happened, a swift, little kick, or stretch. She looked up into his face to see if he'd felt it.

His jaw had firmed, and his lips pressed, but his silver gaze softened, and there was a look of wonder in his expression. *"Sorprendente,"* he murmured.

Amazing.

Her eyes burned, hot and gritty, and she blinked, chasing away the stinging sensation, but she couldn't erase the aching lump in her throat. Quickly, she let go of his hand, suddenly self-conscious, aware that she'd reached for him, creating an intimacy neither of them wanted.

"I'm glad you're here," he said huskily. "I'm glad you came now, so that I can be part of this. Thank you."

Her heart squeezed and she felt more of that terrible pain—yearning coupled with fear, longing layered with anger. Feelings were messy business. She preferred order and structure.

As if he could read her mind, he tipped her chin up, studying her face in the soft light of the rising moon. "Neither of us has absolute control," he said. "But then, no one has absolute control."

And then he dropped his head, his mouth covering hers, and kissed her. She'd imagined that maybe his kiss now would feel platonic, or reassuring, but no, the kiss was just as shocking and scorching as it had been New Year's Eve when his lips made her feel as if she'd touched a live wire, electricity coursing through her.

He must have felt her shuddering response because he drew her closer, his lips moving across hers, deepening the kiss. She thought she'd remembered the pleasure, but this was even more intense, more sensual, and she welcomed the pressure of his mouth, and his hand sliding from her waist down her hip. She leaned into him, giving herself over to him, and when he parted her lips, and his tongue swept the inside of her soft swollen bottom lip, she couldn't contain her sigh, or the desire humming through her.

He caught her soft lip between his teeth, and then his tongue stroked the inside of her mouth, reminding her of how his hips had moved as he'd thrust into her, filling her, making her body come alive.

She was coming alive now, feverishly alive, and she clutched Brando, holding on, legs weak, heart pounding, veins full of honey and fire.

Then his head lifted and he gazed down into her eyes. "I suggest we marry as soon as possible."

Charlotte staggered back a step, dazed, senses swimming. "What?"

"I'll look into the paperwork tomorrow."

"Brando, no." She moved back another step, legs trembling, tension rippling through her. "Marriage isn't the answer, it isn't. There must be another way to make this work. I'll get an apartment in Florence…something not far from yours."

"We should be together, under one roof."

"Then give me a suite of rooms in your house. We'll be roommates."

"That will never work. There's too much chemistry between us. We'll drive each other mad."

"I'm not going to rush into anything. We have time. We have months."

"Let's not tempt fate."

"Months," she repeated firmly, smashing her panic, even as she turned around and started back to the *castello*, her gaze fixed on the tall, magnificent house glimmering with soft yellow light.

CHAPTER FIVE

THE MORNING SUN shone brightly, warming Brando's back as he walked from the house to the vineyard. The dark soil beneath his feet smelled fresh, the air around him fragrant. Summer was coming, and then it'd be fall. Brando was glad to be back on his estate, and he never felt more peace than when he was here, close to the vineyards, able to walk amid the vines. He checked clusters of grapes as he walked between the tidy rows. It looked like an excellent crop this year and he anticipated a good harvest come September.

But that wasn't all that would happen. By the time the grapes were harvested, he would be a father.

He hadn't quite yet become accustomed to the thought. It was still exciting, surprising. Even a little overwhelming. He hadn't been ready to settle down, hadn't imagined starting a family for another few years. Because the Riccis didn't divorce, they tended to marry late, and he was no exception. He'd planned on marrying in his mid to late thirties, but God had a different plan, and he was good with that.

Charlotte, he knew, wasn't.

Charlotte saw obstacles where he saw solutions. He wasn't worried, not yet. He'd find a way to make her understand, but it would mean he needed time, and there wasn't much time, not if she intended to be on a flight to London tomorrow.

He paused at the next row, fingers lightly brushing a leaf, and then the cluster of grapes beneath.

Time together was what they needed. If she was determined to still go to London tomorrow, then he'd go with her.

Better yet, he'd fly her there himself.

None of Charlotte's clients knew she was pregnant, and none of them knew she was in Italy, either. She woke up to dozens of new emails in her inbox, and her phone showed an alarming number of new texts and voice messages needing attention.

Work was good, she told herself, as she sat with her laptop at the breakfast table, responding to emails she could answer now, and making note of what she'd need to do to get back to people.

She had to survive only another day here, she told herself, and then she'd be in England, with her family—not that any of them knew she was coming, in part because she wasn't sure where she should go. But she didn't have to have that figured out yet. Tomorrow was tomorrow, today was today, and she'd devote the rest of her morning to work, and then eventually she'd have to face Brando, and hopefully by the time she did, she'd be more sanguine about the kiss.

The kiss.

Her fingers hovered over her keyboard as heat washed through her. The kiss…

Brando still had such an effect on her. There was something so elemental about him, them, and she couldn't resist him, not physically. Emotionally, that was a different matter. Emotionally, all she had to do was remember Louisa at the door of his Florence house, practically naked, clearly having come to the door from his bed, and that memory still made her recoil.

She knew she couldn't judge him for having others—there was no relationship between them. But how could she make the leap from "nothing" to wife?

It didn't make sense. She couldn't wrap her head around it...or her heart. And for marriage, she needed her heart.

She closed her laptop and pushed it away before crossing her arms over her chest, frustrated and indignant. It was a mistake coming to Florence to see Brando, and an even bigger mistake agreeing to come to this house in the country with him because everywhere she looked, it was his world. She didn't belong here, and she felt trapped right now, trapped in his big, sprawling *castello*, trapped by the beautiful pastoral views, trapped in his world that was both seductive, and consuming.

Brando wasn't like anyone else she had ever known, and she didn't know how to deal with him. She felt hormonal, and restless, agitated and confused. She should have just stayed in California and gone to her yoga class and eaten her healthy salads and worked at her desk and sent him a message that they needed to talk, that she had something important to tell him.

He would have come to see her.

She could have stayed put and made him do the traveling. Why didn't she?

That was easy. She'd secretly wanted the element of surprise. She'd wanted to discover for herself who he really was, not who she imagined him to be. She wanted facts. The truth. Because one night together wasn't anything, one night of sex was just a fantasy. After she'd returned to Los Angeles, she'd built him up in her mind, too, made him special, and wonderful...almost mythic... and she knew it couldn't all be true, that he couldn't really be everything she'd made him out to be. And so, she'd arrived in his world unannounced, shown up on his doorstep to see what she would see—not the fantasy, but the man.

And the man had a famous model in his bed.

The man probably had famous models frequently in his bed. But, why shouldn't he? He was ridiculously wealthy, and impossibly handsome, and he made love like a god.

He'd made her feel things she didn't know she could feel, and he'd made her hope—as impossible as it was— that she was different. Special.

Seeing Louisa on his doorstep dispelled that hope. Charlotte wasn't special, or unique. What they'd done...experienced... New Year's Eve was no different from what he'd done, and shared, with countless other women. Unwittingly she thought of her family, and the affairs—hushed as they were—and the lack of commitment. Both of her parents had been unfaithful. Both of them had found it impossible to honor their wedding vows. If she married Brando, she'd be living with someone who wasn't that different from her father, and it filled her with pain.

But maybe pain was good. Maybe it was better this way, better to deal in facts.

Fact one: she was pregnant.

Fact two: the baby was due in three months.

Fact three: Brando Ricci, Italian tycoon, was the father.

Fact four: Brando didn't love her, but she, Charlotte Parks, might just be a little in love with him…

Footsteps sounded and she glanced up, hoping it was the housekeeper with her cappuccino. She'd had one earlier with breakfast but still craved another cup. Instead it was Brando, and he was carrying a tall bottle of water and a glass.

He twisted off the cap on the bottle and filled the glass with sparkling water before placing the glass in front of her. "Too much caffeine isn't good for the baby," he said. "Water is better for both of you."

"I didn't sleep well. I can't wake up."

"Go for a swim. That will be far more refreshing, and healthier, too."

"I'm not interested in squeezing myself into a bathing suit."

"There is no one to see. You'll have complete privacy."

"I have too much work to do, and sadly, I didn't bring a suit."

He dropped into a chair at the table. "Is there anything I can help you with?"

"No. You've done quite enough, thank you."

"Giving you water instead of coffee?"

"No, getting me pregnant. I think I'll handle everything else from here on out." She shifted in her chair, and drew a slow breath, trying to calm the butterflies in her middle and the tightness in her chest. Just his appearance set her heart racing, and now that he was seated close, she felt breathless. Because this was also a fact—her body liked him, very much.

And then she forced herself to remember Louisa, and Louisa was sleeping with him, and Louisa was his, or vice versa. But the point was, just two days ago he was with Louisa and now he was proposing marriage and the whole thing was ludicrous, and more than a little disturbing.

"How can you suggest marriage when you're still romantically involved with other women?" she said bluntly, unable to hold the words back. "And how can I possibly think marriage is an option when just days ago Louisa opened your door, practically naked?"

"I thought we talked about this."

"She answered your front door."

"She's a free spirit. She knew I didn't want her to, so she ran downstairs before I could."

"You like that?"

"She's playful. Fun."

Charlotte closed her eyes, aware that she was nothing like free spirit Louisa. In fact, Charlotte was the exact opposite of Louisa, and Charlotte couldn't imagine being wild and outrageous. From an early age, she'd recoiled from drawing attention…doing anything outside the norm. And the one time she took a risk, it had been a calculated risk, but still a risk, and Charlotte had ended up pregnant.

"I've told you this already. Louisa and I are not together," Brando said patiently. "There is nothing serious between us. She was in Florence and we met and had dinner—"

"Had sex."

"Yes."

"Probably lots of it."

He leaned forward abruptly, closing the distance between them. "Charlotte, what are you doing?"

There was a bite in his voice and she shook her head,

feeling sick. "This is all wrong," she murmured, looking anywhere but at him. "Every bit of it."

"You must stop thinking about Louisa. She's not part of this equation. No one is, but us. She is completely out of the picture"

She shook her head again, feeling even more frantic. "I can't have your baby. I can't. You will never be faithful. Never be mine. Never—" She broke off and jumped up, neatly sidestepping his hand to escape to the other side of the balcony. "What a mess this all is."

He rose from his chair and followed her. "What's going on? What's happening?"

"I'm just realizing that I've been living in a fantasy world. I've been pretending it's just the baby and me, but it's not. There is you, and you don't fit into my life or my plan. Last night you said we should marry. You said we should raise the baby together, married, but how? It'd never work. You're a bachelor. A virtual playboy—"

"I object. I'm not a playboy and have never been that."

"You have lots of sex with lots of women."

"When I'm in a committed relationship, I'm only with that woman. But if I'm not in a relationship, and I'm attracted to a woman, and she's attracted to me, we might go to bed together. Why not? Sex isn't bad, or dirty. It's physical, it's pleasurable. It's a form of communication and connection—"

"But I don't have sex with every man that is appealing. I don't just make love because I'm attracted to him."

"You did with me."

"And what a mistake that was," she retorted grimly.

He stood in front of her, hands on his lean hips, studying her. "You didn't think so at the time," he said after a long moment.

"I regretted it almost immediately," she answered, glancing at him, and then away, because it was too unnerving to meet his penetrating gaze. "I flew home kicking myself the entire way."

"That must have been a very painful flight," he said deadpan.

She rolled her eyes. "Of course you'd make a joke about it. You don't know me, and you don't understand the first thing about me, because if you did, you wouldn't have suggested marriage as if it were a cure-all. Marriage wouldn't make anything better, Brando. It would make everything worse."

"Explain."

"I just have no desire to be married, much less marry someone who I'm not compatible with. We had chemistry, but you have chemistry with every woman—"

"That's not true."

"And you enjoy your freedom, and the opportunity to be with different women, and I refuse to be the one who takes that freedom from you. You like being a bachelor, so be a bachelor. You can be a bachelor and a father. It's done all the time."

"Not in my family."

"Well, welcome to the twenty-first century, Ricci family."

He ignored the jab. "I was happy being single, but I will also be happy being married."

"I won't be."

"You don't know that, because you haven't even truly considered the suggestion. You've decided outright it's not for you—"

"Because it's not."

"But don't you think that's a little immature? Can

you try to have an open mind? We're having a baby, and we need to come together for our child. I think you're using me as an excuse. I've told you I'm ready, and nothing will change my mind now."

Charlotte looked away, his words weighing heavily on her, eating away at her conscience and heart. She did want what was best for the baby, but the only reason Brando was suggesting marriage was for the baby. Not because he cared for her, and not because he thought it would be good for her, but it would be good for the baby, and the Ricci family name.

In Los Angeles she felt sure of herself, and confident of her place in life. Here…

Here she wasn't Charlotte Parks, but a woman carrying Brando Ricci's baby, the baby who would be his heir.

His heir.

Not hers.

"I liked my life as it was," she said finally. "And I don't think it's selfish or immature to say that I'm a better person on my own. Being independent has been good for me. Being able to be who I want to be, versus what others project onto me, has allowed me to become the me that is successful, and happy." She could feel his gaze on her and she glanced over her shoulder and looked at him. "At the same time, I'm aware that we must come up with some kind of solution, find some middle ground, but marriage isn't it."

"I didn't realize you're so opposed to marriage."

"Not opposed to marriage in general, but opposed to me marrying out of some archaic idea that marriage solves problems. Marriage doesn't solve problems. Marriage creates problems."

"If we were madly in love, would you still feel the same way?"

For some reason his question, in that slightly mocking inflection, made her smile. "I don't know. But then, I've never been madly in love. Have you?"

He moved to her side and leaned against the stone balustrade. "I don't think I've even been in love, period." He looked out toward the valley, his gaze on the horizon. "At least not the way you describe. I've had long and close relationships with women, relationships I cherished, but there was never a sense, or a feeling, of necessity. There was no feeling that it was a forever relationship, one that I couldn't live without. I've been sorry to see relationships end, but I've never felt devastated, or heartbroken."

"Don't you think it's odd that neither of us have been madly, passionately in love?"

"I think it's odder that people fall in and out of 'love' so easily. It makes me think it's not love, but infatuation."

"What do you even think love is?"

He shrugged. "I know familial love. Loyalty, respect, attachment, devotion."

"So, you love your family."

"I do, but that's an attachment formed over time." Brando shifted, faced her. "It's probably why I'm comfortable proposing marriage. I believe together we could raise our children with kindness and respect. We'll be devoted parents, and that devotion is binding…us to them, them to us, and for each other."

"That sounds dreadful. You know that, don't you? Every word you say just sounds dreadful."

"Dreadful, how? It's stability. It's honorable—"

"Devoid of passion, energy, excitement—"

"And yet, you yourself seem to avoid those very things," he interrupted.

She drew back. "What?"

"You deliberately avoid passion and excitement—"

"If that was true, I wouldn't be here, in this situation, now."

"And yet you've admitted more than once that our night together was a mistake."

She felt her face heat. "I don't do one-night stands," she said stiffly. "You were my first, and I realized belatedly that casual sex wasn't for me."

"*I* didn't blow you off, and it didn't have to be a one-night stand. I phoned you while you were on the way in the cab to the airport. I phoned you again after you landed in Los Angeles. You didn't return those two calls. Undeterred, I tried to see you again a couple weeks later, but you pushed me away, saying that while you'd enjoyed our night together, it wouldn't happen again."

"It couldn't, Brando. I've never mixed business and pleasure before. You were the first client I ever got… intimate…with."

"Why did you?"

"I liked you. I was drawn to you."

"And I liked you, and was very drawn to you, too."

"But I don't sleep with my clients," she said firmly. "It's bad business, and incredibly irresponsible of me."

"Don't work with the Ricci family anymore. Problem solved."

"It's not that easy, Brando. The Riccis are important clients. I can't alienate them."

"You can't alienate them, but you can alienate me?"

She sighed with frustration. "You're not helping, especially not when you twist my words. You know what

I mean. I didn't have feelings for any of them… I had feelings for you, and that's a problem." And then realizing what she'd just said, she hurriedly added, "And now that I'm pregnant, we really have a problem. How do we raise this baby, and where?"

Brando was silent, his features shuttered, and then he rolled one thickly muscled shoulder. "Sometimes solutions come when you're not obsessing about them. Perhaps we need a break from talking and thinking. Perhaps we should go do something and just not think."

She arched a brow, curious. "Do what?"

"We could get in the car and drive to Greve, and then stop in Montefioralle, which is up on a hillside, and actually overlooks Greve. Montefioralle is a village that dates to the early nine hundreds and there are wonderful views of the valley from there. Many tourists like to walk to Montefioralle from Greve, but I wouldn't suggest it in your condition, but the drive is scenic and Greve has a charming, historic main square, and several nice spots we could stop for lunch."

Charlotte glanced at her laptop on the table and then out at the valley, and she knew what she wanted to do—escape. Not think. But being with Brando was incredibly problematic. "Can we really not discuss the baby and the future for the next hour?"

"I promise we won't discuss either for the rest of the afternoon. Let's leave serious discussions until later, and just try to enjoy the day. You're not in this part of Italy often. Try to enjoy it."

They drove to Greve in his low-slung sports car and parked in a small alley behind a creamy stone building, and then entered through the back of the building.

It was cool inside, the thick stone walls keeping out the heat, while the interior smelled of oak and wine. "One of our tasting rooms," he said, guiding her past an office to the public rooms where he gave her a brief overview of the Ricci wines being sampled and sold in the shop.

After saying a few words to the staff, he escorted her through the front door, where they emerged onto the medieval town square, the square ringed with handsome buildings filled with picturesque cafés, art galleries and more wine tasting rooms. They wandered in and out of the different shops and galleries and visited a church where the stillness and flickering candles filled Charlotte with much-needed peace. Everything would be fine. She didn't have to panic or worry so much. Brando would be reasonable and they'd find a way through this.

After an hour and a half of exploring the town, they returned to Brando's car for the short drive up a steep hill to Montefioralle.

This time Brando parked at a small restaurant perched on the side of the slope with a breathtaking view of the valley and Greve below. "Hope you're hungry," he said as they were seated at a table on the small patio. "The food here is excellent, and the wine, too."

"Is it wine from your vineyard?" she asked.

He flashed a smile that was as sexy as it was sinful. "How did you know?"

She couldn't help smiling back. He was irresistible when he turned on the charm. "Just a lucky guess."

Brando had been intrigued by Charlotte from the first time he met her in August of last year. She was stylish, stunning, smart and incredibly confident. He was impressed she could hold her own during contentious meetings with his family, and admired her ability to say what needed to be said, even if it wasn't popular. Brando, himself, tended to be blunt, and it wasn't often he met a woman who'd go toe-to-toe with him, rather than shy away from tough topics, but she did. And then when the conflict eased, she'd smile one of her smiles, and maybe that's what had hooked him.

When Charlotte Parks smiled, she lit up a room. Her smile was brilliant and wide, and her blue eyes gleamed, too.

It wasn't until she smiled now that he realized this was the first time he'd seen her smile since their night together New Year's Eve.

He realized how much he'd missed that smile, never mind how much he'd flat out missed her.

Brando hadn't chased after a woman in years, but he'd wanted to see Charlotte last year, after she'd returned to the States. He'd very much wanted another night with her, although he suspected one more night wouldn't be enough for him. He'd gone to LA to see her, but she gave excuses about being busy, and in the middle of a tense situation with clients, but she hoped she could say hello the next time she was in Italy.

She was giving him the brush-off. He'd been equally surprised, and disappointed, because even though she'd said all along it would be one night only, he hadn't believed she meant it. But she had.

He admired that, too.

This wasn't a game for her, either. She truly valued her independence, and it was a refreshing change from the women he dated who were utterly dependent on him, craving attention, desiring to be spoiled, hungry for gifts, big and small. Brando knew he was as much

at fault for cultivating shallow relationships. He preferred giving gifts over giving his heart. It was a tidier
transaction. Fewer complications.

Only now the woman who didn't want him was here,
pregnant with his child, and there would be no tidy transaction. Their situation was enormously complicated.

He leaned across the table and kissed her, a firm,
slow kiss. Her mouth was warm and soft and he felt the
quiver in her lips before he drew back.

Her face was pale with two pink blotches in her
cheekbones, which only made her blue eyes brighter.
He could see the worry in her eyes, though, as well as a
question. She didn't know why he'd kissed her. He didn't
know, either, other than he wanted her. He'd wanted her
from the very beginning, and it crossed his mind that
he would probably always be this attracted to her, and
not just physically, but intellectually. She held her own
with him. She was his equal in every way. She'd make
an excellent wife.

"You'll make an excellent addition to the family,"
he said. "If I didn't know better, I'd think you were a
Ricci already."

Charlotte stiffened, her shoulders squaring, spine
straightening. "We'd agreed we weren't going to discuss the future," she said quietly, flatly, anger washing
through her. "Those were your words, too."

He gave a casual shrug. "I'm not discussing the future. I'm talking about the present. You fit in. You're my
other half. You belong with me," he answered.

"I'm not your other half. You are a whole, and I am
a whole and there is no room in our individual lives for
each other. We are too independent, too headstrong."

"We're smart enough, successful enough to know how to adjust."

She held her breath, unwilling to speak, afraid that whatever she said might be used against her.

"What other choice do we have?" He'd ordered a glass of wine with his lunch and he gave his goblet a slight spin and watched the ruby-red wine swirl. "Not if we're putting our child's needs first, and I don't know a lot about you, but I've heard enough now to understand that your family never put you first. That your fear of families is the fear of being lost, consumed—"

"That's putting it a little strong," she interrupted.

"But I'm right, aren't I? You like your space because you can breathe, and be free, something you couldn't do in your family."

Suddenly parched, she reached for her water glass and took a gulp. "I might need a glass of wine, too, if we're going to be analyzing me over lunch today."

His lips lifted faintly. "No one is trying to psychoanalyze you. I'm just slowly starting to understand you. I think it's important to understand you—"

"Then let me help you understand exactly what I don't want. I don't want to become part of another family. And as much as I enjoyed working with your family, I have no desire to become one of them. I mean no disrespect, and I apologize if I'm phrasing this badly, but your family is every bit as overwhelming as mine—and that doesn't work for me in any way."

"No need to apologize. I agree we are passionate, but there is no malice in any of them."

She didn't immediately reply. Instead she looked away, out across the restaurant's patio toward the verdant valley filled with orchards and vineyards. A vineyard ran down the hill below them, the afternoon sun shining brightly on the tidy rows of grapes, gilding the green leaves with burnished light.

"There's a reason I'm happy in Southern California," she said after a bit. "I'm on my own. I have my own place, my own identity. I don't have to answer to my mother, my father, or any of my stepparents. I can just be myself. It's taken me years to break free and I've no desire to give up that space, and independence."

"But isn't your mother still in Los Angeles?"

Charlotte shook her head. "This isn't something we discuss, but my mother and Bill have been separated for a couple of years. They may even be divorced by now. I don't know, and I don't really want to know. I figure when Mother wants to announce something she will, and until then I'm happy to leave her alone and let her do her thing, and I do my thing."

"Where is she living?"

"South of France at the moment, but I think that's a temporary thing."

"You don't see your stepfather anymore? I thought you two were once close?"

"I like Bill. He's a maverick and colorful and he always invites me to Hollywood parties, as well as his big film premieres. Sometimes I show up because he loves a good red carpet photo with his family all around him, but I haven't since he and Mom went their different ways. But I'm fine with it. I like Los Angeles because I can be no one there. I'm invisible and I like that. I also like the weather, I like being close to the ocean and I like that no one descends on me in Los Angeles. My father hates LA. My brothers and sisters hate LA, too, which delights me to no end. I'm happy with my little house and career. It suits me."

She felt him study her from across the table and it was all she could do to sit still beneath his scrutiny.

"Marrying me doesn't mean you'll lose your identity, *cara*. You will always be Charlotte Parks, even if you become Mrs. Charlotte Parks Ricci."

"What if I didn't want to take your last name? What if I simply wanted to be Charlotte Parks?"

His powerful shoulders shifted easily. "If that is what you preferred, I'd have no objections. You have a career, you have a perfectly lovely name. Marrying you is about giving our baby a home, a family and a family name." He paused. "Or do you take issue with our baby being named Ricci?"

She couldn't believe she was even having this conversation. She wasn't seriously considering marrying him, was she?

She sat silent for a moment, processing everything being said, and realizing she maybe had given an indication that she was open to marrying him... But was she?

Was she even considering this future he suggested?

As if able to read her mind, he added, "It's not as if I live in my family's back pocket. There are family business meetings, as well as periodic family dinners, holidays and birthday celebrations, but my brothers and sister are busy with their own lives and families. They certainly wouldn't be overly involved in our lives, nor would we be expected to be immersed in theirs, not as newlyweds with a young baby."

"You realize I haven't agreed to marry you, nor is it likely that I will accept your proposal," she said.

"Yes, that's understood," he answered gravely, and

yet she could have sworn his lips twitched, as if amused. "So, let's just keep moving forward, and discussing options, aware that no commitments are being made, on either side."

"Fair enough," she said before looking him in the eyes. "How important is it for the baby to take your last name? Would it upset your family terribly?"

His jaw flexed, and he frowned into his wineglass. "I don't know if it would bother them. It would bother me. I'd very much like my son or daughter to have my name."

"I thought you were the rebel."

"I've been a rebel, but I'm older, and wiser, and appreciate my family, and our history here in Tuscany. Riccis have been making wine for one hundred years—"

"But you're the only one still making wine. The others have all shifted to other industries."

"All the more reason for me to want a son or daughter to carry on the winemaking tradition."

She didn't immediately reply, because there was nothing she could say. She understood him, and if she were in his position, she'd feel the same way. It was only later, as they drove back to his *castello*, and passed through the huge gates set in the high stone walls that she said quietly, "We don't have to be married for our child to take your name. You are the father. The birth certificate will reflect your name."

He glanced at her, lips compressing, but that was his only response as they traveled down the private lane lined with tall cypresses.

Brando parked in front of the *castello*, turned the ignition off and faced her. "Do you still intend to go to London tomorrow?"

"Yes."

"I'll fly you there. It'll be easier on you physically. You won't have to deal with long lines and security."

His offer caught her off guard, and yet at the same time, it was a little bit tempting. All London airports were unbearable. You couldn't escape the crowds and lines. But why would he want to fly her back to England? "I'm not sure how flying me to England benefits you."

"Less stress on you is less stress on the baby."

Ah, of course. It was about the baby. She didn't know why she felt a stab of disappointment, but she certainly wasn't going to analyze the reaction here and now. "And there is no other agenda?" she asked, arching a brow. "You're not planning on announcing we're engaged, or something outrageous like that?"

He matched her arched brow with one of his. "How can I do that, when we're not engaged? Really, Charlotte, you have so little trust."

His smirk was galling. But then everything about him was frustrating. He was gorgeous and interesting and he made her feel alive and wistful and confused...

She hated feeling confused. As well as wistful. Both reminded her of being a child, which wasn't a period in her life she remembered with fondness. Being a child, she was forced to rely on others, and the chief lesson from her childhood seemed to be that people weren't dependable, that most promises made were never kept. "I don't trust people very much, no."

"You ought to begin trying to trust me, especially if we're to co-parent."

"I haven't agreed to that, either."

"*Bella*, fortunately for me, that one is out of your

jurisdiction. The law gives us both rights as parents. However, if you feel like agreeing to something, you could agree to marry me so when I do meet your family tomorrow, I can be introduced as your fiancé, and the father of your baby."

"Maybe I should simply take my flight as scheduled. It would be far less complicated."

"Or, I fly you home and meet your family and you can introduce me as the father of your child. I think it would be reassuring for them to know you haven't been abandoned and won't be having to raise the child on your own."

For a split second she couldn't breathe, her chest squeezing, her heart suffused with pain. *That she hadn't been abandoned.* She blinked hard, clearing the hot sting of tears, trying to suppress the emotions that were threatening to swallow her whole.

"Surely your father would be reassured by the news," Brando added, brow creasing. "As well as your brothers and sisters."

"Everyone is quite busy," she said, forcing a smile. "I don't think my pregnancy will trouble them one way or another, but you suddenly appearing with me would cause a fuss. And we don't need the fuss, do we?"

He gave her a long, considering look. "What happens when the gossips discover you're pregnant with my child? That will get lots of tabloid attention, but if that doesn't worry you…?"

"We'll deal with it when we have to. Hopefully it won't be for quite some time."

CHAPTER SIX

CHARLOTTE WOKE SEVERAL times in the night, not feeling well. Her lower back ached. Her lower belly felt heavy and tight. She'd leave bed and walk a bit, and then stretch and eventually she'd fall back asleep.

But the heaviness in her lower back was far worse this morning, and the tightness in her lower belly had become a perplexing cramp. The cramping sensation had become strong, and regular, far too regular. She'd read about Braxton Hicks contractions and wondered if this was what she was experiencing. She even looked them up online, but these didn't quite meet the description. No, hers felt strong, and the dull pain was intensifying to the point she couldn't walk easily anymore.

Something wasn't right.

The cramping was frightening, and the pain was becoming excruciating.

Charlotte had left her cell phone unplugged during the night after researching contractions, and now it was dead, the battery dying in the night.

Limping to the door, she prayed she'd spot one of the staff nearby. Fortunately, one of the maids was walking down the hall with a stack of freshly laundered towels.

"I need Brando," Charlotte said in Italian, panting

and wincing as another sharp contraction hit. "Tell him something's wrong. I think the baby is coming."

"You must lie down," the maid answered. "Let me help you to bed, and then I'll send for help."

Brando was there at her side in less than five minutes. He was wearing jeans, work boots and a thin knit shirt, indicating that he'd been out in the fields again this morning. He leaned over her, his gaze searching hers. "What's happening?"

"Strong contractions. It doesn't feel right."

"You think the baby is coming?"

"I don't know, but I'm scared. It's too soon."

He reached for her hand and gave it a reassuring squeeze. "I've sent for my pilot. He should be here soon. He'll get us to the hospital quickly."

"What if there's something wrong? What if the baby—?"

He gave her hand another warm, firm squeeze. "We're only thinking positive thoughts, *cara*. Be positive, be strong."

Brando stayed with her until the pilot texted that he was on premises and the helicopter was ready. There was a small hospital in the valley that served the local population, but Brando was taking no chances. They were going to go to Florence where there were specialists and a neonatal unit, just in case one was needed.

The moment the pilot indicated they were good to go, Brando scooped Charlotte into his arms and carried her downstairs to the helipad, feeling her contractions as they hit, and soothing her when she expressed pain, and then fear and alarm. "It is all good, all fine," he said, looking into her eyes, letting her see his calm, and confidence.

"Can the baby survive at six months? I think so, but I'm not sure."

"This baby is fierce, and strong, it wanted to be conceived, so yes, I think this baby can survive. Absolutely."

She smiled even as she blinked back tears. "It is a stubborn little thing."

"Maybe because its mother is stubborn, too."

She smiled a little bigger, the smile still wobbly, but he found it hopelessly endearing. "And you're not?"

"I'm the most reasonable, rational man you'll ever meet."

"You forgot arrogant. As long as the baby's okay—" She broke off, eyes filling with tears.

"The baby will be fine. And you will be fine."

"And if something goes wrong?"

"If there are complications, you will know you are being seen by the best doctors, at one of the best hospitals in Europe, and I will be with you every step of the way. Have faith. Trust me."

"I'm trying." She gripped his hand tightly, desperately, as she searched his face. After a moment, she added brokenly, "I want this baby."

"I do, too."

The helicopter had them arrive in Florence in less than twenty minutes, and they were greeted immediately by a medical team.

As he'd promised, Brando stayed by Charlotte's side during the examination. He held his breath as the obstetrician checked her, and then performed an ultrasound.

Thankfully, the baby's heartbeat was steady, and the baby looked fine.

Brando stared at the screen, taking in every detail. He hadn't seen many ultrasounds before, but unless his eyes were deceiving him, that was most definitely a boy baby.

His chest tightened and his throat ached with overwhelming emotion.

Charlotte was pregnant with his son.

"He's really okay?" Brando asked quietly.

Charlotte looked from the doctor to Brando and back to the physician. "It's a boy?"

The doctor nodded. "Yes, and your son looks good. He is fine. But you, Charlotte, are in preterm labor. We're going to try to stop labor, as the best place for your son is right where he is now, safe inside his mother."

"Can you stop the labor?" she asked.

The doctor didn't even hesitate. "Because you sought out treatment immediately, I think we have a good shot at it."

It was a long day, but by midafternoon the contractions had stopped, and finally pain free, Charlotte fell asleep, worn out from the worry and fear. Brando stood by her bed in her private room on the hospital's maternity ward, watching her sleep.

Her color was better than it had been this morning. Her long blond hair spilled across her pillow, her lips slightly parted in sleep.

The tension was gone from her face, and he felt as if he could breathe properly for the first time all day.

He'd been scared, truly scared, and he'd prayed not just for the baby, but for Charlotte, who seemed so determined to be an island and do everything, and manage everything, on her own. He'd seen her panic, and felt her fear, and for the first time, he saw a crack in that perfect, flawless mask of hers. She might not want anyone else to know, but she felt vulnerable, as well as alone, which perplexed him, as she came from a big family and yet it was a family she didn't seem to embrace.

His phone vibrated with incoming messages and he drew his phone from his pocket, scanned the texts and then checked his emails, and seeing nothing that required immediate attention, he pulled a chair closer to the side of the bed and sat down.

When he told her he would be there, with her, he'd meant it.

Charlotte and his son might be out of danger, but there was nowhere Brando wanted to be but here, with her. With them. His family.

His family, he silently repeated, mulling the words over, awed by the implication. He was going to have a son.

Warmth filled him and his chest felt tight with inarticulate emotion. Pride, hope, wonder.

Growing up in a close, overly involved family had made him at times resent the family ties, and then during his early twenties, he'd had a falling-out with his family, particularly his father, whom Brando viewed as overbearing and interfering.

It didn't help that Brando did not feel wanted, or needed, by the family, and questioned why every family member was expected to go to work for the Ricci-Baldi company. He already had two older brothers and a sister working in the business, and they were content. Why was he needed? He wasn't. And the work he was being offered was menial at best. He found every aspect

of working for the family to be boring and mindless—
tasks anyone could handle. After a year of miserably
working for the family, he realized he could go do this
same pointless brainless work somewhere else and be
paid a hell of a lot better than what he was earning
working for his family.

He spoke to his father about his boredom, and his
father dismissed Brando's concerns, stating that everyone was expected to prove themselves, and that as the
youngest, he couldn't expect to ever be in a leadership
position, not when Enzo and Marcello were already
working their way up through management.

His father's answer didn't sit well with Brando, and
in an act of utter rebellion, he returned the call from
a modeling agency in Milan, and said he'd be open to
meeting with the agency if they were still interested in
him. During his teenage years, Brando had been approached several times about modeling, but he knew it
wasn't something that would be viewed favorably in his
family, so he'd turned the opportunities down. But now,
in need of work, he went on his first go-see, booked the
job and proceeded to book almost every other go-see
he was sent out on.

Brando's father did exactly as expected—Brando
was cut off from the family financially, but Brando
wasn't upset. He was relieved. For the first time in his
life, he was standing completely on his own and being
successful. In six months, he made more money than he
had in the previous two years, and by the time he turned
twenty-five he was making so much money he needed
to find investment opportunities, reluctant to leave that
much cash sitting in the bank. He bought stocks, and
purchased real estate, and when those proved to be

good investments, he became a venture capitalist for two small technology start-ups, turning his hundreds of thousands into millions when one of the start-ups went public and became big.

At twenty-six he bought his first small winery. Within two years he'd bought another, and it was at this time his father came to him and asked if he'd come back to the family and work with them since Brando seemed to have a golden touch. Brando was still trying to decide if he would when his father died, and if Brando had one regret it was that his father died before Brando returned to the family, going to work in Florence with his brothers and sister, refocusing the Ricci brands and giving new life to the Ricci wines.

His mother used to say that she was sure Brando's father knew, but maybe it wasn't important that his father knew. Maybe what was important was that those living knew Brando would never shirk his responsibilities, or his familial duty, again.

Family came first, always.

Charlotte woke to the sound of murmured voices and, opening her eyes, discovered Brando at the foot of her bed in discussion with her doctor.

Brando was the one to notice she'd awoken and he immediately approached the bed, a question in his silver gaze. "How do you feel?"

"Better," she said, grateful the contractions had stopped, and there was no more pain. "What time is it?"

"Close to seven. Your doctor was just doing a final check on you before going home for the night."

She glanced over at the doctor as he approached her side. "Thank you for all your help today."

"My pleasure. I'm just glad you could get here quickly. Everything looks good right now," he answered, adding, "You'll be in excellent hands here tonight, and the staff knows I'm on call should you need anything."

Brando walked the doctor out before returning. "Are you hungry? You haven't had breakfast or lunch."

"I am starting to get hungry."

"Good, my personal chef is on the way now with dinner. When he heard we were back in town, he said there was no way we could eat hospital food. He's been cooking all afternoon, and I see you looking worried, but there's no reason for that. I've cleared the menu with the doctor, and the doctor said soup, pasta and a little bit of meat would help keep up your strength."

"You've thought of everything."

"I don't want you to stress. You're to relax, and eat dinner, and sleep well tonight, and tomorrow we'll see what the doctor says. Hopefully you won't have to stay here too long."

It was only then that Charlotte remembered her flight. "I missed it. My flight to London."

"Thank goodness you weren't in-flight. I don't think today's outcome would have been the same if you were on the plane."

"No, I don't think so, either." She slowly exhaled, trying to ease the tension in her chest. "I came close to going into labor."

"*Cara*, you were in labor. The doctors were able to administer medicine to stop it. But another thirty minutes... I don't know the outcome. We might have had our son with us tonight."

"I'm only twenty-three weeks along. I don't think the odds would be very good for him."

"I learned today that half of the babies born between twenty-three and twenty-four weeks survive delivery and have a shot at life outside the neonatal ICU."

"But that doesn't include all the complications premature babies have, does it?"

"No." His expression sobered, and he reached out to smooth hair back from her brow, his touch unexpectedly tender. "Which is why you need to rest and relax and give our son as much time as possible."

She watched the door after he walked out, apparently to make a call, or whatever it was he'd said, feeling raw and shaken. Not just from today's early labor scare, but from his kindness, and his strength, and his calm in the middle of a storm. She always tried to be calm during dramas, but she always felt like a fraud, not truly calm, not truly collected. It was an image she projected, aware that the world preferred strength, and people were drawn to success, but sometimes being strong and successful was isolating.

Sometimes being the one who had it together and needed nothing from anyone meant you had very little support from others.

Perhaps if she'd learned to ask for help, or was comfortable demanding attention, she might feel less alone. Perhaps if she was better at trusting people, she might have had proper relationships... Maybe she'd even be romantically involved with someone.

Instead she admired interesting men from afar, careful to never get too involved, careful to never risk her heart.

At least, until she gave in to her impulse and spent a

night with Brando, and that night changed everything—and she wasn't referencing the pregnancy, but her hopes, and dreams.

She cared for Brando…a lot.

She also knew it was incredibly unrealistic to think he might have genuine feelings for her. He'd proposed because he was old-fashioned, and in his mind it was the morally right thing to do. She knew he would marry her, too, for the very same reasons. But he didn't love her, and she doubted he could be faithful, but she couldn't marry someone who didn't want her, not truly want her.

Brando returned to the room just then, entering with a man in a sharp suit, and the only indication that he might be Brando's chef was that he carried a large hamper in one hand, and an oversize insulated carrier in the other. The chef went to work spreading a small cloth over her table and laying out dishes, and Charlotte keep her attention fixed on the chef so that she didn't look at Brando even though she was incredibly aware of him, and that he was watching her.

No one had ever watched her the way he watched her.

No one had ever paid her as much attention or listened to her when she asked for space. He'd even let her go last winter when she wanted that, too.

Charlotte had met many powerful men, and a few handsome, powerful men, but she'd never met anyone who respected her desires the way Brando did. He could have tried to steamroll over her, but instead he appealed to her intellect and reason, and for that, she was grateful.

The chef was then gone as quickly as he'd arrived. Brando served her and then himself, and they ate the delicate seafood risotto, and while Brando had some of the main course of meat, Charlotte was satisfied.

She watched him as he cleared the dinner dishes, filling the basket before refreshing her water from the large bottle of sparkling water the chef had brought with him. "Thank you," she said, a lump in her throat because honestly, she couldn't remember the last time someone had done so much for her, never mind waiting on her hand and foot.

"My pleasure," he answered. "You do remember there is dessert. Mousse *al cioccolato*. Your favorite."

Chocolate mousse. It was her favorite, and he'd remembered.

They'd had chocolate mousse the night she'd stayed over, and she'd straddled him in bed, feeding him spoonfuls, before deciding it was far too good to share. She blushed, heat rushing through her. "Was this just a lucky coincidence, or did you ask him to make it?"

"I asked him."

Charlotte was dangerously close to tears. She clutched the covers in her hands, holding them tightly. "I'm overwhelmed."

"By mousse?"

"No, by you, today." She felt the hard thudding of her heart, and the strange prickly emotion in her chest, emotion that seemed to zigzag all the way through her. She hadn't been a virgin when she met Brando, and yet he made her feel naive, untutored, inexperienced in the ways of the world. He made her want to believe that better things existed, and that people could be good, and patient, and kind.

Today Brando also made her aware of just how much she needed him, even if she didn't want to admit it.

She didn't know what would have happened if she hadn't been with him when the contractions began. She didn't know how she would have managed without him today. He'd handled everything, and he'd been so incredibly focused, and calm, and strong. He'd said he wouldn't let anything happen to her, and he'd meant it. He'd been incredibly proactive, as well as protective. It was rather humbling to realize how good it felt to let someone else take charge. To let someone else be strong.

"Have I thanked you for today?" she said. "I don't know how I—"

"You have thanked me," he interrupted quietly. "But you don't have to thank me. I wanted to be here. There is nowhere else I'd rather be."

She gave a half nod. "I believe you."

The corner of his mouth lifted a fraction. "Are we making progress, *cara*?"

"I don't know if I'd call it progress, but you should know I appreciate everything, and am grateful, and our baby is grateful, too." And for the first time, the words *our baby* felt right. They felt true. It was their baby and there would be no shutting Brando out, and no fighting over custody. How could she do that to him? He would be a wonderful father, and she couldn't deny him the opportunity to be there every step of the way, or their son the security of a devoted father, either.

Brando misread her contemplative mood as fatigue, and insisted he leave for the night so she could get some sleep. "The nurse knows to call me if you want anything, or if you suddenly crave gelato, or if you're wide awake in the middle of the night and just want to talk."

She smiled crookedly. "I can call you just to chat?"

"If you're lonely or bored, have the nurse call me, and I will keep you company on the other end of the line."

"And if I wanted you to come back and keep me company here?" she asked.

"I'd get dressed and come straight away."

"What if I wanted you to stay here with me to-night?" The words popped out before she'd thought them through.

"Do you want me to? I've been told the little couch makes into a bed."

She eyed the small couch and then looked at him. He was over six feet two, and his shoulders were wider than the sleek Italian sofa. "You wouldn't be comfortable."

"I don't mind, not if it'd give you peace of mind."

She tried to picture him sleeping so close to her, his big body sprawled out, just the way he'd slept with her during their night together when they'd finally stopped touching and kissing and tasting—

"No, I wouldn't sleep a wink," she answered. "Go home and come back tomorrow...if you have time."

"*Cara*, I have nothing but time." He leaned over the bed, kissed her brow and then a fleeting kiss on her lips. "Can I get you anything before I leave?"

And suddenly, just like that, she didn't want him to leave.

Not just now, but ever.

The simmering feelings she'd had for him six months ago had become a fireball, exploding to life.

"No," she said, hating the thickness in her throat, and the aching pang in her heart. "I'm good. Go home, sleep well. I'll see you tomorrow."

Easier said than done, Brando thought, back at his elegant town house in the converted palace. He wandered through the second floor and then up to the third floor, which was his private office suite. Sitting down at his desk, he sorted through mail that had been left for him by his assistant, and documents requiring signatures. He signed where necessary and then leaned back and stared across the room, to the summer sky just now going dark.

He thought of nothing and everything, of Charlotte in the hospital bed, and the ultrasound earlier where he saw his son for the first time, the baby so tiny, but also so very perfect. Brando knew he would do whatever he had to do to ensure his son's safety, as well as his future. What mattered now was Charlotte and the baby. Everything else was secondary.

His phone pinged with an incoming text. He looked at it immediately, in case it had to do with Charlotte. Instead it was a text from Louisa.

Hello, handsome. I'm free now. Are you?

Brando picked up the phone and texted back.

Sorry, no.

He thought for a moment, before sending another swift text.

I enjoyed our time together, but I am no longer single. Ciao e abbi cura di te.

Goodbye and take care.

CHAPTER SEVEN

BRANDO WAS BACK at the hospital in the morning and Charlotte was sitting up in bed, looking anxious and restless when he arrived. "What's wrong?" he asked, leaning over to greet her with a kiss on her forehead.

"I need my phone, and my computer. I can't work without them." She gestured to the short stack of magazines on the bedside table. "The nurse brought me fashion magazines this morning but I don't want to read them. I need to check in with my clients—"

"Easy, slow down," he said, checking his smile as he pulled a chair close to the side of the bed. "You're supposed to be resting, not stressing out."

Charlotte drew a deep breath. "I know, and I agree. But I feel naked without my phone, and it's even worse not having a phone or computer. I'm not used to being completely out of touch."

"Do you want me to have someone drive them up from the *castello*? I can."

Her brow furrowed. "Am I going to be here long?"

"I don't know. That's something we'll have to ask the doctor when he makes his rounds this morning."

She was silent a moment and then nodded. "Obviously if me being here is the best thing, then I should be here. I just would feel better being here if I had my vanity bag, and briefcase with laptop, phone and chargers."

"I'm worried work will create stress for you, though."

"I'd be more stressed not being able to communicate with my clients." She hesitated. "I'll let them know I'm taking the next week or two off and will be in touch soon. I'd feel better about that than just not answering emails."

"Agreed."

She looked at him, brows still knitting together, expression still troubled. "I'm not flying anytime soon, am I?"

"I think it would be incredibly risky."

"I do, too." She looked past him to the window with its view of the city and the hills that framed the capital of Tuscany. "I don't want a repeat of yesterday."

"Neither do I."

"I was terrified."

He saw her bring her hands together, fingers laced tightly against the white hospital covers, and he reached out and covered her clenched hands with one of his. "Everything is good," he said quietly, firmly, determined to keep her calm. Relaxed. The baby needed her to be still, and relaxed.

"For now," she said, a catch in her voice. She glanced up at him, blue eyes shining with a film of tears. "But I can't stop thinking about the what-ifs. What if I'd been on the plane? What if I'd been going through customs at the airport? What if—?"

"But you weren't. You were with me, and we got you here quickly and the doctors were able to stop labor." He squeezed her hands. "And it wasn't all bad. Yesterday we saw the baby and he's healthy, and beautiful—"

She snorted. "I wouldn't go so far as to describe him as beautiful. I'm sure he will be—"

"He was beautiful to me. My son. *Our* son." Brando's voice deepened. "It's a miracle. I wasn't expecting a family and yet suddenly I have one, and I vow to take care of you both, always. Forever."

He hoped his words would reassure her, but instead tears trembled on her lashes before falling.

She pulled her hands free to wipe them away. "I hate crying," she said hoarsely. "Please don't mind me."

His chest squeezed, and he felt a peculiar pang near his heart. "You don't have to be an island," he said carefully, not wanting to upset her. "It's okay to have feelings and cry. Italian women are passionate, and emotional, but those emotions do not make them weak. Emotions are what make us strong."

She swiped beneath her eyes, drying them. "You seem to understand women quite well."

"Somehow you manage to make that sound like a criticism."

"In so many ways you seem so perfect, but then you don't want serious relationships. You aren't married—"

"If I was married, we wouldn't be here today. I would have never had that night with you."

She gazed up at him from beneath wet spiky lashes. "Lots of men have affairs."

"Are you thinking of that survey from a number of years ago that said in Italy, most affairs started in the office?"

"No, but interesting." Two bright spots of pink colored her cheeks. "I just know my parents divorced over affairs, and it was a problem between my mom and her last husband."

"I don't condone affairs. And I don't know if my father ever had an affair, but he cherished my mother, and taught his sons to protect your family at all costs, and you can't protect your family if you're damaging the marriage."

"So when you marry, you won't have one?"

"It goes against everything I believe."

"Then why haven't you married?"

"Because I hadn't found the one I wanted to commit myself to for the rest of time."

Charlotte's heart fell, and she looked away, teeth catching her lower lip to keep it from quivering.

Brando would marry her because it was the right thing to do, but she wasn't the one he would have married. And yet yesterday had made her realize she couldn't manage everything by herself. She'd been prepared to go it alone when she'd felt good and strong, but if there were complications, or if the baby came early, she realized she wouldn't be able to cope on her own. She didn't want to struggle alone.

"Remember when we agreed we'd be honest?" she said, stomach in knots, pulse racing.

He nodded.

"I'm going to be honest with you now, but it's not easy because I like my independence, but it's a problem." She glanced at him, trying to read his expression, but his silver gaze hid whatever he was thinking. "I was wrong. I can't do this on my own." She drew a quick breath and plunged on. "I can't even imagine what I would have done if I were in California when this happened. I don't know what I would have done yesterday without you. I was so scared, and in so much pain." She pressed her lips together, and counted a few counts, giving her time to gain control over her emotions, not easy when her heart felt bruised and she felt overwhelmed by the reality of her situation. "I try so hard to be independent and handle things, but Brando, I've never been so scared in my life. It was too soon for the baby to come, and I just kept thinking of all the problems he'd have if he was born at almost twenty-four weeks."

"It *was* scary, but you're fine, and he's fine—"

"For now." She looked up into his face, her gaze meeting his, and holding. This was serious. Important. She needed him to realize just how serious she was now. "But what if I go into labor again? What if the baby is born early? He could have serious challenges—" She broke off, swallowed and continued. "I was naive to think I could do it all, handle it all on my own. Honestly, it wasn't just naive, it was selfish. He isn't just my baby, he's yours, too, and you need to be part of his life."

"I will be."

She nodded, again biting down into her tender lower lip. For a moment there was just silence and then she added softly, "You were wonderful yesterday. You were such an advocate and so calm and so strong—" She broke off, fighting to hold back fresh tears, uncertain as to why she was falling apart now. She didn't cry and yet she felt as if she were a watering pot, tears springing free. "I realized I can't do this without you. I don't want to do this without you—"

The rest of Charlotte's thought was interrupted by the sudden appearance of the doctor with a nurse, and they entered her room in the middle of conversation, but the conversation ended as the obstetrician approached the bed.

"How are we today?" Dr. Leonardi asked, glancing

from Charlotte to Brando and back again. "I understand it was a restless night for our patient. The night nurse said you were awake much of the night, but we need you to rest."

Brando looked at Charlotte, a black eyebrow lifting. She ignored it, and him, and answered the doctor. "I didn't realize hospitals are so noisy, and every time the nurse came in to check on me I'd wake up and then stay awake." She realized how that sounded and quickly added, "I'm not complaining, I'm just explaining why I couldn't sleep."

"You couldn't pretend it was a fine hotel?" the doctor teased.

"If it was a hotel, I would have phoned the front desk and complained," she answered with a wry smile. "I think I just had too much time on my own, and no way to distract myself. Brando has promised to send for my computer and then I'll be able to work if I can't sleep."

"Is your work very taxing?" Dr. Leonardi asked. "We don't want you to do anything that will create stress. It might be better for you to read a relaxing book, nothing too scary or violent. Maybe a romance. My wife reads them and says they're very good for escaping."

Charlotte forced a pleasant expression, hiding how she truly felt, as she would never, ever be caught reading a romance. A biography, yes. A history, yes. A cozy mystery, yes. Romances were for those who believed in happy endings. She didn't, at least, not anymore.

"Do you have an idea of how long you'll want to keep her here?" Brando asked.

"Another day or two, and then we can evaluate how

she's doing, and how the baby is doing. If both are doing well, I don't see why Charlotte couldn't go home with you, but I'd keep her on modified bed rest."

Charlotte's heart fell. "For how long?"

"Possibly for the duration of your pregnancy."

Her jaw dropped. Three months?

Brando crossed his arms over his chest. "What is modified bed rest?"

"It's a term we use for restricted activity without the stringent dictate to remain completely confined to bed. Every doctor probably has his own definition for it. For me it means limited physical activity, and lengthy morning and afternoon rest periods in bed. I also restrict lovemaking, so no sexual activity, as sex releases prostaglandins that are similar to the medications used to induce labor."

Charlotte blushed. "That won't be an issue," she said unsteadily. "We're not having sex."

"It won't be forever," the doctor replied with a smile. "After the baby you'll need a few weeks to heal, and then you should be able to resume sexual intercourse—"

"Any other concerns?" Charlotte interrupted, embarrassed, and more than a little horrified. "Or do I just stay put for the day?"

"Just stay put, and relax, and I'll be back later this afternoon." The doctor nodded, smiled and walked out with the nurse.

Charlotte couldn't even look at Brando. Everything was so strange, and so uncomfortable. Her life seemed to be spinning completely out of control. "So there's that," she said, plucking at her covers.

"No sex for us—"

"That's not what I'm talking about," she interrupted

quickly, heat rushing through her, making her feel tingly and self-conscious. "And you know it. You're just tormenting me now."

"Sex is what got us into this situation," he said mildly. "And it was good sex. Probably the best sex I've ever had."

She jerked her head up as she looked across her room at him. He was leaning against the wall, one shoulder resting against the window trim, sunlight pouring in, haloing his head with golden light. He had a hint of a smile, and there was a glint in his silver eyes that made her tummy flip and her pulse quicken. He was tall and lean, and incredibly handsome.

And he was hers…or had been for one night.

Two days ago he suggested they marry, which meant he could be hers forever.

Would he be happy, though? Would she?

"We were talking about something important when Dr. Leonardi walked in," he said now, his smile disappearing, his expression turning serious. "Let's finish that conversation."

"I don't remember what we were saying—"

"You'd just said you couldn't do this alone, and you didn't want to." Brando repeated her words back to her, almost exactly as she'd said them. "So what do we do?" he added. "What is our next step?"

Her mouth dried and her pulse jumped, beating too hard in her veins. "You tell me."

"I want to hear it from you. We both already know what I think."

She swallowed hard, her mouth feeling as if she'd been sucking on a cotton ball. It took forever to form words, but Brando waited, saying nothing, just watch-

ing her with those piercing eyes of his. "You think…
you believe…you said, we should…marry."

"And what do you think?" he said bluntly.

She felt another sharp twinge in her chest. "I think
we do what's best for the baby."

"Which is?"

He wasn't making this easy, was he? She drew a
deep breath, feeling tender and shy. "We get married."

"When?"

Her shoulders rose and fell. "Whenever we can?"

Brando needed to head to the Ricci headquarters for
a meeting that couldn't be postponed, but he promised
to be back for a late lunch. He returned two and a half
hours later with lunch and her briefcase and her vanity
bag. She didn't know if she was more excited at being
able to brush her hair or check her email.

Again Brando's chef materialized with lunch, and
after lunch was cleaned up and put away, Brando
opened his laptop and worked, while she worked on
hers. She handled the most urgent emails, and then sent
emails to others letting them know that she was taking
the next few weeks off for a personal matter, but hoped
to be working again by the end of the month.

It wasn't until she got a flurry of email responses
from her clients asking if everything was all right that
she realized her wording was problematic. Normally
Charlotte was an expert at handling sensitive matters
but she certainly wasn't handling her own situation
very well.

She didn't realize she'd muttered any of her frustration out loud until Brando asked what the matter was.

She sighed and rubbed at her temple, trying to make
the headache go away. "I think I've made a mess of

things," she said. "I reached out to my clients and let them know I'd be taking some time off, and it's back-fired. Everyone is asking if I'm okay, and if there is anything they can do." She grimaced. "Someone just now wanted to know how they could help. This is exactly what I didn't want to happen."

"Read what you wrote."

"I said I was taking the next few weeks off for a personal matter, but hoped to be back at work by the end of June." She looked over at him. "I shouldn't have said 'personal matter,' should've I?"

"You could have said 'wedding and honeymoon' and everyone would have been delighted, instead of worried." He saw her expression and shrugged. "It's the perception of things, isn't it? One sounds as if you're in the midst of struggle and sorrow, whereas 'wedding and honeymoon' sounds festive and celebratory."

"I can't tell my clients I'm getting married!"

"Why not? You are. Why not let them be happy for you?"

"But we don't know when we'll get married. It might not be for months."

"*Cara*, we're marrying soon. I'm determined we marry before our son is born, and since he seems to want to arrive early, I don't think we should wait."

She closed her laptop and pressed it to her chest. "How soon?"

"As soon as it can be arranged."

Brando was still with her when Dr. Leonardi returned late afternoon to check on Charlotte but stepped out while the doctor examined her, returning when it was over.

"Everything still looks good. I think she's out of the

woods, but I want her on bed rest for the next few days, and then modified bed rest Friday."

Charlotte glanced hopefully at Brando. "Does that mean I can leave?"

"Perhaps tomorrow."

"But if everything looks good, can't I just rest at home?" she pressed.

Brando's gaze swept the sterile room. "I'd prefer for her to rest at my home. I'm not a fan of hospitals, and Charlotte is right, it's not very restful here. It's noisy and chaotic and I'm not sure how this is the best environment for her, or the baby."

"But we have nurses here, staff here. Equipment here," the doctor answered.

"Can't I get the same equipment for the house? Couldn't I hire a nurse to be with her at home?"

"That's a huge expense—" The doctor broke off when he saw Brando's expression. "But yes, she could be monitored at home. It's essential, though, that she rest, or you'll be right back here, and I don't know if we would be successful stopping labor next time."

"We have no intention of being back until the baby is full term," Brandon said.

Dr. Leonardi nodded. "I'll sign off on her leaving tomorrow. I still want her here tonight, but remember, no stress, no excitement. There isn't to be any drama or pressure."

"Understood."

Charlotte had imagined they'd be going to Brando's city house when she was discharged the next day. Instead the helicopter was waiting to whisk them back to the *castello*.

"There is more fresh air, more peace in the country," Brando said as they made the fifteen-minute trip by air.

Now that she wasn't in pain, Charlotte enjoyed the trip, thinking the Tuscan hills looked like a striking quilt from the air, patches of light green and dark green intermixed with squares of pale gold, which turned out to be villages and *castellos* like Brando's.

On landing at his estate, Brando swept her into his arms and carried her back to the house, despite Charlotte insisting she could walk partway. He ignored her completely, and made short work of the distance, carrying her up two flights of stairs as if she weighed nothing at all.

She'd wondered about the third flight of stairs, and it wasn't until they reached a different bedroom that she realized Brando wasn't returning her to the bedroom she'd had before, but moving her into his room. "What are you doing?" she asked lowly as she was settled onto the enormous bed.

"Keeping you close," he said. "Doctor's orders."

"I thought you were getting a professional."

"I am, for the day. But at night, you'll sleep with me so I can keep an eye on you."

"And you don't think that will be a source of stress or excitement?"

"I think it will be a greater source of stress and excitement if I come check on you three or four times a night."

She pulled herself up, sitting a little taller. "You don't need to do that. I can just shout."

"Right." But his lips twisted. He'd caught her attempt at humor.

She appreciated that, and him. More than he'd ever know. "I don't know that I can sleep in here with you."

"Why not?"

"I don't sleep well with others."

"Build a pillow wall."

"Can I really?"

"No. I need to be able to see you—"

"Nothing is going to happen! I'm not going to disappear in the night or give birth in ten seconds. Everything is fine. I just need to stay put—"

"In my bed."

"Brando, you're causing me stress and excitement."

"*Bella*, you're causing stress and excitement by arguing with me. Accept the inevitable. You're stuck with me." And then he closed the distance, bent down and kissed her, in a long, tender, melting kiss that made the hair rise on the back of her neck and her nipples peak and tighten. By the time he lifted his head, she felt like he'd poured warm honey into her veins. "It won't be all bad, though," he murmured, his lips brushing across hers in another slow, maddening kiss that had her squirming and breathless. "You just have to relax," he murmured, kissing her cheek and then just beneath her earlobe. He'd found an incredibly sensitive spot there, and then another one just beneath her jaw.

She sighed, and arched, pleasure suffusing her. "I'm not sure the doctor would approve," she whispered.

"I promise not to give you an orgasm."

She laughed softly, and the husky laugh turned to a smothered moan as his teeth scraped the side of her neck, setting her on fire, and sending hot sparks all the way down to her toes. She reached for him then, her hand wrapping around his nape as she buried her fingers into his thick, crisp hair. "If your kisses send me back to the hospital, I will—"

"Never forgive myself," he answered, lifting his head, to gaze down into her eyes. He pushed back a heavy wave of her hair, tucking strands behind her ear. "I know you showered at the hospital earlier, but would you like a bath now that you're home? I can send one of the girls up to draw you one."

"I don't need anyone to draw me a bath, and I don't want you to fuss over me. It's enough to know that you're here in case something goes wrong, so please go do whatever it is you need to do, and you can relax knowing I'll be here taking my first nap of the day."

Charlotte was relieved when Brando left the room. Her luggage had already been moved from her bedroom into his, and one of the maids brought up her briefcase and bags from the hospital. Once she was alone, she locked the bathroom door, stripped off her clothes and took a long soak in the deep tub. She washed her hair, rinsed and conditioned it, before climbing out and patting herself dry. With her long hair still wrapped in a towel, she climbed back into bed and fell asleep, grateful to be in a quiet room. Charlotte slept for over an hour and when she woke up, she discovered someone had placed a water bottle and glass next to the bed for her, plus a bowl of fresh fruit and a small plate of biscotti. But that wasn't all. Leaning against the lamp was a tall leather-bound book with a sticky note.

Charlotte, pick out your favorite.

She recognized the handwriting. Brando had written the note and she reached for the book and positioned it on her lap before opening the luxurious soft cream leather cover. *The Ricci-Baldi Bridal Collection*, the title page read.

Puzzled, Charlotte quickly flipped through the pages, from beginning to end. There were maybe twenty gowns in the book, and the entire book consisted of couture bridal gowns, exclusively designed by Livia, Brando's sister, and Livia's designer husband, Luca Baldi.

Brando wanted her to pick out her favorite bridal gown. Was this really happening?

She suddenly wasn't sure she could go through with the wedding, at least, not like this. She was scared, and troubled. Exhaling in a rush, she closed the design book, carefully replacing it where she'd found it, leaning against the glass lamp on the side table.

Intellectually she understood why marrying Brando was a good idea. But emotionally she couldn't see herself wearing a formal white gown, never mind a couture gown from one of Italy's top design teams. She wasn't having a dream wedding. The wedding was business, and the ceremony was for legal purposes. She and Brando were choosing to be responsible, and practical, and she didn't need a formal gown, or veil, or even flowers for that. She could wear a suit, or a smart dress, and Brando would wear one of his tailored suits, and they'd be married quietly, privately, by a government official without fuss.

It was better they not start their marriage under any illusions that this was a love marriage, because she had to manage her expectations, or beautiful, brilliant Brando Ricci would break her heart.

Brando returned from the winery to discover Charlotte had moved herself back to her bedroom.

He entered her bedroom with the briefest of knocks, annoyed that she'd go against his wishes. "What are you doing? Moving things around? Coming to rooms where you'll be alone at night?"

Charlotte drew the duvet up higher, hiding her breasts and bump. "I don't want or need constant supervision. I'm not a child. I'm having a child. Quite a significant distinction, Brando. And I didn't move anything but myself. Your staff carried my things, and I just took my time and walked back here."

He paced around the bed. "And what if something happens at night?"

"I'll call you. We both have phones. We're lucky to live in the age of technology."

He glared down at her. "I'm not amused. You're taking risks—"

"And you're being hopelessly overbearing," she interrupted, "as well as an alarmist. Dr. Leonardi said everything looked better, normal—"

"He never said 'normal.' He wanted you in the hospital. I was the one who insisted you would be able to rest better if you were at home. But I promised you'd be supervised."

"And I am. The midwife starts coming daily tomorrow. I'll have a quiet evening tonight. Just send a tray up for me and I'll have an early dinner, and will make an early night of it, too. I think having some downtime would be good for both of us."

Brando seemed about to protest when he thought better of it. He nodded shortly. "Fine." He started to leave, then turned in the doorway. "Did you see anything in Livia's designs that appealed to you? She's offered to come this weekend for a fitting."

The last thing Charlotte wanted to do was discuss the wedding, or a dress made for her by his famous sister, but she didn't want to offend him tonight. "There are so many beautiful designs, I couldn't even narrow the options down."

"No problem. I can look through them with you tomorrow."

"I don't need help looking at bridal gowns."

"Happy to give you my opinions."

"I'm sure you are. Good night, Brando."

"*Buona notte*, Charlotte."

CHAPTER EIGHT

A BREEZE RUSTLED the leaves of the citrus trees in the ornate terra-cotta pots on the terrace, and the moon, even though only a quarter full, winked white in the purple-black sky.

Brando leaned back in his chair at the table and let the beauty of the night distract him from Charlotte's lengthy explanation of why they didn't need a proper wedding, never mind a reception after.

She'd spent the last ten minutes giving detailed reasons why a formal wedding was a bad idea, and he let her talk as he sipped his after-dinner coffee. It was his favorite kind of night, warm, fragrant, without summer's sultry heat. He'd had a good day in the wineries, and Charlotte looked particularly beautiful tonight, too, wearing an ice-blue sleeveless blouse paired with crisp white silk trousers. Her long hair spilled over her shoulders, and she wore simple sapphire drop earrings that matched the blue of her eyes.

She was stunning and smart, and he felt fortunate that she was to be the mother of his children. She'd be a good mother, a good partner and wife. If she'd just stop fighting him on the wedding. His family celebrated marriages, just as they celebrated births and anniversaries and other special moments.

"I want a proper ceremony, followed by a proper dinner, and a proper cake," he said. "This is our wedding. It should be special."

"Do we need the fuss, as well as the expense?"

"As this is the only wedding I will ever have, *yes*. It should be beautiful. Music, flowers, table decorations, all of it."

"A big wedding, Brando, really?"

"I didn't say 'big.' In fact, I want a small, intimate ceremony here at the *castello* chapel, followed by a reception in the courtyard. That way there is no traveling, no fuss, nothing to stress over, nor would you have to be on your feet very long."

Charlotte listened to his plans, and didn't know how to argue against them, especially as he offered to handle most of the arrangements so she didn't have to be stressed by anything. He did insist on her selecting a wedding dress, or at least, pointing out a few in the design book that she liked, and Livia and Luca would make up something special just for her.

"Your family knows, then?" she asked, careful to keep judgment from her voice.

"Only Livia so far. I will share the news with the rest once we have a wedding date."

Charlotte toyed with her dessert spoon. "What are you telling them?"

"That we're getting married and we'd love them to join us."

"Nothing about the pregnancy?"

"It's not the first thing I'll tell them, no." He lifted a

brow, his expression slightly sardonic. "Would you prefer me to share the news about the baby first?"

"No." She glared at him. "And I don't want to wear a dress that screams 'pregnant bride,' either."

"I'm sure some of Livia's designs will flatter your figure. No matter what you'll wear, you'll look beautiful."

Charlotte's eyes suddenly smarted and she blinked, clearing her vision. "I feel rather lumpy at the moment, and I dread people talking. There will be gossip, you know. I know you don't care, but I'm not there yet. I'm still trying to figure out how to navigate this new world. My success stems from my reputation as someone who doesn't make mistakes. I fix other people's mistakes. And yet look at me—" She broke off, and bit into her lower lip, holding back the flow of words.

"Starting a family is a beautiful thing. We're excited. Remember that."

"You don't think your family will judge?"

"They'll be happy for us. They know you. They like you. Livia is thrilled to be making your dress."

"And your business associates? My clients?"

"They'll think the best, not the worst."

"Which is?"

"That we're head over heels in love and eager to start our new lives together." His silver gaze met hers and held. His voice dropped, and deepened. "And who is to say we're not? Who is to say that this marriage isn't something we both want?"

Her heart did a funny double beat, and butterflies filled her middle. She couldn't look away from the flare of desire in his eyes, the heat radiating out, wrapping around her. "Marriage wasn't on the agenda," she said.

"Maybe not, but you know I want you. If I could have you now, I would. Desire is not an issue between us."

She could see heat and interest shimmering in his stunning pewter eyes. She felt the intense physical pull. She craved it herself, feeling isolated in this strange new body of hers, facing a different future than she'd ever imagined. "Then kiss me," she whispered. "Make me remember why I lost my head over you."

He drew her from her seat, up into his arms, one hand sliding beneath her hair to cup her nape as the other settled low on her hip. His lips covered hers, claiming her, his mouth warm, and firm. He smelled of that spice he wore and as well as a hint of wine. She welcomed the pressure of his mouth, her lips parting beneath his, his tongue tasting, teasing, sending shivers of pleasure through her. He kissed her until she felt boneless and mindless, kissing her until she forgot to breathe and she ached between her thighs, wanting pressure there. His knee moved between her legs, his hard thigh pressed to that place where she was so very sensitive. His hand ran up the length of her, over her hip and waist to cup her breast and then play with the tight, tender nipple, strumming the peaked tip so that she arched, grinding herself against him.

Pleasure screamed through her, bright, hot, intense.

She was so close to climaxing. Just another pinch of her nipple, another rub against his thigh, and she'd come. She wanted to come, craved release, but an orgasm could set off the contractions again.

Panting, Charlotte pulled back, feeling shameless and frustrated all at the same time. "I want you," she breathed, tears of vexation filling her eyes. "But I can't have you."

"You can, but not for a while."

"This is awful." She knocked away the tears, feeling wildly out of control. "We can marry but we can't have sex."

"We'll have sex again, I promise you. But you're right, we can't take any chances now. It's not worth the risk."

Charlotte couldn't fall asleep that night. She was spending so much time resting, so much time in bed, that she felt restless and trapped. The surging hormones didn't help. The relentless desire didn't help, either. She'd never felt sexual, but now, being so close to Brando, desire and awareness hummed through her night and day.

But what she felt for him was so much more than desire, and the feelings were growing stronger by the day. They hadn't even married and yet she felt bonded. Wed. Was it the pregnancy making her feel so connected to him, or was it the way he was treating her…as if she were special…priceless…irreplaceable?

And yes, right now, he was focused on her and the baby, but was it only because of the baby? How would things be after the baby was born?

Would Brando be as attentive? Would he still want her? Would he try to make her feel special?

She pictured Louisa—gorgeous, sexy, fun-loving Louisa—and felt a wave of insecurity. Charlotte hated feeling insecure. She'd had enough of that growing up in her family. It was impossible to get her parents' attention, impossible to get anyone's attention. She'd act out just to force one of the nannies to focus on her, hoping they'd take her to her parents, and yet when she was hauled before her parents, it never resulted in the outcome she'd wanted.

They had no time or patience for her when she was good, and they had even less time and patience when she was naughty. Gradually she learned not to look to others for affection, or validation. She would take care of herself, and learn to be happy and secure through her own actions and achievements. Once she stopped wanting her parents' love and approval, she discovered herself, and became the person she wanted to be.

Since arriving in Tuscany she felt lost, though, and wasn't sure who she was anymore.

She wasn't sure about marriage and forever, either. In her family marriage didn't equal forever. Marriage was just a source of friction and tension, with the friction growing worse until someone threw in the towel and initiated divorce.

The idea of marrying to divorce made her heartsick.

But being married to a man who didn't want her, and might have clandestine relationships on the side, would break her.

Charlotte couldn't escape her thoughts, or the panic rising in her, and she left bed and then left her room and headed upstairs to Brando's bedroom. It was well past midnight and she doubted he was awake but she needed to see him, needed to hear from him that they weren't making a terrible mistake.

She knocked lightly on his door and then opened it an inch. "Brando, are you sleeping?"

"Come in," he said, his voice deep and sleep roughened. "Are you unwell?"

"I'm fine," she said, stepping into his room, leaving the door slightly open behind her. "Everything's fine. I just can't sleep and my brain won't turn off and I'm getting myself worked up."

"Over what?"

"What if you don't like being married to me?" she whispered.

"Come here," he said, drawing back the covers, and patting the bed. "Crawl in with me."

She did, needing his warmth, craving security. He gave her a pillow and then pulled her close, her back to his chest, his arm wrapping around her middle, before bringing the light feather duvet over both of them.

"Do you want to talk?" he asked, his deep voice husky.

"Will you regret marrying me?"

"We're making a family. I will never regret having a family."

A lump filled her throat. It wasn't quite the reassurance she needed. "What about me, though? Will you regret marrying me?"

He kissed her bare shoulder. "Never."

Her chest squeezed, air bottling in her lungs. "Promise?"

"It will not always be easy between us. We're two strong people. But we can make it work, if we want to make it work. Does that make sense?"

"Yes."

He pushed her hair aside and kissed the back of her neck. "We will find our happiness, *cara*. I am sure of that."

And wrapped in his arms, and in his assurances, Charlotte fell asleep.

The wedding plans moved forward quickly, with the date set for the last Saturday in June, which was less than two weeks away.

Brando handled the arrangements, but he ran his ideas past her, making sure she approved. She liked his ideas and agreed with him on virtually everything, appreciating his logic, his tastes, as well as his decisiveness. Her only real objection was marrying in the historic chapel. Charlotte asked if maybe they couldn't say their vows outside, perhaps in one of the gardens, with a view of the valley.

He agreed with her suggestion for a simple outdoor ceremony, and shared his idea for a reception in the inner courtyard, which could be illuminated with strings of white lights, and torches attached to the stone walls.

Ten days before the wedding, Livia arrived to take measurements for Charlotte's dress, but before they could discuss dresses, there were other things Livia wanted to know. "You and Brando did not seem to like each other very much during our meetings. Clearly the rest of us did not know what was really going on behind closed doors."

Charlotte blushed. "Nothing happened during our work together. He and I did have some issues—"

"Too much chemistry, hmm?"

"There were sparks, yes," Charlotte admitted. "But nothing happened while I was under contract. I wouldn't do that to you, not while working for you. It happened New Year's Eve. He'd invited me to Enzo's big party. That was the first time—and the only time—we got together."

"One night and you're pregnant?"

Charlotte grimaced. "We used protection, too. He did, I did." She gestured helplessly to the bump. "But this one wanted to be born."

"That's a Ricci for you," Livia answered with a wink. "Prepare yourself. You're going to have your hands full.

Now let's get your measurements and discuss the kind of dress you'd like for the wedding."

"I don't actually have a preference," Charlotte admitted. "I prefer clean, sophisticated designs, which is what you do. Can I just leave it to you to make whatever you think would look best on me?"

Livia embraced her, and then kissed her on each cheek. "It would be my pleasure. Leave it to me."

A week passed, and the wedding was just days away. The guest list had swelled, with most of Brando's family electing to stay overnight at the *castello* rather than make the drive back to Florence. All the decisions had been made for the wedding, too. Musicians and photographer were booked, flowers ordered, and Brando's chef from Florence was coming to assist the *castello* chef and kitchen staff for the wedding weekend.

All the decisions that needed to be made were done. But Brando, who wasn't a worrier, had concerns. The wedding, while still intimate, was no longer as small as he'd hoped, and the family and friends coming would be up late into the night, celebrating. Brando had wanted a special night for Charlotte, a wedding they'd both remember for years to come. He just hoped that it wasn't going to be too much for her. The last thing they needed was Charlotte being rushed back to the hospital at the end of their wedding night.

From her room Charlotte could see the preparations for the ceremony and reception this weekend. The villa staff swept and scrubbed the courtyard, wiping down stones and the dozen columns supporting the arches of the inner courtyard. Planters were refreshed, topiaries pruned, and long strings of white lights were run across the courtyard, creating a tent-like canopy.

The morning of the wedding, tables were set up in the interior courtyard, and then covered with white cloths. Flowers arrived, and antique silver candelabra lined the long tables, the heavy silver candleholders matching the ornate silverware.

Livia was there to help her dress, and after her hair and makeup were done by a stylist Livia had brought from Florence, Charlotte carefully stepped into her gown.

Her gown was exquisite and what made it so beautiful was that it was perfect for her. It was her style—modern, clean and yet classic. The white silk gleamed in the sunlight, and the luxurious fabric molded to her full breasts, hugging her torso and bump, before forming a full, sophisticated skirt. There were even pockets in the skirt, a touch she adored. Normally she would have avoided such a deep plunging neckline, and yet the dramatic neckline, paired with the wide shoulder straps, looked chic, and drew the eye from her bump to her shoulders and face.

With her hair pinned up, and a long white veil attached to the chignon, she looked like a true bride—radiant, glowing, excited.

Livia walked around Charlotte, adjusting her skirt, and then the floor-length veil. "Perfection," she said approvingly. "Even the pearl earrings. Elegant, classic, discrete."

Charlotte reached up and touched one pearl stud. "My mother's."

"Is she coming?"

Charlotte shook her head. "She couldn't make it.

Most of my family couldn't make it. One of my sisters is on the way. She's coming from London with her husband. They're not here yet, but I think they should arrive soon."

"Not to worry. You have lots of family here," Livia answered. "The Riccis are here. You are one of us now."

In the end, Charlotte thought her wedding was impossibly beautiful, although it wasn't as small as Brando had intimated. Her sister and brother-in-law arrived moments before she walked down the aisle, and of course, all of Brando's family was there—his mother, his mother's sister, his brothers and sister, cousins, so many cousins, plus other guests, people who were "like family" to the Riccis.

They said their vows in the garden overlooking the valley with the gently rolling hills, dark green vineyards and views of the tiled roofs of the village below, and then moved to the *castello*'s courtyard for the dinner and music. The flowers on the table matched her bridal bouquet—the palest pink roses hand-tied with a wide pale pink satin ribbon.

She felt beautiful in the dress Livia had made for her, and Brando looked impossibly handsome in his black suit with the white shirt and dark tie. His hair was sleekly combed back, highlighting his strong cheekbones, jaw and lovely mouth. Her hand had trembled in his as they'd said the vows, but his voice was deep and steady, and he'd held her gaze the entire time, promising to honor and protect her for the rest of their lives.

During dinner Brando insisted she stay seated at the head table, asking guests to come to her. She wondered what he'd said to them as no one seemed surprised, or questioned why she left her chair only to cut the cake, and have a first dance with Brando. The song from the first dance was the same song they'd danced to on New Year's Eve, "At Last" by Etta James. Charlotte was surprised he'd remembered, but also touched. Dancing with him beneath the stars and moon and strings of white lights was probably one of the most romantic moments in her life. Brando might not love her, but he'd gone to great pains to make tonight special. To make her feel special.

"You take my breath away," he said, as the song came to an end.

"Thank you for a beautiful wedding, and a beautiful night," she answered.

His head dropped and he kissed her, there in front of everyone. The kiss filled her with warmth and hope. Their families and friends applauded. Brando lifted his head and grinned. She blushed and smiled.

And then before she knew it was all over, Brando was saying he needed to carry his bride away, and he encouraged everyone to eat and drink and dance as late as they wanted as there were no neighbors nearby to disturb.

Brando literally carried her away, too, sweeping her into his arms and carrying her through the courtyard doors and up the central staircase to his room on the third floor.

She'd been here before but she'd never seen it like this. Tonight, the master bedroom glowed with dozens of white candles. They were everywhere—on the mantel, on tables, on windowsills. There were roses, too, countless white roses, and across the bed lay a delicate ivory satin nightgown with an ivory satin-and-lace robe.

"A gift from Livia," Brando said, putting her down next to the bed. "She said every bride needs something special to wear for her wedding night."

Charlotte suddenly felt overwhelmed by the beauty of the day, and the kindness of Brando's sister, as well as everyone's goodwill. Their guests had been happy for them, celebrating their marriage with toasts, hugs and laughter. "Livia has completely spoiled me," she said, reaching to lightly stroke the satin nightgown. "I hope she knows I'm so very grateful."

"She does." He watched her from the foot of the bed. "How do you feel?"

"Good. A little tired. But happy." She looked at him, and smiled, tears in her eyes. "Thank you for tonight. It was beautiful, all of it, and I'm—"

"Grateful," he interrupted, finishing her words for her. "Yes, I know." His mouth quirked. "But I didn't do this for your gratitude. This was for us, and our son, so we'd have memories and photos to share with our children and grandchildren, and then they can say, *Oh, you were so young!*"

She smiled. "Well, thank you for giving us memories." She glanced down at the shimmering satin nightgown. "I guess I should change."

"Let me help you out of your gown, and then I need to get something from the library and I'll be back."

She turned around and he made quick work of the dozens of small hooks hidden in the seam of her gown. The bodice fell away and she caught the silk, pressing it against her breasts to keep from exposing herself.

"I have seen you naked before," he said, a hint of amusement in his deep voice.

She blushed. "Not like this. There is so much more of me now."

"I think you're absolutely beautiful pregnant."

She didn't know what to say, and so she stood up on tiptoe, and kissed him. He caught her by the arms and pulled her closer, his mouth claiming hers, hunger and heat and possession in the kiss. Desire shot through her, bright and fierce. She wanted him badly, wanted the pressure and sensation, wanted touch and release. Everything in her craved more of him—more of his time, more of his attention, more of his heart.

She loved him, and yet she feared the love because she didn't know how she'd ever survive this marriage if he didn't love her back.

Brando lifted his head, gazed down into her eyes, before pressing the pad of his thumb to her full, tender lips. "There are so many things I want to do to you. It's incredibly difficult to keep my hands off you."

It wasn't a declaration of love, but it was something, she thought, as he left the room and she removed her veil, and unpinned her hair, brushing it smooth before taking a bath and changing into her satin nightgown, the delicate fabric impossibly soft and light as it followed her every curve.

Brando returned, and his dinner jacket was off, and the tie gone. He'd unbuttoned his dress shirt, exposing the upper planes of his muscular, golden chest. He was carrying a bottle and two crystal flutes. "Come," he said, going to the French doors and opening them onto his private balcony.

She followed him out, smiling as he popped the cork from the champagne and filled the two flutes. "Just a sip," he admonished, handing her one flute. "Just for a toast."

She took the pretty flute and glanced down at the pale gold champagne, the bubbles rising and popping.

"To you," he said, lifting his glass. "To your beauty, to your amazing mind, to the miracle you carry. I'm lucky to call you my partner, and wife."

Her eyes burned and a lump filled her throat. "Thank you," she whispered, lightly touching her glass to his.

As she sipped her champagne, a loud popping sound came from the corner of the castle, and then fireworks filled the sky, a dazzling display of light.

She could hear their guests cheering below, and Brando reached for her, and kissed her as the dark sky lit up with all the colors of the rainbow. It was an extraordinary surprise, and a wonderful way to cap a magical evening.

He'd given her absolutely everything this evening but his heart.

CHAPTER NINE

THE *CASTELLO* WAS still full of guests the next day, with Brando's friends and family staying over to enjoy a leisurely Sunday morning brunch before an afternoon departure.

Charlotte came downstairs for the late breakfast, hoping to see her sister Alice, but Alice and Philip had already left to catch their flight back to London. Charlotte felt a pinch of disappointment, aware that she'd exchanged only a dozen words with her sister last night, but at least Alice and Philip had appeared to be having fun, sitting at the same table with Brando's brothers, and talking the evening away with Marcello and Elena, Marcello's wife.

Elena and Livia were together, drinking coffee, and Elena waved Charlotte over now. "Last night was beautiful," Elena said to Charlotte as she joined them at their table. "And those fireworks! Did you know?"

"No, it was a complete surprise," Charlotte answered. "I was shocked, but I shouldn't have been. Brando did most of the planning for the wedding and it went off perfectly."

"It did," Livia agreed. "And you were the most radiant bride. Brando couldn't keep his eyes from you."

Charlotte grimaced. "He watches me constantly, afraid that I might go into labor." She saw her sister-in-laws' confused expressions and explained, "We had a scare a couple weeks ago. If Brando hadn't flown me back to Florence in his helicopter, who knows what would have happened. But fortunately we got there quickly and the doctors could stop the labor. That's why he's so protective of me now. We want the baby to stay put as long as possible."

Elena glanced at Livia, murmuring, "Aren't you glad Brando married her, and not the other one? That would have been awful."

Livia gave her head a slight shake, discouraging Elena, before smiling warmly at Charlotte. "We've been hoping he'd settle down, and so very glad it's you. We're already quite fond of you."

"And we also know you're not after his money like the other one," Elena added. "Thank goodness Marcello convinced Brando to take a paternity test before the wedding—"

"The wedding?" Charlotte interrupted. "Was Brando engaged before?"

Elena looked at Livia. "Would you call it an engagement, Liv? I don't think it was that formal. She was pregnant and he was going to marry her. Wasn't that pretty much how it was?"

Charlotte's heart fell, and her insides went icy cold. She clasped her hands together, feeling chilled to the bone. "When was this?"

"A couple of years ago," Elena answered. "I don't even know what's happened to her—"

"I thought the flowers were gorgeous last night,"

Livia said, cutting Elena off. "They were roses and pe-onies, weren't they?"

Charlotte nodded vaguely, unable to focus on the question. Brando had been through all of this before? He'd nearly married another woman because he thought she was pregnant, and apparently, all his family had known.

And here he was, years later, going through it all again. No wonder he was good at planning weddings. The whole celebration last night had been a show...a sham...

My God, what had his whole family been thinking last night as they watched him marry her? Charlotte put a hand to her middle, suddenly feeling as though she might be sick. "I think I need to get some food," she said unsteadily, rising. "If you'll excuse me, I'll see what I can find."

She waited until late afternoon and everyone had gone before approaching Brando about what she'd learned from Elena and Livia. She found him in his ground-floor study so lined with antique volumes that it probably was a former library. He was at his desk, reading through a document, looking relaxed and bronzed as if he'd spent his afternoon swimming.

He looked up with a smile as she entered the room with its golden paneling and rich wood accents. "How was your rest?"

"Boring." She took a seat across from his desk. "Not very restful." She hesitated, trying to figure out how to broach the subject that had troubled her all day. The more she'd thought about it, the more upset she became. "I heard a story today," she said carefully. "Elena told me. But Livia was there and verified it. Apparently they nearly got a different sister-in-law a couple of years ago. Elena says they didn't like her much. Thankfully she likes me more." Charlotte stared at a button on Brando's shirt, unable to meet his eyes. "It was a bit embarrassing to realize you've been through all this before—"

"I haven't."

"Apparently, you have. You get a woman pregnant, and you marry her."

"I've never been married before. There have been no weddings, no engagements, no babies. You're the first."

"But this other woman… You would have married her if it had been your baby?"

"Yes."

Her heart did that awful freefall again, plummeting all the way to her feet. Charlotte wasn't special. He had no real feelings for her. Brando was just going through the motions.

"But Charlotte, it wasn't mine. We didn't marry. None of this is relevant," he said, leaning forward in his seat. "You can't let Elena upset you over something so trivial—"

"Trivial?" Charlotte interrupted. "Marriage changes everything, and marrying you has turned my life inside out. Having a baby would have been a significant change, but this…becoming your wife…moving to Tuscany… I've given up everything I am, and everything I've known, for you—"

"Not for me, for our child, for our family."

"No, Brando," she corrected, getting to her feet, hands clasped tightly together. "I agreed to marriage because I would be marrying you. Just for clarification, I wouldn't have married anyone else. I married you because it's you."

She left his study then, and headed outside to walk the rose garden, and then circle the *castello* grounds, ending up near the fountain in the historic walled garden.

Brando found her in the walled garden, pacing around the gravel like a caged animal. "The walking doesn't seem to be calming you."

She shot him a look of reproach. "I'm not calm, no."

"You're getting yourself agitated over nothing. Charlotte, there was no one else—"

"Oh, Brando, please. Don't say that. Let's not pretend there has never been anyone before me. Your bed is never empty. You never lack for female company."

"When I'm in a serious, monogamous relationship, it's serious and monogamous."

"Define 'serious relationship,'" she said, hands on her hips as she faced him.

"Affection, attachment, respect, monogamous."

"Is that what we have?"

"You're my wife. My family."

His words were beginning to make her feel a little mad. "Yes, but you feel affection, attachment, respect for me?"

"Yes."

"We're to be faithful to each other?"

"Yes, absolutely."

"And this is what you offer your significant others? This is the most you offer? Affection, attachment, respect?"

His jaw set, his eyes narrowed. "Last night you were content with me, and hopeful about the future. Today, you throw it all back in my face? Because Elena thoughtlessly mentioned someone from my past?"

Furious tears burned the back of her eyes. "I'm not a replacement bride—"

"No, you're not. But I don't know what you want from me, Charlotte. I don't even know how to talk to you right now. We had a beautiful wedding last night. We had our friends and family here. You thanked me last night for making it a special day, but suddenly, based on something Elena said, it's not enough?"

She didn't know how to explain, but she felt as if there was an injustice here. In marrying him, she'd lost everything she'd known—her home, her name, her identity, her independence. And he'd lost nothing other than his ability to sleep with whomever he wanted. Because he hadn't really given up anything. He didn't have to change, or even feel too much, because he didn't feel too much.

"This was a mistake," she said hoarsely, mouth dry, stomach in knots. "I didn't marry out of duty. It's not why I agreed to this."

"We're doing this for our son," he answered.

"This marriage will make us miserable. I refuse to raise a baby in a home where we're miserable."

"I'm not miserable."

"Because you don't love. You lust—"

"Charlotte."

"Where are your emotions? And what do you really feel for me? Affection…desire?"

"Yes."

"It's not enough."

"Our attachment will grow."

She was already attached, though. She already cared. What was she supposed to do, wait for him to catch up? Hope he might one day have more feelings for her?

"I don't want this marriage," she said lowly. "I don't want to be part of any of this. You're not who I thought you were. We don't have what I thought we have."

He closed the distance between them, hands settling on her upper arms. "You're working yourself up over nothing. Adele meant nothing to me. I swear—"

"Isn't that the whole issue?" she cried, looking up into his face. "You don't care about any of them you've been with. You love sex, the act of sex, but you don't love the women you're with, and you will never love me." She tried to pull away but he didn't release her. Charlotte pushed his chest, and still he held her. "See, it's already a trap. I'm trapped. I knew this would happen. It's what marriage does... It changes people... changes the power balance between two people."

He gave her a gentle shake. "Nothing has changed, Charlotte."

Her chest burned and her heart was beating so fast she couldn't catch her breath. Her emotions were chaotic, her control splintering. Where was the Charlotte who was so capable of dealing with crises that she could virtually do it in her sleep? She needed that Charlotte to show up, right now. "I shouldn't have agreed to marry you. I shouldn't have let you convince me it was the right thing to do. It's not, and I can't pretend like you, can't fake happiness." She struggled to pluck his fingers from her arm. "I can't live with you. I won't live with you—"

"The baby—"

"The baby will be fine. I promise you I'll make sure of that." She reached up and pressed a hand to her eyes to hold back the tears. She wouldn't cry now. She had to keep it together. "I'd like to return to Florence. I'll get a small apartment for the rest of the summer—"

"That's absurd."

"I'll be close to the hospital should anything happen," she added, continuing as if he hadn't interrupted. "I promise to keep you informed. I won't take any risks. You won't have to worry about me."

"I don't understand any of this."

"That's the problem, Brando. You don't understand this, because you don't understand me. I didn't marry you to give the baby your name. I didn't marry you to do the right thing. I married you because—" She broke off, tears filling her eyes. "I married you because I wanted to be with you."

"And that's changed?"

She couldn't hold the tears back. *"Yes."*

"Why? Because you've heard some story about Adele and her pregnancy that had nothing to do with me?"

"You were prepared to marry her. You would have married her—"

"It wasn't my child. I didn't get her pregnant."

"It doesn't matter. What matters is that we're all interchangeable in your eyes. You love making love, but you don't really love, and then when you're faced with the consequences, you think you're doing the right thing, but marriage isn't the answer, not when there's no love."

"It's a little late for regrets, though. We've said our vows, we've made a commitment. There's no backing out of it now." He released her then and she took a step back, and then another, her chin high, spine straight.

For a long moment she just held his gaze, expression defiant, before regally turning around and walking away from him, aware that his gaze followed her every step of the way.

Brando watched Charlotte return to the *castello*, gut on fire, head throbbing. What the hell had just happened?

How had everything gone sideways?

She'd been happy last night, radiant in her bridal gown, and breathtaking in her shimmering satin nightgown. He'd slept with one arm around her last night, savoring her warmth, her softness, feeling overwhelmed with his desire to protect her. And then the baby kicked, right against his hand where it rested on her belly, and he'd known then that he would sacrifice everything for them, his wife and son. They would want for nothing. They would always have him, a devoted husband and father.

All day he'd felt renewed. Purposeful. There was a reason now for him to work harder, to push to be more successful. Everything he did would be for them... And yet Charlotte now wanted none of it.

And nothing from him.

He was baffled, but also angry. Angry that she didn't trust him. Angry that she would judge and condemn him. Angry that she'd be so selfish that she'd put her needs before their son's needs...before the needs of the family.

Apparently, he didn't know her.

Apparently, she wasn't who he'd thought she was, either.

There was no honeymoon, and they spent the next week living like strangers in the *castello*. Charlotte moved out of the master bedroom and back into hers. He never once commented on her decision.

After she returned to her own room, they still had dinner together twice, but each evening they barely spoke, the atmosphere tense, so severely strained that Charlotte couldn't manage a bite. After the second miserable dinner, she told him she couldn't eat with him anymore, it was too upsetting, and it was true. After that last dinner, she threw up after crying so hard. This wasn't the life she wanted. This wasn't the marriage she'd agreed to.

Days passed and the first week of July had come and gone, the summer heat making the air hot, and heavy. The heat gave Charlotte a headache and she stayed in her room, in the dark, heavy coral silk curtains drawn to keep her room cool and dim.

She felt listless and lost, confused as to why she was here in this place, living this way. Brando didn't seem to care that he never saw her anymore, either, and he came to her room only after hearing she hadn't gotten out of bed again one day.

He didn't bother knocking. He opened her bedroom door, stood on the threshold, gaze sweeping the room, before crossing the floor and drawing back the heavy silk drapes, allowing sunlight to pierce the darkness. "Are you having contractions? Is there pain?" he asked brusquely.

"No," she whispered.

"Then what are you doing still in bed?"

"I'm on bed rest, Brando."

"The midwife said you should get up and walk a little. She said you need fresh air."

"I'm fine."

"You're not fine." He crossed to the side of the bed,

narrowed gaze raking her, the curl of his upper lip revealing disdain.

"I want you to get up."

"Why?" she asked, rolling onto her back to look up
at him.

"Because this isn't good for you, or the baby."

She hated his tone, hated his arrogance, hated his
superiority. She pushed herself up, the covers heavy on
her legs. "Do you only care about the baby?"

He rolled his eyes. "That's absurd, and you know it.
I care about you. I'm concerned about you. You can't
keep this up. It's not healthy, and it's not good for any
of us—"

"You don't seem overly troubled by it. You've gone
about your life this past week without any trouble."

"I was giving you space."

"Thank you for the profound emptiness."

"I was respecting your wishes."

"You don't know me at all, do you?"

"I don't play games. I didn't think you played them,
either."

"You're above all of this, aren't you? How nice not
to have emotions—"

"Charlotte, I'm genuinely worried about you. You're
clearly having a breakdown of some sort."

She stared at him in wonderment. "What is your solution to the problem, then, Brando?"

"Get some sun, go for a swim, take short walks,
read something interesting, take the focus off you." His
broad shoulders shifted carelessly. "You're not the only
one whose life has changed. We both have adjustments
to make."

"And yet this is your house, and your country. You

are surrounded by your family and your employees, and your friends. The only thing you have lost is your ability to bed new women." Her lips curved, but it wasn't a smile. The pain inside her was blistering and raw. "Is that your hardship, Brando?"

Brando couldn't remember the last time he was this angry. He felt as if he'd married a stranger. Who was this woman in his house? What had happened to the Charlotte he knew? Where was the woman he'd been so enamored with? "Do I need to call the doctor?" he asked, struggling to contain his temper. "Should I make an appointment for tomorrow?"

She averted her face. Her lower lip quivered. "I'm not sick."

"Something is clearly wrong, though. You're not yourself. If you don't try to pull yourself together, then I'll find help."

"You don't need to find 'help,'" she said, still not looking at him. "I'll be fine once I'm away from here. I need a break. I need to go somewhere for a while. I'm suffocating here."

"No, I'm not going to let you go 'somewhere.' You're not running away. You've made a commitment. We both made a commitment, and we're going to honor the commitment."

Her head jerked around. Her gaze met his, eyes flashing fire. "You're not my father. I don't work for you. I don't belong to you, which means you don't get to tell me what to do, or how to behave."

"You're my wife. That gives me some authority—"

"Authority?" she laughed. "Oh, that's fascinating, but also wrong. You have no authority over me, and you

trying to manage me will backfire. It'll destroy everything I feel for you."

"Obviously, you feel very little if you're already determined to leave me."

"Speaking of feeling very little, Brando, just because
you throw huge sums of money around doesn't mean
you're being kind or loving. It means you're paying for
things, but I don't need your money, and I don't need
you to buy things for me, and you can't buy me. Maybe
everyone else is taken in by your extravagance and generosity but I know the truth. You dazzle with your gifts
and your generosity, because it's all you offer. Our elegant wedding…the dinner reception…even the fireworks… It was to make up for the fact that you don't
love me, and you will never love me. Instead I'm supposed to be satisfied—"

"You don't know what you're saying." His hands
balled into fists. He was at the end of his tether.

"No? Then tell me about one woman from your past
that you deeply loved. Tell me how it broke your heart
when it ended, and you didn't think you'd ever be able
to continue without her."

"This is ridiculous. You're hysterical. It's not good
for you, and it's not good for the baby. Clearly you need
space, space I'm happy to give to you. I'll be heading
out to the vineyard near Greve and then having dinner
with my winemakers. I'll have my phone with me. Call
if there's an emergency. Otherwise I'll check in on you
after I'm back."

Hands bunched in the covers, heart thudding hard,
Charlotte watched him leave her room, and listened to
him close her door, firmly.

Part of her wanted to fling pillows at the door. Part of her wanted to hurl insults at him, because who was he to tell her anything? Who was he to lecture her on behavior? He was the one who'd slept with legions of women, never truly caring for any of them. But on the other hand, she'd known who he was when they went to bed together. She knew he was a powerful, sexual man who had no intentions of settling down.

If she wanted to cast blame, she could only blame herself for falling for him, and worse, allowing herself to become so terribly attached. The attachment, the love, the passion... It was what made her hurt now. It was maddening that she felt so much for him, and he felt nothing at all.

The dinner with his winemakers went later than he anticipated and the *castello* was dark when he returned. Brando locked the front door and headed upstairs, hesitating on the second landing, wondering if he should still check on Charlotte at this late hour.

There was no light shining beneath her door and he remembered their fight earlier. Perhaps it was better to let her sleep. She needed sleep, and so did he. He'd have breakfast with her in the morning and begin working on untangling their knotted relationship, because ignoring her, and their problems, hadn't worked so far.

The next morning Brando asked his housekeeper if Charlotte had requested a breakfast tray yet. The housekeeper looked at him, expression bewildered.

"She left yesterday, signor," she said. "A car came for her a little after you left."

Brando didn't believe it. He went through his room, and then her former bedroom, but all traces of her were gone. He called her but her phone was turned off, and he was sent to voice mail. Brando struggled to stay calm as he threw his things into his leather duffel to return to Florence.

He spent the drive to Florence trying her phone—still off—before making some calls. She wasn't at his house in Florence. She hadn't checked back in at the hotel she'd stayed at before. Florence was a city filled with hotels. She could be anywhere.

He called a half-dozen hotels while he drove, and none of them had her under her name, or even his.

His frustration mounted with every call. This was ridiculous. Such a waste of time, as well as dangerous for her and their son. She was supposed to be on modified bed rest, not running off somewhere making it difficult for her to be found.

In Florence, he went straight to his house, asked his staff to help make discreet calls, but even after two days no one could find a trace of her. Brando was certain she wouldn't try to fly, not in her condition, but where had she gone? And why? Why go through the motions of marrying him, if she'd never intended to stay?

Those questions haunted him over the next week and continued to trouble him for the rest of the summer as it seemed Charlotte had vanished completely.

CHAPTER TEN

TWO MONTHS WENT by, two months without a word from Charlotte, months that passed with agonizing slowness for Brando.

Where had she gone?

And why had she cut him out so completely?

He knew she'd seen Dr. Leonardi at least three times over the past eight weeks, because ten days ago Brando had cornered the doctor and demanded information. Dr. Leonardi didn't know where Charlotte was staying, but he confirmed that she'd come in for her regular appointments and all was well.

So Charlotte was in the area still—that was a plus.

But where, he didn't know, and he couldn't find her, despite repeated searches. Knowing she'd remained in Florence helped calm him, though. He still didn't understand why she'd leave, but he was grateful she wasn't taking unnecessary risks by traveling.

The baby's due date was September 24. If it wasn't harvest season, he'd be permanently in the Florence town house, but as harvesting had begun, he was at the *castello* in Chianti, waiting for word, should word come that she'd gone into labor.

Word arrived far earlier than he expected, though.

It was just the first week of September when Brando received a call from Livia telling him to get to the hospital immediately, that Charlotte had gone into labor.

It was on the tip of his tongue to ask how Livia found out, but instead he hung up and drove straight to the hospital. Thankfully it was the middle of the day and there was no traffic, and he made it to the Florence hospital in under an hour.

Brando was met in the emergency waiting room by Livia. "There are complications," Livia said bluntly. "They've taken her to surgery."

"The baby?"

"Is fine. He's here, small, but healthy. It's Charlotte. She's hemorrhaging. They're trying to save her now."

Brando shook his head. "What do you mean, *save her*?"

"Her blood pressure dropped very quickly. Her heart—"

"You're not making sense."

"Because you're not listening. Charlotte is in critical condition, and I was told to prepare you—"

"Prepare me for what?"

"She might not make it, Brando. The surgeons are going to do the best they can, but there was a lack of blood flow to her vital organs."

"I need to see her."

"You can't. She's in surgery."

"I'm her husband, Livia."

Livia gave him a pitying look. "And what will you do once you're there? How can you do anything to help her?"

"You don't think I should be with her?"

"Where have you been all summer?"

He froze, and then slowly turned to stare at his sister. "What do you know about this?"

"I've taken care of her all summer." Livia lifted her chin. "She's been with me."

"I've been to your house. She wasn't there."

"She's been staying in the apartment over my studio. I've been taking her meals and making sure she gets to her doctor appointments. My daughter has been helping, too, keeping her company so she wouldn't be lonely when I had to work."

"You never told me."

"Charlotte asked me not to."

"Why?"

"She was terribly unhappy. She needed a friend."

"I am her husband."

"Yes, but not her friend."

Livia's reproach stung. His hands knotted. "You shouldn't have gone behind my back."

"What would you rather I did? Turn my back on my new sister, pregnant with your baby? Tell her I don't care? But I care, and I took her in, because I know somewhere in your hard heart, you care."

"I do not have a hard heart, and I have always cared. I was never unkind, never impatient—"

"But was there love?"

"Of course there was love. She's my wife, the mother of my son."

Livia sighed. "Brando, you're so very shrewd in so many areas, but you don't understand women, and you don't understand Charlotte. Charlotte loves you, so much so that I think she's dying because her heart is breaking."

"She's not dying."

Livia's shoulders twisted. "Fine. You know best. You know everything."

Her icy, dismissive tone gave him pause. "You're not being dramatic?"

She shot him a look of scorn. "You have a newborn son, and a wife dying. Why should I be dramatic?"

"I don't know," he admitted. "Maybe I'm in shock."

"Then prepare yourself. It's probably going to get worse."

His chest tightened, his pulse felt heavy and slow. "She can't die. We have a son—"

"You'll find another wife. It'll be fine."

Brando drew back, appalled, sickened. "What in God's name?"

"Her heart stopped, Brando. It will be a miracle if she makes it. But you'll find someone else to marry and raise Charlotte's son—"

Brando walked away from her then, going to the nurses' desk and demanding to be allowed into the surgical room. "I'll scrub in. I need to be there. My wife needs me."

"That's not permitted, signor. I'm sorry—"

He dropped his voice, speaking in measured words. "I am one of the largest benefactors for this hospital. I'm not asking to participate in surgery, but to be allowed to be in the room. I will not interfere with anyone. I just need to be near her."

The nurse said she'd check, but she couldn't promise anything.

Brando refused to look at his sister while he waited for the nurse to return. Brando watched the hands on the clock slowly move. It seemed to take forever for the nurse to return, but it was maybe just five minutes.

"They're just finishing now. She's to be taken to ICU, where they will monitor her recovery. I'll take you to her once she's there. It will be another ten, maybe fifteen minutes."

"So, she's okay? She's stable?"

"I wasn't given any information about her condition, only that she's to be closely monitored." The nurse hesitated. "Would you like to see your son, though? I can take you to him until you're able to join your wife."

Brando stood at the window of the neonatal intensive care unit staring at his son in the Isolette. His son looked tiny and red-faced, swaddled in a blue-and-white blanket with a little blue knit cap on his head.

A nurse joined him outside the window to explain that the incubator was protecting the baby from infections, allergens and excessive noise. He'd had a stressful delivery and the hospital was doing what it could to regulate his environment with optimum oxygen, humidity and warmth. "It's a lot to go from his mother into the outside world," the nurse said with a smile. "But overall he's doing well." She shot him a side-glance. "It's his mother we're worrying about. How is she?"

"I don't know yet. I'm supposed to go to her once she's in recovery."

"Let me make a call."

The wait again felt endless, and Brando stared at his son, unable to imagine his child growing up without his mother. Without Charlotte.

He couldn't imagine life without Charlotte. She was meant to be with him, part of everything. She was part of him. How could she go? How could there be a future without her?

Brando's gut burned, and the fire spread to his chest, creating a searing pain. None of this made sense.

How had they even gotten to this point?

And yet how had he thought this would turn out?

The nurse returned. "I'll take you to her."

Charlotte might have been taken to recovery from surgery, but she wasn't awake. She lay utterly still, her skin so pale that it looked like alabaster. Tubes were attached, as well as machines that monitored her.

Her long hair had been gathered into a side ponytail, the vivid gold strands the only color against the white sheets.

The nurse who'd walked him to ICU stood next to him for a moment. "She'll remain sedated for some time," she said quietly. "Don't expect anything."

Brando gave a brief nod that he'd heard the nurse, but he couldn't look away from his wife. He still couldn't process it all. That she'd been with Livia all this time. That his family had been taking her meals and keeping her company. That even his mother had been to see her.

Everyone had been with her but him.

The nurse silently slipped out and Brando drew a chair close to the bed. He watched the shallow rise and fall of her chest, watched the pulse at the base of her throat, watched the monitors measuring her every breath and beat of her heart.

She looked so small and fragile. So terribly alone.

Regret filled him, regret and pain. He'd caused her pain, and everyone could see it, and everyone could feel it, and everyone wanted to do something about it…everyone, it seemed, but him.

Brando slipped his hand through the tubes and cords

and covered her hand with his, careful not to bump or disturb anything attached to her.

Carefully, gently he squeezed her hand. Of course, there was no response, and yet her very lack of response drove home how vulnerable she was. How vulnerable they all were.

"We made a beautiful baby," he said to her, voice low and rough. "He's in the nursery where they're taking good care of him. But he needs you, *cara*. You are his everything. You're the only one he knows. You're the only one he loves. He trusts you. He depends on you. Don't leave him, Charlotte. Don't break his heart."

There was no response from her, no flicker of her eyelids, no movement in her fingers. She was so still it was as if she was no longer there.

And yet she was here. She was somewhere in there, resting, quiet, waiting.

Waiting for what?

He thought of Livia's words. *But was there love?*

He'd answered that of course there was love. He married her. He was starting a family with her.

Charlotte loves you, so much I think she's dying because her heart is breaking...

But that didn't make sense. He loved Charlotte. It's why he'd followed her to Los Angeles. It's why he wanted her in his life—forever. How could she not know how he felt? How could she not believe he cared deeply?

He stood up, and leaned over her, gently kissing her forehead. "It's not just the baby that needs you, *cara*. I need you," he whispered, his lips brushing her cheek, and then her lips. "I love you. I always have. I always will. Now come back to me. You've made your point. I'm paying attention. Give me a chance to make it right."

She woke late that night, groggy and weak, but her eyes opened, and she saw him and for a long moment just stared at him. "The baby?" she croaked, voice raspy. "How is he?"

Brando left the chair he'd been in all day, all night, and stood next to her. "Good. But he'll probably be happier once he's with you."

"He's really all right?"

"Yes." He could see the fear in her eyes as well as the extreme fatigue. She'd been given transfusions, but she was still pale, dark shadows etched beneath her eyes. "You're the one we're worrying about."

"I'm fine."

And yet her voice sounded hollow and there was no light in her eyes. She wasn't fine. She hurt. She didn't feel safe, didn't feel loved. He felt an ache in his chest, hating that all this time he'd caused her so much pain. "I have missed you," he said. "I looked for you everywhere. I called everyone in your family. No one knew where you were."

"Hiding right beneath your nose," she answered.

"I've been worried sick."

"I took no risks. I kept all my doctor appointments. Your family has been really good to me."

He felt another lance of pain. "I should have been the one taking good care of you."

"I don't think we belong together—"

"But we do," he interrupted quietly, firmly. "I haven't expressed my feelings properly, and I apologize, and vow to become better, and more communicative, but you must know that just because I struggle with words, doesn't mean I don't feel, and don't care. Charlotte, I love you. I care for you so much that I can't imagine a future without you in it. I don't want a future without you in it. You are my future."

Her head turned and she looked up at him, her eyes slowly filling with tears. "You have your son now. You don't need me. I did my job. I gave you what you wanted. Now I just want you to let me go."

"*Cara*, baby."

The tears shimmered in her eyes, turning the blue irises aqua. "I can't live like this anymore." Her eyes closed, and a tear spilled. "I don't want to live like this. Let me go."

"I love you, Charlotte."

"Don't lie to me."

He bent over her and wiped away the tear before kissing her near the corner of her mouth. Her lips trembled. "I love you, Charlotte."

Another tear slipped free. He wiped that one, too. "I love you, Charlotte," he repeated.

"They're just words."

"But they're the words you needed to hear, and I should have told you. I should have said them before, not just once, but over and over, until you felt safe, and loved. Because you are loved. You are my heart, Charlotte. Come back to me. Stay with me. Give me a chance to show you I'm the one for you."

Her mouth quivered as she gave her head a faint shake. "I can't do more pain."

"There's no more pain. We've done that part already. It's time for happiness. Time for love. Time for change. I promise. I swear. I give you my word."

Her eyes slowly opened and she looked at him. "I don't want your word. I want your heart."

"You have it, *cara*. You have all of it."

"Why do you feel now, but you didn't before?"

He used the pad of his thumb to dry her cheek. "I feel. I've always felt things, sometimes so strongly that I keep those emotions under lock and key."

"Why?"

He shrugged. "I was the youngest in a big family. Everyone else was important. Everyone else had a voice. I was the baby, dismissed as shallow and silly, a boy with a pretty face. I learned to hide things, especially the things that affected me deeply. It's become a terrible habit, and I promise to never again shut you out."

Her hand reached for his. Her fingers circled his. "I need to know how you feel. We need to know, your baby and me."

"Our baby," he corrected. "And, yes, I agree."

CHAPTER ELEVEN

It was a week before she was released from the hospital but now they were all back at the *castello*, a family having come home.

The grapes were close to being harvested, and the days were long and warm. During the morning and early afternoon, Brando was in the fields, and with his winemakers, but late afternoon he always returned to her. Now Charlotte drowsed in the lounge chair beneath an umbrella by the pool, their newborn asleep on her chest, while Brando swam laps. She could hear the lazy hum of bees in the flowers in the big terracotta pots and the warble of a distant bird. Now and then she opened her eyes to watch him swim, marveling at the ripple of bronzed skin and muscle against the sparkling water.

He was magnificent.

And he was hers.

Finally.

The baby stirred against her and Charlotte nuzzled him even as she rubbed his tiny back. He smelled heavenly. Of milk. And love. He was so very loved.

"You know, we really need to give him a name," Charlotte said as Brando climbed from the pool before wrapping a towel around his lean waist. "We can't just call him 'the baby' forever."

"Why not?" Brando retorted, leaning over them, to drop a kiss on her mouth and then on the back of his son's head. "I was called 'baby' for years in my family."

She laughed softly, appreciating his humor. Brando grinned down at her, white teeth flashing, silver eyes filled with warmth.

"Aren't we supposed to name him after one of your father's brothers or something?" she asked. "Remind me again of the Italian tradition? I find it very confusing."

"Don't worry about the tradition. I don't think we need to follow any rules. We should give him a name that we think will suit him, a strong male name, as he's a strong boy."

"A miracle boy. He was determined to come into the world."

Brando nodded. "Determined to be made."

Her heart turned over. "Determined to bring us together."

Brando crouched next to them and kissed her again. "And he did. Our miracle. Our angel."

Charlotte's eyes met his. "Angel. Angelo."

Brando was silent a moment and then kissed her, and then the baby's cheek. "We love you, our Angelo."

Charlotte's heart was so full. She blinked back tears as she reached up to caress Brando's hard, chiseled jaw. "And I adore you, Brando. Thank you for loving me. Thank you for giving me this amazing family."

"And thank you, *cara*, for being mine. I love you."

"I know." And she did.

EPILOGUE

September, two years later

IT WAS HARVEST season and life at the *castello* was un-
usually busy, with two babies and a very busy husband
who spent more time in the vineyards than he did at
the house, but Charlotte understood and was almost as
excited as Brando about this year's harvest.

After feeding the newest addition to the family, another boy, seven-month-old Joseph, Charlotte left the
contented babies in care of their day nanny, and put on a
hat, and left the house in search of her missing husband.

She hadn't gotten very far before she saw him approaching. He was on his way back to the *castello*, his
white shirt damp and sticking to the hard planes of his
chest.

He smiled when he spotted her. "Where are you
going?"

"I was looking for you."

"Is everything all right?"

"Everything's perfect, and I thought maybe, just
maybe, I could steal you away from work... But only
if you've time."

"It depends on why I'm needed."

She loved the teasing light in his silver eyes and the husky note in his voice. Everything about him was so impossibly sexy. "I've had lots of time with the children, but I could use some adult time." She gave him a pointed look. "I could use some of you."

His smile widened, and he lowered his head to drop a warm, melting kiss on her lips. The kiss was full of promise and she pressed herself closer to him, desire flaring, hot and hungry. "You can use me all you want," he said against her mouth.

"Good. I intend to."

Brando wrapped an arm around her, holding her firmly to his chest and hips. She could feel the hard ridge of his erection through his work jeans, the ridge of his shaft rubbing her right where she was sensitive. "You still make me crazy," she whispered, arching against him, wanting all of him. "You make me want you morning, noon and night."

"Which is probably why we have a second baby already."

She smiled. "I have a feeling we're going to end up with a big family."

"As long as there are no more difficult pregnancies, I'm good with that."

"Last one was easy."

"Yes, it was. Thank you, Joseph." Brando swung her into his arms and cut across the gravel path, making a swift detour to the gated swimming pool.

She hummed with excitement and that electric heat that always crackled between them. "Where are you taking me?" she asked.

"Somewhere we can get some privacy." He pushed

open the gate, and carried her into the pool house, and locked the door behind them.

The shutters were closed and the inside of the small stone building was dark and cool, smelling of lavender and citrus. Brando stripped Charlotte's clothes off and walked her backward to the oversize chaise, before nudging her down. He dropped to his knees, and kissed her right knee, and then the left, and then higher, up her tense thigh.

She sighed his name, her breath no longer steady. He pressed between her thighs, parting them wider, making room for his body, but instead of filling her, he kissed her, there where she was so wet and tender, where every flick of his tongue created licks of fire. Her hips danced of their own volition, her body desperate for him. These kisses were maddening. His flicking tongue was maddening. What she wanted was the heavy weight of him, the consuming pleasure that only he could give her. She needed him, needed him desperately, now and forever.

Brando never tired of the taste of his Charlotte, or her soft urgent cries. He loved the feel of her in his arms, the silk of her pale gold hair, and the shimmer in her eyes as she reached for him. Her passion for him was matched only by his need for her. He loved how much of herself she gave, whether they were making love, or being a family. As he made love to her on the chaise, he didn't just give her his body, he was giving her his heart. Making love was more than sex, more than sensation. It was a pledge between them, to always put their love and family first.

Charlotte was still independent, and strong, but he'd come to understand that what she needed most was loyalty, commitment and stability. She needed hope and family. He wasn't perfect but he understood these things, and knew that this was a promise he could keep. To protect his Charlotte. To protect their children. They were his life now, and he cherished this life with them because it was full of hope, and love. Always love.

And maybe another baby.

* * * * *

PROMOTED TO
HIS PRINCESS

JACKIE ASHENDEN

For Sparta

CHAPTER ONE

CALISTA KOUROS CONCENTRATED on the slight prickle of her woollen uniform chafing against her wrists, needing something to focus her attention on that wasn't the half-naked man pacing back and forth across the expanse of the massive living area, a phone jammed to his ear as he argued with someone on the other end.

The glorious man, who was currently wearing a pair of worn jeans and nothing else, was proportioned very much like the Greek gods his ancestors had no doubt worshipped thousands of years ago.

Broad, powerful shoulders, muscled chest, six-pack abs, lean hips, long legs. Olive skin and short black hair. A face that was all exquisite angles, sharp, sculpted cheekbones and a high forehead. Straight nose. A beautifully carved mouth that somehow managed to be both hard and sensual at the same time. A deep, rich voice with a faintly rough edge, like black velvet or melted bittersweet chocolate…

You're staring at him again.

Annoyance shot down her spine.

She should *not* be staring at him. That was the one thing she shouldn't be doing. As a palace guard, she was there to protect him, which meant she should be alert for threats, not gawking at his body.

He'd stopped in the middle of the cavernous room, his back to her, facing the huge plate-glass windows that looked out over the lake on which the royal villa was situated. It was dark outside, the moon glittering on the water.

His voice rolled over her, sin and smoke. 'You were expected to be in Axios today. What? Yes, I'm aware you had a council meeting to attend, but I'm afraid that's not my problem.' There was a pause. 'I don't care. The gowns are here and you were required to attend a fitting.'

Calista stared at his sleekly muscled back and the magnificent tattoo of a lion that stretched from one powerful shoulder to the other.

The royal lion of Axios.

Only one other man in the country was permitted such a tattoo: the king.

'No,' Prince Xerxes Nikolaides of Axios said tersely. 'I'm not couriering them to you. The designer needs to be back in Paris by tomorrow, which means she needs to make the final alterations tonight.'

Calista dragged her gaze from him, fixating on the middle distance instead. But it was difficult and that annoyed her acutely—a problem when one had a volatile temper that needed effort to keep controlled.

For the past month, ever since she'd been promoted to the prince's personal guard, she'd been finding it very, very difficult—sometimes next to impossible—not to simply ogle him like a teenager would their favourite pop star.

It was an issue. Especially when she'd never had this issue with men before.

She was a soldier, a member of the elite royal guard tasked with ensuring the protection of the king of Axios and his family, a position for which she'd worked very hard. The Axian army included women, but the royal guard didn't. Or, at least, it hadn't until she'd been assigned to it a month earlier.

She was the first woman to be an active royal guard and she took her position extremely seriously. One day she hoped to be promoted to the king's personal guard, perhaps even making captain as her father had, but she wouldn't until she'd made an impression as part of Prince Xerxes' detail. And she had to make a good impression.

His official title was Defender of the Throne, a title that all second royal sons were given, and his duties included being the head of the Axian army. Which meant if she was going to be promoted to the king's guard, she would need his good word.

Not an impossibility, but it was difficult trying to do her best for a man she personally didn't think much of.

Prince Xerxes had not been popular when he'd been appointed, mainly because he'd been disinherited and exiled from Axios by his father, King Xenophon, ten years earlier. The rumours went that it was for cowardice, which was on a par with treason to most Axians, and his behaviour—that of a spoiled, self-centred playboy touring the bedrooms of Europe—certainly didn't enhance his reputation with the army.

After the old king had died and his eldest son, Adonis, had succeeded the throne, Adonis had brought Xerxes back to Axios, and, despite strong disagreement from the generals, Adonis had reinstated him, titles and all.

The army had been openly scathing, but Xerxes' acceptance of responsibility for his own reputation and the rumours that dogged him, and his determinedly spotless behaviour since returning to Axios, had somehow mitigated the generals' disapproval. That he had proved to be an excellent strategist, a decisive leader, and possessed of a huge amount of personal charm also helped. He'd en-

deared himself to the rank and file with his easy camaraderie and his almost perfect recall of their names. He
had the ability to make people feel special and somehow
the tide of approval had turned in his favour.

Calista still found him deeply troublesome.

Despite his charm, she suspected he was a rule-
breaker. A secret rebel. There was a casualness and lack
of deference to him that offended her rule-following, ordered nature.

But that wasn't the worst part.

The worst part was that somehow, despite her best
intentions, she wasn't immune to his physical beauty or
his intense personal charisma, a legendary magnetism
that had once brought half the female population of Europe to their knees.

She hated that. It reminded her that no matter how
hard she tried to be like her comrades in arms, to make
sure she wasn't treated differently because she was a
woman, there was still some part of her that remained
intrinsically female. And that female part of her found
him absolutely fascinating.

She despised that part of herself. Despised it utterly.

'I see.' The prince's usually warm voice was distinctly
cool. 'Well, don't expect me to care if you turn up to our
engagement party in a gown that doesn't fit properly.'

A small, electric jolt coursed down Calista's spine.
She shouldn't have been listening to the conversation
and was irritated that she was even conscious of it. Then
again, the prince didn't seem to care about the members
of his staff, be they civilian or military, listening in on
his conversations.

Even private conversations with his soon-to-be fiancée.

King Adonis had ordered his brother to marry to safeguard the succession of the Nikolaides royal line, and,

though it was well-known that Prince Xerxes wasn't entirely happy about it, an announcement had been made that the prince would be formally engaged to one of the princesses of one of Europe's more progressive countries and that an engagement party would be given.

Hence, presumably, the fitting of dresses. Which his fiancée-to-be would now not be attending.

Calista didn't know why that strange little jolt had hit her at the mention of his engagement party. The marriage would certainly be good for the prince. People would be less inclined to gossip about his past if he married and settled down.

'No, and that's not my problem either,' Xerxes snapped, and he must have disconnected the call because he tossed the phone down onto one of the low couches that were scattered around the room. He didn't like living in the palace for some reason, preferring his luxuriously appointed lakeside villa instead, with its couches of butter-soft white leather, and thick pale carpet, white walls and glass and steel furniture.

It was all very clean and modern, unlike the ancient stones of the palace.

Calista shifted minutely on her feet. She'd be dismissed for the night soon with any luck, which meant she could go back to the barracks and…

Her thoughts came to a dead stop, the weight of another person's gaze settling on her.

His.

Instantly she snapped to attention, her chin coming up, her shoulders straightening.

He'd turned around and was gazing at her, a distinctly speculative look on his impossibly handsome face.

He had that knack of looking at a person and making

them feel as if they were the centre of the universe. As if he saw *them*.

Calista didn't like it. She was just one of his guards; she wasn't special. She didn't stand out and she didn't want to. And besides, she was a firm believer in royalty maintaining their distance, so the prince's laid-back attitude was another thing she disapproved of.

Though there was nothing laid-back about him now.

Deep in his dark eyes, gold flecks gleamed like coins at the bottom of a night-shadowed sea, making her heartbeat accelerate. Then his beautiful mouth quirked, as if he found her amusing in some way, sending a burst of irritation through her; she didn't appreciate being laughed at.

She didn't let it show, though she did click her heels together rather more ostentatiously than she would have normally. 'Highness,' she said crisply.

He smiled and lifted a hand, crooking a finger. 'Come here, soldier.'

Calista had been following orders and taking commands her entire life, including many from the prince himself. So obeying this one shouldn't have made her think twice. Yet, she hesitated for a split-second. His smile was arrogant and that crooked finger annoyed her, plus his bare chest was still irritatingly on show, and he didn't comport himself the way a prince should.

All of which shouldn't have any impact on her ability to obey orders, yet somehow did. Which was wrong. She shouldn't let her personal opinion of him affect her behaviour as a soldier and especially not compromise her emotional control. And most especially not if she wanted a promotion to the king's guard.

Shoving away her irritation and hoping he hadn't noticed her hesitation, Calista stepped forward from her post by the door. 'Your Highness.'

'Closer,' the prince murmured. 'I'm not going to bite, I promise.' The gold in his eyes gleamed brighter. 'Well, at least not very hard.'

Even though she hadn't been working for the prince long, she'd learned that the gleam of gold in his eyes, and the slightly edged, amused tone in his beautiful voice, was usually a sign that he was in a temper. And that it was wise not to disobey him when he was in this mood.

Still, the comment made more irritation prickle over Calista's skin and she couldn't think why. It was very strange.

'Highness,' she repeated, and took another step, coming smartly to attention once again and giving him a steely-eyed stare.

He stared back a second, then let out an annoyed-sounding breath and strolled up to her. 'When I said closer, I meant closer.' His smoky gold gaze looked down into hers. 'Like so. Are we clear?'

For a second Calista's brain blanked. All she could think about was that he was, indeed, *very* close. Mere inches away. That distracting bare chest, broad and powerful, all smooth olive skin and sharply cut muscle, was right in front of her. Close enough for her to feel his heat, catch his scent, spicy and warm, reminding her of pine forests and sun-drenched earth.

Are you insane? You're his guard. You're not supposed to notice anything but threats.

The royal guard was largely ceremonial these days, but still. She took her job seriously. She should not be getting distracted by a bare chest, and especially not *his* bare chest. He was Commander of the Armies, a superior officer. She shouldn't even be noticing it.

'Yes, Highness,' she said crisply, with any luck masking the thick note in her voice.

His gaze narrowed and then, much to her shock, he gave her a very thorough, very deliberate scan from her head to her feet.

The prickle of irritation became something else, electricity whispering over her skin.

Slowly, he began to circle her with the same kind of fluid, predatory grace as the lion tattooed on his back.

'Yes,' he murmured, his deep voice nearly a purr. 'Yes, I think you'll do.'

The strange, electric sensation got worse.

Calista fought it, putting iron in her backbone and steel in her shoulders the way her father had taught her: lifting her chin high and staring straight ahead; ignoring the way he was looking at her. 'Excuse me, Highness?'

He stopped circling, coming to stand in front of her again. A satisfied-looking smile flickered around his mouth. 'Calista, isn't it?' he asked. 'Calista Kouros?'

Another small shock pulsed through her that he knew who she was, though it shouldn't have come as a surprise. He knew the name of every single person who worked for him, plus those of the soldiers under his command. And besides, she was the only female guard on his staff; he would know her name.

'Yes, Highness,' she said.

His smile lost its satisfied edge and became warmer, more charming. 'I need you to do something for me, Calista.'

It was very strange. The way he said her name made her entire body shiver.

She ignored that, too. 'Certainly, Highness.' She was nearly off-duty, but when royalty commanded, she obeyed. No matter how annoying she found said royalty.

One perfect black brow arched. 'You're not going to ask me what it is?'

'No, Highness.'

'What a good soldier you are.' His voice became languid and lazy, like melted chocolate. 'Maybe I should be marrying you instead of the rather unreliable Princess Eleni.'

Yet another of those strange shocks went through her. Marry her? Did he mean…?

No, of course he didn't. What a ridiculous thought.

'Yes, Highness,' she said again, keeping both her voice and her gaze level.

'And you probably would, wouldn't you? Like a good little soldier…' He trailed off, staring at her once again, and she had the uncomfortable impression that it was definitely *her* he was looking at, the woman under the uniform.

The woman she'd successfully ignored for years, just as she ignored the thump of her heart, and the distracting, mesmerising presence of the impossibly beautiful prince in front of her.

'Luckily,' he said, this time without the seductive edge, 'I have something else I require of you. And don't worry, it's not particularly onerous and you'll be safely tucked up in your barracks before you know it.'

'Of course, Highness.'

'Good.' Finally, he took a step back and smiled, and there was something slightly wicked about it this time that made her breath catch for no good reason. 'I have some dresses for you to try on.'

The guard in front of him was doing a good job of hiding her surprise, but Xerxes caught the flicker of it as it passed over her face.

She was possibly only a couple of inches shorter than

he was and he liked that. It was refreshing not to have to bend to look into a woman's eyes.

And she certainly was a woman. Beneath the black and gold of her uniform, there were very obvious curves, full breasts and generous hips. Long legs, too. Her figure was Amazonian and very like Eleni's. Which made her perfect.

The rest of her wasn't like Eleni, though. She didn't have Eleni's delicate features or long, golden hair. No, this woman was determinedly plain, though she did have a rather lovely mouth, and her eyes were a startling light amber framed by long, thick, dark lashes. And, with her brown hair ruthlessly pulled back and coiled in a tight bun at her nape, the elegant shape of her neck and golden skin was revealed...

Not that those things mattered. It was her build that counted.

Xerxes studied her face, noting the minute tightening around her eyes and mouth, sure signs of disapproval. He was extremely good at reading people—something he'd used to his advantage in the army before his exile and afterwards as he'd tried to pick up the shreds of his life in Europe—and he knew when someone was unhappy with him. And this soldier was unhappy with him, no matter how well she tried to hide it.

Then again, he'd noticed her disapproval the minute she'd joined his personal guard detail a month ago.

It didn't bother him. He didn't let anything bother him, these days.

Besides, most of the army had been extremely disapproving of his reinstatement as Defender of the Throne and there wasn't anything to be done about it. He couldn't hide his past or conceal his reputation and so he'd done neither. What he had done was accept responsibility and let his actions speak for themselves.

It was annoying, but he did need the army on his side, because his role as Defender was important to Adonis, and anything that was important to Adonis was important to him. It was also a position for which his father had thought him unsuitable, which naturally meant he had not only to claim it, but to make it his own. Which he'd done. It hadn't been easy, but he'd dragged a good proportion of the army over onto his side through a combination of honesty and pragmatism, not to mention healthy doses of charm. Some of the generals weren't convinced, but he was confident they'd follow eventually. Certainly marriage would help that.

Perhaps it would help him with this particular soldier, though, given the way her gaze followed him, as if she couldn't help herself, perhaps not. Because he knew that look. It was as familiar to him as breathing, and he frequently saw it on the faces of some of his female staff—and some of the male, too.

It didn't bother him—he'd never laid a hand on anyone who worked directly with him—but sometimes it caused problems. He hoped it wouldn't here, since she was the first female royal guard and her presence was a sign that Axios was making small inroads to progress. If there were difficulties with him, it would be a setback. He'd hate to have to dismiss her if it got out of hand. Especially as she was the daughter of Timon Kouros, the captain of the royal guard.

'Excuse me, Your Highness?' Her voice was very clear, with a sweet note that he should have found cloying but didn't. 'I didn't quite catch what you said.'

'No need to catch it.' He turned towards his bedroom. 'Follow me.'

The designer had left the gowns there in preparation for Eleni to try on, since everyone assumed he and Eleni were already sleeping together. They weren't. He hadn't touched her and he wouldn't until after the wedding.

Not that he particularly wanted to, since they weren't at all attracted to each other. A good thing in many ways, since it was less likely they'd get attached to each other.

How ironic that the one lesson of his father's that he hadn't rejected, the most painful lesson of all, had been the one on the dangers of caring too much. But he'd learned that lesson and he'd learned it well, so now he didn't allow himself to care much about anything at all. Anything except his brother.

He strode down the long white hallway that led to his bedroom, not bothering to check if Calista was following him—he knew she would since obedience to authority was the core of every Axian soldier's belief—and feeling slightly annoyed at said brother.

Adonis was obsessed with securing the succession—and fair enough, he was the king after all—but he could stand to be a little less rigid about it. Yes, he'd lost his queen a few years back, but, since the union had given him a daughter, he had his heir.

The real issue was that Adonis refused to marry again, which meant he wasn't going to have any more children, thus all the pressure for more heirs fell on Xerxes.

Xerxes had no desire to marry either, but, since Adonis had given him no choice in the matter, he'd acquiesced. Adonis was the only person in the world Xerxes would obey, if not without question, then at least with a limited number of questions.

It would be an arranged marriage and, as Adonis had already had a bride in mind, Xerxes had let him make the match since he didn't much care who his fiancée ended up being.

Eleni was a princess from a very progressive principality near France with a strong international political influence that Adonis had deemed useful for Axios. In return, Axios would provide access to the world-famous Axian army.

It was an extremely valuable alliance, and one that Xerxes essentially had no problems with, except for the fact that Eleni was turning out to be rather more difficult than he'd hoped. And now he was annoyed, which he did so hate to be.

Striding into the master bedroom, he found the designer fussing around with the gowns hanging on the rail near the bed. The woman kept glancing at him from underneath her lashes, which again was a look he was very familiar with. Sadly for her, he was no longer the playboy he'd once been, otherwise he might have given her a little taste of what she was missing out on.

Not that he had either the time or the inclination tonight. Not only was he irritated at Eleni for conveniently 'forgetting' about the dresses and making excuses about council meetings—she wasn't any happier about this engagement than he was but she was prepared to do it in return for the army—but he was also annoyed at having to fuss around with the choosing of appropriate gowns.

However, as much as he didn't care about gowns, appearances mattered to Adonis, and a beautiful woman in a charming gown it had to be.

The designer gave him a coy smile that only faltered when her gaze shifted to Calista standing behind him.

'The Princess Eleni won't be joining us tonight,' he said casually. 'My guard is about her height and build. She can try on the dresses instead and then you can make the adjustments to fit her.'

The designer inclined her head. 'Yes, Your Highness.'

Xerxes glanced at Calista, just catching the look of

shock on her face as she stared at the rail full of dresses, her expression smoothing as she realised he was watching her.

Interesting. Not the reaction most women would have at the prospect of trying on a lot of pretty gowns. At least, not the women he knew.

'You have an issue, soldier?' he asked.

The shocked look had gone, her chin lifting, her shoulders squaring. 'Not at all, Your Highness,' she said, her tone absolutely neutral.

Too late, though. He'd seen that expression on her face and the way she'd masked it. She didn't want to put those dresses on, that was clear.

He should have left it alone, gone and finished dressing since Eleni's call had dragged him out of the shower. But, as he didn't have anything better to do and he'd always been insufferably curious, he strolled closer to her, watching with interest as her level gaze dipped a moment to his bare chest. She betrayed no emotion this time, her expression fixed, but a flush stained her cheeks.

So he'd been correct in his initial assumption. She found him attractive, which was completely understandable. He was fully aware of his looks and had spent a good few years of his adult life shamelessly using them to get what he wanted.

Once, he might have toyed with her, purely for his own amusement, but he was supposed to be above that now, the little sermon his brother had delivered when his exile had been revoked and his title reinstated still resounding in his ears even a couple of years later. It had been about the kind of behaviour expected of a prince, as if Xerxes didn't know. As if Xerxes hadn't sacrificed everything he was on the altar of princely expectation already.

Still, he'd given his brother a pass on that since Xerxes

hadn't exactly comported himself with dignity in Europe, and it had been a good reminder of all the things that had bound him before he'd been exiled. All the things that he'd been forced to give up when his father, King Xenophon, had disinherited him.

Things like honour and dignity and responsibility.

Things like self-respect.

Yes, Adonis had handed those things back to him when he'd returned to Axios, but they had come at a cost. And he wasn't the same biddable boy he'd once been. The earnest, easily manipulated boy who'd only wanted to do his best and make his father proud.

No, he was a man now and he recognised the twin cages of title and name that the boy had been trapped in. It wasn't a cage he would willingly enter again.

At least, not without a key.

He wandered closer to his very stiff-looking guard, studying her face, though what he was looking for he didn't know. Perhaps for another glimpse of the person he thought he'd seen beneath the mask of the soldier.

Not just a person. A woman.

A small jolt went through him. Yes, she *was* a woman, and he even though he shouldn't find that as interesting as he did—just what drove a woman to want to be a guard, for example?—he couldn't un-notice it, as it were.

'No need to look so horrified,' he purred, coming to a stop in front of her. 'It's only a couple of gowns.'

She looked startled for a second, as if she hadn't expected anyone to notice her slip. Then that too was quickly masked, her expression like granite. 'I'm sorry, Your Highness.'

Curiouser and curiouser. She wasn't a fresh-faced recruit, which meant she should have had more control over her reactions than that. His father would definitely not have approved.

'No need to apologise. I'm just curious as to why a woman wouldn't want the opportunity to try on a couple of pretty gowns.'

Something gleamed in her amber eyes and he thought it was probably temper. 'Not all women like pretty gowns, Your Highness,' she said coolly.

Something stirred inside him. Very definite interest.

If he wasn't much mistaken—and he seldom was— there had been a slight note of challenge in her voice. Which wasn't exactly wise in a soldier, especially when responding to a commander. Was she like this with all her superiors? Or just him?

The thing inside him stirred again, rousing. Oh, he hoped it was just him.

Careful. You're supposed to be on your best behaviour.

He always was, though, wasn't he? Ever since he'd returned he'd been nothing but good, giving his brother no cause for concern. But it had been a long three years. And, now he was getting married, those years would turn into a lifetime.

Surely a minute or two's enjoyment with an interesting woman was allowed?

'No, indeed,' he said lazily. 'What would you prefer? A good flak jacket? Some hard-wearing boots? A sturdy pair of trousers?'

'Those are all very useful items,' she agreed stonily, 'but I assure you, I have no problem with gowns.'

'Is that so? Your expression, soldier, would say otherwise.'

Her lips were pressed together, temper sparking in her eyes again, and the hungry beast inside him, the one he'd had to leash since coming back to Axios, pulled on its chain.

It had been a long time since he'd allowed himself female company and he missed it. Women had been his saving grace while he'd been exiled—and not just physically. He'd enjoyed their company, too. His childhood had been largely male dominated since his mother had died young. His father had never remarried, turning ever more rigid and austere as time had gone on, making the palace a cold place to grow up in.

As a child, he'd tried to make friends with the daughters of a couple of the palace staff, because he'd been lonely, but his father had put a stop to it soon enough. Those friendships had been innocent, but Xenophon hadn't approved, teaching Xerxes his first and most painful lesson in the importance of detachment: that the personal needs of a prince were insignificant compared with his county and his duty. Those two things came before everything else.

This soldier wasn't a girl, but she was still staff and she was employed by him, and if he wanted female company there were others who could fulfil his needs.

Still, he couldn't deny he was intrigued by her show of spirit. It gave him a hint of the woman behind the military mask, and the contrast was…interesting to him.

Obedience was valued highly in the royal guard; questioning orders was not allowed and disdain for authority was not tolerated. Yet twice now she'd given herself away, both in her disapproval of him and her clear dislike at what he'd asked her to do.

Clearly there was some passion in her.

'I'm sorry, Your Highness,' she said with only the faintest trace of apology. 'I'll try not to be so obvious with my expressions in future.'

Just think how much fun it would be to get her to lose her cool.

Xerxes contemplated it for a split-second. Then his better self stepped in. No, he couldn't afford to risk stepping out of line. Not only would his brother be highly irritated, but showing interest in one of his guards wouldn't improve his standing with the army. Especially not with the first female guard.

But you're going to be engaged soon and then you won't be able to do this any more.

Ah yes. As if he needed that reminder.

'I'd advise it,' he murmured, letting an edge of warning creep into his voice. 'I'd hate for your father to find out you were less than thrilled with your orders.'

Her gaze sparked, that temper igniting yet again. 'I have no feelings about my orders, Highness. I haven't refused an order before and I won't now.'

The second part might be the truth, but the first was definitely a lie. She did have feelings about her orders.

He stared at her, realising with a sudden start that, actually, she was far from plain. He'd got that wrong. Her forehead was high, her cheekbones sharp, and her jaw was strong. Bold features. Not pretty, nothing so anodyne, but fierce.

Possibly even beautiful.

A current of heat moved through him, a heat that shouldn't be there.

He liked to be surprised. He liked that more than anything. But an inexplicable attraction to one of his guards was not the kind of surprise he was looking for.

Xerxes turned sharply and gestured at the designer, who was waiting patiently beside the rail of clothes. 'The blue, I think. Let's try that one first.'

CHAPTER TWO

CALISTA'S HEART WAS beating uncomfortably fast and she wasn't quite sure why.

The prince had turned from her, striding across the bedroom to where the designer stood with the rail of gowns, the play of lean muscle that moved beneath his taut amber skin making her breath catch.

She felt as if she'd been standing in the path of a blazing forest fire, preparing to be burned, only for the fire to turn abruptly at the last minute and blaze somewhere else.

What had happened? Because she was sure something had. The prince's dark gaze had been focused so unerringly on her, so intense it had made her skin prickle and her uniform feel suddenly far too hot.

He saw your slip.

She gritted her teeth, forcing away the sudden rush of shame. She'd been certain her instinctive recoil at the sight of those gowns hadn't shown. Certain, too, that her irritation at the Prince's prodding wasn't obvious. She'd never had a problem with her emotional reactions before, had always been the perfect soldier. Strong. Steady. Emotionless.

Surely a couple of gowns and one irritating prince hadn't been able to get under her skin so quickly?

Ah, but he's not just any prince.

Xerxes had taken one of the dresses off the rail, luminous blue silk falling over his hand and contrasting beautifully with his olive skin. The designer was saying something to him, batting her eyelashes rather obviously, and he smiled. It was practised—Calista knew by now which of his smiles were natural and which were not—but nevertheless, it was one of the most beautiful smiles she'd ever seen.

A smile should not have the power to make her feel this hot. It shouldn't. And maybe he wasn't just any prince, but she wasn't just any soldier.

She was the daughter of the captain of the guard, the first woman to be appointed to the royal guard, and she had a duty to uphold. A point to prove and a promotion to earn. And no prince, no matter how gorgeous he was, would be getting in her way.

There had been an incident once, back when she'd first signed up, where some male recruits had teased her and she'd let her temper get the better of her. She'd ended up weeping tears of rage like the stupid, weak little girl she'd thought she'd left behind the day her mother had walked out. That incident had given her a reputation for being overly emotional—always a bad thing in the army—which meant she had to try extra hard to be impervious.

She couldn't have any more slips. Couldn't let her disapproval show. Couldn't let *anything* show. Her father had been very clear: good soldiers never let their emotions rule them and they always obeyed their commanding officer no matter what.

Clearly she needed to try harder.

The prince laid the blue silk gown over the black velvet quilt on his bed, and glanced at her. 'This one first, if you please. Aimee and I will let you get changed—'

'No need.' Calista strode towards the bed, ignoring the fact that she'd just interrupted a prince. 'I'll get changed here.'

She didn't wait for him to reply, lifting a hand to undo the buttons of her jacket and pulling it open. She had no hang-ups about her body. Military training had stripped away any self-consciousness she might have had about it. Her body was a machine that did her bidding, that required fuel to keep it running and exercise to keep it performing in top condition, but that was all.

You're not at all trying to prove something to him.

Of course not. He wanted her to try on a ridiculous gown and so she would. All she was demonstrating was her obedience. It didn't matter that the gowns reminded her of the times her mother would let Calista try on her dresses, smiling as she pirouetted and turned in front of the mirror, telling her how beautiful she was and what a heartbreaker she'd grow up to be. Those memories no longer had the power to hurt her, especially now she'd turned herself into something better than a useless, pretty creature who broke men's hearts. Something better than her mother.

She had turned herself into a hardened soldier. She could kill men instead.

Tossing her jacket down onto the bed, Calista then kicked off her boots. Unfastening the buttons on her black trousers, she pushed them down, stepped out of them and put them on the bed, too. Someone—the designer probably—made an inarticulate sound, but Calista ignored her. She unbuckled the body armour she wore under her jacket and quickly pulled off the tight-fitting black T-shirt that was under that.

Then, standing in nothing but a pair of black briefs and a black sports bra, she turned and faced the prince head-on. 'I'm ready, Your Highness.'

He said nothing, and if she hadn't known better she would have said it was shock that flickered over his ridiculously handsome features. Shock that disappeared almost as soon as she'd seen it, to be replaced by what looked oddly like anger. Which was strange. What did he have to be angry about?

The gold flecks in his eyes gleamed brightly as he stared at her and her breath caught, unfamiliar self-consciousness creeping over her. Making her aware that no matter how hard she tried, she was still a woman. And he was very much a man…

'Out,' he ordered in a low voice.

It took a moment for Calista to realise that he was talking to the designer, not her.

The woman scurried off, but Calista wasn't watching, held captive by the prince's dark gaze as it raked over her. The self-consciousness intensified, but she fought it, standing straighter, taller.

She wasn't a coward and there was no reason for her to be self-conscious. Her body was only a machine, and his looking at it didn't mean anything. She was a soldier, impervious to emotion.

And physical excitement.

'Excuse me,' the prince enquired silkily, 'but what the hell do you think you're doing?'

Calista didn't know what was annoying him so much, especially when she was only doing what he'd asked her to do. 'I'm obeying your orders, Your Highness.' Turning, she picked up the blue silk gown that he'd laid across the quilt and gingerly began to pull it on. The fabric felt fragile in her hands. She'd probably rip it the second she stepped into it.

He made an irritated sound as she clumsily tried to

put the gown on, striding over and taking hold of the material himself.

'Let go,' he ordered. 'I'll hold it for you.'

She did as she was told, shocked as he crouched down in one fluid motion, holding out the gown so she could step into it.

Royalty was not supposed to be at her feet. She was supposed to be at his.

He looked up at her and a pulse of heat shot through her. 'Put your hands on my shoulders.'

Calista caught her breath. 'I'll be fine—'

'The gown is very expensive and I'll be very unhappy if you tear it.' Iron edged his voice. 'So put your hands on my shoulders. That's an order, soldier.'

Her hands itched and she wasn't sure why. Touching royalty was forbidden, yet he'd ordered her to, which meant she had to obey, didn't she?

You didn't have to take your uniform off though.

No, she hadn't. She could have waited until he and the designer had left the room. She hadn't needed to strip down in front of him.

What are you trying to prove?

Nothing. Well, maybe her obedience. Plus, he'd threatened to tell her father, which had flat out made her angry. It had been one minute slip, nothing more, but her father would definitely have something to say about it if he found out. She couldn't have that.

Ignoring the voice in her head, Calista shoved away the tension snapping and crackling in the air around them and followed orders, putting her hands on his broad shoulders to balance herself.

His bare shoulders.

His skin was hot—hotter than she'd expected—and very smooth. Velvety almost, and she could feel the shift of hard muscle beneath her palms. As if he'd tensed as she touched him.

And she realised she was staring down at him, looking into his dark eyes, watching the gold burn bright, like treasure at the bottom of a dark river. She'd put her hands on men before, of course, in training and on missions. But it had never felt like this, as if she wanted to run her fingers over him, stroke him…

One corner of Xerxes' mouth curled. 'I wouldn't look at me like that, if I were you. Not if you don't want me to start getting ideas.'

Her jaw tightened, a flood of embarrassment washing through her. Getting ideas? How ridiculous. Presumably he was talking about sex, but she was a guard and he was a prince and about to be engaged, so why would he say that?

'Apologies, Your Highness,' she said stiffly, trying for her usual flat monotone. 'I wasn't aware I was looking at you like anything. But I won't do it again.'

'Perhaps not taking your clothes off would be a start.' He said it lightly, but there was a certain tension in the words. 'I was going to offer to leave the room like a gentleman, but you didn't give me time.'

Calista ignored the velvety skin beneath her palms and stepped into the circle of blue fabric he was holding out. 'Again, apologies, Your Highness,' she repeated, staring at his glossy black hair, since there wasn't anywhere else safe to look. 'You seemed impatient.'

Slowly, he rose to his feet, pulling the gown up with him. 'Hold out your arms.'

She did so and he carefully tugged the sleeves over her hands, sliding them up her arms to her shoulders. His fingers didn't touch her bare skin, not once, and she was profoundly conscious that he hadn't. It made her skin feel overly sensitive, as if it craved the brush of his fingers.

But no, that wasn't right. She didn't wish that. He was her ultimate superior and her job was to protect him, even though her position was largely ceremonial and she disapproved of him. And besides, despite his thoroughly deserved reputation, there had never been any hint of impropriety since he'd returned to Axios, and certainly not with his staff.

What a pity.

Calista pretended she hadn't had that particular thought.

'You should be more circumspect, soldier,' the prince murmured, settling the gown on her shoulders. 'You must be aware of my reputation. Taking your clothes off in front of a man like me will only cause gossip. Not exactly what either of us wants on the eve of my engagement.'

Calista stilled, an icy feeling creeping through her. Oh, she really hadn't thought of that and she should have. What was happening to her? She was always calm and controlled, and she never let her emotions get the better of her. Never.

You must do better.

Gritting her teeth, she looked him in the eye. 'I'm sorry, Your Highness. I hadn't considered that.'

He was very close. His hands had dropped to his sides but he didn't step back. And he was looking down at her, his dark gaze unreadable. She was a tall woman, but next to his height and broad, muscular strength she felt small. Dainty almost.

Almost female.

'You're full of apologies.' He adjusted one sleeve of the gown. 'But words are empty.' He tweaked a bit of fabric on the other sleeve. 'It's action that matters. Or, at least, that's what I learned when I was in the army.'

She stared. Somehow, the fact that he'd once served as a common soldier had slipped her mind, though it shouldn't have.

'You look surprised,' he said when she didn't speak. 'All princes of Axios are required to do military service.' His mouth curved in one of his practised smiles. 'Me? I prefer words. They're so much less painful than bullets and they don't tend to kill you.'

Bitterness had crept into his voice, a note so very slight that if she hadn't been staring straight at him she might not have heard it at all.

Curiosity gripped her and before she could stop herself a question slipped out. 'You didn't enjoy your service? Why was that?'

His eyes widened as if the question had taken him by surprise, then something else flickered across his beautiful face. Something that she thought looked like pain. But it was gone so fast she wasn't sure she'd seen it at all.

Of course he didn't enjoy it. He was disinherited and exiled for rank cowardice.

There were many theories about why he might have been banished, but no one knew for sure. King Xenophon had never given a reason and after he'd exiled his son he'd never spoken of him again.

But Xerxes only gave another smile, practised and empty, the gold in his eyes taking on a sharp glint. 'Because there were no pretty women in the barracks, of course.' He stepped back and circled around behind her. 'No flirting, no drinking. No sex. Not my thing at all.'

Calista began to turn around to face him again, because he was lying. That wasn't the reason.

Except he murmured, 'Keep still.'

She froze, very conscious of his warmth at her back, of the bare skin of his chest so close to her own. The scent of pine forests and hot sun surrounded her, reminding her strangely of her childhood, of the games she'd used to play in the woods behind her house before her mother had left, of being a princess rescued by a knight from a dragon.

Now she was the knight. And she did her own rescuing.

The gown tugged as he slowly drew up the zip, the fabric closing her in its silken grip. His breath was warm on her shoulders and she didn't know why she was noticing it.

You know why. You're attracted to him.

She took a soft, silent breath. Surely not. She'd never been attracted to a man before and there was no reason she should be now. The army was her life and she thought the army would end up being her husband, too, and that was what she wanted. As a teenager she'd given up parties and boyfriends and hanging out with friends in favour of school work and the hard, physical discipline her father had insisted on. And when she'd enlisted at eighteen, she hadn't looked back.

The military was her vocation. It was her religion.

And there was no room in there for an inappropriate reaction to the prince she served, especially a prince such as him, a living refutation of everything the Axian army stood for.

A living refutation of everything Axios stood for as a country.

Calista straightened, squaring her shoulders, coming to attention. She couldn't forget herself. He kept calling her a soldier and that was exactly what she was.

'Hmm,' the prince murmured. 'Coming to attention in a gown. You're a soldier to your core, aren't you?'

That he'd recognised what she was doing felt exposing in a way she didn't like, but she couldn't hide what she was so she didn't bother. 'Yes. A soldier is all I wanted to be. Ever since I was a girl.'

'Is that so?' His fingers were doing something with the back of the gown, the fabric tightening around her. They were disconcertingly soft. 'You know what I always wanted to be?'

'What?'

'A rubbish-truck driver.'

Calista blinked, forgetting all about the gown for a second. 'You did?' she asked in surprise, unwillingly charmed by the thought of Xerxes, a prince of Axios, driving a rubbish truck.

'Yes.' The warmth at her back increased, his breath ghosting over the back of her neck like a ray of sunshine. 'But don't tell anyone. It's a state secret. And one only you know.'

Really? Only her? But before Calista had time to process that, his hand settled at the small of her back and he was turning her around, propelling her towards the bank of mirrors that lined one wall of the bedroom.

'Come on, Cinderella,' he said. 'Time to see what magic your fairy godmother has done.'

Calista stared at herself in the mirror and this time there was no hiding the shock that spread itself over her strong features. She'd said she'd always wanted to be a soldier—had she ever even seen herself in a dress? If not, no wonder she was shocked.

Because she was beautiful.

The blue silk hugged her statuesque figure, showing

off the delicious golden skin of her shoulders and arms, while skimming the full curves of her breasts and hips. Then it flared out, swirling around her thighs before falling in a pool of silk to her feet.

It was a simple gown, designed to highlight the beauty of the woman wearing it, and highlight Calista's it certainly did.

It's not supposed to be for her, remember?

Of course not. It was for Eleni, and he hadn't forgotten. But it was good to get a general impression first, and it seemed that gown fitted her beautifully, no adjustment needed.

He frowned at the thick black straps of her sports bra. They ruined the look.

'May I?' He met her gaze in the mirror, lifting his hands to indicate the straps.

'What?' Her face had gone pale, highlighting little freckles that he somehow hadn't seen before, a scattering of gold dust on her cheeks. There was no 'Your Highness' this time. It was as if she'd forgotten who he was.

He found he didn't mind that. 'The bra straps interfere,' he said. 'I want to move them.'

'Oh. Uh...yes.'

The uncertainty in her voice made him narrow his gaze at her reflection in the mirror. Why was she so pale?

Why do you care?

He wasn't sure. Perhaps it was that curiosity of his. Or perhaps it was only because she was female. He hadn't been this curious about his male guards and, after all, he was a simple man. There was also this physical attraction, which, though surprising, couldn't be denied.

Yes, perhaps it was merely chemistry. And maybe he cared more than he should or ought to, about the impending engagement. He'd told himself it didn't bother him that he was tying himself to someone he didn't want or even like for the rest of his life, but it seemed that he had more feelings about it than he'd anticipated.

The whole situation reeked of the kind of virtuous self-denial and sacrifice his father had so often espoused, reminding him of the cage he'd escaped during his exile. The cage of responsibilities and expectations from which his banishment had set him free.

Yes, he'd chosen to come back and take up the royal mantle once again, but only because his brother had asked. If it had been left up to him, he'd have happily continued sleeping his way around Europe and wasting his life.

Liar. You weren't happy.

Xerxes ignored that thought, concentrating on the woman in front of him.

It didn't escape him that she would make a particularly sweet last rebellion.

She was beautiful. Strong. And there were those tantalising glimpses of spirit in her eyes, signs of a passionate yet hidden nature. He'd always found that fascinating, and add to that a period of enforced celibacy and, perhaps most of all, the forbidden element…

Oh, she was perfect.

But… He'd promised his brother that he'd be good. That he'd leave his life of indulgence and pleasing no one but himself behind. The role of Defender was one he'd been born to and one he'd desperately wanted to fulfil when he'd been younger, before his father had tainted it. He couldn't let Adonis down for one night of completely inappropriate pleasure, no matter how perfect it might turn out to be.

Ignoring the rush of heat flooding through him, he settled his fingertips lightly on the straps of her bra, easing the fabric off her shoulders and tucking each strap beneath the sleeves of the gown, hiding them.

She watched him, the lovely amber of her eyes darkening, deepening into an even lovelier coppery brown.

The air around them got that dense, electric feeling it always did when physical chemistry was involved. And it came to him that he hadn't felt it so strongly before. Not that he could remember.

Who was this woman?

Her breathing was faster now, and although she faced the mirror she didn't even give herself so much as a glance. She was looking at him as if he was a lifeline she had to hold on to, and he suspected it wasn't only because of their chemistry.

It was something more.

'Tell me,' he said. 'What exactly is it about a gown that makes you go so pale?'

She blinked as if a spell had been broken. She didn't look so pale now, colour staining the clear golden skin of her cheeks. 'Nothing. Is this the gown you want, Your Highness? Or is there another you want me to try on?'

His curiosity tightened. He wasn't used to being denied, especially when it came to women who were interested in him, and she was interested, of that he was certain. That she was trying to put him at a distance was also obvious, though he supposed she had good reason, given who they were.

Then again, it was delightful, since he'd always liked a chase.

Don't be a fool. You've put all of that behind you now.

True. But he wasn't going to touch her. He just wanted to know more.

Briefly, he considered ordering her to tell him, but that wouldn't be nearly as satisfying as her telling him because she wanted to. Which she might, if he played this right.

'The gold, I think,' he murmured.

Stepping away from her, he went over to the rail and pulled a gold satin gown off it. Then he went to the bed and laid the fabric across the quilt. 'If you please, soldier.'

She followed him over to the bed, walking carefully in the yards of blue silk, then came to a halt and reached around behind her for the zip. Her forehead creased as she fumbled for it, so he moved behind her, taking hold of the tab and slowly drawing it down. The fabric parted, exposing the elegant length of her bare back, and he had the almost irresistible urge to run his finger down it, to touch her skin. What would happen if he did? Would she shiver? Would her breath catch?

That would be a mistake.

Luckily, he didn't have to make what would probably be the wrong decision, because she moved away from him, going over to where he'd laid out the other gown. She let the blue silk slip from her shoulders, stepping out of it without a trace of self-consciousness. Undressing before him the way she had previously. As if he were a statue. As if he wasn't a man at all, let alone a man with a certain reputation.

A reputation you can't afford to revisit.

Xerxes clenched his fists then opened them again. She'd taken him by surprise the first time she'd stripped in front of him, because it had been the last thing he'd expected her to do, and he'd been a little angry with her about that.

So, really, a second strip show shouldn't have either surprised him or affected him, yet it did both. The former because he'd thought she would have remembered him telling her to be circumspect and she hadn't, and the latter because she was beautiful. Her figure, as he'd seen already, was long and lean, and toned. Athletic. Powerful.

His groin hardened as she bent to pick up the golden gown, wearing nothing but black briefs and that determinedly practical sports bra. Golden skin and strength. A fierce, warrior beauty. Like Artemis, the huntress his ancestors had used to worship.

He could worship her. He'd be her most attentive priest. He'd shower her with glory and all sorts of other... pleasures.

Stop.

He took a deep, slow breath. Yes, he should very definitely stop. Yet his mind kept drifting to his engagement and the feeling of that cage closing around him. It reminded him of things he didn't want to think about— pain and betrayal—and a capsule in his hand that he hadn't swallowed.

A capsule that would have killed him.

A capsule that had ultimately led to his banishment and exile, that had saved him and condemned him at the same time.

He didn't want to go back to that and yet here he was. For his brother's sake. Committing himself to a life of duty and responsibility, and a marriage with no passion and no chemistry. Not even any friendliness or camaraderie.

Since when do you care about that?

He wasn't supposed to, yet the cold feeling inside him was there all the same. Oh, he would do this; he wouldn't shirk his responsibilities to his brother, but...didn't he deserve something for his sacrifice? Surely one last taste of freedom wasn't asking too much?

Calista had picked up the golden fabric and was already stepping into it, drawing it up; clearly she didn't need his help this time, even managing to get the zip up herself.

He forced that little disappointment away. 'The mirror, please.'

Obediently, she went over to stand in front of the mirrors while he prowled up behind her. Again, she didn't look at herself, her gaze off to the side.

He came to a stop, staring at her reflection, his breath catching.

Yes, he was right to think of her as a goddess. That was exactly what she was. A tall, golden goddess, the colour of the gown highlighting her lovely skin and deepening the clear amber of her eyes.

It would have been perfect except for the black sports bra getting in the way.

'The straps again,' he said. 'They ruin the line of the gown.'

Her gaze flicked to her reflection and away again. Then before he could say anything more, she reached behind her, undid the zip a little, then tugged the sports bra up and over her head before discarding it on the ground.

Looking away would have been the decent thing to do, but he'd never been decent, and he certainly wasn't now. He actually couldn't. He was riveted by the glimpse of her breasts, round and full, her nipples a deep rose, before she tugged the gown up, reaching for the zip once again.

Desire swept through him, his groin aching, his muscles tight. He was standing very close behind her and her scent was fresh and a touch sweet, like a bouquet of freshly cut wildflowers. He wanted to curve his hands over those beautiful breasts, bury his face in her hair and inhale her.

It had been too long and he was weak.

You've always been weak, though, haven't you?

The thought echoed in his head as he caught her watching him again in the mirror.

She felt the charge between them; he knew she did. And yes, he was weak.

'Why won't you look at yourself?' he asked to break the agonising tension.

'I don't need to look at myself.' Her chin lifted as if he'd challenged her. 'I'm a soldier, not a socialite.'

She did *not* like him insisting. Why was that?

'There's nothing wrong with socialites. Nothing wrong with putting on a pretty dress and enjoying a few parties.'

'That's not my purpose.'

'I see. And what is your purpose?'

'To protect Axios.' The look in her eyes changed, the spark of temper becoming one of pride. She looked like a new recruit, on fire with the desire to throw her life away for her country. Such patriotism. He'd once felt that same urge and it had nearly destroyed him.

'I see.' His temper coiled, shifting unexpectedly like a sleepy beast inside him. 'You're a zealot, then.'

'If wanting to serve my country to the best of my ability makes me a zealot, then yes, I am.' Her back was ramrod straight. 'Better to be a zealot than a…' She stopped herself just in time.

'Than a selfish playboy once exiled for cowardice?' he finished for her.

A muscle twitched in her jaw, the coppery glints in her eyes bright. She looked even more goddess-like, golden Artemis in full flight, hunting with her bow drawn. 'If the shoe fits.'

There was a sudden, deathly silence.

No one spoke of his exile. Not the generals, not the army, not the people of Axios. Not the press. His father had silenced them. But not entirely, because rumours had spread all the same. About how he'd refused a mission. How he'd gone AWOL. How he'd cowered like a dog in the street while his men had been shot all around him.

He'd never bothered with the truth because he'd convinced himself so completely that he didn't care. But he did care. For some reason, staring into this woman's beautiful eyes, he found he cared rather a lot. And he wasn't sure why. His brother knew the truth and he was the only person in the entire world who Xerxes cared about.

What did it matter what this woman thought of him? Why was her judgement so important? She was only a guard, burning with that same blind loyalty and dedication to her country that he remembered feeling all those years ago. She needed to be careful. Those emotions could be used, could be manipulated. Could lead to betrayal.

Better not to care about anything at all.

But what would that passion look like in bed?

The thought was instinctive, sending a raw heat coiling through him. Yes, far better to think about sex than his own destruction. That was simpler, easier, and a whole lot more pleasurable.

What would she look like naked and beneath him? Would her eyes glitter with the same dedication and pride as he pushed inside her? Would she apply that zealot's fervour to making him come?

A rush of colour flooded her face, as if she'd read his thoughts. 'My apologies, Your Highness. I should not have said that.'

Oh, yes, that was right. She wasn't thinking of sex. She'd just insulted him.

'You disapprove of me,' he said, deciding he wasn't

going to let her off the hook. And he didn't make it a question, either, because it was obvious she did.

More emotions flickered over her face, as if now she'd let her mask slip, she couldn't quite put it back on. 'It's not my place—'

'Don't lie to me.'

Her lovely mouth compressed. 'Your Highness—'

'It's a simple question, soldier,' he drawled. 'Yes or no?'

She was silent for a long moment and he thought she wouldn't answer him. But her gaze was defiant, clashing with his in the mirror as she said, 'Yes. I do.'

There was no denying that challenge.

She'd flung the truth at him like a gauntlet, daring him to pick it up.

Well, if she thought he wouldn't, she was wrong.

'You forget yourself,' he murmured, anticipation rising inside him. He liked a fight, always had, and fighting her would be…

It should be nothing. You must step away.

But he couldn't. And when she lifted her chin higher, not backing down, he knew he wouldn't. 'You wanted the truth, Your Highness. What does it matter what I think anyway? I'm just one guard.'

Good question. Perhaps it was her idealism he wanted to confront, the idealism he'd once had long ago. The idealism that had led him to a capsule in his hand, the weight of what he knew was expected of him weighing him down, the knowledge that he was utterly and completely expendable.

You should have taken it.

No, he shouldn't. He'd done the right thing in not taking it. His mistake had been letting himself care and he would not make that mistake again.

'It doesn't matter,' he agreed lazily, reaching for the pins that kept her hair coiled in its tight little bun, unable to stop himself. 'You don't need to approve of me in order to die for me.'

She froze as he pulled the pins out one by one, deliberately slowly, dropping them carelessly on the floor and watching her as he did so.

Her breathing had quickened, the pulse at the base of her throat accelerating.

Yes, he was pushing her. Wanting a challenge, wanting a fight. And it was dangerous; it was playing with fire. But he'd always liked a little danger, and getting burned could be fun.

'I *would* die for you, Your Highness.' Certainty glowed in her eyes. 'That's my purpose, too.'

'Would you?' He pulled out the last pin and dropped it on the floor. 'You'd die for a man you don't know, much less like?'

'What I think of you doesn't matter. It's the royal house of Nikolaides that's important, and that's what I'm protecting.'

It's never you. Did you really think it was?

The thought was a snake winding through his head. Of course. She meant that she would die for the prince, not for *him*. The country and the throne were the only things that mattered. The only things that had *ever* mattered. The man wasn't important, and once he was engaged, the man would be gone, crushed beneath the weight of the crown.

But you won't care. You'll have become your brother. Cold. Hard. Rigid. Exactly what your father always wanted you to be.

Ice sat in the pit of his stomach, spreading through his veins. He didn't know why that thought should cause him so much dread, when it hadn't before. When the last ten years of his life had been dedicated to proving he didn't care much about anything.

When he'd been a boy, all he'd wanted was to be Defender of his brother's throne. The position hadn't been filled in years, since his father had had no siblings, and Xerxes had been desperate for the honour. But that was before he'd learned what a cage being royal was, before he'd understood the demands it would lay on him, the sacrifices he would have to make.

He knew now though. Oh, yes, he knew.

She was watching him in the mirror again, her gaze sharp, as if she could see inside his head. See all his doubts.

See the weak man you really are.

Xerxes ignored the thought, tugging on her bun, uncoiling it so it fell down her back in a thick, tangled skein. Initially he'd thought her hair was plain brown, but it wasn't. There were strands of gold there, and tawny, chestnut, caramel and a deep mahogany like fox fur. Her hair shimmered in thick waves, curling at the ends. He'd never seen anything so lovely.

He wanted to wind his fingers in it, wrap it around his wrists, spread it all over his chest, silky and soft.

She made no sound, made no move to stop him, merely watching with that same steady, amber gaze.

She's not looking at the prince.

His breath caught, his temper shifting yet again, coiling tight. He shouldn't care what she was looking at. Whether it was the flawed, broken man he'd once been or the sulky playboy he'd turned himself into. It shouldn't matter. So why did he feel angry? Why did he feel exposed?

Either way, he needed an angle and he'd always preferred to attack and take the enemy by surprise.

'Such blind obedience.' He pushed his fingers into the silky mass of her hair, combing it out so it cascaded over her shoulders. 'If you'd die for someone like me with no questions asked, purely because you were ordered to, then what else would you do?' His fingers closed into a fist as he drew her head back gently. 'Tell me, soldier. If I ordered you to unzip your gown and stand naked before me, would you do it?'

CHAPTER THREE

CALISTA'S HEART WAS beating very fast. The prince was behind her, all heat and hard male strength, his hand in her hair. He wasn't holding her tightly and it wasn't painful, but she could feel his grip, the slight tug of it sending shivers down her spine.

Every part of this was a problem.

His proximity, his touch. The weight of his dark stare gleamed in the mirror. The scent of him was pine and sunshine, and something else musky and delicious.

She shouldn't have lost her grip on her temper. Shouldn't have told him she disapproved of him. Definitely shouldn't have said she'd die for him.

She should have kept her answers to *Yes, Your Highness* and *No, Your Highness*.

But she hadn't.

She'd let his presence get under her skin. The way he looked at her, the way her body reacted to him as if it had a mind of its own. The seductive darkness of his voice. The gowns he'd made her try on and the shock of seeing herself looking not at all like the soldier she was, reminding her of the little girl she'd once been, who'd loved trying on her mother's clothes. Who'd once wanted nothing more than to grow up pretty and fun and smiley just like her. Sunshine to her father's dour raincloud presence.

The little girl who hadn't ended up being anyone's sunshine, who had ended up destroying her parents' marriage instead.

Looking at herself in the mirror had felt impossible, so she'd looked at him instead, mesmerised by the flickers of emotion that had glinted in his eyes. Pain and anger, so quickly masked she wasn't sure if she'd seen them at all.

He shouldn't be so fascinating to her. She shouldn't want to ask him what had happened to him, why he'd been exiled, and why he'd returned when he was reputed not to care about anyone or anything. So many questions she wanted to ask, but she couldn't.

He was her prince and she was only a guard, and she had no right to any of them.

His eyes in the mirror gleamed and she knew that he was angry. That what she'd said about dying for his royal house had got to him in some way. But how? And why? He knew her purpose as well as she did, so why should that make him angry?

Why would he let the opinion of one lowly royal guard get to him in this way?

'Well?' His breath was warm on the bare skin of her neck and shoulders. 'Tell me the truth. If I ordered you to get naked for me, would you do it?'

Yes, he was angry. She must have hit him where he was vulnerable and now he was snapping like a tiger, going on the attack.

Fascination wrapped itself around her, holding her tight. He was so strong and so powerful, invulnerable almost. Yet she'd found a weak point in his armour and that intrigued her, thrilled her.

'Yes,' she said, purely to see what his reaction would be. 'I would.'

'Would you?' His grip on her hair shifted, his fingers

easing down to the nape of her neck and pressing lightly. 'And if I ordered you into my bed, you'd do that too?'

He didn't mean it, she knew that. He was still angry and that tiger was still snapping. Yet that didn't stop a shiver from chasing over her skin at the thought of obeying his orders, unzipping her gown and being naked in front of him, of moving over to that bed and slipping between its sheets, waiting for him...

There was a dragging kind of pressure between her thighs, a pulse directly related to the hard, muscular wall of his chest at her back and the slight brush of his fingers on her neck. She knew what they were: her feminine urges. But she would not surrender the way her mother had surrendered. Unlike Nerida Kouros, Calista was loyal.

Which makes this a dangerous game you're playing.

Perhaps. But she was strong. And a soldier did not give ground.

'Yes, Your Highness,' she said levelly. 'I would do that, too.'

'You shouldn't be so honest,' the prince murmured. 'An unprincipled man might take advantage of it.' His fingertips brushed lightly over her nape. 'A man such as myself, for example.'

His touch felt like sparks scattering all over her skin, lighting tiny fires wherever they landed.

She shivered. No one had laid hands on her like this, not with such gentleness. Every touch she'd had over the years had been in training and it had all been violent and physical. Punches and kicks, the purpose to incapacitate, to kill. But this wasn't violent in any way. It was light, soft. Teasing. Almost as if he liked it and was doing it for his pleasure. And hers...

She swallowed, trying to resist the sensations. Physical pleasure made you weak and she could not give in. 'Why would you do that?'

'Why would I want to order you into my bed?'

'Yes.'

'Why would I not?' His fingers began a gentle, hypnotic stroke up and down the sides of her neck, making those fires blaze. 'You're beautiful. And soon I'll be engaged to a woman I don't want and who doesn't want me. A woman who isn't passionate like you. Who doesn't burn like the sun the way you do.'

She should pull away. She shouldn't stand there letting him stroke her, making her feel soft and pliant. Like melted wax. But his voice was warm, with a roughness threading through it, a darkness that captivated her, getting under her defences like a sapper crawling beneath a wall.

Beautiful? She was beautiful?

'What a pretty daughter I have,' her mother had said, pulling her daughter in for one of her special hugs as Calista had twirled in front of the mirror in one of Nerida's pretty party dresses. *'You'll break so many hearts when you grow up...'*

Except it was her mother who'd ended up being the heartbreaker and the heart she'd ended up breaking had been Calista's father's.

And yours.

Yes. That was true. Which was why her heart now wore its own armour. She'd taken a leaf out of her father's book and had tempered it, hardened it. And it would take more than a prince's empty, pretty compliments to make it soften.

Yet a small, traitorous tendril of pleasure curled through her anyway, as if there was some part of her that had remained that weak, soft little girl, who'd loved her mother's praise. Who'd loved her hugs and loved hugging her in return. Who'd believed it when her mother had told her that she loved her.

Be careful. Be very, very careful.

Yes, she had to be on her guard. He was exactly like her mother, pretty and faithless, and she couldn't allow herself to be fascinated or intrigued by him. Couldn't allow herself to get distracted by him physically either. That way lead to weakness. Softness. Disloyalty.

Anyway, he was only playing with her because she'd hit him somewhere vulnerable. He didn't actually want *her*.

'So you'd be faithful to your wife even when you don't want her?' It was a rude and impertinent question to ask anyone, let alone a prince, but she wouldn't allow him to put her on the defensive. Strike first, strike hard, that was her father's attitude.

'Ah, what a question.' He sounded amused, but a faint bitterness tinged the words. 'I suppose I shouldn't expect you to think differently, though. My reputation hasn't exactly been stellar.' His thumb glided over a knot in her shoulder and pressed down, easing a tension she'd had no idea was there. 'But yes, to answer your question, I would be faithful. It may not look like it, but I take my duties very seriously.' The ghost of a wicked smile turned his mouth. 'My brother would have my hide if I didn't.'

She *really* needed to pull away from that touch, put some space between them. Yet she didn't, staring at him instead, caught by the edge of sincerity in his voice.

Did he really take his duties seriously? It was true, his conduct since he'd returned to Axios had been impeccable. But could a leopard really change its spots just like that? People said all kinds of things and didn't mean them, so why should she believe him?

Of course he can't change. If he could, he wouldn't be touching you.

But was that because he was still angry with her and her questions, or was it because he wanted a woman and she was the closest one?

Why do you care?

She didn't know. Perhaps she was only searching for evidence that he was a leader worth following. A commander she could trust. That her loyalty to the crown hadn't been misplaced.

'You always do what your brother says?' she asked, testing him.

There was the slightest of pauses, his thumb finding and pressing on another knot in her shoulder, and she had to grit her teeth against the insidious wave of pleasure that went through her as the tension was released.

'Yes.' There was no amusement now in his voice, no lazy drawl. 'He's my king.' His face was devoid of those empty smiles and there was no trace at all of the charm he used like a weapon. Instead something fierce and bright burned in his eyes,

He meant it. He meant every word.

His sincerity shot through her like lightning and she recognised it. Recognised herself. Because she'd felt that same ferocity when she'd first enlisted, that determination to do her country and her father proud. To prove her loyalty and strength. To give her all to Axios, because if there was one thing she knew to be true, it was that her country would never betray her.

She turned around, looking up into his dark gaze.

He didn't smile, that fierce thing burning so brightly she couldn't look away.

'Is that why you came back?' she demanded. 'Because he asked you to? Why do you pretend not to care about anything? What happened to you—?'

'No.' His voice was quiet, but very firm. 'No more questions now.'

'But—'

He laid one long finger across her mouth. 'No more.' The light touch was another shock, echoing through her entire body. 'I meant what I said, Calista Kouros. I'm an unprincipled man. I obey my king, but I don't take orders from anyone else. And I get what I want when I want it.' He took his finger away, but the heat in his eyes remained. 'Which means that you should leave, because right now, what I want is you.'

The blunt statement hit her like a bolt of electricity, making her mouth go dry and anger collect inside her at her own traitorous body.

'No, you don't,' she said, just as blunt, trying to distance him. 'You're angry at being questioned and you want to punish me.'

Something rippled over his face but it was gone before she could tell what it was. 'How astute of you. But also incorrect.'

'You could have any woman you wanted,' she insisted. 'You don't want me.'

'Is that right?' His eyes glinted. 'Perhaps you'd better leave before I decide to prove you wrong.'

Her heart beat like a drum, a fluttery kind of feeling gathering deep down inside her. A feeling she didn't want. Why was she continuing this conversation? Because surely it didn't matter to her why he wanted her? She didn't want him to want her at all.

Liar.

No, she wasn't lying. His attention meant nothing. And his touch didn't make her doubt herself or put at risk the years of iron discipline she'd put herself under.

Despite the crown, he was just a man and men were

all the same. If you didn't present yourself as a target, then you couldn't become one.

'I don't understand. Why me?' Perhaps if she knew what it was about her that had caught his interest then she could guard against it the next time.

'I told you why.' He took a step back from her and inclined his head towards the door. 'Out.'

It was a command and one she should obey, yet Calista didn't move. She needed to know the answer so she could shore up her vulnerabilities, defend herself.

'No,' she said flatly. 'Answer me.'

The beautiful lines on his face hardened, the light gleaming on his black hair and his tawny skin. He suddenly looked every inch the powerful prince, a commander of armies.

And you just commanded him.

Her gut lurched. She'd forgotten herself and her position. She'd let him get to her, with his male beauty and the glimpses he'd given her of another man. The man behind the prince. A sincere man who, far from not caring about anything, clearly loved his brother.

And she'd been addressing the man, not the prince. Not her superior officer.

That had been a mistake.

See what happens when you forget yourself?

If she had any sense, she should apologise and do as she was told—leave the room.

'Excuse me?' The prince's voice was cold. 'Surely I didn't just hear you issue me with a demand?'

She knew she should turn around and walk away. But her feet wouldn't move. There was something inside her, a weakness, a flaw. Some part of her that wanted more of his attention, his light, gentle touch. That was hungry for softness and pleasure, and to feel beautiful. To feel cared for.

She knew she couldn't give in to it. Yet she couldn't stop herself.

Calista drew herself up, her heart hammering. 'It wasn't a demand. It was a question.'

'It did not sound like one.'

It was useless to fight this. She couldn't do it. And besides, it was just a question. She didn't have to let the answer mean anything.

'I only wanted to know why it was…me you wanted.'

His stare focused on her like a beam of concentrated sunlight, burning hot. 'Why do you want to know that?'

She couldn't tell him. Couldn't reveal her own weakness, her flaw, the terrible need inside her that she'd thought she'd overcome but clearly hadn't.

So maybe you just need to give in to it.

The thought was searing, like a brand pressed against her skin, freezing her in place, making her conscious of that nagging pulse between her thighs and how sensitised her skin was. Of the space that separated them. Of him and the work of art that was his body, all hard, chiselled muscle and male power. Scars marred his skin. She hadn't noticed them before, but she could see them now. Long slashes on his chest that must have come from a knife and the tell-tale round circles of bullet wounds on his taut stomach. There were other scars, too, from weapons or injuries she didn't know, but they all told a story. He wasn't some pampered prince, kept safe and in luxury. His body was that of a warrior and he had the warrior's scars to prove it.

Desire gripped her hard. Did it really matter why he wanted her? Perhaps it only mattered that he did. That right here, right now, she wanted him, too. And after all, she'd denied herself so many things in order to get where she was right now. Had sacrificed many pleasures in favour of hard discipline. Hadn't allowed herself anything that would compromise her dedication or make her weak—touch, closeness, warmth, the pleasure of feeling different, of feeling special.

In the army you weren't special. You weren't different. In the army you were the same as everyone else, a cog in the machine, and she liked that. She hadn't wanted to be different or special, because by being a woman she already stood out.

You want to be a woman tonight, though.

She took a breath, a tremble shaking her. Yes, maybe she did. And maybe if she was, maybe if she took what she wanted tonight, this terrible need inside would go away.

'Why do I want to know?' Her voice sounded strange even to her own ears. 'Because I'm just a guard and you're a prince. What could a prince possibly see in me?'

He stood very still, the gold flecks in his eyes glittering like stars in the darkness of the night. 'I meant what I said. You burn like the sun, Calista. And right now, I'm not looking at you as a prince, because I don't see a guard. I'm a man and I see a woman.'

She didn't need to see his expression to know he was deadly serious. It was obvious in every word he said.

You've always wanted to be someone's sunshine.

Everything fell away in that moment. The army, her country, her position, her iron discipline.

For one shining second, he was a man and she wasn't a soldier. She was a woman. The woman she'd never let herself be.

Her pulse thundered in her head, her hands curled into fists at her sides. 'And so? Is that all?'

'What more do you want?' He took a half-step towards her. 'Do you want me to take you? Is that what you're trying to say? Because if so, you'd better be very, very clear.'

This could be her chance. A moment to relax the discipline of years and allow herself to have something more. Something that wasn't about hiding herself or proving herself. That was about pleasure and release. About feeling good, feeling wanted, because he did want her. Out of all the women he could have, it was her he'd chosen.

So why not take what he had to offer? Why not step beyond the boundaries she'd set for herself? Throw off the armour she'd encased herself in? Unlock the cage?

Just for a night. Just for a night she could be free.

'Yes,' she said hoarsely. 'That's exactly what I'm trying to say.'

He'd gone very still, the gold in his gaze molten. 'I hope you understand what you're asking for, Calista. Because I have nothing to offer you but one night. I will be marrying Princess Eleni and I will not be changing my mind.'

But that was perfect. One night to indulge these feelings, to explore them, satisfy them. One night to be a woman. And then she could return to being a soldier with no regrets and no looking back. Yes, she didn't want or need anything more.

'One night is all I want.'

'And afterwards, I can never acknowledge you. It will be like it didn't happen.' His voice was rough, hard. 'My loyalty first and foremost is to my brother and I need to maintain the reputation I've built here for his sake. Word that I have spent a night with you cannot get out.'

'I don't want it to get out.' She stared fiercely at him. 'This can't jeopardise my promotion to the king's guard or my standing within the palace guard. This would derail my entire career.'

'It won't. I give you my word.' And he meant that, too, it was clear.

Somewhere inside, she was trembling with a strange combination of excitement and fear, which was puzzling. The thought of pain and death was a soldier's constant companion and she'd made her peace with both of those things. But pleasure? Baring her body to someone else? That was a different story. She'd been in her armour a long time. What would it be like to take it off?

Freedom...

A shudder worked its way through her as he stared at her, and she could feel tension building in the space between them, an electric energy that snapped and crackled over her skin.

'Be sure, Calista,' he said softly. 'Sometimes getting what you want isn't at all how you'd expect.'

But it was too late for second thoughts. Now he was within reach and those barely acknowledged desires were close to becoming reality, she wanted them. She wanted them badly. She'd be free in his arms, she knew it deep in her soul. Free in a way she hadn't been for years, if ever. Free of her armour, free of her discipline. Free of having to be so controlled and so locked down all the time.

Free of the soldier.

Yes, that too. How could she walk away from that?

'I'm sure,' she said, her voice sounding breathless.

He studied her face a moment longer, then abruptly turned, striding to the door of his bedroom, shutting it and locking it before turning back.

'No titles tonight, Calista,' he said in that dark, rich, silken voice, beginning to prowl towards her. 'No *Yes, Your Highness* and *No, Your Highness*. No *Sorry, Your Highness*.' He moved like the lion marked on his back, fluid and predatory, lean and hungry, ready to hunt. 'My name is Xerxes.'

Too quickly he was right in front of her, surrounding

her with his heat, his scent, overwhelming her with the force of his presence. 'Say it.'

Instinctively she obeyed, stumbling slightly over the word. 'X-Xerxes.'

The expression on his face blazed. 'Again.'

'Xerxes.' This time there was no stumble and the prince fell away. Leaving the man standing in front of her. Passionate and fierce and wild.

Her heart crowded in her throat, the intense rush of adrenaline making it hard to breathe. She wanted to touch him, half lifting her hands to reach for him, but by then he'd buried his fingers in her hair and covered her mouth with his.

She'd never been kissed before. Never had a man touch her like this. And she'd never thought she'd want either of those things. But she was wrong. Very, *very* wrong.

She ached. She burned. It was as if all the emotion she kept locked away had been transformed into a fierce hunger she couldn't contain.

Calista closed her eyes, the forest fire blazing over her, burning her up. But she didn't care, because this time she was part of the blaze.

He tasted rich and dark and decadent, like all the things she never allowed herself, the simple, physical pleasures she'd denied herself in pursuit of her army career. But she wasn't going to deny them now. His mouth was on hers and she wasn't going to stop him, not when his tongue was tracing the curve of her bottom lip so carefully, coaxing her to open for him.

A low moan escaped her as she did, the kiss deepening, becoming hot and demanding as he began to explore. How strange. She hadn't known it was possible to tremble with pleasure—fear yes, but not pleasure. Yet here she was, trembling, and she couldn't stop.

She put her hands on his chest, his skin shockingly hot, the contrast between smooth velvet and the slight prickle of hair intoxicating. His muscles tensed, hard and powerful, and a sudden rush of desire swept through her.

She'd trained with men, knew how to gain the advantage over someone stronger and bigger than she was, using her speed and dexterity to win. But she hadn't thought there was another way to defeat a man, and some deep part of her recognised it in the flex and release of Xerxes' muscles beneath her touch, in the hunger of his mouth as he kissed her. In the clench of his fists in her hair.

He wanted her. She affected him. And there was power in that. A very female kind of power and it was hers.

Calista curled her fingers against the hot velvet of his skin, digging her nails in, leaning into his heat as the kiss turned from hot to even hotter, his mouth devouring and tasting, exploring and inciting. He wanted her to respond and she tried to, tentative at first. And then when he made a deep sound of male appreciation, her confidence grew and she kissed him back harder, her armour beginning to burn away, letting the demanding woman out to play.

His fingers tangled in the long strands of her hair, pulling her head back, the kiss getting even deeper. She wasn't used to having her hair loose or to having someone touch it, and the slight tugs he gave it sent sharp, electric jolts of pleasure racing through her.

She arched against his powerful body, pressing herself to him, wanting something she couldn't quite name. A big, warm hand settled into the small of her back, urging her closer, her hips against his, and she could feel him pushing against the satin of the gown she wore. Long, thick and hard.

The blatant evidence of his desire made her shudder, desperation coiling tight inside her. It felt as if every second of all the years she'd been without his kiss, without his touch, were weighing down on her, crushing her.

She spread her hands out on his chest, testing him, wanting more, desperate for it. He muttered something harsh against her mouth and she felt his hand at her back shift, the zip being tugged down, and then the silky fabric of the gown was sliding over her skin and away.

She took a sharp breath as her bare breasts brushed against the hot wall of his chest, sending sparks of pleasure through her. Sparks that ignited into flames as he pulled her harder against him, the heat of his body against hers almost dizzying.

Then something cold hit her back and she realised he'd pushed her up against the mirrors, the glass warming almost instantly with the combined heat of their bodies.

She shuddered, the sensation of being trapped and held, confined between the glass and a powerful male body unbearably arousing. All that mattered was that he touched her, that he kissed her, that he gave her more, because she was so hungry for it. Desperate for it.

She sank her teeth into his bottom lip in demand, her fingers tracing the carved muscles of his abdomen, loving how they flexed beneath her touch. He made a growling sound, his mouth leaving hers and trailing down the side of her neck, his teeth against the delicate tendons there, nipping her, sending lightning strikes of pleasure pulsing through her.

Calista groaned, sliding her hands up his glorious chest to his shoulders, her nails digging into hard muscle. He was so strong and hot, and he made her feel so good.

She hadn't realised before, hadn't understood that because he didn't know her as anything but a guard he had no expectations of her as a woman. She didn't have to prove herself or contain herself. She didn't have to be… anyone.

Emotion rushed over her, a wave full of currents she couldn't identify, that she would have ignored and locked down hard not a few hours earlier. But she didn't now, letting it wash over her, letting those strong hands of his hold her, keep her safe.

It was a puzzling thought for an elite soldier to have. She could kill a man with her bare hands if need be and she shouldn't need anyone to protect her, yet this was different. This involved her emotions and she'd spent so many years forcing them down that she had no idea what to do with the emotional storm sweeping through her now.

She was shaking and her eyes were prickling with tears, her throat closing. Her father would have been appalled at such a loss of control, but her father wasn't here.

Only the prince was. And there was no judgement from him. No contempt. He didn't tell her to harden up or to control herself. He only stroked her gently, easing her trembling body with his hands, whispering wordless reassurances in her ear. As if she was a skittish animal he had to calm.

She leaned into him as he eased her briefs down, baring her. Her breathing was fast, almost as fast as the sound of her heartbeat thumping in her head, an intense, intolerable pressure building between her thighs. 'Xerxes,' she heard herself gasp, 'please…'

'Patience,' he murmured, kissing her throat, his mouth tasting the place where her pulse raced.

But she had none. Her nails scraped his back and she arched against him again, pressing her hips insistently to the hard ridge behind the denim of his jeans. She could feel the rough brush of the fabric against her sensitive flesh and she shuddered, realising that she was naked.

It didn't bother her. It only made her even hungrier. She reached down between them, desperate to touch him, only for him to grab her hands and lift them, pressing her wrists to the glass above her head. She was strong, but his strength was effortless and she was no match for it; somehow that excited her even more.

The gold in his eyes blazed as he looked into hers. 'Another second and I'm not going to be able to stop.' His voice had lost the smooth richness, becoming rough as gravel. 'I'll need to get protection.'

It took her a moment to understand what he meant.

'Oh, I'm on the pill,' she said breathlessly. She took it to have control over her hormonal fluctuations, never thinking she'd need it for contraceptive purposes.

He murmured something she didn't catch that sounded like relief, and when she flexed her hips against his, pressing even harder, he said roughly, 'Ah, God...you're killing me.'

She loved his roughness. Loved that her own desperation was somehow fuelling his, and that she wasn't alone with it. That they were both feverish and wanting, and unafraid to show it.

Keeping her wrists pinned in one hand, he dropped the other to the fastenings of his jeans, pulling them open, and she felt heat against her stomach, making her breath catch hard. Then his hand was sliding down the back of her thigh, catching her behind the knee and lifting her leg up around one lean hip, tilting her back against the mirrors. She trembled helplessly as she felt the press of his hard length against her bare sex, steel covered in velvet, rubbing gently against the sensitive place between her thighs.

A moan escaped her as that length slid through her slick folds, pushing against the entrance to her body, teasing her. When he thrust in, she groaned, feeling herself stretch impossibly around him, her body giving way to his.

It hurt, but pain was something she was used to and so she barely registered it beyond tensing slightly. The next instant it was gone and then there was only him pushing deep inside her, filling her. It was a strange feeling, an invasion almost, and yet so good. Who knew surrender would be quite so pleasurable?

He'd lifted his mouth from hers and was staring down at her, and she stared back, astonished at the intimacy of being so close to another person. She could feel him inside her, hot and powerful, could see the deep gold flecks in his eyes. Could see the pleasure darkening them, pleasure that she felt, too, pleasure that they shared.

There was astonishment in his fascinating eyes, too, as if he was just as shocked as she was. But surely that couldn't be? He'd done this so many times, after all.

The thought was a fleeting one, because then his hips moved, drawing back, pulling away before sliding inside her once again, a delicious rhythm that had her gasping.

She tugged against his imprisoning hands, but he didn't let her go, holding her pinned with that delicious strength and the brilliant gold of his eyes, as the pleasure deepened, widened, coiling tighter and tighter.

She couldn't look away from him.

There was something between then, something familiar and real. A connection she'd never allowed herself, not since her mother had turned her back on her. This man felt like someone she knew, someone she liked. Someone she could trust.

This man would never betray her, she knew that in her heart of hearts.

His free hand cupped her cheek, a moment of gentleness. He smiled, so natural and so warm it made her throat close. It was as if he knew exactly what was going on in her head. As if he felt exactly the same way.

Then his hand dropped to her hips, guiding her to follow the rhythm of his, the movement allowing a friction that made her shudder every time he thrust, and she couldn't stop the helpless sounds he drew from her, couldn't stem the rush of feeling that overwhelmed her when he made the same kinds of sounds, only deeper, rougher. Male pleasure.

He liked what she was doing to him.

This prince could bring you to your knees.

Oh, he could. And that made some part of her suddenly afraid. But her body was greedy and she could feel the tight knot of sensation beginning to build beyond her power to contain it. She gave a desperate sob, and then his hand was sliding between them, down between her thighs to where she needed it most, stroking her. At the same time, he gave one hard thrust and her armour shattered completely, leaving her soul naked and flying free.

'Xerxes…' Her head went back against the mirror, lights bursting behind her eyes, her mouth opening on a scream of pleasure. Only to have his mouth cover hers, quietening the sounds she made, his hold on her hard as she convulsed around him.

She had a dim awareness of him moving harder, deeper, and then his own low roar of release as he came.

And all she could do was stand there, deliciously crushed between the mirrors and his powerful body, with the inescapable knowledge that he'd changed her on some fundamental level. That he had wrecked her.

He'd given her a taste of freedom and she would never be the same again.

CHAPTER FOUR

THE LIMO STOPPED outside the huge stone palace, the home of the Lion of Axios. A red carpet had been laid on the imposing stone staircase that led up to the massive double doors, and already the assembled news media were waiting with their cameras and phones at the ready, taking pictures of the glittering array of European aristocracy, politicians, movie stars and a smattering of internet celebrities that were making their way up the steps.

Xerxes surveyed the scene without pleasure.

The engagement party had been delayed and delayed due to various issues with Eleni and her schedule, and Xerxes had begun to think that she was delaying now just for the hell of it.

He understood she wasn't happy with the match. But he'd accepted his fate and now she needed to accept hers so they could both get this over and done with.

At least she'd managed to get herself to Axios for the party, sitting beside him now, fussing with the blue silk gown Calista had modelled for him weeks ago. She probably would have preferred the gold, but Xerxes hadn't even shown it to her. He'd told himself that it was because the gown wasn't right for the occasion, but, of course, that wasn't the case.

It was because every time he looked at it, all he could

see was Calista. Not that Eleni wearing the blue was much better. He could still see Calista's golden skin and the warm amber of her eyes. Hear the gasps she'd made as he'd pushed inside her. Feel her thighs wrapping tightly around his waist as her sex clenched around his.

The sound of his name in her sweet voice, husky with pleasure, and the way she'd looked up at him in astonishment and wonder as he'd paused deep inside her, as if she'd never seen anything as amazing as him.

He'd forgotten how it felt to have a woman look at him like that. To have *anyone* look at him like that. The women he'd been with in Europe had all been experienced, and although they'd appreciated his passion and his expertise, they hadn't looked at him the way Calista had. Perhaps no one had ever looked at him the way Calista had.

And you don't want them to, remember?

That was true. He didn't care what people thought of him these days.

Yet despite his best efforts, his groin hardened at the memories and he had to catch his breath and force the thoughts of Calista from his head.

It shouldn't happen. Once he'd had a night with a woman, it was over; he never thought of her again. Yet the memories of his one night with his beautiful palace guard kept returning again and again.

He'd had to put effort into ignoring her and not letting his gaze linger on her as he passed her, or speaking any differently to her. To not giving even the slightest hint that anything had happened between them. A prince was always watched and so he had to be doubly careful to protect both his reputation and hers.

He'd made very sure that no one knew about their

night and so far no one had found out. It had to stay that way.

Sleeping with her had been a mistake.

Maybe. But when she'd looked at him and told him that she wanted him, the iron mask of the guard slipping to betray the woman underneath, a woman full of wild passion and hunger… Well, he'd forgotten all the promises he'd made to his brother.

One night, he'd thought. One night of freedom before his engagement. No one need know, least of all Adonis. What could it hurt?

He'd thought it would be easy to go back to seeing her as merely one of his guards. But it hadn't. Not when every time he looked at her, all he could see was her naked in his bed, her hair across his pillow, her amber eyes gone dark with passion.

She was like a painting he passed by every day, never seeing it, never even noticing it, until one day the light hit it differently. And he found himself standing in front of it, examining the richness of the paint, observing the colours, the gold leaf. The beauty of the subject.

And he knew he'd never pass by that painting unseeingly ever again.

He had to pretend that he didn't see the gold buttons gleam on the jacket of her uniform, or see that same gold echoed in the bun that was coiled tightly at her nape. Didn't catch that sweet scent of wildflowers whenever she was near, and didn't feel the inevitable pulse of hunger.

It put him in a foul temper, made worse by the fact that it shouldn't be happening and he shouldn't care even if it was.

One of his guard detail—mercifully not Calista—opened the limo door and he got out, reaching down a hand to help Eleni from the car. People shouted and camera flashes went off, the crowd that had gathered at the steps to watch roaring.

They were deeply approving of their prince's engagement, and he supposed he should be grateful, since it meant their acceptance. Yet he didn't feel grateful. He only felt as if the bars of that cage were closing around him.

You've been caged before. Literally.

Xerxes ignored the ice collecting in his gut and the ghost of old pain sparking along his nerve-endings, reaching for his usual detachment. Because feeling nothing was better than bewilderment and the cold, sick knowledge that you'd betrayed someone important.

She made you feel something. And that was better than nothing.

Xerxes caught his breath, finding himself scanning his guard detail the way he always seemed to be doing these days, for Calista. He knew them all, but she wasn't there. Strange. She was supposed to be on duty tonight, he was sure of it.

Eleni's fingers were cool in his though she didn't hang on to him. Her lovely face was serene as they ascended the steps, pausing every so often for photo opportunities. He pulled her in close as they smiled at the crowds, her body tensing as he did so. Yet more proof, if he needed it, that she didn't want him.

Well, their personal wants and desires didn't matter, only the political influence for Axios that she would bring. And an heir in return for Axios' armies. A fair trade all in all.

But no passion. No heat. No fire.

He turned from the crowds, tugging Eleni with him. There was no point to these thoughts. He'd chosen to return for Adonis and, though there was a price, it was a price he'd pay willingly. Especially when he owed his brother so much.

Besides, time and proximity might help with the lack of chemistry between him and Eleni. She was a beautiful woman, after all, and he wasn't exactly inexperienced. Surely he'd have enough passion for both of them.

The engagement party was being held in the palace's grand ballroom. One side of the vast room was glass doors that led out onto a large terrace that looked down onto Itheus, Axios' capital. The palace had been built centuries ago into a hillside high above the city, where it was most defensible. Defence wasn't so much an issue these days, and it was the views that astounded most people.

Tonight, all the doors had been pushed wide open so the terrace was accessible, and strings of fairy lights hung from invisible wires that had been strung between the parapet and the roof, making it look like a waterfall of light rushing over the heads of the guests.

As he and Eleni approached the doors to the ball-room, the music from the small orchestra set up in one corner quietened, palace staff who had been circulating with food and drink pausing. One of the palace officials announced them and soon he was in the middle of the ballroom in a crowd of well-wishers.

He turned on the charm automatically, listening with half an ear while the rest of his attention roved over the ballroom, scanning for…someone. And it took him at least a couple of seconds to realise that he was scanning the room for Calista.

Ridiculous. Why did he keep looking for her? She'd been his for one night and it had been good. Very good. But it was over now and soon he'd be officially engaged. He had to stop thinking of her.

The party proceeded with all the usual nonsense that so often accompanied a royal occasion and Xerxes tried to force his recalcitrant thoughts back to the present and not keep focusing on the past or on a woman he shouldn't be thinking of when the woman who should be occupying his thought was standing right beside him.

He was in the middle of introducing Eleni to a couple of the staider Axian aristocrats, when one of his aides whispered discreetly in his ear, apologising for disturbing him at so important an occasion, but someone needed to speak with him urgently and could he spare a couple of minutes?

He couldn't, not when he was expected to lead a formal dance with his new fiancée in approximately fifteen minutes, but he was getting tired of pretending to be ecstatically happy with the proceedings and wanted a distraction, so he excused himself and followed the aide out of the ballroom and onto the terrace.

Small groups of people clustered here and there, the lights above the guests sparkling off jewels and sequins, glittering just as brightly as the lights of the city below the palace. The night air was warm, carrying with it the promise of another long, hot Axian summer.

Xerxes frowned as he followed his aide to a darker corner of the terrace, out of sight of the main doors and the guests. He wasn't concerned about his own safety, not here in the palace, but his curiosity was piqued. Who could be wanting to speak with him under cover of the shadows?

The aide stopped and bowed, withdrawing as a figure moved in the darkness near the parapet. 'Thank you for meeting me, Your Highness,' a familiar clear, sweet voice said.

And he felt it rush through him like a hot current, a burst of intense desire.

Calista.

She stepped out of the shadows and his heart seized in his chest. She wasn't in uniform tonight, wearing a simple T-shirt and jeans, with a black jacket thrown over the top. Her hair was caught in a ponytail and there were dark circles under her eyes.

She was pale and looked as if she hadn't slept in days.

He stared at her, unable to stop himself from examining her from head to foot, because for at least the past couple of months he hadn't let himself look. He'd had to make sure his gaze coasted over her as if she were just another guard in his detail.

But she would never be that, not any more, and looking at her now made him feel like a thirsty man finally allowed to drink water after months in the desert. Except, though they might be in an apparently unobserved part of the terrace, there were always eyes around, especially tonight, for his engagement.

So he merely arched a brow. 'Calista, isn't it? Aren't you supposed to be on duty tonight?'

Her amber gaze wavered, an expression he couldn't identify flickering across her face and then vanishing. 'Yes.' Her voice had an edge to it. 'I'm sorry to disturb you, Your Highness, but I…needed to speak with you urgently.'

A whisper of foreboding brushed over him. There weren't many reasons for her to come directly to him. In fact, he couldn't think of a single one, especially not one that would involve interrupting him during an important official occasion, not wearing her uniform or going through official channels.

He studied the pale cast to her cheeks and the circles

under her eyes. He might have only spent one night with her, but he knew she wouldn't interrupt him if it wasn't important, not when she was such a stickler for protocol and authority.

No, whatever it was, this was serious. Serious enough that she'd come to him in secret, too. She didn't want anyone to know...

'What is this about?'

She glanced apprehensively over his shoulder to where the guests stood, the party going on just a few feet away. Music drifted out of the ballroom. Soon it would be time for him to dance with Eleni.

'Can we go...elsewhere?' Her hands were clenched at her sides and she radiated nervous tension.

Foreboding gripped him more tightly. Normally she was emotionless. Expressionless.

'Where else do you suggest? This is the middle of my engagement party, after all. Not really the time for heart-to-heart chats.'

It was unfair of him to say that, because he knew she wasn't here for anything as insignificant as a declaration of love or desire. Not when she'd ignored his existence as completely as he'd ignored hers. He'd wondered if he might run into difficulties with her, but he hadn't needed to worry, as it turned out. She'd acted as though it had never happened. Looking through him as though he wasn't there.

And you didn't like that.

Ridiculous. It had made things significantly easier and he'd been glad of it.

'I...' She stopped and took another breath, her hands opening and then closing again. 'I didn't really want to tell you like this. But I thought you should know immediately.'

'Know what?'

Calista's eyes were very dark in the shadows, her face even paler. 'I'm sorry, Your Highness, but... I'm p-pregnant.'

The prince had gone very still, like a figure carved from rock, his expression utterly unreadable.

Nausea twisted in Calista's stomach, though that could have been nerves rather than related to the pregnancy. She hadn't been feeling sick at all in the weeks leading up to this point, and there was no reason to now, not at this relatively 'late stage'.

But then, wasn't it any wonder she was feeling so ill? She'd only just come from the doctor's and was still reeling from the shock of finding out that she didn't have a virus or the flu. What she had was a classic case of pregnancy. And probably facing Xerxes now was a terrible mistake, but she couldn't in good conscience wait. He had to know and the sooner the better.

Your timing is awful.

Yes, but then, the whole thing was awful and there was never going to be a good time. And she'd wanted to tell him before his engagement was announced so he could decide what he wanted to do about it. Not that she expected anything from him.

He was a prince and she was a guard and their reputations—

Oh, God...

Another wave of nausea churned uncomfortably in her stomach. Her mouth was dry, her heartbeat through the roof. Her fingers had gone cold and they were tingling and she had no idea why.

Xerxes stood there, impossibly handsome in his black-and-gold uniform, the roaring lion pin that denoted him Defender gleaming against the inky fabric. The uniform suited him, accentuating his height and the dark charisma that surrounded him. His beautifully carved face was expressionless, his eyes as shadowed as the night around them, no gleam of gold hidden in the depths this time.

Longing coiled helplessly through her, the longing she'd been fighting for weeks. The physical pull that dragged on her whenever he was around. The need inside her that ached for one more night, one more touch. Even a glance in her direction.

But he'd done exactly what he'd told her he would: he'd ignored her.

She'd tried to do the same. Had thought it would be easy. That she could put the armour of the soldier back on, find her discipline and her commitment once again, go back to being who she was before that night with him.

Yet it had been impossible. Her armour had cracks running through it, vulnerabilities she hadn't noticed before, vulnerabilities that he'd put there when he'd stripped it from her. And it didn't protect her any more, not the way it needed to, the way it had been doing for years before he'd shown up.

That terrible longing had worked its way through those cracks. The ache filled her soul whenever she thought of that night and the freedom she'd found in his arms. And no matter how hard she tried to patch those cracks, fix those holes, those forbidden emotions somehow found their way in all the same.

She didn't understand why. She'd been so sure one night would be enough for her to indulge those inexplicable urges of hers, get them out of the way and over for good. That what they'd shared was physical only. So why she still felt these things, she had no idea.

You know how that ends.

The nausea inside her doubled and she had to fight to keep it down.

The prince lifted his other perfectly arched brow. 'I beg your pardon?'

Surely he wasn't going to make her say it again? Surely.

She searched his face for any sign of the man who'd held her in his arms, who'd kissed her passionately, taken her fiercely. Who'd told her that she was killing him…

But there was no sign of that man, only the imperious prince, looking at her as if she was merely something dirty he'd happened to get on his shoe.

She wanted to meet that look with her usual steel, to ignore the tangling emotions inside her. And once upon a time that had been easy. Once, she'd been able to just pretend they didn't exist.

But now it was as if her ability to do so had been broken and she couldn't do it.

Her throat closed up, her eyes prickling. And all she could think of was that this had been a mistake, an awful, awful mistake. He didn't want to know that she was pregnant. Of course he wouldn't. Why would he? She was merely some guard he'd slept with and here she was, at his engagement party of all things, telling him she was pregnant with his child.

She was lucky she hadn't been thrown out on the street, though there was still time for that.

It was a warm evening but she felt cold and sick to her stomach. And when she opened her mouth to repeat herself, he only raised a hand, silencing her. Then he turned his head and someone in royal livery appeared at his elbow, the same staff member she'd pleaded with to get him to speak to the prince just before.

And then things happened very quickly.

Without a word, the aide took her arm and hustled her into the palace and she thought that she was indeed going to be thrown out on her ear. But they weren't going in the direction of the main entrance or even the staff entrance. She was being led down various stone corridors and up a flight of stairs, towards the wing where the royal family lived instead.

Then, much to her shock, she was led into a small room that was warm and furnished with a couple of plush armchairs, a small fire burning in the grate.

'Wait here, please,' the aide said, not unkindly, then withdrew, leaving her alone in the room.

It was very quiet, no noise at all from the engagement party penetrating the thick stone walls.

Calista shivered. Why had she been taken here? What was Xerxes going to do? She shouldn't have come. She'd been shocked and probably wasn't thinking straight; she wasn't thinking straight now either. Perhaps she should simply leave…

But she was cold and she needed a quiet moment to pull herself together, to find her usual control, so she moved over to the fire, holding out her hands to the flames, trying not to feel as if her world was slowly crumbling into dust around her.

For weeks she'd ignored the strange fatigue that had crept through her bones and the odd bouts of nausea that had come and gone seemingly at random. She'd thought she had a virus, that she'd been working too hard, training too much. Pregnancy had never entered her head, because it hadn't seemed a possibility. She was on the pill and she didn't get periods because she made sure she didn't. And besides, she and Xerxes had used condoms as well for the rest of that night; the chances of a pill failure were very slim.

But apparently not impossible. The doctor had been very clear.

Calista began to pace before the fire, her thoughts going around and around in circles. She had no idea what to do or where to go from here. All her dreams of being appointed to the king's guard were now ashes. And what was she going to tell her father? Oh, God, her father…

She stopped and gritted her teeth hard, fighting the despair sitting like ice in her stomach.

'You did the right thing, Calista,' he'd said, the night he'd told her mother to leave, that he never wanted to see her again. 'And I'm glad you told me. You're loyal. You'd never disappoint me the way your mother did.'

She'd been so full of rage after her mother had brushed past her without even saying goodbye, so angry at her mother's betrayal, that right then and there she made the decision that she would never disappoint him. She *would* be loyal. And, most importantly of all, she'd never be her mother.

Her father had always wanted a son and so she'd become that son for him, the way she'd tried to be her mother's beautiful daughter. With total commitment and determination, she'd worked her way up the ranks to palace guard, and she knew she'd done her father proud. That she was everything he'd wanted her to be.

Except now she'd failed him. She'd fallen into the same trap as her mother, letting her own wants and desires rule her, putting at risk everything she'd worked so hard to achieve.

Tears pricked her eyelids. She never cried, not since that day she'd lost her temper and burst into tears of rage in front of her comrades. What on earth was happening to her?

'Come, now, soldier,' a dark, rich male voice said. 'It's not that bad, is it?'

Calista looked up.

Xerxes had come into the room, shutting the door behind him, a tall, imposing presence, every inch of him royal.

She forced down her despair. 'I'm sorry, I—'

'Sit,' he ordered, nodding in the direction of one of the armchairs.

Her body was moving before she was even aware of it, going over to the chair he'd indicated and sitting down. Her legs just about gave out as she sat—another shock. She shouldn't be going to pieces like this, surely?

Xerxes said nothing and she was about to speak when there was a discreet knock on the door. The prince opened it without a word and a palace staff member came in bearing a tray. The man put it down on the coffee table near her chair and then left as silently as he'd entered.

Calista blinked at the tray. A tall glass of iced water sat on it, along with another glass of orange juice, and a small plate full of artfully arranged fresh fruit.

'Eat.' Another order issued quietly as he came over to the armchair opposite hers and sat down.

'I'm not hungry,' she muttered.

'Did you have any dinner tonight?'

No, she hadn't had dinner. She'd lost any appetite she'd had after she'd seen the doctor.

'Eat,' Xerxes repeated and he must have correctly interpreted her mutinous expression because this time the edge of command was in it. 'And while you eat, you'll tell me exactly what our situation is.'

Our situation. Not hers. *Ours.*

Something kicked hard in her chest. 'You're assuming the baby is yours,' she said flatly.

He let out a laugh that held no amusement. 'I never considered otherwise.'

'I could be lying to you.'

'You're not lying.' He sounded so smug and certain her temper flared, making her want to kick him. 'Do you even know how?'

Calista curled her fingers into her palms. 'Don't you want proof? You must get this all the time, women claiming they're carrying your child.'

'In the past there were a few.' His tone was dry. 'But they were easily disproved. Contrary to what you might expect, I don't have hundreds of bastard sons and daughters running around Europe.'

Her mouth was dry, her throat a desert. She didn't want to be weak and give in, or take the food and drink he'd given her, though for what reason she didn't know. Perhaps to prove to herself that she had some restraint, though that particular horse had long since bolted. But the glass of water at least looked very inviting and she couldn't resist.

She leaned forward and picked up the glass, taking a sip. The water slid down her throat, cool and delicious.

'And no,' he went on, his voice just as cool as the water she was drinking. 'I don't require proof. I believe you.'

She hadn't expected that. In fact, she had no idea what she'd expected. Thrown out on the street, ignored, punished…

You knew he wouldn't do that.

But she didn't know. She knew nothing about him other than that he was a selfish prince with a terrible reputation, who didn't care about anything except his brother, and who growled when she kissed certain parts of him. That was the sum total of her knowledge.

He wasn't selfish, not with you. He made you feel special. He set you free...

She forced those thoughts away, sipping on her water while her stomach growled helpfully. 'The pill failed.'

'Clearly.' His tone was even drier.

'I didn't lie about that either. I was taking it and I—'

'Again, I believe you. You're nothing if not honest.'

Why did he make it sound as if that was a thing to be ashamed of?

She glanced at him, which was a mistake. Because he was staring intently at her, his gaze focused, the light from the fire glinting off the gold flecks buried in the darkness.

A thrill of heat went through her and she had to catch her breath.

'So,' he went on, not looking away, 'how long have you known about this?

She could feel herself blushing, which was ridiculous because she never blushed. Ever. 'Since tonight. I went to the doctor this afternoon because I'd been feeling tired and I'd put on some weight, which I normally don't do.'

'But not the palace doctor.'

She took another sip of water. 'No. I didn't want…'

'You had a suspicion,' he finished for her. 'And you didn't want him to know.'

It was true. Deep down there had been a kind of certainty that she hadn't wanted to admit to herself. She'd been hoping her suspicions weren't correct.

'I wasn't feeling sick. Just tired,' she said, not wanting to talk about that. 'And I thought I had a virus, but…' She stopped again, glancing at the plate of fruit, since that was easier than looking at him.

She felt calmer, as if in response to his presence, which

was very strange when she had no idea what he was going to do.

'Eat the fruit,' he said, a current of authority running through his voice. 'You're going to need it.'

She didn't want to keep doing what he said, but found herself putting her water down, reaching for a piece of apple and putting it in her mouth anyway. It was crunchy and delicious and slightly sour, and she suddenly wanted to devour everything on the plate.

But she stopped herself from taking another piece, because she had to at least start getting herself under control. She'd find something to eat later. She'd done her duty and informed him of the situation, and now she needed to leave. He was in the middle of a party, after all. His engagement party. And she couldn't outstay her welcome.

'Your Highness,' she began, keeping her hands firmly on the arms of the chair and not giving in to the urge to rub her palms on her thighs, 'firstly, I don't expect anything from you. I just thought you should know the situation. Secondly, I won't be asking for any money or any—'

'Spare me the speech,' he murmured, the gold in his eyes glinting. 'And eat the fruit. I'll order you some more food.'

A surge of irritation went through her. 'No, thank you. I'll need to be getting back to my—'

'No. You will not be going anywhere.'

She blinked. 'What?'

One black brow rose. 'You really think I'm going to let the mother of my child out of my sight? No, that's not what will be happening.'

Yet more shock rippled through her. 'But…you're in the middle of your engagement party. I'm sorry about the timing, but I thought you'd want to know immediately.'

'And indeed I did.' He had that lazy drawl again, the

one that was deceptive because it hid so much steel. 'Eleni is going to be very relieved.'

'What do you mean?'

'You're carrying a lion or lioness of Axios, Calista. What do you think I mean?'

She frowned, picking up her glass again for another sip of water. 'I think you'd better be clear, Your Highness.'

His beautiful mouth curved in another of those smiles that held no amusement. 'Very well. You'll not be going anywhere tonight, Calista Kouros, because in approximately half an hour I will be informing my brother that I've had a change of heart.' The gold in his eyes flared, bright and fierce, his smile like a wolf's, white and predatory. 'I won't be marrying Eleni after all. I'll be marrying you instead.'

The glass dropped from Calista's nerveless fingers and shattered on the floor.

CHAPTER FIVE

SHE'D GONE EVEN whiter than she'd been when he'd first seen her on the terrace, but then, that was to be expected. It wasn't every day a woman got a proposition of marriage from a prince, after all.

Not that it was a proposition as such. It was more of an order, though that wasn't a bad thing when it came to Calista. She was a soldier and she obeyed orders.

And if she doesn't obey this one?

Oh, she would. There would be no disobeying him this time. This time his word would be law.

The moment Calista had told him she was pregnant with his child, it had felt as if something had clicked inside him. A key turning in a lock. A sense of rightness, of certainty. Because it had come to him very suddenly that *this* was why he was here. Why he'd answered his brother's call to come back to Axios. This was his second chance, his purpose.

This was his destiny.

He'd failed at so many things—protecting his brother, protecting his country, protecting his men. But he would not fail at this. He would not fail to protect his child.

Which meant that letting her go was out of the question. He wouldn't let any child of his be born away from him, where he couldn't protect them or look out for them.

The way your father failed to protect you.

Yes, that was a lesson he couldn't ignore. He'd be a better father than his own had ever been. He wouldn't torture or betray his child under the guise of 'training'. He wouldn't banish them for not ending their life when they should have. He wouldn't call them 'weak'.

No, he would be different. And he would not fail.

As for the marriage, there was no question it was necessary. He wanted his child to have a mother, a family. Legitimacy. He also wanted her. Returning to Axios had involved a certain loss of choice about a great many things, including marriage. But this changed things. This gave him the perfect excuse to choose his own wife, and so he'd choose Calista. It was true that Eleni bought political benefits to Axios, but an heir was more important. And he would marry the mother of his heir.

All that fire and passion...all that feeling will be yours.

And why not? Hadn't he sacrificed enough? Didn't he deserve something for himself?

His brother wouldn't like it, but Adonis wouldn't argue. Not when he found out Calista was pregnant.

He won't like that, either.

Marriage would solve any doubts Adonis had about his reputation. His brother couldn't say that Xerxes didn't take responsibility for his actions.

'Oh, dear,' he murmured. 'You appear to have dropped that glass.'

Calista didn't notice the glass. She'd shoved herself upright, her eyes gone dark, the dusting of freckles across her nose and cheekbones standing out against her pale skin. 'You can't be serious.'

Xerxes got out of his own chair and strolled casually over to the door. He pulled it open, spoke a word to the staff member standing outside then turned back as one of the housekeeping staff scurried in and set to work cleaning up the broken glass.

'I'm completely serious.' He thrust his hands into the pockets of his trousers. 'As you can tell from my very serious demeanour.'

She shook her head as if that would somehow change things. 'No. No. You can't.'

'Why not?'

'Because I'm a—' She stopped dead and looked down at the staff member kneeling on the floor and sweeping up the broken glass. Her teeth worried at her bottom lip.

There was no soldier's mask now, no thousand-yard stare, no iron control. All those powerful emotions he'd seen the night they'd spent together were laid bare, shock flickering over her strong features and darkening the liquid amber of her eyes. The light from the unnecessary fire had caught the differing shades of gold in her glorious hair and he was suddenly, almost forcibly reminded of how he'd wound that hair around his wrists and used it to guide her mouth on him.

Desire pulsed through him, a thick, hot wave of it, and deeper this time, an edge of possessiveness creeping in. She would be his and there would be no cold bed for this particular marriage. He was tired of feeling nothing. He wanted to drown himself in her heat and her fire, which meant she would be his wife in every way.

The staff member finished up with the glass, making sure every shard had been collected and the water mopped up, then they scurried away as noiselessly as they'd entered.

Xerxes shut the door again and moved over to the coffee table, picking up the glass of orange juice and holding it out to her. 'Drink this. You're looking pale.'

'No.' Disbelief was stark on her face. 'I'm a palace guard and you're a prince. I can't marry you.'

'*Au contraire*, soldier. I can marry anyone I choose because I'm a prince.'

'No, you can't,' she insisted. 'Your engagement to the princess—'

'Has been put on hold, soon to be cancelled.' He moved over to her, took her nerveless hand in his and closed her fingers around the glass. Her skin felt cold against his. 'Don't drop it this time.' He deepened his voice, putting a note of command in it that seemed to work so well on her. 'Drink at least half, and that's an order.' She needed the glucose to combat the shock.

Reflexively she lifted the glass and took a couple of swallows.

Satisfied, Xerxes went on, 'I have already informed my brother that I need to speak with him urgently. In about…' he glanced down at the heavy platinum watch that had been made just for him '…twenty minutes. And I will inform him of my plan.'

Calista's eyes were wide and shocked, but her cheeks had lost that overly pale look.

Xerxes took the glass from her—she'd swallowed almost exactly half as ordered—and put it down on the coffee table. Then he laid a hand at the small of her back and guided her to the chair again. She didn't resist, the heat of her body seeping into his palm, making the desire already smouldering inside him flare.

But as much as he'd like to kiss those red lips, taste the sweetness of her again, he wasn't going to. Not yet. She needed some time to come to terms with her new situation and he could be patient when he wanted to be. He'd had practice since coming back to Axios, after all.

'Sit down before you fall down,' he murmured, easing her back into the chair.

She did so, looking up at him, her face still whiter than he would have liked. 'You can't...' she whispered. 'You can't.'

'I can,' he said with a certain amount of gentleness, and crouched down in front of her chair, reaching out to take her fingers in his and chafing them to warm them. She let him, as if she wasn't aware he was even doing it. 'I'm going to tell the king that you are pregnant with my heir and that I need to marry you quickly. Eleni won't care. She'll be relieved, since she didn't want to marry me anyway. We'll come to some arrangement about the armies we promised her country; it won't be an issue.'

He wouldn't let it be an issue. His own father had put everything before the welfare of either of his sons; nothing was more important than the throne, than Axios. A prince had to be made of rock and stone, since human flesh was weak, and so he'd tried his hardest to crush the humanity right out of them.

Xerxes still remembered that stone room in the bowels of the palace, with no windows and no furniture except a chair and one bright light. A test, Xenophon had called it afterwards. But it hadn't been a test his father had put him through, but torture.

No, he would not do the same to his child. *Never.*

Calista was shaking her head. 'But all those people in the ballroom...'

Of all the possible issues she should concern herself about, the people in the ballroom were the least important. He'd half considered presenting her to the assembled dignitaries right now so that it was done. But it was clear she wasn't ready and he had no desire to put her through that.

Later, when she'd come to terms with it, he'd dress her in that golden gown and a tiara worthy of her new status. Array her like a goddess, Artemis with her bow and arrow, ready to hunt. He'd present her to his country as the prize she was. *His.*

Hunger and possessiveness wound itself around his throat, clawing at him. The sudden rush of feeling would have worried him, since possessiveness wasn't exactly a hallmark of detachment, but he ignored it, refusing to examine it.

Instead, he kept his touch on her fingers businesslike. 'The people won't care. They'll have enjoyed a party with free champagne and it'll end in a scandal, which will thrill them. I'll be speaking to Eleni before I see the king and ensure she's well taken care of. She might want to score a few points off us for it, but I'm sure we can come to some arrangement.' Ideas had already begun to turn themselves over in his head, his brain flicking through options the way it had used to do when he was in the army. 'In fact, I'll probably offer some military support in recompense and she'll be pleased. Even more pleased if I tell her that she can be the one to break off the engagement. Tell everyone I'm not suitable. No one will be surprised.'

Calista's fingers were warming in his hands now, the cold leaving them, and he had a sudden urge to kiss them. Instead, he closed his own around them, giving her a reassuring squeeze.

Instantly, as if remembering herself, Calista jerked her fingers from his, leaning back in her chair away from him. There was a set look on her face, the beginnings of anger glowing in her eyes. 'You're totally serious, aren't you?'

He remained where he was, crouching in front of her

chair. 'Of course I'm serious. That's what I've been trying to tell you for the past ten minutes.'

'And if I refuse?'

Slowly, Xerxes rose to his full height. 'You won't.'

The anger in her eyes leapt, hot as the fire in the grate. 'I can and I will.'

Desire clenched harder, urging him to match himself against her, take her challenge, turn her anger into something far hotter that would consume both of them the way it had consumed him that night in his bedroom. Make her forget any objection she had.

God, he was so tired of feeling nothing, of this cold void around him. He was Hades in the Underworld and she was Persephone, bringing heat and fire and passion, bringing life to him. Literally. He wanted to wrap himself up in her, cover himself with her, lose himself just for a moment.

But there was no time for that now. He had an engagement to break.

'You will not,' he said flatly. 'You're pregnant with my heir and I will not allow any child of mine to grow up without the protection of the throne behind them.'

Calista shoved herself unexpectedly out of the chair again, standing so she was right in front of him, bare inches away. There were sparks in her dark honey eyes, anger suffusing her cheeks, bringing much needed colour to them.

And he realised suddenly that he'd spent weeks watching her, weeks looking for some kind of reaction to him, weeks being disappointed when she betrayed no reaction at all. He'd wanted that soldier's mask of hers to slip, just once, yet it never had.

It was slipping now though. Now, if he pushed a little harder, it might come right off.

'I can't marry you, Your Highness,' she said forcefully. 'I'm afraid it's impossible.'

He stared at her, right into those gorgeous eyes. The shock had gone, leaving anger flaming in its wake. A goddess full of righteous fury.

The desire was so strong now it just about strangled him, and all he could think of was how badly he wanted to pull her closer, to take her lovely mouth. Show her all the physical benefits that a marriage to him would bring.

He hadn't had a woman in weeks. In fact, the last woman he'd had was her, so no wonder he was feeling it so acutely.

She'll be the last woman you'll ever have.

Yes, she would. And he was not disappointed about that in the least.

'It's not impossible, soldier. It's inevitable.' A rough edge crept into his voice. 'And I wouldn't get that close to me if I were you. It's been a while since I've indulged myself with a woman and I have no issues with taking my fiancée to bed before we're married.'

Her strong features hardened. 'I'm not your fiancée.'

'Not yet.' He lifted a hand before he could stop himself, taking her chin between his thumb and forefinger, holding her fast. 'Give me five minutes.'

She went very still. 'I'm not even going to get a choice?'

'I'm sorry, was that not clear?' His fingers tightened as her anger blazed, his own will rising to meet it. 'No. You don't.'

Her hands half lifted then closed into fists, and he smiled, because he knew exactly what she'd been going to do. 'Attacking one's future husband is very bad form. Especially when one's husband-to-be is second in line to the throne.'

The sparks in her eyes had become flames, blazing unchecked. He thought she might lay hands on him anyway, and he wanted her to. He wanted her to attack, to fight, because he knew how that would end. He'd turn her rage into passion and they'd end up on the floor of this room, naked and panting.

Maybe she knew it, too, because her gaze flickered, dropping to his mouth then back up again. And for a second tension crackled between them, electric and hot.

She was aware of him now, he could tell. Physically aware. Aware that the chemistry that had ignited between them that night in his bedroom was there still. It was written all over her face. He thought she might go up on her toes and kiss him, take his mouth the way he wanted to take hers.

But she didn't. Instead she lowered her hands and jerked her chin out of his grip. 'I'm not marrying you, Your Highness. I won't.'

So that was how it was going to be. Well, he could work with that.

'You will,' he said calmly, stepping back from her, because it was probably wise for them both to have some distance. And besides, it was time to go and see Eleni and then his brother. 'And that's not a request. That's an order.'

Then he turned on his heel and went out.

CHAPTER SIX

CALISTA WOKE UP the next morning and for a second couldn't work out where she was.

The room was far bigger than the barracks she was used to and there was certainly a lot more furniture. A low couch against one wall and a dresser. A couple of side tables and then the bed she was lying in, big and wide and very comfortable. The walls were stone and there were a couple of paintings hanging on them, a rich, thick silk carpet on the stone floor...

And then memory came rushing back, of a small room with a fire flickering in the grate, the sparkle of smashed glass on the floor, and the taste of orange juice in her mouth. Dark eyes staring into hers revealing a will as formidable and immovable as a mountain.

Xerxes.

Marriage.

Calista sat bolt upright, feeling as if a bucket of ice water had been emptied over her head, the image of Xerxes informing her that, since she was carrying his heir, she'd be marrying him and that she didn't have a choice about it, replaying over and over.

She still couldn't believe it. He hadn't got rid of her the way she'd feared he might, but she certainly hadn't expected him to claim her hand in marriage. That had seemed unreal. It still did and she didn't understand it.

She was a soldier in the palace guard. She didn't come from wealth and her family wasn't important. She was nothing, a nobody. And yet, he wanted to marry her, to break off an engagement that had already been agreed upon, and all because she was carrying his child?

It didn't make any sense.

She wasn't sure why she'd got so angry with him. But his calm and the way he'd taken her chin in his hand, looked at her with that flicker of deep gold in his eyes, had almost broken her tenuous control.

She'd almost laid hands on him, almost shoved him away. And he'd seemed to understand exactly where her temper had come from, his smile making her anger burn hotter and something else inside her tighten.

Her control had gone from tenuous to almost non-existent and she'd been seconds from kissing him. Seconds from rising up on her toes and covering his mocking mouth with hers. In that moment it had seemed like the most logical, most obvious way to handle the burning tangle of emotions inside her and to claim some of her own power back.

Except a deeper part of her knew—even if she hadn't been fully conscious of it herself—that if she did that, it wouldn't end there, and she'd seen the confirmation deep in the glittering darkness of his eyes. In the tension around them.

And so she'd managed to pull herself back, her heart hammering.

Then he'd left and she'd waited five minutes before jerking the door open, intending to go back to the barracks, grab her belongings and leave the palace immediately. To escape him, escape Itheus, and lose herself somewhere else—though quite where she hadn't thought.

But the moment she'd pulled the door open, a couple of guards she didn't recognise had materialised with instructions to escort her to one of the palace's guest bedrooms. And it was clear that she had no choice in the matter.

By this stage, her hot rush of anger had gone as quickly as it had appeared, leaving her exhausted, and she didn't have the energy to protest. She'd gone without a word to the guest bedroom provided, and as she'd entered she'd seen them station themselves outside the door; it was clear they were there not to protect her from people coming in, but to stop her from leaving.

She was, essentially, a prisoner.

She'd thought she wouldn't sleep, that her anger at Xerxes and her fear of what was going to happen to the life she'd planned for herself would prevent her. But she'd run through a few of the disciplinary exercises she'd used back in basic training to calm herself down and get herself under control again. Then she'd lain down on the bed fully dressed…and the next minute she was awake and it was morning.

Her eyes felt gritty though and exhaustion had soaked into her bones. She still hadn't quite processed how completely her life had changed in the space of a few hours. How she had been planning for a future promotion to the king's guard, only to find herself ordered to marry the very prince she'd been guarding only a day or so ago.

It didn't feel real.

Hauling herself out of bed still fully dressed, Calista went through into the en-suite bathroom and splashed some water onto her face, trying to work out what she was going to do now.

Because one thing was certain: she couldn't marry the prince.

It wasn't only the difference in their stations that made it impossible, it was also that Axios had her heart and she was dedicated to defending it. She didn't want or need anything else in her life.

What about your child?

But she was saved from having to think about that as a knock came on the door and when she went to open it she found another couple of guards waiting outside. Again, they weren't people she recognised, which was a relief, but then she was informed that she was to be escorted out to the palace's helipad immediately, which wasn't.

Her heart thumped painfully hard behind her breastbone, her confusion deepening as one of the guards went past her into the room and picked up the leather bag sitting at the end of the bed—a leather bag she hadn't even noticed.

And there was no chance to even ask what it was, because then she was ushered out of the room and marched through the echoing stone corridors, down a flight of stairs, then outside into the sunshine. They followed a curving path lined with cypresses that led to the wide, flat area of the helipad, where a sleek, black helicopter waited, a man moving purposefully around it.

It wasn't until she got closer that she realised the man was Xerxes and that he was making last-minute checks with the kind of casual competence that spoke of experience.

The guards approached the helicopter, and Xerxes spotted them, finishing up whatever check he was doing and coming to intercept them.

Calista stiffened as the guards came to a stop and Xerxes approached.

He was really too beautiful to be real, the epitome of the handsome prince in a tight-fitting black T-shirt and jeans, sunglasses held carelessly in one hand as he came towards them. Sunlight glossed his night-black hair and he was smiling his usual charming smile, but the look in his dark eyes missed nothing.

'Good morning, Calista,' he said, his deep voice winding around her like soft black velvet. 'Are you ready for your flight today?'

One of the guards had moved to the helicopter with the bag he'd picked up from her room and was now stowing it.

'Flight?' Her heartbeat thumped even harder. 'What flight?'

'I thought a little trip was in order. A chance to work out our differences before the engagement announcement.' He gave a minute nod to both guards and the two then turned and marched away, leaving her and Xerxes alone.

'Engagement announcement? But I'm not—'

'Time to board,' he said calmly, moving over to the helicopter and pulling open the door, indicating she was to get inside. 'I'll answer your questions as we fly.'

Calista's mouth had gone dry and she felt sick again. She'd eaten only fruit the night before and she'd had no breakfast this morning, and now she was being taken by helicopter God only knew where by this prince…

'No,' she said, trying to keep her voice level. 'You need to answer them now.'

He lifted a brow in that infuriating way he had. 'Issuing orders now, I see. That's good. A princess needs to know how to lead.'

She ignored him. 'I'm not going anywhere until you tell me where we're going.' Her hands had closed into

fists yet again, her temper straining at the leash. She'd
never felt so close to the edge, and that was a bad thing.
She couldn't look weak, not in front of him, not when
she'd let her guard down with him once already. He was a
warrior, a predator. He'd take shameless advantage of all
those cracks in her armour and, since pregnancy played
havoc with emotional regulation, she would have to be
extra careful.

His gaze narrowed, roving over her, assessing her.
'We're going to my villa on the coast for a while—at least
until the news of my broken engagement has been dis-
seminated and the scandal has had a chance to die down.'

He'd broken it off. He'd really broken it off.

'You can't—' she began.

'I did,' he finished, amusement flickering in his eyes.
'You have to marry me now, soldier, or else I'm ruined.'
His hand came beneath her elbow, urging her gently towards the helicopter. 'Come on, it's not a long flight and
you'll have food waiting for you, I promise.'

And even though she wanted to stand her ground and
protest, she found herself moving, drawn along by his irresistible strength and by the shameless need inside her
for the warmth of his hand on her arm.

'But who's flying the helicopter?' she asked as he
helped her up into the machine.

He grinned, a hint of boyishness in it that she didn't
want to find charming. 'I am.'

Before she could ask any more questions, he'd shut
the door and moved around to the pilot's side. Then he
got in himself and five minutes later they were airborne,
the palace and Itheus falling away beneath them as Xerxes headed north, towards the mountains and the coast.

He handled the machine expertly, as if he'd done nothing but fly helicopters all his life, which, given that he'd

spent a good proportion of his exile touring the beds of socialites all over Europe, couldn't possibly be true.

'Where did you learn to fly?' she asked, desperate to fill the tense silence with something, anything to distract herself from the riot of feelings inside her.

He flashed her a glance, his mouth turning up as if he was pleased with the question. 'The army.' Even over the headset mike, his voice sounded like melted honey, rich and warm. 'I loved flying, so I kept my hand in even after I left the military.'

She knew she should keep quiet, that talking would only betray her own nervousness and uncertainty, but he was so confident and sure that she couldn't help wanting to do something to put a dent in him.

'Why did you leave the military again?' she asked, knowing full well what the answer was.

He gave a low laugh. 'My father banished me for cowardice, as I'm sure you're well aware.'

He wasn't looking at her, his attention on the controls, his profile seemingly untroubled. And yet she heard the slight edge in his voice.

So, she'd got to him, had she? Good.

'Why?' she asked bluntly, taking the opportunity to put the pressure on him for a change. 'What did you do?'

He flashed her another glance, his expression enigmatic. 'You really want to have this discussion now?'

'Why not? I've got nothing else to do.'

He looked away, lifting a casual shoulder, as if it was nothing to him. 'I was captured by the enemy on a mission in the Middle East. We all had cyanide capsules to take in case of torture and we were all expected to take them to safeguard military secrets. I should have taken mine, but I didn't. I ended up being rescued by my brother, who went against orders to do it. My father was furious. He told me I should have died and that by not killing myself I'd endangered the entire country. So he exiled me.'

Calista's gut lurched. His voice had been utterly normal, as if relating a story about something innocuous and not about capture and death. As if it had happened to someone else.

So that was the truth about why he'd been disinherited and banished. The truth about his so-called cowardice. He was supposed to have killed himself and hadn't.

'I…didn't know,' she said hesitantly. As a soldier, she should have treated this admission with the disgust it deserved, since a loyal soldier would always die before betraying his or her country's secrets. Yet…it wasn't disgust that she felt right now. It was something else. Something she couldn't identify.

'No, of course you didn't.' He adjusted something on his controls. 'My father refused to speak of me after I left.'

The emotion clenched tighter and more questions bubbled up inside her. Why hadn't he taken the pill? Why was his father furious? Wouldn't the king have been happy his son was alive?

But no, she shouldn't be getting curious about him. She shouldn't want to know. What she should be doing was trying to get him to drop this marriage idea, because it was insane.

She knew how to kill a man, how to march for miles with a heavy load, how to disassemble a firearm in seconds and then put it back together again. How to stand at attention for hours, alert to the slightest movement.

She'd put work and effort and time into her military career and she did not want it to be derailed because she'd somehow forgotten all those lessons in control her father had taught her, about the dangers of giving in to your own wants and needs, of putting yourself first.

Her country was the most important thing in her life aside from her father, and she couldn't allow one mistake to jeopardise it.

Calista turned away to look out at the mountains passing beneath them, gritting her teeth against the stupid tears that pricked behind her eyes.

Why was she crying? She was a soldier. She was strong. Which meant it had to be the pregnancy hormones affecting her. Perhaps she'd leave off asking questions and instead try to come up with a plan so he'd drop the idea of marrying her.

So all she said was, 'I'm sorry.'

He only shrugged and said nothing more.

The rest of the trip was spent in silence, but, as he'd promised, it wasn't a long one. Barely an hour later, they were coming down to land on the flat stone roof of a palatial villa built into the cliffside. A small beach covered in perfect white sand lay below it, with a deep, crystalline blue ocean lapping at the shore.

Immediately the helicopter landed, they were met by a swarm of staff, one taking her bag and a second bag that must have belonged to the prince, while another few surrounded Xerxes, obviously receiving orders.

A few more surrounded her, preparing to usher her inside, but the prince waved them away and abruptly they were alone again, standing on the roof while a fresh sea breeze smelling of salt and sunlight played with the ends of her hair.

'Come,' Xerxes said, making no move to touch her this time. 'Do you want to eat first or shall I show you around?'

Calista squared her shoulders, standing at attention. 'Neither, Your Highness. I'd prefer to go home.'

He gave her another of those measuring looks. 'Food, I think. We'll discuss it over brunch.'

Calista opened her mouth to protest, but he was already walking away towards the stairs that led down to the rest of the house. Which left her with two choices. Either she could stand here stubbornly waiting until he saw sense, or she could follow him.

Glancing regretfully at the helicopter—she'd never learned how to fly, though it was something she'd always wanted to do—Calista sighed. Waiting here would be pointless, since if she wanted to change his mind she'd actually have to talk to him. And besides, a soldier needed strength to fight and she was certainly intending to fight.

Forcing her sullen temper away, she followed him reluctantly.

The villa was amazing. Constructed of white stone and over several levels, it tumbled down the side of the cliff in a series of boxes and terraces, with huge windows that made the most of the astonishing views over the sea.

On one of the terraces was a long, deep blue infinity pool, while on another there was a garden with pots of trees and shrubs and flowers.

A long, heavy, rustic wooden table shaded by grapevines growing over a wooden frame stood on yet another and it was here that brunch had been laid out, the table covered by a white tablecloth and set with fresh, crusty bread, butter, all kinds of preserves and a carafe of coffee and glasses of orange juice. A basket of pastries stood near the coffee, while a platter of crispy bacon made her stomach growl.

Xerxes flung himself down in one of the heavy

wooden chairs, the seat covered with bright cushions, and gestured at her to do the same.

She felt an irresistible urge to stand just to spite him, but she wasn't quite that petty, so she sat, unwillingly pleased at how comfortable the seat was.

The prince reached for the coffee, pouring out two mugs and pushing one to her, before grabbing a plate and filling it with bacon, the fresh bread and some pastries, which he also pushed in her direction. 'Eat that before we start,' he ordered. 'You look like you're going to pass out at any second.'

He wasn't wrong. The food smelled so good and it was making her feel light-headed. Irritated both at herself and at him, Calista began to eat, trying to ignore him as he ripped a piece off the bread with those long, competent fingers and buttered it for himself, slathering it in honey.

It made her wonder if he had a sweet tooth, and then immediately she was irritated yet again at herself for even wondering about it in the first place.

She didn't care if he had a sweet tooth. She didn't care about him.

What she was going to do was eat, then tell him in no uncertain terms that marrying him was impossible and that she needed to go back to the palace before anyone realised she was missing.

And the baby? What are you going to do about that?

That she would work out later.

'So,' he said at last, after she'd eaten at least two pieces of bread, numerous rashers of bacon, and three pastries. 'Let's hear your objections to marriage.'

Calista took a sip of her orange juice, surprised he was giving her a voice. 'I thought my objections didn't matter?'

'They don't. Nevertheless, I'd still like to hear them.'

He was honest, she'd give him that.

She sat back in her seat and gave him a level look. 'I'd have thought it was obvious what my objections were.'

'It's not obvious, which is why I asked you to tell me.'

She held up a hand, ticking them off on her fingers. 'First, you're a prince and I'm a palace guard. Second, I have dedicated myself in service to my country and there is no room in my life for anything else, let alone a husband. Third, we don't know each other, let alone love each other. And fourth…you didn't even ask me what I wanted to do.'

Xerxes' dark eyes gave nothing away. 'And what is it that you wanted to do?'

That was the issue. She didn't know, not when it came to dealing with the child. Children had not featured anywhere in her future plans for herself and never had. Neither had a husband. All she'd wanted was to serve her country, be the kind of loyal, true soldier that her father…

Oh, God. Her father.

Cold crept through her, winding deep into her heart.

'I want to serve Axios,' she said, trying to ignore it. 'That's all I've ever wanted to do. And perhaps be promoted to the king's guard. I…hadn't thought of children.'

Xerxes didn't move and yet a sense of threat radiated suddenly from him, the powerful force of his will pushing against her. 'You'll be keeping it.' There was a whole world of certainty in those words that left no room for argument.

Of course. She hadn't considered her options, had she? And adoption was one of those options. But as soon as the thought occurred to her, something twisted in her gut.

Could she really give this child to someone else? Abandon it to suit herself and her own needs?

You've put yourself first before and look how that turned out.

No, she'd followed her mother that day after school because she'd been suspicious. It didn't have anything to do with her own anger because Nerida had cancelled a much anticipated shopping trip.

And she'd been right to be suspicious, as it had turned out. She'd seen Nerida kissing a man who wasn't Calista's father, and so she'd gone home straight away and told her father.

She was a good and loyal soldier, exactly as he'd said.

It certainly wasn't a betrayal simply because you were furious and hurt.

Calista forced that thought away, looking down at her stomach, still flat though perhaps a little softer than it should have been. There was a life inside there, a son or a daughter to protect and defend.

Realisation moved through her, shifting to certainty. Yes, she was a soldier and a soldier's duty was to protect. She'd dedicated her life to her country, but there was room for a child, too. She would make room.

She wouldn't be her mother, walking past the daughter she'd once said she loved more than life itself and ignoring her as if she wasn't there. Never speaking to her again, not even after the divorce.

She wouldn't abandon this child the way her mother had abandoned her.

Calista put a hand on her stomach, feeling suddenly fierce. 'Of course I'm keeping it. This child is mine.'

'And mine.' Warning tinged his voice, the predator guarding what was his. 'Don't forget that.'

He's strong. He'll keep the child safe, too.

The thought was instinctive, the primitive response of a mother wanting safety for her child, and it made her uncomfortable. She didn't want to have to acknowledge him in any way.

'I could hardly forget,' she snapped.

'See that you don't.' He leaned back in his chair, all that taut muscular power deceptively casual. 'So, where were we? Ah, yes, your objections. Let me answer them. First—' he held up one long-fingered hand and began to count them off as she'd done earlier '—yes, I'm a prince and you're a guard, but if I say it doesn't matter, then it doesn't. Second, to be a royal of Axios whether by birth or by marriage *is* to dedicate your life to your country so that wouldn't change. Third, neither love or like is required in a royal marriage. Fourth, if you want me to ask you, I will.' The smile he gave her was ridiculously charming. 'As long as the answer is yes.'

Calista sat on the edge of the wooden chair, her back ramrod straight, one hand on the arm of the chair, one resting protectively over her stomach. She still looked pale and she couldn't have slept well because those dark circles under her eyes seemed as heavy as they had been the day before. She needed rest and good food, and a little cosseting wouldn't go amiss.

He wouldn't mind cosseting her. Especially if that cosseting involved a bed and being naked. Except it was clear she wasn't ready for that, which meant he'd have to take things slowly. That was fine. All of this had come as a shock; she'd need some time to come to terms with it.

But come to terms with it she must. No other choice was permissible and especially not now. Last night he'd seen Eleni and broken the news to her, which meant his course was now set. Eleni had taken it well and had been more than happy that his offer of military support would still stand. She'd also agreed to still provide Axios with political support, as long as she was seen to be the one ending the engagement. It was what he'd been planning to offer anyway, and so she'd rushed off to talk with her PR people.

The interview with his brother, however, had been less satisfying.

Adonis had been furious with him, especially about the pregnancy, and had had a few choice words to say about Xerxes' reputation, his position, and how he'd promised to uphold Axian values, et cetera, ad nauseam. It wasn't anything Xerxes hadn't either heard before or expected to have thrown at him, and because strategy had always been his strong point, that was when he'd told Adonis that he would marry Calista.

Adonis still hadn't been happy, but he'd had no choice but to approve the marriage after that.

Once that had been dealt with, Xerxes had decided a period of absence would be best while the news of his broken engagement to Eleni circulated, mainly to give time for the scandal to die down. Then another announcement would be made concerning Calista. He'd told Adonis in no uncertain terms that the pregnancy would need to stay a secret until after he and Calista were married, as he wanted no hint of scandal to touch her. His brother had been scathing, muttering something about horses and barn doors, but Xerxes had been adamant. This had to be managed and managed carefully.

Scandal would happen—there was no avoiding it—but he wanted the wedding to take place with the minimum of gossip if he could possibly help it.

Both of them being absent from the palace and official duties would help, as well as giving Calista some time to come to terms with the idea of marrying into the family.

The expression on Calista's face now, however, was

anything but accommodating. 'What if I don't want to say yes?'

'This is not a debate, Calista.' He reached for the coffee pot and poured himself a mug. 'This is non-negotiable.'

And he was prepared to fight for it. His father had told him just before he'd banished him that he was weak, that he was a vulnerability neither Adonis nor Axios could afford, and that had left him with a choice to make.

He could prove that his father had been wrong about him, and make himself strong. Or he could admit his father was right and drown himself in self-pity, giving in to the weakness inside himself.

Or he could simply choose not to care.

Up until now he'd chosen the third option and that had worked well enough. But it would not work any more. To be a good father, he had to care about the child and so he would. He was nothing like his own father, after all.

She watched him put the coffee pot down, anger glowing in her eyes. 'So what I want doesn't matter at all?'

'Not when it comes to the safety of our child, no.' He cradled the mug in his hands and studied her. 'What is it in particular that you don't like? Or is it only that you weren't given a choice?'

Her jaw hardened. 'It's not "only" that I wasn't given a choice. You're essentially ordering me to change the entire course of my life for you.'

'Not for me,' he amended. 'For our child. And the entire course of your life will have to change anyway. Or did you think you could continue to serve Axios while nine months pregnant?'

A flush stained her cheekbones. 'I…hadn't thought about it. It's not as if I've had time.'

He gestured with his hand. 'Well, here is your time.

Think, Calista. Your life will change regardless, so marrying me isn't going to make it any worse. You'll have a roof over your head, support for you and the baby. You won't have to worry about money; everything will be taken care of. There will be no down side.'

'Except I'll be married,' she said flatly. 'To you.'

'Is that really a down side, though?' He smiled, allowing her to see a bit of the heat that was burning inside him. 'I can make being married to me extremely pleasurable.'

Her flush deepened. 'I don't want to be married to you. The army is the only life I ever wanted. Serving Axios is all I ever wanted.'

Again with the army and Axios. He loved his country and he would lead its armies, but that wasn't all he wanted, not now. Where had her dedication come from? This one-eyed view of what life could be? It didn't have to be so all-or-nothing. Even in the dark days in Europe, he'd allowed himself some consolations, such as sex for example. But she didn't even want that?

'Why?' he asked, curious. 'There are other ways to serve your country that are much more exciting than following Adonis or me around all day.'

'My father was a soldier. He was a captain and I wanted to follow in his footsteps.' She paused, then added, 'And our country is important to me. I want to help protect it, defend it. I've worked hard for years to get where I am and I don't want to throw that all away on marriage.'

He understood that. She must have faced many challenges to get where she was today; he knew what an army career was like all too well.

'Is it the glory you want?' he asked. 'Is that the big drawcard?'

She sat ramrod straight, at attention like the soldier she was, and he had an urge to put down his mug, and go over to her, put his hands on her stiff shoulders and massage away those little knots of tension.

'No.' Her voice held conviction, but there was something else flickering in her eyes that he couldn't identify. 'I don't care about glory. I love this country and I can't think of a greater privilege than serving it.'

That sounded like his father. Too like his father.

'And your child?' he asked, because she would have to understand this sooner or later. 'Where does that leave the child? If you don't marry me, what will you do instead? Mothers can certainly be soldiers, but if they are they usually have a partner to look after their children, or day care to send them to. Tell me, who will be looking after our child, Calista? Or will they have to come second to Axios?'

That unidentified emotion flickered across her face again, and it looked like shock. Then she glanced away abruptly, her jaw tight. 'I don't know, but I'll think of something.'

A strange feeling shifted in Xerxes' chest, one he wasn't expecting. Sympathy. He knew what it was like to be stripped of your choices, to feel—as well as to be literally—trapped. He didn't enjoy doing the same to her. But it had to be done.

Failure was not an option.

Calista looked back at him again. 'Why are you being so insistent about this?'

She was one for blunt questions, wasn't she? She had been up in the helicopter, and he'd surprised both of them by telling her the truth about why he'd left the military. It wasn't something many people knew, and part of him had wanted to tell everyone when he'd returned to Axios, precisely because his father had never spoken of it. But Adonis had counselled otherwise. It was better to let it go, his brother had advised. Let it stay forgotten. And because he hadn't cared one way or the other, that was what he'd done.

He still didn't care, not about that. So why not tell her? The truth wouldn't hurt.

'Because I've failed a great many people in my life.' He met her level gaze. 'But I will not fail my child.'

'How will marrying me help?'

'Because I want him or her to live with me in the palace, where I can protect them. And they'll need a mother. They'll need a family. Marriage will give them that.'

Calista's knuckles whitened on the arm of her chair as her grip tightened. 'And where do I fit in to all of that?'

He watched the sun slide over her hair, igniting shades of gold and caramel and gilt, and his hands itched, wanting to touch it. 'Where do you fit? In my bed, of course.'

Her gaze snapped back to his and it was clear that she did not like that, not one bit. The flare of her temper was like heat from a furnace, bursting up through the cracks in her discipline like flames through an iron grating, and he could feel his own rising to meet it, adrenaline flooding through him.

God, what he wouldn't give to channel her anger into passion and pleasure, to ease the tension he could sense inside her. He'd done that for her once before and she'd loved it. She'd been so hungry for it.

'That's all you want from me?' she demanded. 'Sex and my child?'

'Our child,' he corrected. 'And as far as anything else, what more can you offer me?'

Her chin came up, amber eyes glittering with gold fire. 'Don't play these games with me, Your Highness.

I'm not one of your pretty little toys. I could kill you where you stand.'

Such a warrior. He loved it.

He smiled, every muscle in his body tightening at the thought of her attempting to do exactly that. 'Try it, soldier. See how far you get.'

For a second he thought she actually might, the look in her eyes blazing. The pulse at the base of her throat was beating fast, the dappled sunlight coming through the grapevine above their heads shining on her skin like drops of pure gold.

He wanted her to get up from her chair and reach for him. And he would put his hands on her, gather her anger and change it, turn it into pleasure.

But she didn't move, her expression hardening, going utterly rigid. It was as if she'd poured cold water on the fire of her anger and doused it utterly. 'I need to rest now,' she said, her voice stiff. 'Please show me to my room.'

You have hurt her.

He couldn't have said what gave it away, but he knew he had. And he didn't like that. It made him aware of the power gap between them, of the fact that she really didn't have a choice, while he did. She couldn't refuse him, and even if he allowed it, it was she who'd be left with the child.

She's vulnerable.

A soldier who wanted only to serve her country. Who'd worked hard to get where she was. A soldier who'd made one mistake and who now was paying for it. She was right. Playing games with her wasn't fair.

But…she was more than just a soldier. He'd seen glimpses of the woman she was, a passionate, fiery sort of woman, and it was the woman who interested him the most. Didn't she know that it was okay to be that woman sometimes? And if she didn't, why not?

However, now wasn't the time for such discussions, not when she looked so shattered. So he said carefully, 'I am Defender of the Throne. That's my official title. And my purpose is to head the army, to defend Axios. It will be my wife's purpose, too. In fact, the job of any prince or princess of Axios is to defend this country. It's not the army, I realise, but the end goal is still the same.'

Her gaze flickered, a little of the stiffness bleeding out of her. 'I...hadn't thought of it quite like that.'

'Don't be blinded by titles or the differences in our social standing, Calista. There's a reason Adonis and I wear the tattoo and that's because we're soldiers of the cause, the same as you. We're the ultimate protectors of this country, and by marrying me you will join our ranks.' He hadn't expected to start sounding like his father, or, rather, like the ghost of the idealistic boy he'd once been. And it should have disturbed him. Yet he was rather surprised to discover that he meant every word.

She stared at him, a slight crease between her brows. As if she was surprised. As if he was telling her something new.

'Yes,' she murmured, after a moment. 'You're right. We're both serving our country, aren't we?'

'Of course I'm right.' He studied her face. 'Why do you want to serve Axios so very badly?'

'My reasons are my own.'

'You'll be my wife, Calista. Your reasons are now mine.'

'But I'm not your wife yet.'

He smiled. 'Did you ever think that goes both ways?'

'What do you mean?'

'If you're my wife, I'll also be your husband. You tell me something, I'll tell you something.' It had suddenly occurred to him that convincing her wasn't simply a matter of laying out logically why this was a good thing. That might convince the soldier, but she wasn't only a soldier, as he already knew. She was a woman, too, and though he might admire the soldier, it was the woman he wanted in his bed.

And that involved a seduction. Laying breadcrumbs was the trick, that and knowing which approach to take. The direct approach wouldn't work with Calista when it came to this marriage, and if he hadn't known already, he did after today. No, she required a subtler approach. Luckily, he was very good at that, too.

Her expression became measuring. 'How do I know you'll tell me? That you won't lie?'

Clever soldier. He could get angry about that, be offended that she doubted him. But he'd given her no reason to trust him.

Maybe your marriage starts here.

If he didn't want things to start off antagonistically then they would have to start somewhere. And although he liked the prospect of a fight, he wanted her surrender more. But she'd have to be given some enticement.

'I swear on my brother's life that I will be truthful,' he said, holding her gaze. 'And I will uphold my end of the bargain.'

She gave him a long, narrow stare then nodded. 'Okay. Well, to answer your question, yes, I do have personal reasons for wanting a military career.'

Of course she did. No one was that dedicated without something personal pushing them.

Her fingers traced the carving on the arm of her chair. 'My father always wanted a son, but my mother left him when I was a girl and he never remarried. So I decided I'd be that son for him.'

Not unsurprising. Timon was a stern, upright man,

very like Xerxes' own late father; he definitely had a soldier's sensibility, so no wonder it had rubbed off on his daughter.

'I hate to say it,' he murmured, sipping on his coffee, 'but you look far too female to be his son.'

Calista didn't respond to the gentle tease, her expression hardening. 'Looking female has nothing to do with it.'

Xerxes studied her, sitting upright and rigid, always the soldier. And a memory came back to him, of her standing before the mirrors in his bedroom, wearing a magnificent gown yet refusing to look at herself.

'I think it might have something to do with it,' he said, testing gently. 'And I think you don't like that.'

Her eyes glittered, the embers of her temper glowing. 'Being a woman in the army is a liability. You have to work harder than everyone else, be stronger, not show even the slightest weakness. And you can't ever look female, because when you look like a woman, that's all people will see.'

She looked so proud sitting there, proud and defiant and strong. But he had the feeling that she wasn't directing that conviction at him. No, it was at someone else.

'That sounds personal,' he said, innate protectiveness squeezing tight inside him. 'Did something happen? Did someone hurt you? Take advantage of you?'

'Why should that matter?'

'Because I am the head of the army, which means I'm ultimately responsible.'

'Oh, of course.' She took a little breath. 'No one ever physically touched me. But some of the men liked to get me…angry.'

Carefully, Xerxes put his mug down so he wouldn't crack it. 'Angry? Why?'

She lifted a shoulder. 'To test me, probably.'

'And what happened?'

The flush was back in her cheeks, creeping down her neck, but her jaw was tight. 'I cried.'

It was clear from the look in her eyes that crying had been a crime worse than death, and he could well imagine it. In the army, strength was everything and emotion was a weakness, a terrible vulnerability.

You understand that.

Of course he did. He knew that better than anyone.

'I told you something,' she continued stonily, not waiting for him to speak. 'Now it's your turn to tell me something.'

So it was, and he'd promised her. And who knew? Perhaps she would find his own weakness, his own loss of face, useful.

'When I was captured, it took Adonis a week to find me,' he said. 'And every day for a week I held that capsule in my hand and thought about taking it. But I didn't. Because I told myself that my brother needed me. I was his Defender and if I was gone, who would be left to defend him?' He paused, back in the concrete cell they'd kept him in, which was oddly reminiscent of that room under the palace. With no food and no water, beaten every day. 'But the truth was, I didn't choose not to take that pill for Adonis. I didn't take that pill because I wanted to prove my father wrong.'

The stiffness had bled out of her entirely, her gaze was glued to his. She was curious, that was clear. 'Wrong about what?'

'He thought I was weak,' Xerxes said. 'He gave me that pill because he thought I would break under torture.' The beatings had been painful, the water deprivation worse, yet he'd endured. 'So I didn't take it. And I didn't break. Not this time.'

Calista's eyes widened. 'What do you mean, "not this time"?'

The room under the palace. The bright light. The knife. The cigarette. He'd been terrified. He hadn't known it was a test.

And he'd failed.

You were weak. You still are. Nothing can change that.

Yes, he'd been weak once. But not again. He knew the dangers now, wouldn't fall into the same old traps. He would stay strong for his child's sake.

'Xerxes?' She was frowning. 'You said *not this time.*'

But he was done with the subject all of a sudden. He didn't want to talk about this, and anyway, he'd meant to end the conversation before because she looked so shattered. He couldn't think why he'd prolonged it.

He put his hands on the arms of his chair and pushed himself to his feet. 'I think that's enough for one day. Do you still want me to show you to your room? Or better yet, perhaps you'd like me to show you your bed?'

Her gaze turned measuring, as if she knew very well what he was doing. 'You can show me to my room. But I'm not sleeping with you.'

He wanted to tell her that he hadn't mentioned anything about sleeping, but he'd lost his taste for suggestive flirting. So all he said was, 'Certainly. Follow me.'

She said nothing as she followed him into the house, up a couple of flights of stairs and down some of the light, airy corridors to the room he'd assigned to her, that was conveniently a couple of doors down from his.

He pushed open the door and stood aside so she could go in. But she didn't. She stood there, looking at him and frowning. There was something in her eyes that made him feel strange, as if someone had taken his heart in their hands and was slowly twisting it.

Why had he told her that? She was a soldier through and through, and she'd judge him the way his father had. View him with disdain and contempt the way the rest of the army did. Not that her opinion mattered to him one way or the other.

'Don't look at me like that,' he said. 'Or I'll start thinking you want to sleep with me after all.'

He'd meant to push her away, but apart from a slight twitch of her brows, she paid no attention to his petulant remark. Instead she said, 'It bothers you, doesn't it? That you didn't choose death.'

His jaw hardened. 'Cowardice is a crime. Though I guess it's not in the same league as weeping in front of a roomful of soldiers.'

The words dripped with sarcasm and they had the desired effect.

He wasn't surprised when she abruptly turned away. What he was surprised about was the disappointment he felt when she shut the door in his face.

CHAPTER SEVEN

CALISTA WOKE TO light coming through the windows that was the soft, dusky pink of twilight. She must have slept half the day away, though maybe that wasn't any surprise, given the shocks of the past twelve hours.

She'd been exhausted after the conversation with Xerxes downstairs and had simply lain down on the big white bed in the big white room he'd shown her to and gone to sleep.

Possibly she'd been so tired because of what they'd talked about, since she hadn't expected to confess those things to him. Hadn't expected him to confess things to her, either.

Such bleak things, too. Things she'd never guess a prince would be subjected to. He'd been tortured. And, despite not taking that pill, he hadn't broken and his father had still exiled him.

Why? Why had his father assumed he would break? Why had his father assumed he was weak?

You think you're weak for weeping...

She let out a breath and rolled onto her back, staring at the ceiling, contemplating his last sarcastic comment and how it had hit her somewhere vulnerable. He hadn't liked her asking him questions and so he'd turned into the tiger again, snapping at her with those sharp teeth.

She'd been tired, and she'd felt vaguely ashamed of how large her own weakness had loomed in her life, especially when his had been infinitely more serious.

She should have found it contemptible that he'd failed to swallow that capsule, that he'd put his own obvious anger at his father ahead of the good of his country. Yet... she didn't. And maybe that was because it so obviously bothered him that he hadn't. He'd clearly expected her to judge him for it, too, though why her opinion would matter to him, she had no idea.

What she did know was that he wasn't weak. Nothing about him was. He was so strong physically and it must have taken a tremendous amount of mental strength to return to a country that he knew had condemned him.

And it was clear, also, that he felt very strongly about keeping their child safe, and she couldn't help but respect that. She was a protector herself and his total commitment to the child they'd created was admirable.

She did want to know why he felt he'd failed people, though, because he had told her that. And that he wasn't going to fail again.

So who had he failed? His father? His brother? Who else?

Perhaps that didn't matter though. What mattered was that this was clearly a mission for him and one he was determined to complete whether she wanted it or not.

So where did that leave her? She could keep on refusing to marry him, but that wouldn't stop the little life inside her from growing. Or from needing protection when it was born. No, she hadn't asked for this to happen, but she'd made an error and this was the consequence, and she couldn't avoid taking responsibility.

Xerxes certainly wasn't, which meant she could do no less. She'd been thinking with her heart, not her head, so maybe she needed to think like a soldier and regroup, re-strategize.

He'd said that the role of a prince or princess was to defend, to protect, to serve, and she hadn't thought of it like that before. It made sense. If she married him, she'd be a princess, which meant she would still be serving Axios. And she'd be protecting her child, too.

In which case, if he was going to be her husband, it would probably be a good thing to do a little reconnaissance on said husband, check out the lay of the land, so to speak. She'd made a start already downstairs, but that had only left her with more questions.

She rolled over and stared towards the big windows that looked out over the sea. The gauzy white curtains had been drawn over the glass, making the light diffuse and milky, but she could still see the sea sparkling beyond. It was very peaceful here with nothing but the faint sound of the waves breaking against the rocks and the cries of the gulls.

What would Xerxes be like as a husband? What did marriage even mean? The only example she had was her parents and that wasn't a stellar example. Her mother had been so sweet and loving, and yet she'd ended up betraying both her husband and her daughter, leaving them for another man, another life.

A better life than what she had with you.

Pain dug sharp claws into her, though she tried to ignore it. No, her mother had been weak, that had been the issue. She'd wanted love, or so she'd shouted at Calista's father, but she'd had love. Calista had loved her with all her heart, but in the end that hadn't been good enough for Nerida. She'd walked away from her husband and her daughter without a backward glance.

No, Calista's father had been right that night when

he'd told her that love was a lie. That it was a weakness. That it had no place in the life of a soldier. And, since she would still be a soldier married to Xerxes, it would have no place in hers.

Xerxes himself wouldn't care. He didn't love her and, as he'd already told her, love wasn't a requirement for a royal marriage and so he wouldn't be expecting it anyway. And that could only be a good thing.

Sick of thinking about it, Calista pushed herself up and brushed her hair back from her face. Perhaps she'd have a shower, then maybe find something else to wear, as she'd been wearing the same clothes since the day before.

The shower in the en-suite bathroom was large and had the perfect pressure, and once she felt refreshed Calista wrapped a towel around herself and went back into the bedroom. The bag that the guard had taken out of the helicopter had been put on the sofa that faced the windows, so she moved over to it and unzipped it. Inside were a number of brightly coloured, silky items that appeared to be underwear and nothing else.

Calista dug around for anything that was less revealing than the long, dark blue silk negligee that had for some reason been included, but apparently actual clothes had not been packed for her, which meant it was the negligee or nothing.

She'd never worn anything so feminine before—if she didn't count the gowns she'd tried on a couple of months back—and she didn't like the idea of wearing it now. But she wasn't going to wander around naked, so she put it on, as well as a fresh pair of lacy gold underwear. Then she found a matching blue silk robe that at least covered up the fact that she was dressed only in a nightie, and put that on over the top.

Feeling underdressed and oddly vulnerable, she

opened the door and went to find Xerxes. With any luck she wouldn't run into any staff curious about why she was wandering around in only a silky dressing gown.

There were no staff members around, as it turned out, which was a relief, the big house seeming empty. All the rooms were large and all were facing the incredible views of the ocean, the sun setting fire to the sky as it sank below the horizon. The furniture was low-key and rustic, the walls white, while silk cushions and rugs provided bright pops of colour here and there. There was nothing fussy or formal about the decor; it was a house meant to be lived in rather than admired and she liked that very much.

Eventually, drawn by the sounds of splashing coming from one of the terraces, she walked out onto the cool white stone to find Xerxes swimming in the infinity pool.

The big glass doors that separated the terrace from the house had been pushed back, so she wandered out into the pool area, standing on the side, watching him as he powered down the length of the pool.

His strokes were strong, and he pulled himself through the water as if he were climbing a mountain, his muscles flexing and releasing as his arms rose and fell. His skin glistened in the fading light of dusk, the water flowing over the tattoo of the lion on his back.

He was beautiful to watch, raw masculine power and strength, sleek and predatory as a shark in the water.

A pulse of hunger and deep longing went through her.

She'd tried so hard not to think of him over the past few weeks, or of the specifics of the night they'd spent together. Tried so hard to keep everything about that night locked down and in the past. But she could feel that need inside her, twisting and turning, trying to penetrate the armour she wore, stealing through the cracks and forcing them wide. He was the one who'd done that. Who'd cracked her armour apart. And now she'd had a taste of what it was like not to wear it…

God, she wanted more.

Another benefit of marrying him.

Her mouth dried as the thought hit her. If she married him, she *could* have that. He'd made it clear that he wanted it, so she wouldn't have to deny herself or pretend she didn't feel it. She wouldn't have to be quite so disciplined. The expectations of a princess were different from that of a soldier and so maybe she wouldn't have to wear that armour. At least, not all the time.

The thought was like a stone thrown into a still pond, each ripple getting wider and wider, setting up a reaction that echoed through her entire body, making her shudder.

Why not? If you keep it only physical, what harm could it do?

Perhaps no harm. And she could be free…

Xerxes must have spotted her, because he slowed then came to a stop, putting his head back and standing up. Water streamed down his body, running off every carved inch of him, the setting sun sending his olive skin a deep gold, and striking sparks from the gleam of it in his dark eyes. He raised a hand, pushing his fingers through his wet black hair, and she was mesmerised by the flex and release of the muscles of his biceps and chest, by the lift of one powerful shoulder.

The hunger inside her deepened.

He smiled, his sheer physical charm almost an affront, because surely no man was allowed to be that gorgeous. 'Good evening, Calista. How did you sleep?'

'Very well.' Her voice was scratchy and breathless, and she couldn't quite get it under control.

Do you need to? You've already lost control with him once before...

Another thought that sent ripples through her. Of course, she'd lost control with him that night, hadn't she? And he hadn't cared. He hadn't judged. He'd simply taken her passion and driven it higher, using hers to fuel his own so that they'd lost it together...

Her heart thudded hard in her ears as he gave her a long look up and down, and she remembered abruptly what she was wearing, her face heating at the blatant appreciation in his eyes. 'I knew that would look superb on you.'

She tried to get some much-needed air into her lungs, resisting the urge to cross her arms protectively over her breasts. 'There doesn't seem to be anything else for me to wear.'

'No, there isn't.' He moved through the water to the side of the pool. 'I didn't pack anything else.'

'Why not?'

'Because you don't need anything else.' He put his hands on the white stone of the pool's edge. 'I'd really prefer you to be naked, but I thought the underwear and negligee would save your blushes.'

Calista opened her mouth to respond to that particular insanity, but just at that moment Xerxes pushed himself up and out of the water in one fluid, powerful movement, and everything she'd been going to say went straight out of her head.

He straightened, the sheen of the water on his skin outlining every muscled inch, and Calista found herself staring. Then she blinked as she realised something.

He was naked. Completely, gloriously naked.

Wild heat rushed through her. 'You're not wearing anything,' she said stupidly.

'No. It's my pool and the staff have all gone home for the day.' His mouth curled in that seductive way. 'Why don't you join me? You look like you could do with some cooling off.'

She barely heard, unable to stop looking at him. He was a work of art, the setting sun making his skin gleam, the hard lines and white scars a map she wanted to follow with her fingers, or like braille, a story she could read just by touching him.

Something caught in her chest, and before she knew what she was doing, she was walking slowly towards him. He didn't move, watching her approach, an answering heat flickering in his eyes.

She stopped inches from him and lifted a hand to one of the long, slashing scars across his abdomen.

His fingers closed hard around her wrist.

Calista looked up in surprise.

He wasn't smiling now, the lazy seductiveness had vanished, leaving behind it something fierce she didn't understand.

He said nothing, only looked at her, his grip on her wrist almost painful.

There was a tightness in her chest. He didn't want her touching him, that was obvious. But she didn't understand why, not when he hadn't had a problem with it before. Was it the scars? Or something else?

'What?' she asked. 'You didn't seem to have a problem with me touching you the other night.'

He was silent, a muscle leaping in his jaw. Then, very deliberately, he let go.

Her heartbeat thumped hard behind her ribs. She shouldn't push him, because she could see that for some reason this was painful. But she wanted to know why.

And she had the sense that he wouldn't give her any explanations, not if she didn't push.

So, carefully, keeping her gaze on his, she brushed her fingers over the faded white scar. His skin was damp and cool from the water, and he tensed, his eyes darkening into black.

'Does it still hurt?' Calista asked softly.

'No.' His voice was rough, the word bitten off.

But something did, that was clear.

'Is it from when you were captured?'

'No,' he repeated. 'Another time.'

She frowned. 'What time?'

He said nothing and the only warning was a flare of gold deep in the darkness of his eyes. Then he pushed one hand into her loose hair, pulling her head back, and his mouth was on hers.

The kiss was raw and it was hungry, and there was anger in it. No, he did not like her touching that scar.

She thought about pulling away and insisting on an explanation, but then his teeth sank into her lower lip and all thought scattered and dissolved like smoke in the wind.

The need she'd been fighting, the hunger she'd been trying to deny, flooded through her, sweeping away everything in its path. Her resistance, her armour, her control, all of it was gone.

She'd put both hands to his chest before she was even aware of what she was doing.

His grip in her hair tightened, the kiss deepening. His mouth was so hot and he tasted of freedom, of everything good and delicious she'd ever denied herself. It was a kiss that took, that conquered, that demanded her surrender, and she melted against his hard, wet body, giving it to him without even a thought.

The moisture on his skin dampened the silk of her

robe, making it stick to her body. Making her aware of how hot she was and how cool he felt. She was burning up, sweat breaking out all over her, and she needed him to put out the flames.

Calista pressed herself against him, desperate, kissing him back hungrily, and he made a low, male sound of satisfaction. Then his powerful arms were around her and he was picking her up, carrying her over to one of the sun loungers near by and depositing her on one of the white cushions.

He knelt between her thighs and there was a tug and the sound of tearing fabric as he ripped the silky underwear from her body. Then he pushed her legs wide, settling himself between them, stretching himself out on top of her. She gasped at the delicious coolness of his skin against the blinding heat of hers, her hands on his powerful shoulders then sliding down his back, holding on. His mouth claimed hers again as desperation tightened on both of them.

He shifted his hips and she felt the long, hard length of him sliding against her, sliding inside her, ripping another moan from her throat. He stretched her, pushing in deep, his hands beneath her bottom, tilting her hips and opening her up to him.

The pleasure was so sharp and raw she had to close her eyes against the sudden burn of tears.

Oh, yes, this was it. This was what she wanted. Him inside her, setting her free from her control and her own expectations. From the limitations and boundaries she'd placed on herself. Him, setting her free of the soldier.

He didn't wait, drawing his hips back and thrusting, setting up the same intense, driving rhythm she remembered from their night weeks ago. But there was something different in it this time, an edge of ferocity, of desperation.

Her nails sank into his back and she nipped at his bottom lip, giving herself up to the passion inside her, wanting more of his taste, more of that delicious coolness to ease the blinding heat. But he wasn't cold any more, his body as hot as hers, maybe hotter, and there was nothing but flames everywhere.

'Xerxes.' His name escaped the kiss and she was hardly aware of even saying it. 'Xerxes, please...'

He shifted again, laying one hand against her throat in a gentle grip, kissing her harder, changing the angle of his thrusts, making lightning flash behind her eyes.

She couldn't bear it. The feel of his body on hers, of him moving inside her, the pressure of his fingers at her throat, the edges of his teeth against her sensitised lip, were all too much. And when he gave one deep, hard thrust, the pleasure exploded around her, and she screamed against his mouth, blinded, shattered. Overwhelmed by the waves of ecstasy rolling through her.

She was hardly aware as the brutal rhythm of his hips intensified, as his whole body suddenly stiffened. But she heard her name whispered like a prayer, low and deep and rough, as he followed her into the maelstrom.

Xerxes lay on Calista's warm body, half stunned by the orgasm that had descended on him with the finality of a building falling, crushing him completely.

He couldn't move, couldn't speak, was conscious only of her hands moving lightly up and down his back, stroking him, and the warmth of her skin beneath him, the sweetly musky scent of sex and woman surrounding him.

He wasn't quite sure what the hell had just happened to him.

All afternoon he'd been unable to settle, the conversation he'd had with her on the terrace kicking up the dust of old memories, making him restless and unable to concentrate. His thoughts kept going around and around in circles, how she'd told him about her experience in the army, how she didn't want to be seen as a woman. Then there were his own confessions and how, despite the years and his determination not to let it matter, it had been surprisingly difficult to tell her.

And then, when the restlessness had become unbearable, he'd taken himself down to the pool to cool off. She'd appeared at the side, a golden vision of strength and beauty in the robe he'd brought for her. And instantly the restlessness had poured itself into a single, aching thought: he wanted her.

A simple seduction, that was all he'd meant it to be. Slow and lazy lovemaking, where he'd call all the shots, he'd be the one making her scream.

He hadn't expected her to touch that scar on his stomach, the first knife cut in that room underneath the palace, where everything had been so horrifically real.

He hadn't expected, either, the rush of anguish that had come with the touch, or for his hand to reach out and grab her wrist to stop her. She'd looked at him in shock and he'd had to force himself to let her go, to find his usual detachment.

But he couldn't find it. And when she touched him again, he could think of only one way to distract her.

He hadn't meant that kiss to consume them, but it had, burning all his plans of long and lazy sex to ashes on the ground.

It wasn't supposed to be like this. He wasn't supposed to feel anything but physical pleasure. But his chest felt tight, his nerve-endings raw, the detachment he usually cultivated hanging by a thread.

She'll break you if you let her.

Well, that was one problem that was easy to solve. He simply wouldn't let her.

She could touch his body, but nothing else, nothing that would threaten the careful walls he'd constructed around his emotions, those deep flaws within himself.

He'd tried hard to get rid of them after that day in the cell beneath the palace, when he'd discovered that the torture had only been a test of his endurance. But after his capture in the desert, after the decisions he'd made there, he realised that it was impossible. Those flaws would always be with him, and the only thing he could do was to wall them off. Pretend they didn't exist.

And that had worked until she'd appeared, waking him up, making him aware of how he'd been lying to himself, of how all the pretending he'd been doing hadn't made those flaws go away. Of how deep they went, those cracks he'd never be rid of.

He couldn't allow her to do that. She'd got to him, but he couldn't allow her to get any further.

He shifted so the majority of his weight wasn't lying directly on her, then pushed himself up so he could look down at her.

Her golden skin had flushed deep pink, her riot of beautiful hair spread all over the white linen of the cushions beneath her head. Her amber eyes had deepened into that gorgeous dark copper, and her mouth was red and swollen from his kisses.

She looked like a woman well-tumbled, no trace of the soldier remaining.

Good. The soldier was far too sharp and direct for

his liking. Right now, he preferred the soft, hot, passionate woman.

He brushed back a lock of hair sticking to her forehead. 'Are you all right? I didn't hurt you?'

'No.' Her sweet voice was slightly husky, her hands still moving on his back. She smiled, making his heart almost stand still in his chest. 'Not at all.'

No, he didn't want this. Didn't want her smiling at him. Didn't want the maddeningly light brush of her fingertips. He wanted her nails scoring him, her teeth biting him, her legs around his hips, squeezing him, not this... gentle touching.

'Good.' He bent and kissed her mouth again before moving down, trailing kisses along her neck, tasting the hollow of her throat, her pulse leaping against his tongue.

'What happened?' she asked. 'Why did you stop me?'

He didn't need to ask her what she meant; he already knew. But he didn't want to talk about it, so he nipped the side of her neck instead. 'I think I should make it clear,' he murmured, nipping her again, her breath catching as he did so, 'if it wasn't clear already, that our marriage will definitely *not* be in name only.'

'Xerxes.' She shivered, her hands coming to his chest.

He nuzzled the side of her neck, just beneath her ear. 'I like the way you say my name.' Moving lower, he brushed his mouth over her sensitive collarbones. 'Say it again.'

Her hands pushed against his chest. 'Xerxes. Stop.'

Dammit.

He lifted his head again, not bothering to hide his anger. 'I don't want to talk about this right now.' Shifting on her, he fitted the growing hardness of his shaft against the soft, sweet heat between her thighs. 'I have other things I want to do.'

Her body shivered beneath his, but she didn't look away.

She was deceptive. He'd thought the woman wouldn't be quite as confrontational as the soldier, but apparently that was not the case. 'I tell you something, you tell me something,' she murmured. 'Wasn't that what you said?'

Yes, he had said that. Clearly, he'd been an idiot.

'But I did tell you something.' He ran a hand down her side, stroking her then lingering to cup one full, round breast. 'Which means it's your turn.' His thumb brushed over her rapidly hardening nipple. 'Or you could do something else instead.' He circled the taut peak, teasing it. 'I'm sure you'd find that infinitely more pleasurable.'

She gave a little gasp as he pinched her gently, her eyelashes fluttering half-closed, her back arching into his hand. She was so responsive. He remembered that from their night together. Which was excellent, since it made her easy to distract.

'When I was around twelve, my mother promised to take me out shopping for my birthday,' she said huskily. 'I loved her so much, loved spending time with her, and I was so looking forward to it. But when the day came, she told me she had a meeting she couldn't change and we'd have to cancel it. I was so upset and angry. To this day I don't know why I followed her, but I did. I got on my bike and followed her into the city.'

Xerxes stopped touching her, the emotion in her voice making something inside him pause.

'She didn't go to her office building like I thought she would,' Calista went on. 'She went to a park instead and there was a man waiting for her by the fountain. The man took her in his arms and kissed her, and that's when

I knew it wasn't a work meeting. She was meeting her lover.' Calista's eyes remained half shut. 'I was so angry. So very, *very* angry. I went straight home and told my father. And he was angry, too. That night I heard them shouting in his office and so I crouched outside the door, trying to listen to what was going on. She'd been having an affair for a year, because she felt my father didn't love her. And he…said that she was a faithless whore and that he never wanted to see her again. Mum burst out of the door, tears on her face. I'll never forget the way she looked at me when she found me outside.' Her voice thickened. 'I loved her so much, and I wanted to be her when I grew up. But the absolute loathing in her eyes in that moment… She shouted at me that it was my fault, that I'd ruined her life, and then she walked away.' Calista's eyes opened suddenly, looking up into his. 'I never saw her again.'

Her gaze was dark with old pain and he was seized by the sudden need to kiss her lovely mouth, stroke her silky skin, make her feel better.

'Dad told me that it wasn't my fault,' she went on. 'That I'd been right to tell him what I saw. That I would never disappoint him like she had. That I was loyal. But sometimes I wonder if I really did do the right thing. Sometimes…' She swallowed. 'Sometimes I can't help feeling like… I betrayed her.'

The note of anguish in her voice made his chest constrict, and all he could think about was that of course she would think she'd betrayed her mother. Given the strength of her commitment to her country, she was deeply loyal and felt things very intensely. Both were valuable, admirable traits, but also a double-edged sword; it was clear her mother's abandonment had hurt her terribly.

He cupped her cheek in his hand, the way he'd done

the night they'd spent together, giving her some gentleness. 'You didn't ruin anything,' he said. 'If your mother was having an affair, then it was already ruined. It would only have been a matter of time before it all fell apart.'

Calista's throat moved as she swallowed. 'I shouldn't have got so angry about that stupid shopping trip. I shouldn't have told Dad. I should have talked to her or something. But I didn't. All I could think about was that she'd ruined Dad's life, and she'd ruined mine, and that I wanted to ruin hers back.'

His own mother had died very young; he barely remembered her. But he knew what it was to feel anger at a beloved parent. To feel betrayed by them. To feel abandoned.

He brushed his thumb over her mouth then bent and kissed her, soft and sweet. 'You were twelve,' he murmured. 'Of course you would feel that way. And she shouldn't have been angry with you. She was the one who had the affair. It was her issue, not yours.'

Calista's eyes were very dark. 'I wanted to ruin her, Xerxes. So I did.'

'You loved her and she hurt you. It's not wrong to feel angry. And all you did was hasten something that would have happened anyway.'

'But she walked away. I never saw her again.'

Anger twisted inside him, a hot, irrational anger at her mother for hurting her so badly. 'Then she was a fool,' he said fiercely, looking down into her eyes. 'It wasn't your fault she turned her back on you. That was her decision. And it was the wrong one. She should have been there for you no matter what you'd done because that's what being a parent is all about.'

'But maybe if I hadn't been so angry, if I hadn't let

my emotions get the better of me… Maybe if I hadn't been so weak—'

'You weren't weak,' he interrupted flatly, so there could be no doubt. 'She was the weak one to turn her back on her child. Not you.'

She didn't speak for a long moment, only looking up at him, the currents ebbing and flowing in her gaze. Then she said, 'I've told you something. Now it's your turn.'

But he didn't want to do that, to have her painful past get lost in the mire of his, so he only shook his head and kissed her again, slow and sweet.

She'd given him a gift and he wanted to mark it.

'Xerxes, stop,' she murmured against his lips, but without any real conviction.

'Let me, Callie,' he whispered. 'Let me make it better.'

And when she sighed, her hands against his chest starting to caress, he kissed her deeper, tasting that fire, the hot passion she tried to hide beneath the mask of the impassive guard.

Well, he didn't want her hiding it. He didn't want her locking it down or thinking it was a weakness. He wanted her passionate. He wanted her wild. He wanted her burning for him.

He resumed his trail of kisses, down her neck and further down, finding her breast then flicking his tongue across one hard nipple. Then he took the tip into his mouth, sucking on her gently at first, then harder, making her cry out.

He tormented the taut peak, teasing it with his tongue and then the edges of his teeth, before turning his attention to her other breast.

She shuddered, twisting beneath him, panting, her body lithe and strong and so achingly beautiful. Her skin was flushed with pleasure, her eyes closed, her mouth open. She looked thoroughly and completely seduced.

He kissed his way down her flat stomach, spreading her thighs, finding his way to the soft nest of curls between them. She was all slick and wet and hot, her hips shifting restlessly, wanting more, so he gave it to her, laying his mouth on her. She cried out, her body jerking, and when he parted her slippery flesh with his fingers and began to explore her in earnest, she sobbed.

He drew it out for as long as possible, giving her as much pleasure as it was in his power to give, making her sweat and drawing more raw, desperate cries from her.

And then, when she was as balanced on the knife edge of pleasure as he could get her, he pressed his palms down on her thighs, holding them wide. 'Scream for me,' he murmured against her damp skin. 'I want to hear how well I've satisfied you.'

Then he flicked his tongue against her one last time and she screamed and screamed and screamed.

CHAPTER EIGHT

A FEW DAYS LATER, Calista got up after a lazy afternoon nap, pulling on one of the sundresses that Xerxes had finally relented and bought her. She'd wanted something more practical, but he'd told her the soldier was currently on leave, which meant she could let the woman out to play.

Initially she hadn't been entirely comfortable with that, but after a day or two of passion in his arms she'd let herself relax, and when he'd sat down with her and a laptop, getting her to choose some pretty dresses from a high-end designer website, she'd given in. And after five minutes her reluctance had turned into delight as she found herself admiring fabrics and styles. Something she hadn't let herself do in years.

Xerxes had bought everything she'd shown an interest in and they were brought the next day by helicopter. He'd insisted on a fashion show, which had then turned into a strip show as she'd changed out of different dresses in front of him, teasing him in a way that made him laugh as well as making his gaze flare with heat. Until he'd finally taken her down on the floor of the lounge in a bout of passionate lovemaking.

The white cotton dress with the straps that tied at her shoulders was his favourite, mainly because it was so easy to take off, and so she put that one on then padded down the hallway, hungry and wondering where he was.

They'd fallen into an easy rhythm over the past couple of days, one that consisted mainly of sex and food, followed by lazy conversation, sleep and then maybe a dip in the pool or a visit to the beach at the foot of the cliffs beneath the house, and a swim in the sea.

Calista forgot about her control. Forgot about her armour. She loved that he flirted with her, making her laugh with his outrageousness, and then demanded that he teach her to flirt with him. She ended up being a natural and every time she made the gold in his eyes gleam and his beautiful mouth curve, it felt like a victory.

But she was still missing one thing.

She'd hoped that by forcing herself to tell him about her mother, he'd reciprocate with something about himself. To talk about the significance of the scars on his body and why he hadn't wanted her to touch him, but he didn't. He didn't mention them again.

Yet the more days that passed, the more desperate she was to know. That it was a painful topic, she understood, and she didn't want to cause him pain. But talking about her mother with him and having his fierce protectiveness turned towards her had felt like balm to an aching wound. She hadn't had someone care about her feelings, about how she'd been hurt, for a long time.

And now she wanted to do the same for him. To be the balm to whatever wound had hurt him. Of course, she shouldn't be wanting that, because that was getting emotional and emotions weren't supposed to be part of what they had together.

But that didn't stop her wanting it.

Voices drifted down the hall and she followed the sounds to the living room, pausing in the doorway as she discovered a restless Xerxes, pacing up and down in front of the windows, glaring at a tablet that had been propped up on the coffee table.

On the screen, the king's massive, powerful frame was stretched out behind a desk as he signed a stack of official-looking papers. It looked a little strange. Adonis Nikolaides, the Lion of Axios, was a man built for the battlefield, not the boardroom.

'I don't know why you simply assumed I would lie for you, Xerxes,' Adonis was saying, not looking at the camera, signing the paper in front of him and then putting it to one side before picking up another and scanning it quickly. 'She's already pregnant, and besides, a love affair between an infamous playboy and a palace guard is the stuff of fairy tales. No one will ever believe it, especially not given your reputation.'

Xerxes had his hands shoved in the pockets of his jeans. 'If the press release comes from you, Adonis, people will believe it.'

His brother looked up from the stack of papers, his blue eyes glacial. 'Are you giving orders to your king?'

Adonis' deep voice was mild, but Xerxes clearly wasn't deceived. 'No,' he said flatly. 'I'm giving orders to my stubborn-as-hell, hidebound brother.'

'A king does not condone a lie,' Adonis said implacably.

'A king can bend the rules however he likes,' Xerxes shot back. 'I won't have any hint of improper behaviour attached to Calista's name, are we clear?'

Her heart gave a little kick against her breastbone, though she wasn't sure why, when he was defending his reputation as well as hers. Then again, the way he'd said it made it sound as if he cared about how it would affect her, too.

Did you really expect him not to?

Maybe not. He'd been nothing but wonderful to her the last couple of days.

'Perhaps you should have thought of that before you took her to bed,' Adonis was saying, glancing back down at his papers and pulling another one towards him.

There was a pause as Xerxes came to a stop, glaring hard at the tablet. 'Are we going to go there, then? Are you going to tell me that I owe you my life? Remind me of the promise I made to you when I returned? The promise I broke? Are you going to make me beg for it, brother?' His eyes glittered with a very real anger. 'Because I have to tell you, I've been there, done that, and for your sake, already.'

Some kind of fierce expression flickered across Adonis' granite features, but it was gone so fast Calista wasn't sure if it had been there at all. 'You know I wouldn't do that to you. I'm not our father, Xerxes.'

'But the throne is more important than anything else, am I right?'

'More important than what you want?' Adonis said. 'Yes.'

There was a pause.

Xerxes said nothing, gazing at the tablet, his jaw tight, his figure tense.

'She matters to you, doesn't she?' Adonis was looking directly at the camera now and Calista's gut lurched. She shouldn't be here, eavesdropping like a spy. This was a private conversation and she didn't need to hear it.

You want to, though.

No, of course she didn't. Yet she didn't move.

'Will you help her?' Xerxes demanded, not answering the question. 'She'll be a royal princess, after all, so keeping her pregnancy out of the news until we're married will be in your interests as well.'

Adonis was silent. Then abruptly he looked away, back to his stack of papers. 'You're causing a scandal, Xerxes. But I suppose that's nothing new. Very well. You can have your story of some kind of ridiculous love affair, and I'll back you up. I'll give you my approval to marry her.' He picked up another piece of paper. 'But if you're unfaithful to her, if you create another scandal for me to deal with, then make no mistake, I'll strip you of your titles and banish you a second time. Is that understood?'

Calista took a breath at the ice in the king's voice. There was no give in it, none whatsoever.

'Yes,' Xerxes bit out. 'Your Majesty.' Then he reached forward, touching the screen of the tablet, and Adonis disappeared.

He straightened, his back to Calista, shoving his hands into the pockets of his jeans once more. 'You saw all of that, I take it?'

Shock coursed down Calista's spine. He'd known she was there all along.

'I'm sorry.' She pushed herself away from the doorframe. 'I didn't mean to eavesdrop.'

Xerxes turned slowly to face her.

His gaze was dark and absolutely unreadable, and he didn't smile, the warm, easy lover of the past few days vanishing. He was so tense, she wanted to go to him and put her hands on his shoulders and massage it away.

Yet some instinct told her that he wouldn't welcome it, so she stayed where she was.

'What's the issue?' she asked, keeping her voice carefully neutral.

'He's very concerned with appearances and didn't

want to condone the story I gave him about us having a love affair.'

'Oh,' she murmured, not sure what else to say.

'He thinks no one will believe it.' Bitterness had crept into his voice. 'Apparently the idea that I might genuinely care about someone is utterly preposterous.'

She scanned his face, noting the anger glittering still in his eyes. 'And do you care?'

His gaze focused on her, his expression sharp and edged. Then he turned away, striding over to the windows and pausing in front of them, looking out over the sea beyond. 'No, of course I don't. Why would you think otherwise?'

But that bitterness in his voice gleamed bright as a blade and she knew suddenly what it meant.

He'd been so fierce when she'd told him about her parents, his gaze so concerned... Of course he cared.

She crossed the space between them, stopping behind him, staring at his strong, powerful back. There was so much tension in his posture. Was it just his brother's refusal to lie? Or was it something else? Something to do with their father?

A sudden memory of the ferocity in his eyes as she'd touched that scar on his stomach flashed before her. He hadn't stopped her since, but she hadn't asked about it since.

It had something to do with that, she was sure.

'Why are you so angry with him?' she asked into the silence of the room, the urge to touch him, give him some comfort, almost overwhelming.

Xerxes gave a short laugh. 'Who? My brother? It's not him I'm angry with.'

'Then who? Your father?'

He turned his head to the side, his perfect profile hard.

'If you want me to give you something, you'd better get naked first.'

Calista didn't move because she knew him better now and she knew when she'd touched a nerve. 'Don't snap at me,' she said softly. 'Not when it's not me you're angry with. Why won't you tell me what's wrong? I already gave you something, remember? But you never reciprocated.'

For a second he remained silent, then he turned suddenly, the gold bright in his eyes. But it wasn't warm. It was icy, hard. Frozen.

Threat radiated from him, danger charging the air around them, but she'd never been afraid of him before and she wasn't now. He was the tiger forced into a corner, left with nowhere to go but to attack.

'Is that so?' He laughed, the sound cold. 'Give me one reason why I should.'

She stared back, not giving ground. 'Because you promised.'

He cursed, low and filthy. 'What do you want to know? The details of my capture? How I put that pill in my mouth every day but couldn't make myself swallow it? How I justified my own cowardice by thinking that perhaps my father wouldn't want me to die? That he would come for me? Or perhaps you want something else?' He stepped back from her and suddenly pulled his T-shirt up and off in one fluid movement, baring his magnificent chest. He flung the T-shirt onto the floor, fury suddenly stark on his face. 'Perhaps you want to know about the interrogation games my father played. How one day, when I was thirteen, a man in a mask kidnapped me from my room. He blindfolded me, took me to a stone cell and tied me to a chair. Shone a light in my eyes. Told me that I had to give him the palace layout, details of guard movements, everything, or he would hurt me. I held out against the knife.' His hand dropped to the slashes across his stomach. 'I held out against the burns.' His fingers brushed some shiny round scars. 'He broke my finger and I held out against that, too. But then he told me he had Adonis in the next room and that if I didn't tell him everything, he would kill him. I didn't believe him, but then he played me the sound of Adonis shouting for help on his phone. So...' Xerxes was breathing fast, his chest rising and falling as if he were running a race. 'I told him. I told him everything.'

The look on Xerxes' face drove all the air from her lungs. She couldn't breathe.

'But that wasn't the worst part,' he went on, his voice vibrating with rage. 'The worst part was after, when I'd given up everything, when I thought I'd killed my family, destroyed my country, the man pulled his mask off and it turned out to be my father. None of it was real. It was a test. And I failed it.' His mouth twisted. 'He made no bones about how disappointed he was in me. He'd seen me being friends with the daughter of one of the palace staff and thought I needed a lesson in detachment. He expected me to fail it and I did. Because I was weak. I'd let my love for my brother overrule my love for my country. And I would have to prove myself to him if I wanted to claim my title of Defender of the Throne, because a defender was supposed to protect the throne, not betray it.'

Calista's heart squeezed in her chest at the anguish and rage in his eyes, sympathy for him hitting her unexpectedly hard. As a soldier, torture was something that was always a possibility. But not for a teenager. And to be tortured by his own father, a parent who was supposed to protect him...

That was nothing short of a betrayal.

And you know what that feels like.

'He threatened your brother,' she said fiercely. 'How were you to know it wasn't real?'

'That was the whole point, though.' His voice was harsh. 'I was supposed to think it was real. And I was supposed to hold out. It was a test of my strength and I failed it.'

'You were thirteen!' She took a step towards him, her own anger rising, but not at him. At the man who'd hurt him. Who'd given him a test as a teenage boy that even a battle-hardened soldier would have trouble passing. 'How can you blame yourself for that?'

'Easily.' There was contempt on his face, but it was clear it was aimed at himself. 'I broke again in the desert. I should have taken that pill and I didn't. I lived when I should have had the guts to die.'

'Xerxes,' she said hoarsely. 'You did it—'

'I did it to prove a point. To prove to my father that I wasn't weak, that I was stronger than he thought I was. That my rightful place was beside my brother.' The fury in his eyes abruptly drained away. 'But all I proved was how flawed I was. How I let my emotions get in the way of my country's security.'

She knew how that felt. Hadn't she felt it herself? The desire to prove that she was strong, that she could be what her father wanted her to be. That she wasn't the foolish girl who'd betrayed her mother. That she was loyal.

Yes, she knew. And she knew, too, the pain of failing. Of not being strong enough, no matter how hard she tried.

Her heart twisted and she wanted to touch him, but he'd turned away.

'I did it again that night with you,' he said, his voice distant.

She caught her breath, not expecting that. Not expecting the bolt of hurt that came with it either. 'Do you regret it?' she asked, unable to help it even though she knew she shouldn't, because it would reveal far too much.

He didn't move for a second, not looking at her. Then he glanced back and this time the gold in his eyes burned hot. 'No.' He looked down at her stomach for a beat. 'You and our child are my second chance.'

That's all you are? His second chance?

The thought was barbed and oddly painful. Which was strange, because since when did she want to be more than that to him? Since when did she want to be anything at all to him?

Since the night he set you free. You want to be his sunshine the way you could never be your mother's.

No. She didn't. She would enjoy his company, enjoy spending time with him, but nothing more. Even the sympathy and hurt for him, the anger she felt on his behalf for what his father had done to him, all the strangely intense emotions currently tying knots in her chest, shouldn't be there.

She had to pull back. Had to wall herself off, find her armour again. Emotions hurt, they destroyed. They made her weak and she couldn't be weak.

But she didn't want to leave him with nothing, so she came closer, reaching out to touch him, to offer him what she could, because he'd done the same for her down by the pool that day.

Her fingers brushed over the scar of the knife, the scar his father had put on him, and she looked up into his eyes. 'You held out,' she said with quiet ferocity. 'You held out as long as you could against superior forces and you were thirteen. Yes, you broke, but you didn't give up. You kept on fighting. Even in the desert, when you were captured, you didn't give up.' She touched another scar, one of the burns. 'Don't be ashamed of these. These are marks of strength, Xerxes. Taking that pill would have safeguarded the secrets of the country, too, it's true, but in a way, it's also an escape, don't you think?' She moved her hand, brushing another scar. 'A way out. You could have left it all behind for everyone else to deal with. But you didn't. You stayed. And when you left Axios, it was because you were banished, not because you ran away.'

'Calista—'

'You came back again, too, didn't you? Your brother called you home and you answered. You didn't have to; you could have stayed in Europe. Who would blame you after what your father did to you? But you didn't. You came back to a country that condemned you, to make it right. To claim your rightful place at your brother's side. And that's not weakness, Xerxes. That's strength.' She stared at him, willing him to see the conviction in her eyes, not sure why this mattered to her so very much, only that it did. 'That's endurance.' Her hand lifted to his heart and she placed her palm over it. 'I don't see a coward when I look at you. I see a hero.'

She stood in the sunlight coming through the windows, the white fabric of her dress highlighting the deep gold of her skin. Her hair tumbled down her back, shining, all the colours deep chestnut, caramel, gold and gilt and every other colour in between.

She looked like a woman, but the expression on her face as she looked at him was that of a warrior, a soldier. Direct and fierce, and full of pride.

A hero, she'd said. And when she looked at him that way, he almost felt like one. Could almost believe he wasn't flawed, that he hadn't let anger and bitterness eat away at him, corroding him like rust in an iron bar.

'Do you really believe that?' He tried to make it sound as if he didn't care either way, but he knew he'd failed.

He wanted her to believe it. He was desperate for her to believe it, because if she did, then perhaps there was some hope for him after all.

Strange to think about hope. He hadn't ever thought about it before, had never even noticed the lack. But he did now...oh, he did now.

Her fingers were light on his skin, gentle, and her touch hurt for some reason, but he didn't push her away.

'Yes.' Conviction shone in her eyes. 'I do.'

The anger inside him, the bitter self-loathing, melted away like snow under spring sunshine.

She saw strength in him. She saw a hero. How could he not believe her? If she thought he was one, then perhaps it was true. Perhaps there was indeed hope.

Hope that he could be equal to the trust his brother had placed in him.

Hope that he could be a good father, a father their child could be proud of and look up to.

Hope that he wouldn't fail.

And what about her? Hope that you can be a good husband to her?

His hunger rose, everything focusing on the woman in front of him, standing tall in the sunlight, looking as if she was covered in gold.

His golden goddess. His soon-to-be wife.

His.

Her touch was gentle, yet it felt as though she was brushing away years of scar tissue and emptiness, years of feeling nothing, replacing it all with sunshine and heat. With warmth.

He lifted his hands, cupped her face between them,

staring into her amber eyes. 'Oh, Callie,' he said softly. 'What did I do to deserve you?'

Her cheeks flushed. 'It's the truth.'

'In that case, it's a truth no one else saw in me. All my father ever saw was everything I wasn't.'

'He was wrong.' Her gaze was very direct and very fierce. 'He shouldn't have done those things to you. Shouldn't have said those things to you. And he should never, ever have hurt you. A father is supposed to support their child, not undermine them.'

Something caught in her voice, and if he hadn't been looking right into her eyes he might have missed it. He stroked her cheekbones with his thumbs, her skin soft and hot against his. 'Yours did?'

'He did what he could.'

Which wasn't an answer. But he knew what the answer would be anyway.

'What didn't he give you, Callie?'

Her lashes lowered. 'He wasn't my mother.'

The mother who'd loved her. The mother who'd walked away from her in the end.

'You tried to be your mother's daughter, and then you tried to be your father's son,' he murmured. 'That's what you told me.'

'Yes.' She kept her gaze turned away.

'But were you anyone's?' he asked softly. 'In the end?'

She tensed and tried to pull away from him, but he firmed his grip, holding her still. And that was his answer. No, she hadn't been, and it hurt her.

Strong fingers closed around his heart. 'Did you have anyone, Calista? Anyone at all? A lover at least?'

She was still, but he felt the tension in her. 'No. Not a lover, either. Not until you.'

He felt no shock or surprise. Only the same sense of

fate settling down on him as it had when he'd realised she was pregnant. The sense of rightness, of purpose. Of destiny. He wasn't only here for his child. He was here for her.

Gently, he tilted her head back, forcing her to meet his gaze. 'Then that makes you mine,' he said simply. Then he lowered his head and took her mouth like a vow.

She froze. Her lips were hot and she tasted sweet, the perfect antidote to all that bitterness that had been living inside him. The perfect cure for all that self-loathing that had nearly corroded him away.

He kissed her deeply, slowly and with purpose, because she was his purpose now.

She was the goddess he'd been put on earth to worship.

She was the reason he hadn't taken that pill all those years ago. Somehow he'd known, even years ago, that there was a reason he had to stay. That it wasn't only his brother or his anger at his father that was keeping him here. That there was another reason he'd endured, that he'd come back to Axios three years ago, even though he hadn't wanted to.

She was the reason. He was here for her.

He kissed her more deeply, keeping it slow and gentle, exploring her with thorough deliberation. She made a soft, eager sound and her hands were on his chest, sliding up around his neck. She came up on her toes, her mouth open beneath his, suddenly desperate, clinging onto him as if she were drowning and he was her last chance of rescue.

But he didn't want desperation now. He didn't want fast or furious. He wanted long and slow and gentle. He wanted to make her his with purpose and intention, not through a loss of control.

He gentled the kiss, easing her. He stroked the sides

of her neck and her shoulders, her skin silky and warm beneath his fingertips.

'Xerxes.' She shivered, pressing herself against him. 'Please…'

'Hush,' he murmured against her lips. 'Keep still for me. Keep very still.'

'But I don't—'

He stopped her protests with his mouth in another long, achingly sweet kiss. She shivered, trying to kiss him back, impatient and hungry. Her hands began to rove all over him, his chest and his stomach, down to the fastening of his jeans, stroking him urgently. Lightning followed in her wake, and he was hard almost instantly.

But if there was one thing he was good at, it was this: a slow and sweet seduction. And that was what she deserved. That was what she needed.

She thought he was a hero. He would be that hero for her.

He took her wrists in his and drew them behind her, holding them together in one of his hands at the small of her back. She fought him, but he was stronger and she couldn't break his hold. Not unless she went into full combat mode.

'Xerxes,' she pleaded, desperate. 'Please.'

'Patience.' He let the fingertips of his free hand drift to one of the ties of her dress, brushing her skin. 'Good things come to those who wait.'

'I don't want to wait.'

'I know you don't.' He stroked her shoulder, sliding his fingers beneath the tie, caressing her, brushing his lips over her mouth. 'Impatient girl. But you will wait for me. Because you're mine, Callie. Understand?'

She shook her head and he didn't know whether it was because she didn't understand, or because she didn't want to be his. Either way it didn't matter. He was going to show her what that meant right now.

He took the end of the tie in his fingers and tugged gently, undoing the bow that held one side of her dress on, the material slipping down, exposing one beautiful breast.

She gave a little moan, pulling against his grip, but he tightened his hold, kissing her, keeping it slow and gentle, sweet and hot. Then he touched her, stroking the satiny golden skin that had been revealed, letting her know with each touch what being his meant. That he would keep her, hold her, worship her.

Adore her.

The fingers around his heart closed tight, squeezing hard. Yes, he would adore her. He'd thought that the moment he'd seen her in that gown in his bedroom. Possibly even before that. Maybe even the second he'd looked at her standing by the doorway in his living room, tall and straight in her uniform. Proud and strong.

A woman a man would want to be worthy of.

And she'd made him feel worthy. Now it was his turn to repay her.

He let his fingers stroke down to the curve of her bare breast, sliding beneath it, taking the soft weight in his palm. She gasped, arching into his hand, pressing herself to him, demanding more.

But he refused to be rushed, squeezing her so gently, brushing the tips of his fingers around her nipple, feeling it harden responsively under his touch. She shivered, pulling harder against the hold he had on her. He let go of her breast and reached for the other tie, pulling that, too, so her dress came completely off.

She was naked underneath it, trembling as she tried to press her body against his, her skin hot and silky, the wild-flower scent of her underlain with the musk of her arousal.

Beautiful soldier. *His* beautiful soldier.

He reached behind her, taking her wrists in both hands now and holding them at her back. Then he fell to his knees in front of her, ready to worship.

'Oh,' she whispered. 'Oh, Xerxes. No.'

But he ignored her, leaning forward and nuzzling against her stomach, glorying in her scent, pressing hot kisses to her skin. He finally let go of her wrists and ran his fingertips up and down her sides, stroking as he kissed down to the sweet little nest of curls between her thighs.

She tried to move, but he put his hands on her hips, holding her still. 'No,' he murmured. 'Just wait. Let me give you this.'

'You shouldn't.' Her voice sounded thick. 'You shouldn't kneel to me.'

He glanced up at her, taking in her flushed cheeks and the darkening of her amber eyes. But there was distress there, too. It made that grip on his heart squeeze.

He stroked his thumbs over her hips gently, keeping his gaze on hers. 'Why not?' he asked softly. 'You're a goddess, Calista. And I want to worship you.'

'I'm not. I'm just a soldier, and a prince shouldn't kneel.'

'But you're not just a soldier.' He spread his fingers out on her sides, stroking her, letting her know how beautiful he found her. 'And I'm not just a prince. I'm a man and you're a beautiful woman. Why shouldn't I kneel to you?'

'I…' She stopped, shivering, a confusion in her eyes he didn't understand.

She wanted him, it was clear. And yet this was distressing her and he wasn't sure why. Over the past few days she hadn't found his touching her difficult, so what had changed?

You are making this about her. That's what's changed.

Understanding filtered through him. The sex they'd shared here had been about the act itself, about sating the hunger, indulging the chemistry. He hadn't thought about the emotional connection.

But this was different and he could feel it. He wanted to give her pleasure, make her feel good, show her she was special, and not for his own satisfaction, but for hers.

He couldn't pretend he didn't care any more; that excuse was long gone.

He cared. He cared about her.

But she was fighting it.

'You can't,' she said, suddenly and fiercely, picking the thought right out of his head. 'You can't care about me.'

So, was this where the battle was to be fought? Fine, he was ready.

'Oh?' He lifted a haughty brow so she would know that he was not going to back down, not on this. 'And why not?'

'Because I don't want you to.' She took a shaken, ragged-sounding breath, her amber eyes wild. 'A prince can't care for a soldier.'

It was about more than that, he could tell, but now wasn't the time to push and besides, he wasn't a man who took orders from anyone. And he wasn't a man who gave up. She was the one who'd shown him that.

'A prince can do whatever he wants.' Xerxes met her fierce gaze. 'And so can the man. Let me show you.'

'Xerxes…'

But he was ready to fight and he ignored her, kissing her lower and lower still, gripping her hips tightly and holding her in place as he nuzzled between her thighs.

She shuddered, and when he began to explore her with his tongue she moaned.

She didn't pull away or tell him to stop again. Her fingers settled in his hair instead, twisting tightly as he explored, tasting the sweetness at the heart of her.

And only when her knees were weak, and she was gasping and shaking, did he finally rise to his feet and pick her up in his arms, carrying her over to the sofa and laying her down on it. He paused only to get rid of his own clothing before following her down onto it.

She reached for him, pulling him to her, wrapping her legs around his waist as he settled himself on her. Her body was hot, her skin like satin, all firm muscle and soft curves, and she smelled like sex and desire.

He put his mouth to her throat and kissed her there, the taste of her skin making need tighten inside him. Making him hungry. Her hips lifted beneath his, the press of her wet sex against him stealing his breath, turning his blood into lightning in his veins.

She lifted her hands to his shoulders, sliding them down his back, nails digging into his skin. Her mouth found his and she bit him, her teeth sinking into his bottom lip.

It felt as if she was fighting him or punishing him, or something in between, but that was fine. She was a soldier and all she knew was how to fight.

But he would teach her differently. He would teach her that she didn't need to fight, that sometimes surrender could be just as sweet. So he ignored her bites, refused to rise to her demands, took them and turned them instead into slow, hot kisses and long, lazy caresses. She tried to push him, writhing beneath him, trying to make him desperate, but he wasn't desperate. Because he had nothing to be desperate about.

He knew what he wanted and he had patience. He had strength and he had endurance and he would use all of that to show her that a prince could indeed care about a soldier. It was possible. It was inevitable.

He pushed his hand between them, finding the soft, wet heat and the most sensitive part of her, stroking as he kissed her, taking her desperate cries and choked sobs into himself and giving her back more pleasure.

And then he thrust deeply inside her, holding on to her hips, the sounds of her pleasure echoing in the air around him. A storm of sensation chased him, the feel of her, the scent of her, the sounds she made.

Every sense he had was focused on her. She was the centre of the universe. His universe.

He moved harder, deeper, driving both of them higher, looking down into her darkened eyes as he did so, letting her see that this was a fight he would win.

This would be a marriage in every sense of the word, not just physical but emotional, too, and she had to know it.

The pleasure gripped him tight, stretching him thin. And he reached down between her thighs, stroking her so that she gave a desperate sob, her body convulsing around his as she came.

Then he let go of his control, thrusting harder, deeper, until the climax swept through him, hot and dark and overwhelming.

'Don't care about me,' she'd told him.

But it was too late.

He already did.

CHAPTER NINE

A WEEK LATER, Calista stood in front of the mirror in the bedroom she'd been assigned on her return from the coast. She'd been half-afraid, half-hopeful that Xerxes would insist on her sharing his rooms, but he hadn't.

It was for propriety's sake, he'd told her, to help bolster the illusion of a love affair that hadn't been consummated. It was the story they'd both agreed on, to help shield her from any negative public opinion, and she knew that it was best if they had separate rooms in the palace. But the past couple of nights she'd missed him.

He'd spent the time in meetings with his brother and with the press, the scandal of his broken engagement to Eleni and the gossip about his love affair with a palace guard having settled down somewhat. Of course, the fact that there would be a second formal engagement party, where she would be introduced to the people of Axios as his fiancée, gave the gossip columns plenty of material, but with any luck once the party had been held everyone would be more excited about their wedding than the circumstances surrounding it.

It helped that all requests for interviews with her had been officially denied by the palace.

She'd had an audience with Adonis, which had been very formal, the king himself not friendly but also not outright rude. Xerxes hadn't helped though, standing protectively at her side virtually bristling with threat. But at least it hadn't been a disaster.

After that, she'd been poked and prodded by the palace doctor, the health of the baby checked and confirmed. Then there had been an array of visits from clothes designers that covered fittings for a new wardrobe, not to mention a wedding gown. Various palace staff also visited, with instructions on what she could expect once she married the Prince, and what her duties would be. Lessons in protocol and media training also followed, along with stylists, make-up artists and other staff that would now be assigned to her.

It was all a little overwhelming.

Her father hadn't visited, even though Xerxes had told her that he'd paid a personal visit to him, assuring him that his daughter would be well taken care of.

She tried not to be hurt by the fact that he hadn't contacted her, staring at herself in the mirror as the stylist tweaked some fabric of the gown she'd be wearing at the engagement party instead.

Her hair was in an artful, gleaming tumble down her back, and she wore the same gown that she'd tried on the night she'd met Xerxes. The gold satin skimmed her every curve, highlighting the deep amber of her skin. The stylist had brushed some gold powder over her shoulders and collarbones, making her gleam, picking up the same golden lights in her hair and eyes. A delicate tiara sat on her head, a corona of white diamonds fashioned to look like a delicate web, with large golden diamonds caught in it like raindrops.

It was beautiful. She was beautiful.

She barely recognised herself and, while a part of her was thrilled by it, another part found it deeply unsettling.

Nerves fluttered in her stomach. Xerxes had reassured her that tonight all she'd have to do was smile and look lovely, that he'd do the rest. She'd be introduced to the Axian court and aristocracy and the assembled media, there would be some mingling required, then she and Xerxes would lead a dance, and that would be it.

It wasn't exactly a battlefield or even basic training, but still she felt out of her depth. She'd felt out of her depth a week ago when she'd approached the palace during that first engagement party. Then, she'd had little idea she'd end up being the star of Xerxes' second party.

You shouldn't be here and you know it.

She did know it. Here she was, wearing a beautiful gown, about to be formally engaged to a handsome prince, to be a princess the way she'd once pretended she was all those years ago. It should have been magical. Special…

He will want you to love him. He'll demand it.

Her hands shook as she smoothed down the satin of the gown. She'd warned him not to care about her, that emotions could not be part of this marriage. She didn't want them to be.

A knock came on the door but whoever it was didn't wait to be admitted. The door opened to reveal the king himself.

The flutter in her stomach increased.

The king said nothing, merely gave the staff who'd been helping Calista prepare a look and instantly they vanished out of the door, leaving her alone with him.

Adonis Nikolaides was slightly taller and broader than Xerxes, a warrior rather than a diplomat. His features were rougher, blunter, a statue of a god that had been worn over time rather than freshly carved like his brother. And carved out of granite rather than marble.

Power, authority, and brute strength radiated from every inch of him, his piercing blue eyes sharp as swords; he looked as if he should be on the battlefield in armour, wielding an axe, rather than dressed in the black-and-gold uniform of the Axian army, his chest covered in medals and ribbons.

Instinctively, Calista clicked her heels together and bowed.

The king's straight black brows rose. 'Since you're not in uniform, a curtsey would be more appropriate,' he said, his voice harsh, like stones grinding against one another.

Calista flushed. 'I apologise, Your Majesty.'

He said nothing, merely eyed her.

There was a long moment of silence and Calista felt every second.

'Your Majesty,' she said at last, unable to stand it any more. 'How can I be of—?'

'Are you in love with my brother?' the king interrupted. 'Because if you're not, if the baby is not his and you're merely using him to get a better life for yourself, I will make things very difficult for you.'

Shock swept through her, along with a chill that settled right down in her gut.

This wasn't only the threat of a king, it was also the threat of an older brother who'd do anything to protect his younger sibling.

What did you expect? That the king himself would welcome you with open arms?

Calista swallowed, the memory of that day in the living room of the house on the coast replaying through her head. Of Xerxes, tall and strong and powerful, a prince in every line of him, kneeling in front of her as if she was the one who was royal.

It had made her feel afraid, made doubt catch hard inside her.

He shouldn't have knelt to her, shouldn't have looked up at her, fierce and full of heat, as if she was something worth looking at. As if she was worthy.

As if he cared about her.

He does care. And you know it.

Her throat closed up, her heart tight and painful behind her ribs, because it wasn't fair. It wasn't fair on him that she could never care for him in return.

The king was looking at her, obviously wanting an answer, but she had only one to give him.

'No,' she said, ignoring the hoarse edge to her voice. 'I don't love him. And for what it's worth, Your Majesty, I'm not using him. I didn't actually want to marry him, but Xerxes had other ideas.'

'Did he?' The king's blue gaze glittered. 'And what did you want?'

Calista lifted her chin. 'I only wanted to serve my country. But—'

'Xerxes had other ideas?' he echoed.

She flushed, but didn't look away. 'Yes.'

There was speculation in the king's eyes. 'So why are you marrying him?'

'Because he didn't give me a choice.' She smoothed her hands down her gown again, the cold feeling inside her getting stronger. 'And because this baby needs a father.'

'I see. And if you weren't pregnant? Would you still marry him?'

A bitter, hard truth settled inside her.

'No,' she said, her voice almost a whisper. 'I wouldn't.'

The king didn't show any surprise or shock. 'Why not?'

She took a breath. 'Because he…cares for me, I think.

And I will never be able to give that back to him. I will never be able to give him what he deserves.'

Something flickered over the king's granite features. 'You're honest, I'll give you that. And you're right, he deserves more. He's endured much these past few years and none of it has been easy for him. I don't want to see him hurt.' The king paused, studying her a little longer. 'You should not have to give up the life you wanted either. Would you like to be given the choice, Calista? To stay or to leave?'

Did she? She wasn't sure.

'I can't leave. He'll follow me.'

'Yes,' the king agreed. 'He will. In that case, after the party, come to me. I can help you to leave if you choose to, hide you from my brother, if that's what you want. You and your child will be cared for, I give you my word.'

Calista stared at him, at his hard face, at the glitter of something fierce in the ice of his eyes. It was clear he cared about his brother as much as Xerxes cared about him.

Xerxes deserves better. He deserves better than you.

Something inside her dropped away. She felt dizzy and a little ill. 'Yes, Your Highness,' she said blankly, her lips numb. 'I'll consider it.'

He gave a nod. 'See that you do.'

The door opened suddenly, and Xerxes came striding into the room.

He was dressed in the same uniform as his brother, black and gold, with medals and ribbons, but perhaps not quite as many as the king. He didn't need them though. He was the most beautiful thing she'd ever seen, the gold in his uniform echoing the gleam of gold deep in his dark eyes, the black highlighting the inky darkness of his hair.

The uniform fitted him to perfection, outlining his

wide shoulders and narrow hips, his muscular chest and powerful thighs. He was every inch the handsome prince, radiating strength and authority, and his own special brand of lethal charm.

He is worth so much more than what you can ever give him.

Calista's fingers were cold, so she curled them into her palms to warm them.

Xerxes stopped dead as he spotted Adonis, and frowned. 'What are you doing here?'

His brother lifted a shoulder. 'Merely saying hello to my future sister-in-law.'

'Well, now you've done so, you can leave,' Xerxes said gracelessly. 'Goodbye, Your Majesty.'

Adonis' granite expression betrayed nothing. He merely gave Calista one more piercing look before withdrawing from the room.

'What did he want?' Xerxes came over to her, reaching out and drawing her close, as if he couldn't stop himself from touching her. 'Was he threatening towards you? Disrespectful?' His gaze was fierce. 'I won't allow anyone to upset you tonight.'

He was so protective. It made her ache.

'I'm fine,' she said, forcing the ache away. 'He only wanted to make sure I wasn't going to hurt you, I think.'

'Hurt me?' A smile curved Xerxes' mouth. 'Was he worried you might be an assassin?'

'No.' She didn't want to tell him what the king had actually asked her. She didn't want to have that conversation now. 'Is it time to go?'

His gaze narrowed, as if he was debating whether to push her, but he obviously decided there was no time, because he nodded and held out his arm. 'I'm afraid so. Try not to look like you're heading to your doom.'

Calista tried to smile, to ignore the growing coldness in her stomach. She put her hand on his arm instead. 'I'll try, Your Highness.'

He reached out and cupped her cheek, bending to brush a kiss over her lips. 'That's Xerxes to you. Remember that.'

But it was impossible to remember that as he took her down to the ballroom, as they were introduced to the greedy eyes of society. As he moved, tall and strong, through the crowds, his charm and easy wit making people smile. Making them nod approvingly at him and at her, too.

He introduced her to people, whispered stories in her ear about them to help her remember names—a trick he'd learned in Europe, apparently. Some of the stories were scandalous, some of them clever, some of them designed to amuse her, but all were whispered with a smile, the boyish glint in his eyes that was for her and her alone.

It made the ice in her gut spread out, freezing the rest of her, hurting her.

He *did* deserve more. He was honourable and brave and strong. He was the kind of soldier she'd always wanted to be. The kind of son her father should have had. And he deserved someone who could make him feel the way he made her feel.

But she wasn't that someone. Her love was a toxic thing. It was a weakness that led to anger, and it hurt people. It had hurt her mother. It had ruined their whole family. And if she wasn't careful, it could ruin him.

The evening felt interminable and towards the end of it Calista slipped out onto the big terrace that overlooked Itheus, tucking herself away down one end in the shadows, where she couldn't be seen. Just for a couple of minutes to clear her head, that was all.

It felt strange to be standing here in a golden gown, a beautiful crown on her head, when a week ago she'd been here in jeans and a T-shirt, still reeling from her pregnancy news.

She put her hands on the parapet, the stone cool underneath her fingertips, and looked out over the city below, and took a ragged breath.

'There you are,' a soft, deep voice said from behind her, concern edging the words. There was movement, a steadying hand settling at the base of her spine. 'Are you are okay, Callie?'

The affectionate shortening of her name scraped along her nerve-endings, hurting her. The way his gentle hand at the base of her spine hurt her.

She shouldn't be prolonging this and she didn't know why she was. It wasn't fair on him. What she should have done was accept the choice that the king had given her straight away, not gone through with this…farce.

Leaving now would hurt him immeasurably, perhaps beyond repair, but that would be a lesser pain. A ruined party and a ruined month or two rather than a ruined life. And then he'd be able to find someone else. Someone who'd love him the way he deserved to be loved.

Because she couldn't allow herself that luxury. She was a protector, protecting was what she did, and she would protect him. Even if that meant protecting him from herself.

'Yes,' she said. 'I'm okay. Just tired.'

She would go to the king after this. Tell him that her choice was to leave, and he would take her away and hide her. She would never bar Xerxes from seeing his child, but she wouldn't have to see him again herself, not if she didn't want to.

And if he insists? If he wants the child back in the palace?

She would cross that bridge when she came to it. Maybe she'd have to give up her child. But maybe that would be for the best. Who knew what kind of mother she'd be, after all? Given how she'd hurt her own mother, perhaps not a good one.

You can't tell him you're leaving.

No, she couldn't. She knew him; he'd do everything in his power to stop her, and she couldn't have that. Eventually, he'd see it was for the best.

His hand at the small of her back was warm and she wanted to lean into it, but she denied herself. There'd be no more of that and she'd have to get used to it.

'Tell me,' she said, before she could stop herself. 'Would you have married me if there was no baby?'

He let out a breath. 'Interesting question. What makes you ask that?'

She had no idea. No idea why her heart ached so much, why she felt as if she was falling apart inside. 'Just thinking about your previous engagement party and how that went.'

'Ah, yes.' He gave a soft laugh. 'Well, to answer your question, a couple of weeks ago, no. I wouldn't.'

It felt like an arrow piercing her. A stupid question. Of course he wouldn't have.

But then there was pressure at her back, his hand urging her to turn and face him, and when she did, when she looked up into his dark eyes, there was gold shining in the depths. Buried treasure just for her.

He cupped her face in his palm the way he had done back in his bedroom months earlier, his thumb soft against her cheek, and this time she couldn't stop herself from leaning into it, craving one last touch. 'But I would now,' he added.

Her throat closed, her heart shredding itself inside her chest. 'Why? I don't bring you anything. I don't bring political influence or money. Or connections or—'

'I don't need you to bring me anything. All you need to bring is you. You have everything I need.'

That gold shining in his eyes… It made her feel cold inside.

'I told you not to care, Xerxes,' she said, her voice hoarse.

He shrugged, as if that didn't matter. 'And I told you a prince will do what he wants. And if he chooses to care about you, then he will.'

She had no answer to that, because it was an argument she knew she wouldn't win. And it was a fight she didn't have the strength for. So all she did was lean up and kiss him, and hope that would cover the sound of her own silence.

If he noticed it, he didn't say, and when they went back together into the ballroom for the dance they would lead, he didn't push. He merely held her in his arms and watched her as they danced together, his gaze steady and clear.

As the evening came to a close, she thought it might be difficult to slip away without him noticing, but apparently the king had meant it when he'd said he'd help her, because some palace staff came up to Xerxes as they prepared to leave the ballroom, drawing him away in conversation.

Calista took her opportunity. She slipped silently out of the ballroom to find one of the king's guard waiting for her, and without a word followed him down a long corridor and through a series of interconnecting rooms.

The king was waiting for her in what looked like a study, still dressed formally in his uniform. 'Have you made a decision?' he asked neutrally.

'Yes.' Calista lifted her chin, straightened her shoulders and shoved away the sudden, tearing pain. She pulled on the cracked remains of her armour, the iron discipline of the soldier. 'Please take me away, Your Majesty.'

CHAPTER TEN

XERXES STRODE INTO his brother's office and slammed his hands down on Adonis' desk. 'Where is she?' he demanded, the room echoing with the sound of his fury. 'What have you done with her?'

Adonis looked up from his computer screen, expressionless. 'Who?'

'You know who I'm talking about,' Xerxes snarled. 'Calista.'

'What makes you think I know where she is?'

'Because she's not in the palace. And I know because I've torn the place apart looking for her.'

He'd been detained a good quarter of an hour by some palace protocol nonsense, and then by a last-minute well-wisher who'd pulled him aside to talk to him about the condition of the Itheus sewerage system, of all things, and how it needed upgrading urgently. By the time he'd got rid of the man, another half an hour had passed, and he wanted to see where Calista was.

The strange conversation out on the terrace earlier had bothered him for some reason he couldn't put his finger on, and he wanted to talk to her about it.

But he couldn't find her. She wasn't in her bedroom, or his. Or anywhere else where she potentially might have been. And after he'd rounded up the entire contingent of palace guards and ordered them to find her, it soon became clear that she wasn't in the palace at all.

Given the level of security, it was impossible for her to have been kidnapped by outside forces, which meant that someone on the inside had taken her.

Either that or she'd escaped herself. But even then she'd have needed help.

And there was only one person who had the power to help her disappear so thoroughly: his brother.

He'd interrupted something before the engagement party, that had been clear, but Calista had shrugged it off. There had been some distress in her eyes, but he hadn't had time to push her about it, deciding he'd do it after the party.

He'd known the whole week since arriving back from the coast that something hadn't been right with her. She'd seemed quiet and withdrawn, and, due to all the things he'd had to organise and deal with, he hadn't spent the time with her that he ought.

A mistake now, he could see that.

Adonis leaned back in his chair and stared at him. His brother's blue eyes were glacial, his expression rigid. Not that he ever had any other expression that Xerxes could remember. Adonis had taken their father's lessons in detachment and elevated it into an art form.

'Does it matter where she's gone?' he asked coldly.

Xerxes had never wanted to punch him so badly in his entire life. 'Of course it matters, damn it! She's my fiancée and the mother of my child!'

'Language,' Adonis said. 'You're not in the barracks now.'

Xerxes bit out an even fouler curse. 'What have you done with her? Answer me!'

His brother was silent for a long moment, staring at

him. He'd once been a playful boy and a caring older brother, but that had been before their mother had died and Xenophon had turned into a rigid, hard, emotionless father whose prime concern was turning both his sons into rigid, hard, emotionless versions of himself.

Xerxes had once wanted to be exactly like that. To be the kind of prince his father had wanted him to be. To be that kind of man.

But looking at Adonis now, at the ice in his eyes and the granite in his heart, Xerxes knew with a sudden burst of realisation that he didn't want that for himself. That maybe he'd chased it for a while in Europe, had tried to turn himself into something similar after he'd returned to Axios. But the basic truth was that he'd never wanted it.

He wanted the passion he'd found in Calista's arms. The heat in her eyes. The fiercely proud expression on her face as she'd looked at him, as if the way he'd broken under his father's torture and his failure to end his own life weren't flaws, but signs of strength. Of courage. Of endurance.

He wanted the fire that lit his heart whenever he thought of her. Whenever he looked at her. Whenever he held her.

He just wanted her.

'I asked her whether she wanted to marry you,' Adonis said after a moment. 'And she said she didn't. But that she didn't have a choice. So I gave her one.'

Fury vibrated through every cell of Xerxes' being. 'What do you mean, you gave her one?' he ground out.

'I told her she could come to me after the party and I'd provide her with an escape, if that was what she wanted. And she did. And I provided her with one.'

Xerxes felt as if someone had punched him hard in the gut, winding him.

She'd walked out. She'd walked away. Without a single word.

Not without a word.

Ah, yes, out there on the terrace, that strange note in her voice as she'd told him not to care. The sweetness in her kiss. That had been a goodbye, hadn't it?

Something opened up inside him, a deep, abiding pain. It felt worse than anything his father had ever done.

'And my child?' he demanded hoarsely. 'What will happen to the baby?'

'She said that if you wanted the baby with you, she would allow it. She was very concerned that the safety of the child was paramount, regardless of whatever…issues the pair of you might have.'

'Issues?' Xerxes said in disbelief. *'Issues?'*

'Well?' Adonis lifted an eyebrow. 'Aren't they issues?'

'No.' He leaned over Adonis' desk, pinning his brother in place with a furious stare. 'I care about her, you absolute fool!'

Finally, anger sparked in Adonis' electric-blue gaze. 'But she doesn't love you,' he snapped, pushing himself suddenly to his feet. 'And so I was trying to protect you. You deserve better than that, Xerxes. You always have.'

Xerxes shoved himself away from his brother's desk. 'I don't need your protection,' he spat. 'Or your opinion on what I do or don't deserve. Tell me where she is.'

'She told me so herself,' Adonis went on implacably. 'I asked her whether she loved you and she told me she didn't.'

No, that was a lie. She felt something for him, he knew she did. It was in the way she'd touched the scar on his stomach, the way she'd told him that he was a hero, even when he didn't feel it himself. The way she'd kissed him goodbye out there on the terrace. In the distress he'd seen in her eyes.

Why had she lied?

Why does that matter?

The thought sliced through him, sharp and deadly as a blade, pinning him to the spot.

Because it mattered. It mattered to him.

He hadn't thought about love. He hadn't thought about anything beyond fate and destiny and purpose. He hadn't thought about anything beyond duty.

He hadn't thought about what he wanted for himself except passion.

She was his goddess to worship, but worship was only one-way. A priest didn't expect his god or goddess to answer. A priest didn't require to be worshipped in return.

But you do.

Something burned in his heart, something he'd always hoped for but had never asked for. Something that, deep down, he'd never thought he was worthy of.

He wanted to be worshipped. He wanted to be loved.

By her.

Because he loved her.

Love for him had always been pain. Always been failure. But this didn't feel like either of those things. It felt like power. It felt like strength. It felt like glory.

It felt like something he wanted and not for his king or for his country, but for himself.

And it mattered because he didn't think he could survive without it.

'Fine,' he snapped, because he was certain now. He had to find her, talk to her, tell her what he felt. 'I'll find her myself.'

He turned on his heel, striding towards the doors.

'I don't want you to have what Sophia and I had,' Adonis said roughly. 'I didn't love her, but she loved me and that killed her in the end.'

Sophia, his brother's queen. Who'd died just before Xerxes had returned, leaving Adonis a widower and their young daughter motherless.

Adonis never spoke of her.

Xerxes stilled.

'I don't want that for you,' Adonis went on, more quietly. 'You deserve better than that, Xerxes.'

'I have better than that,' Xerxes said, staring at the doors ahead of him.

'Are you so certain? And do you think confronting her will work? That telling her what to do will work?' The breath went out of him. No, of course it wouldn't, not with Calista. She was stubborn and strong, meeting his will with her own. Fighting because that was all she'd ever done. Fighting and pushing herself, denying herself. Trying to be something she wasn't, not at heart. Because the heart of her wasn't a soldier.

The heart of her was a lover.

Except she didn't believe that, did she? No, she thought she had to stay strong and keep fighting. She didn't understand that she didn't need to do that with him. That he wanted her exactly as she was, the determined soldier and the passionate woman.

And what she needed was something he should have given her days ago: a demonstration of faith, of belief in her. A demonstration without a guarantee and without proof. Without a demand for something in return.

He wouldn't give her a battle. He would give her love.

'No,' he said into the silence. 'It won't work. But I have a better idea.' He swung round and met his brother's gaze. 'Will you help me?'

Adonis said nothing for a long moment. Then he nodded. 'What do you need?'

* * *

Calista sat on the terrace of the little stone house in the mountains, looking out over the olive groves that stretched away beneath it. After Adonis had brought her here—one of a number of houses he had scattered around Axios, he'd said—she'd pretty much spent the first couple of days in bed. She'd slept mostly, curled around the ache in her chest and the constant feeling that she was missing something.

After that, she'd forced herself to get up and do things, some gentle exercise, reading books on birth and parenting, watching movies, making herself food to eat. It was boring, but placid. Once, a doctor had visited and checked her out again, making sure she and the baby were healthy. Everything was on track, so she supposed that was something.

But as the days had gone by, the feeling of missing something hadn't grown any less. If anything, it had only grown stronger and stronger, developing into a pain she couldn't shake.

Her heart. She was missing her heart. And she suspected she knew where it was.

She'd left it in Xerxes' strong, capable hands.

But that surely couldn't be true. She'd been so determined not to care and she was sure she didn't, so she tried to ignore the feeling, to lose herself in the small, everyday pleasures of existence.

Yet it didn't work. There was a grief inside her, a loss that wasn't getting any better.

She'd thought that once she left him, she'd forget him, but she couldn't forget him. The baby inside her reminded her every day of what she'd given up, as did every time she woke in the middle of the night and reached for a warmth that wasn't there.

It didn't matter, though. She'd made her choice. She'd given him up to protect him, so he could have someone better, someone who could love him the way she couldn't, and that was how it would have to stay.

So it shouldn't have affected her when she spotted the helicopter flying overhead. It shouldn't have made her whole body go tight, made tears start in her eyes when she saw the livery on the side of it.

And when it landed with a roar on the lawn beside the house, she shouldn't have been torn by the simultaneous desires to leap to her feet and run away, and straight towards the figure ducking beneath the rotors and heading for her instead.

But it wasn't Xerxes. It wasn't even the king.

The man in royal livery came up to her, handed her an envelope and turned away, heading straight back to the helicopter and getting inside. Then it lifted off and flew away, leaving her sitting there in shock, holding an envelope with her name on it.

Calista's hands were shaking. She didn't want to open it, but even so, she did.

A heavy, creamy sheet of paper was inside, and when she unfolded it she saw it was an invitation to a wedding. A royal wedding. The wedding of Prince Xerxes Nikolaides, Defender of the Throne, to… Calista Kouros.

Tears filled her eyes, thick and hot, her own name wavering and swimming in her vision.

The king had told her he'd handle all the details of the wedding cancellation. Yet it was clear that Xerxes, stubborn to the last, was having none of it. Despite the fact that she'd walked out on him without even a goodbye, he still thought she'd marry him.

The arrogant bastard.

Fury rose in her then, white hot and unexpected, and

she took the invitation and ripped it to pieces with trembling hands.

But after her anger had subsided and she was left standing in a pile of white confetti, she knew the truth: he was leaving the final choice up to her.

And she had no idea at all what to do with that.

Calista went into the house and tried to busy herself with doing other things, with books and exercise. With cooking and TV. Boring, mundane things that had provided her with distraction for the past week or two, because she didn't want to have to think about him.

Didn't want to think about the choice he'd apparently given her or what she would do about it.

But nothing helped.

In three days there would be a wedding and he would be there. He'd stand in front of his country, in front of his king, in front of his people. He'd stand there, waiting for her.

And if it was still going ahead, it was because he believed she'd be there. He believed she'd come.

She didn't know whether to be offended at his presumption or comforted by his conviction.

Why was he going through with it? What did he think would happen? Did he really believe she'd turn up? She'd told him over and over again that she didn't want to marry him, so why hadn't he given up?

He never gives up.

Calista couldn't get that out of her head.

The next day arrived and then the next. She wasn't going to go, of course she wasn't. She'd decided not to marry him and her decision was absolutely the right one.

It was up to him if he wanted to risk his dignity and reputation in front of the entire country. If he wanted to look like a fool when she didn't arrive, then who was she to stop him? It would be a hard lesson for him to learn, but perhaps then he'd realise how ridiculous the whole idea was.

Except the more she thought about it, the more she ached. The more justifications she invented, the more hollow they sounded and the more empty she felt.

She woke on the morning of the wedding, more tired than she'd ever felt in her life, and when she got up she simply sat on the terrace of that little house again, watching the sun rise as the knowledge she'd been trying to escape for weeks now unfolded in her heart.

There was a reason those justifications had felt so hollow: they were excuses. Distractions from the real issue.

She was afraid. Not of the gap in social hierarchy between them or anything else, but of what lay in her own heart. Of the strength of what was in it. She'd always felt things so deeply and strongly, and after she'd ruined her mother's life and with it her own relationship with Nerida, she'd locked all those feelings away, committed herself entirely to the armour she put on, poured all her desperate love into her country. Because a country could never betray her. Not the way her mother had done.

But a country couldn't love her back and the armour she'd put on was constricting, and those feelings hadn't gone away. They were still there and they were still powerful, and they frightened her.

You want to be loved back. You want it desperately.

Calista watched the sun come up, the realisation cold and sharp, because yes, she did want to be loved. And she'd had that back there at the palace, or at least the potential for it. But instead of taking it, instead of standing her ground and fighting for it, she'd retreated. No, worse than that. She'd broken and run away. And not even from an enemy bent on killing her.

She'd run away from herself and all those feelings in her heart.

She'd run away from the one man who could give her everything she'd ever wanted.

She'd told herself that she couldn't love him to protect him, but it wasn't him she was protecting. It was herself. Because she'd fallen in love with him. She'd been in love with him for weeks, possibly months. Maybe even since that night he'd cupped her cheek in his big, warm hand and smiled at her.

She loved him and she was afraid. Because it was so strong and so frightening.

It made her weak, made her vulnerable, caused her pain. That was why she wore armour. To protect her heart.

But you can't wear armour and love him, too.

Calista wiped her eyes as tears streamed down her cheeks, feeling hollow and raw. Because that was true. And the choice had always been one or the other for her. There was no in between. She couldn't do both.

But he did.

A shiver shook her then, right down to her core. And all she could think about was Xerxes. He'd been broken, but he'd got back up. He'd been tortured and afraid, but he hadn't let it beat him. He'd been banished and he'd returned. Because he loved his country and he loved his brother.

It had been his love for Adonis that had kept him from taking that capsule, no matter what he thought. And it was that same love that had brought him home.

Love had never made him weak. Love had made him strong.

How can you repay that strength by walking away from him? When it's what your mother did to you?

Her heart froze in her chest, the pain shattering her.

Yes, that was exactly what she was doing. She was leaving him as if he wasn't important, as if he didn't matter, but he *did* matter and he *was* important, and she couldn't do that to him.

She couldn't leave him the way her mother had left her. Somehow, she had to find the strength that would take her back to him.

But she knew where that strength would be found. It was in her love for him. And it would bring her home.

Calista stepped out of her armour, burned it to the ground, and set herself free. She let love surround her instead, making her whole, making her strong.

Then she pushed herself out of her chair, went into the bedroom, showered and washed her hair. She went to the wardrobe where the clothes she'd brought from the palace were and took out the uniform that was hanging there.

Her uniform. And she dressed slowly and carefully, brushing all the dust and lint from it, polishing the buttons to make them shine.

Yes, she was a soldier. She had a soldier's courage and a soldier's endurance. But she was also a woman, with a woman's strong heart. A woman's deep love.

It might not be what he wanted. It might mean she'd end up being hurt.

But he was worth the risk. He always had been.

She waited, and when the helicopter arrived to pick her up she got in without a word.

The trip to the palace didn't take long and she was surrounded by guards when she got there, men she knew, who nodded to her, escorting her to a room where a wedding dress hung, along with a long white veil, a make-up artist, and a stylist ready to turn her into a vision.

But she shook her head as they approached. She didn't

need that. She would come to him as she was, offer him what she had. And hope that it would be enough.

She only paused for one thing—the veil. Taking her cap off, she put the veil on her head, along with the tiara that went with it, because after all, she wasn't just a soldier, and, still dressed in her uniform, got back into the car that would take her to the cathedral in the middle of Itheus.

There were people everywhere when she arrived, and news media, crowds of people thronging the streets. And they all looked at her as the door was opened, and just for a second her heart quailed inside her chest.

But it was only for a second. Because he was here, waiting for her. And love had made her strong. So she got out of the car with her chin held high, in her uniform and veil, walking straight up the steps, the crowd roaring in her wake.

Just inside the great double doors her father waited.

He said nothing as she appeared, giving her an up-and-down look. And she met that look, let him see her pride. Let him see her love. Because it wasn't a weakness, no matter what he thought.

Her father gave a single nod and offered her his arm, and then the doors into the cathedral itself were opening, and the aisle was in front of her.

The vaulted space was full of dignitaries and aristocracy, but she didn't see them.

The only person she saw was the man at the other end, waiting by the altar. Tall and strong and powerful in his uniform. His gaze met hers across the acres of space, and even from where she was she saw the flare of his expression on his face.

The hope. The joy. The pride. The love.

Her heart throbbed, full and painful. There were tears in her eyes.

Music played and then she was walking down the aisle, looking nowhere but at him, and with every step she felt herself grow taller. Grow more sure, more certain.

None of the people in the cathedral mattered. Nothing mattered.

The only thing that did was the look in his eyes as he watched her come to him, and the fierce emotion that glowed so brightly she could barely meet it.

But she did meet it. And she smiled, letting her own love for him shine in her eyes, because she wasn't afraid, not any more.

She arrived at the altar at last, and the look Xerxes gave her was intense and hot, encompassing her uniform and her veil, his approval clear in his gaze.

'Are you here for me, soldier?' he asked, for her ears alone, as she took her place beside him. 'Are you here to be my wife?'

'Yes,' she said with purpose. With conviction. With love burning inside her. 'Are you here to be my husband?'

He smiled, bright and fierce and passionate. 'I would never be anyone else's.'

And then the bishop began the ceremony, and when the ring slid on her finger Calista felt as if something had slipped firmly and quietly into place inside her.

Her future.

Xerxes lifted her veil and his kiss changed the world, set fire to her heart. And after they went down the aisle as husband and wife, when they reached the steps outside, he swept her up into his arms.

The crowd roared their approval and Calista looked up into his face, everything inside her aching with happiness. 'I love you,' she whispered. 'And I'm sorry I walked away, that I left without a word. But I was scared of what I felt for you. I loved my mother so much, yet I ended up hurting her, and I couldn't bear the thought of one day hurting you. So I told myself I couldn't love you. And that when I was gone, you'd find someone better.' She swallowed. 'Does that make me a coward?'

That smile of his was the summer sun on an icy winter's day. 'No. It makes you a soldier. You protect people and that was what you were trying to do.'

'It was myself I was protecting.' She put her head on his shoulder, the strength of his arms around her after weeks of not having it making her want to weep. 'I shouldn't have left. I should have been brave enough to face you. To tell you at least. But I thought you wouldn't have let me leave if I had.'

'I wouldn't have, that's true.' He began to walk down the steps, still holding her because it was clear he didn't want to put her down. 'So what changed your mind? Why did you come back?'

'I came back for you. You showed me that love isn't a weakness. It's a strength. It gave you the strength to endure everything you did and it brought you home.' She reached up and touched his beloved face. 'And I realised that it could bring me home, too. I couldn't walk away from you the way my mother walked away from me, Xerxes. I had to come back to you.'

He turned his head and kissed her fingertips. 'It was good you walked away, though. Because I didn't realise until after you'd gone that I wanted you to have a choice. I wanted you to choose me because you wanted to be with me and not because I forced you.' There was molten gold in his eyes now and his arms tightened. 'And I hoped you would choose me. In fact, I didn't cancel the wedding because I believed you would. And you did. And you know what that means, don't you?'

They were nearing the car that would take them away

and she couldn't wait. She wanted nothing more than to be alone with him.

'What?' she murmured, nestling against him, right against his big, strong heart.

'It means you're mine. For ever.' He looked so smug she laughed.

'So, do I get to hear it, husband?'

'Hear what?'

'I said I love you and you said nothing.'

They would be at the car soon, and there were people taking pictures, the world's media seeing the prince with a soldier in his arms.

'I was formulating a response,' said Prince Xerxes Nikolaides, Defender of the Throne. 'But it's a very long response and it's going to take a while to tell you all the details.'

'Oh?' She ran a finger along his beautiful mouth, because he was hers now and she could touch him whenever and wherever she pleased, and she didn't care who saw. She didn't care at all. 'How long?'

His gaze turned very, very intent. 'Probably for ever.'

Calista smiled, her vision wavering through happy tears. 'Then you'd better start now, hadn't you?'

'Well, I can give you the short version immediately.' He paused, bending to kiss her, long and sweet. 'I love you, Calista Kouros. My goddess. My wife.'

She would never get tired of hearing that. Never.

And then they were getting in the car, and at last, as the doors closed, they were alone.

Xerxes pushed the button that raised a privacy screen between the driver and the back seat, and then proceeded to show her the rest of his response.

And he wasn't wrong.

It did take for ever.

EPILOGUE

THE BIRTH WAS long and hard, but his princess was also a soldier and she held her ground. And a day later, Xerxes held his daughter in his arms as his wife lay back in the nest of pillows he'd arranged behind her head, and wondered if it was possible for a man to have too much happiness in his life.

'She's a fighter,' he said, looking down at the baby nestled in the crook of his arm, his heart two sizes too big for his chest. 'Like her mother.'

'She's also stubborn.' Calista's smile lit up the room. 'Like her father.'

Xerxes laughed and bent to his wife, kissing her. 'You're amazing,' he murmured against her lips. 'I'm so proud of you. My sunshine.'

And he was. She'd proved not only to be a perfect princess, but she was also leading the charge to recruit more women to the Axian army, as well as mentoring existing recruits into elite positions. Her own security detail was all female and she was encouraging the generals to provide more support for female soldiers, as well as better training for males.

She was a born leader and he could only thank his lucky stars that she'd made the choice to meet him at the cathedral that day.

Calista flushed, fierce and proud, and all his.

And he realised he'd been wrong to think that the purpose of his life had started months ago in the little house by the sea.

It started here. With his family. And that his purpose wasn't just to protect and defend. It was also to love.

And he did.

With all his flawed heart.

* * * * *

COMING SOON!

We really hope you enjoyed reading this book.
If you're looking for more romance, be sure to
head to the shops when new books are
available on

Thursday 6th
August

To see which titles are coming soon, please visit

millsandboon.co.uk/nextmonth

MILLS & BOON

Coming next month

CONFESSIONS OF AN ITALIAN MARRIAGE
Dani Collins

"Get in," Giovanni said.

The sight of him struck like a gong, leaving her quivering. He had a shaggy black beard and dark glasses, and his black hoodie was pulled up to hide all but his familiar cheekbones, but his legs stopped above the knees and she recognized the tense line of his mouth.

Alive. Her heart soared so high, it should have shattered the sky.

At the same time, a thousand furies invaded her like a swarm of killer bees. There was no triumph in learning she was right. There was only a crippling heartbreak that he had abandoned her. If he'd been truly dead, she would have been angry, but she wouldn't have blamed him.

This, though? He had put her through horrifying hours of actually believing he was gone. She had endured his gut-wrenching funeral, convinced it was a sham. Then, two short weeks later, she'd suffered another unbearable loss that would never heal.

He'd forced her to go through all of that alone.

For every minute that had passed since that awful day, she had longed for him to reveal himself, but now her feet only carried her forward so she could bitterly hiss, "Go to hell."

"Where do you think I've been?" he growled.

"I'm calling the police!" Teresina yelled from deep in the alley. Two of Teresina's employees were recording everything on their phones.

A man in a suit was running toward her. She instinctively moved closer to Giovanni, heart jamming with fear.

Giovanni's hard arm looped around her and he dragged her into the back of the car. He clutched the door for leverage, but his strength was as annoyingly effortless as always.

She didn't fight him. In fact, once he grabbed her out of her stasis, she helped, kicking against the edge of the door to thrust herself inside, desperate for whatever sanctuary he offered.

They wound up in a heap on the back seat while the man who was chasing her came up to the open door and reached for her leg.

She screamed and kicked at him with her sharp heels. He dodged her shoes and threw the yards of silk in after her, then slammed the door before he leaped into the passenger seat in front of Giovanni.

"Go," Giovanni said to the driver, and he pushed himself upright.

As the SUV sped into traffic, Freja rocked deeper into the seat, stunned to her toes.

Continue reading
CONFESSIONS OF AN ITALIAN MARRIAGE
Dani Collins

Available next month
www.millsandboon.co.uk